KILLING FEVER

KILLING FEVER
A Virtuoso Press Trade Paperback Book

Published by
The Virtuoso Press

Editorial Offices:
University of California
Humanities & Social Sciences
UCSF (Box 0850)
490 Illinois Street, Floor 7
San Francisco, CA 94143-0850

COVER: Details from Map of the British Empire (John Bartholomew,
1850s); Lord Viscount Canning, Governor General of India (circa 1858),
detail from an engraving by D.J. Pound from a photograph by John
Jabez Edwin Mayall; Portrait of Princess Helena (daughter of Queen
Victoria), 1861. Albumen Carte-de-visite by John Jabez Edwin Mayall;
'Sonthal Aboriginal,' Watson & Kaye, *The People of India* (1868).

Library of Congress Control Number: 2023944624
ISBN: 978-1-7355423-7-9

Printed in USA

ANDY WARWICK

KILLING FEVER

V

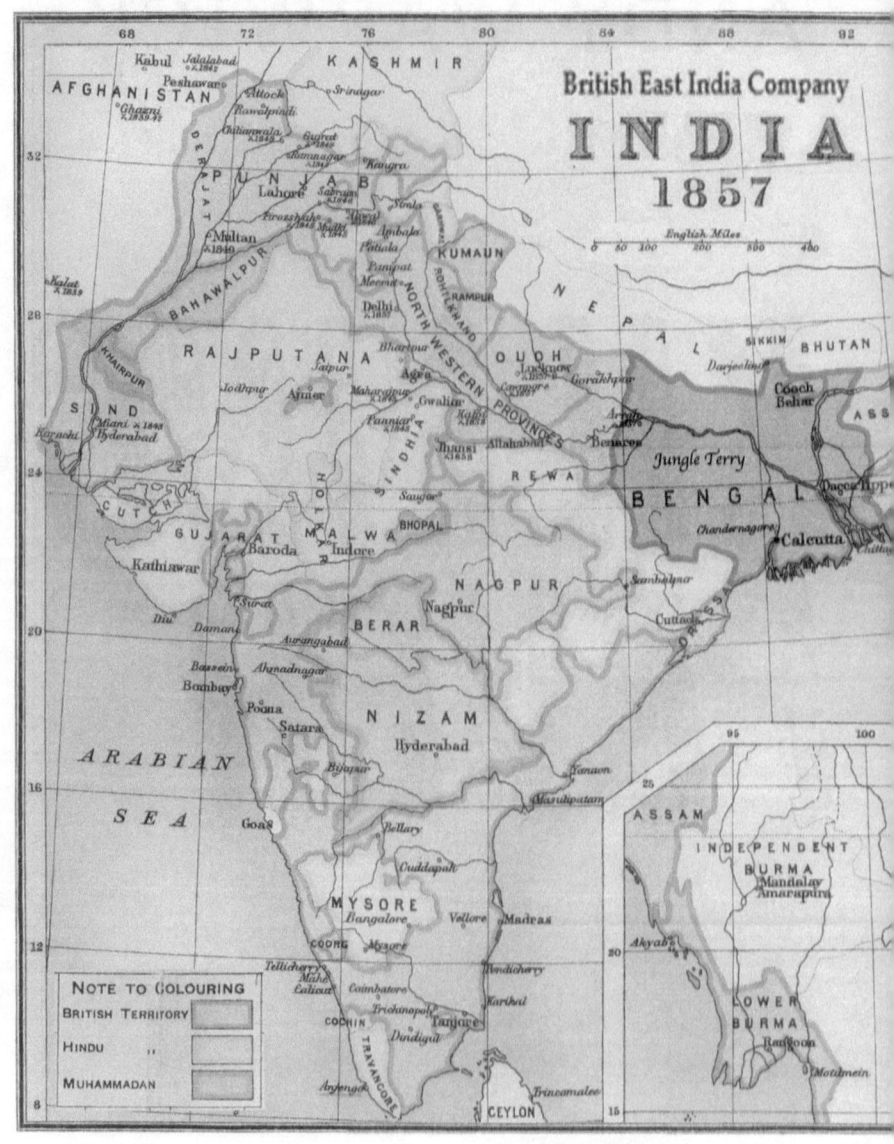

Jungle Terry Bengal

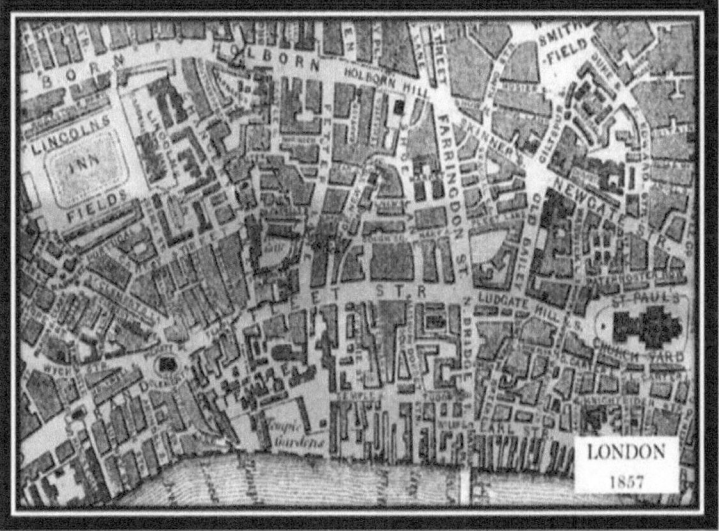

LONDON
1857

Prologue

The Santals or hill-tribes of west Bengal are well-built men, about five feet seven, weighing eight stone, without the delicate features of the Aryan, but undisfigured by the oblique eye of the Chinese, or the heavy physiognomy of the Malay. They are men created to labour rather than to think.
– William Hunter, The Ethnical Frontier of Bengal, 1868

A British rent collector has acquired among this wild people a power which is almost regal. He has increased the revenue paid to Government, from two thousand to forty-three thousand rupees a year, and this with so little oppression, that the Santals have increased in number to 82,795 souls.
– The Friend of India, Calcutta, 1852

Wealth, wealth
O mother wealth
Where was your birth?
I was born
In the soil
I was born
In the splash of rain
– Traditional Santal Song

Part I

Preparation

59.

THURINGIAN PORCELAIN MORTARS, thick in the body, with large spouts, glazed outside, biscuit inside, all with PESTLES.

59. Hemispherical, with large spout and foot, $3\frac{1}{4}$ inches wide, 1s. 9d.

John Griffin, *Chemical Handicraft*, 1866

Part 1

Preparation

One

NOT MANY MEN know where and when they'll die.

I did. And I knew how. I watched them build the gallows from my cell in Millbank Prison. Three men arrived this morning with a handcart full of timber. It's a simple affair, a gibbet on a high table with a trap door. Banged together with nails.

At 6am they'd tie my hands and ankles, put the noose around my neck. Slip the bolt and let me drop. Last things I'd see were the Houses of Parliament, smoke from factories south of the River Thames. In theory the drop would break my neck, what they'd call a civilized execution.

The first of my people I saw hanged by the British were lynched from a Banyan tree near a silk factory in the Bengal jungle. They were dead, turning like game in the summer breeze. My mother said they'd refused to plant indigo instead of rice. I was seven years old. It wasn't the worst thing I saw that day.

My cell's small and sparse with a vaulted ceiling like a crypt. My ankles are shackled to a chain that's fixed to the wall. So I've nothing to do but look out the window. Listen to a clock in Westminster chime the quarter hour, like a death knell. And think.

Whoever wanted me to hang had done a good job. No doubt about it. They'd fixed the police. Fixed the judiciary. Even fixed the Home Secretary, Sir George Green. What kind of man could do a thing like that? And why? That's what I was thinking about. Because

1

once that rope snapped tight around my neck everyone would think I'd murdered Henry Bullock.

And not just murdered him. Beaten him. Tortured him. Wrecked his shop. I didn't do any of it. I told them that. I've knocked a few men senseless in my time, but I've never killed anyone.

The thing was, Henry owed me ten guineas. Don't get me wrong, it wasn't about the money. He was a friend. But Henry took liberties. Give him the idea I'd work for nothing he'd never pay me again. And I'd bought a ticket to Handel's Messiah at St Paul's Cathedral. I'm no Christian, but we Santals have our own messiah, *Thakur Jiu*, and the Hallelujah Chorus works just as well for him. I'd be humming for days on end, '*Lord of lords... Hallelujah!*'

Anyway, Henry was a druggist. Had a shop in Ivy Lane near St Paul's. If I called in before the concert, took him for a couple of pints in The Ship, he'd pay up sweet as a lamb. But when I got there the shop was dark. A printed card in the window said 'Closed'. I cupped my hands to the glass. No sign of Henry at the counter so I took out a copy of the unpaid bill to post through the letterbox. For some reason I tried the door handle, found it wasn't locked, which was odd. I stepped inside.

Henry sometimes mixed medicines in a back room but when the doorbell jingled, he'd pop out like a jack-in-the-box. Not that evening. I called his name. No reply. Then I heard a noise from the basement, like a groan. Went down the stairs to take a look.

That was my first mistake.

The room's chilly, gloomy like basements are. And the air's a bit ripe. Henry'd left two buckets of dung uncovered in a corner. Typical. A street-finder told him he made fifteen bob a week collecting 'pure'. That's dog shit to you and me. It's called 'pure' because it purifies things like leather. So Henry hatched a plan to get it direct from the dog kennels, set up a sort of refinery south of the river, sell 'fortified-pure' to the tanners in Bermondsey. There was always a scheme about to make him rich.

Two half-light windows were set near the top of the front wall, both thick with grime and cobwebs, heavily barred. You could see people's feet as they walked by. An oil lamp hung over the worktable, or what's left of it. Someone had hurled it on its side, scattering kit across the room. Cases of books and chemical apparatus the same. The floor was chaos.

In the middle a rotund figure lay flat on its back, half buried in the wreckage. I unhooked the lamp, climbed over the table and crunched through the broken glassware.

What I saw when I held the lamp near the body turned my stomach. I've seen plenty of messed-up dead'uns in my time, some so bad it took a while to realize they'd been human. But it's different when you know someone. Henry could be difficult all right. Thought everyone was out to rook him, even when they weren't. And when his temper flared he'd shout accusations, vicious stuff. I told him more than once to mind his tongue. But when I first came to London, had nothing, he put some work my way. Lent me bits of apparatus from this very room. I hadn't forgotten, never would.

It looked as if he'd gone fifty rounds with Bill Perry, the Tipton Slasher. His head's beaten to a pulp, swollen half as big again as normal. One eye's so bloated you couldn't see the eyeball. Blood had crusted round his broken nose. More than a few teeth were missing, a couple poked through his top lip. But when I looked closer I saw it wasn't just a beating. This was surgical violence, calculated to cause agony. The teeth had been torn out with pliers, tongue crushed. Ears twisted half off his head. I'll spare you the rest.

The vacant stare told me he was dead but I crouched down to make sure. That's when I saw the bottle. Henry's right arm was thrown out perpendicular to his body. The bottle lay in his palm as if he'd held it tight as he died. I set the lamp down, picked up the bottle. The label said, *Poison. Prussic Acid*. His left arm lay at his side, fist clenched.

I laid the unpaid bill on his chest and prized the fingers open.

There in his palm was the stopper belonging to the bottle. I gave the body a quick onceover, wondering what to make of it.

Then the bell upstairs jingled and someone shouted, *"Shop!"*

"Down here," I called.

That was my second mistake.

A MAN TROD cautiously down the stairs, wrinkled his nose at the stink. The uniform said a sergeant in the City of London Police, but I'd seldom seen a man looked less like a copper. You'd think he was an actor in costume. For a start he's too young, mid-twenties at most. His face was fresh, cheeks pink, more like a writer or a professor. The eyes were big and curious, lips full. His mutton-chop whiskers ended in a shaved vertical line below the corners of his mouth.

What I saw was a handsome young man, strongly built but trying to look older than his years, wanting some social gravity. When he saw me, he stopped and drew a truncheon from his belt. Then he crouched a little, held out the weapon and crept on down. At the bottom he crunched forward trying to make sense of the scene. A couple of paces from me he stopped.

"Get up!" he said, in curt Glasgow Scots.

I knew the accent from British soldiers in Calcutta. A policeman there would've questioned a Santal with a kick, a beating with his *lathi*, a bamboo cane. I got up, lifting my hands to show I meant no harm.

"What happened?" I said.

The sergeant's wary, waving the stick like he's ready to use it. Which I didn't doubt. He's on his own in a dark cellar with a dark-skinned man and a dead body. He might've hit me already but for two things. I dress like an Englishman, and I speak like one, more or less. A little slower perhaps, more clipped, more nasal, with just enough of my native Bengal accent to remind me who I am. But tailored cotton and a schooled tone make a difference.

He waved me back a pace and stared down at the body.

"It's Henry Bullock," says I. "Dead."

"I can see that," he grunted.

He nodded at the bottle in my hand. "What's that?"

"Prussic acid. Cyanide."

He drew back a fraction, eyes wide. "That a threat?"

I shook my head.

He tugged a pair of Darby handcuffs from his belt.

"Turn around," he said. "Hands behind you."

I wasn't being cuffed. Not by him. So I stood my ground, arms still raised, and stared him in the eye. I'm tall for a Santal, lean and well built.

The sergeant stood his ground too. "You resisting arrest?"

They wouldn't have asked that in Bengal. Just thrashed you senseless with the lathi. "No need for arrest," I said. "I came to collect a debt, that's how I found him. The bill's there on his chest."

Now the sergeant's uncertain, eyeing the bottle of cyanide. What if I throw it at him? The floor's littered with pots and pans, furniture, shards of broken glassware. It's no place for a violent struggle. He tucked the Darby's away and drew his rattle. It's a stick with a sprocket on one end, a hardwood clacker that chatters over the teeth when it's whirled. Makes a hell of a row.

"I can have half a dozen men here in two minutes," he said.

And the rest. The alarm would bring every copper, every do-gooder, every busybody for a quarter mile, running. I didn't want that. So I thought about what I had. A young sergeant who seems intelligent, ambitious, in a hurry. I re-stoppered the cyanide bottle and held it out like peace offering.

"That'd be a pity," I said.

He made a curious frown, said nothing.

"You'll lose your lead."

"What lead?"

"Knowing how Henry Bullock died."

"You know something about it?"

"It's my business, forensic medicine. Look at the bill"

The sergeant glanced at the paper on Henry's chest. Then he jabbed the stick like a warning, ducked down and picked up the bill. My name and business were written at the top. He read it, tucked the sheet in his tunic.

"That's mine," I said.

"It's evidence."

"Of what?"

"Murder."

I shook my head. "Suicide."

"Suicide! You're pulling my pisser. Look at him, man!"

"You look. Cold blue sheen on the skin, visible eye glistening. Lips reek of bitter almonds. It's a text-book case of cyanide poisoning. His torturers knew their business, how to cause agony without risk of death. None of the injuries are fatal, I checked."

"So they finished him off with poison."

They ... not me? I shook my head, explained how the bottle and stopper were gripped in Henry's hands.

He looked down, screwed up his face in disgust. "Dear God," he said, "why beat a man like that?"

I pointed to the rough brickwork in the front wall.

"That might be your answer," I said.

The sergeant followed my finger, nodded slowly. Then he came to some kind of decision. He tucked the rattle back in his belt and waved me towards the brickwork with the cosh. I went ahead, took up the lamp as I passed the body.

Behind me I heard him stop. When I turned he'd crouched over what looked like a crumpled sheet of butcher's paper on the floor. For a moment he poked at it with a finger. Then he rolled it into a rough tube, folded the ends and slipped it into his pocket. He nodded me forward.

I'd pointed to a safe on a stone plinth under a half-light window, set deep in the brickwork. Not any old safe. It's a Price's Double

Door, best money could buy. Henry'd told me about it. Pickproof. Fireproof. Gunpowder proof. Kind of thing you'd find in a City bank. It's a yard tall, a yard wide, weighed more than half a ton. Henry must've had it built in. Try to pull it out you'd bring down half the house.

The sergeant followed my line of thought. You want to get inside a safe like that, well, there's only one way. You need the key. Actually you need two keys because a Double Door has two locks, one for each door.

"Jesus," he said. "What's he got in there, the crown jewels?"

Now I happened to now there's a lot of cash in that safe. Henry told me himself. We'd had a skin-full of Hanbury's ale in The Ship one night, just after he came back from India. He didn't often drink but when he did he took it like medicine, a tumbler of whiskey with every pint, chucked back in one. After five or six he's tight as a boiled owl, started sharing confidences. Mostly he wanted to tell me about a safe he'd bought, the Price's Double Door.

"New design," says he, "George Price challenged the locksmiths to pick it, or blow it open. *Couldn't do it!*" he spat in my ear. "Wrote a book about it, Price did."

Then he began a long explanation of the safety features, like the locks are such you can't pour in any quantity of gunpowder. As it happened I knew all about Price's safes but I let Henry rabbit on.

"You might wonder," he slurs, "why I'd spend forty pound on a safe. Me, who's careful with every farthing."

I'd had five or six myself so I just sipped my beer, inquisitive.

"Banks!" says he, suddenly angry.

"What happened?" I said.

"Never trust'em", he growled. "Take your money but they don't want to give it out. I'm keeping mine in that safe. I don't need banks, not me."

Then, quieter and sort of nasty, he said, "There's something in there you'd like to know, Baboo. Wouldn't you just." He called me

Baboo when he was drunk so people wouldn't think he's too friendly with a black. Not even one in a nice suit. Henry knew at once he'd said too much about the safe. Told me to forget it. Got up, lurched out. I sat wondering what he meant while I finished my pint. We never discussed it again.

I wasn't telling the sergeant that story. Instead I set the lamp and the bottle of cyanide on top of the safe. The sergeant tried both handles. Locked. He patted the top.

"There's something in here worth a man's life," he said.

"Seems like it," I replied. But I thought, *there's something in there Henry'd rather die than hand over*. Which is a very different matter.

"You say you knew Bullock?"

I nodded.

"Any idea where he kept the keys?"

"Nope."

He picked up the bottle of cyanide. "Poisoned," he said. "Suicide, eh?"

I read his mind. What I'd said could be true. Except it might be me who wanted those keys, who tortured Henry, who poured cyanide down his throat.

The sergeant gave the bottle a thoughtful stare. "Look," he said, "you're the expert on poison. Will you not come to Old Jewry, write down what happened? The Super won't believe me."

I looked at my pocket watch. Nearly half past six. I'm supposed to meet Bea – Beatrice – on the steps of St Paul's at seven thirty. She's not the kind of woman you kept waiting. If I didn't hurry I'd miss her. And I'd miss the concert, Hallelujah and all. But the sergeant's right. No one would believe how Henry died. Not unless I laid it out in black and white. I owed him that. And I'd a feeling the sergeant might use the rattle if I didn't cooperate.

"All right," I said. "I'll come."

That was my third mistake, the big one.

Two

IT'S A SHORT walk east from Ivy Lane to Old Jewry. As we went I asked the sergeant why he'd come into the shop. Turned out it's his beat. He'd seen the 'closed' sign, tried the door just as I had.

"Won't be easy opening that safe," I said. "Without the keys."

"Aye. What about next of kin, wife or someone like that?"

"Henry lived alone over the shop. Kept his own company. He once mentioned a sister ... Ethel or maybe Emma?"

"Know where she lives?"

"No idea. But she's married so she won't be a Bullock now."

We turned up Old Jewry, went left through a wrought iron archway into a courtyard, approached a redbrick building with a columned entrance of Portland stone. On the lintel was chiselled, Chief Office, City of London Police. Inside the big oak door was a reception area with a counter and a duty officer. The place looked and smelt institutional.

"This way," the sergeant said, guiding me to a side door.

The duty officer followed me with hard, suspicious eyes. I don't suppose they got a lot of Indians in frock coats dropping by. The sergeant gave him a nod to say all's well. Then he took my arm and zigzagged me along the corridors to a sparsely furnished room. In the middle's a table with a pile of paper, a blotter, a ha'penny inkpot and a pen. Tall windows faced a courtyard. A mahogany and brass clock ticked on the wall.

The sergeant nodded at the table. "You know what we need?"

I nodded. Then an odd thing happened. When he left, the sergeant locked the door. Didn't say anything. Just gave me a look, then *click*.

I wanted to get going so I dipped the pen, wrote my name and what I'd seen, my conclusion, my signature and the date. I'd done it a dozen times before for the Metropolitan Police. I blotted the ink. Sat back, waited. Watched the big hand twitch round to a quarter past seven. Waited. Got up and rattled the door. Called out. No response. Waited. Half past seven. Thought about climbing out of a window. That's when it registered there were iron bars on the outside. I was a prisoner. Eight o'clock.

WHEN I HEARD a key in the lock I was ready to give the sergeant a piece of my mind. But he wasn't alone. Four other men trooped in with him. The atmosphere cooled ten degrees before they'd shut the door. Two were young constables with heavy side-whiskers. One's thickset, like a wrestler, the other's taller with a gaunt face and greasy hair. Made me think of a sewer rat.

The fourth's a superintendent, pale faced with flabby jowls hanging over his tunic collar. He's wearing a stovepipe hat, even though we're inside. Clean shaven, around fifty. In his hand was the poison bottle from Henry's shop. He set it carefully on the table. Then he pulled out a chair and sat so stiffly you'd think someone's taking his photograph. He pointed to a seat on the other side.

"Sit down, boy" he ordered.

I didn't sit. I don't answer to the name, 'boy'. Rule one: never show fear.

The fifth man's different. Tall and bony, wearing a scarlet tunic prettied up with gold lace and blue lapels. White gloves and black boots. The uniform says he's a major in the East India Company army. His face was long and thin, tapering to a narrow chin. He'd an intellectual forehead topped with a mop of tangled black hair. Looked like he'd rolled out of bed and combed it with his fingers. There's three days' stubble on his chin, a walrus moustache drooping over his top lip. But the eyes—deep set, hooded and unforgiving, staring like the dead.

The sergeant and constables lined up behind me. The superintendent read my deposition, told me again to sit down. Since he and the major were seated, I obliged. As I pulled out my chair I turned and asked the sergeant what's going on.

"I'm in charge here," the superintendent said. The voice was abrupt. Face as hard as a marble mantelpiece.

"And who're you?" I said.

"Superintendent Cartwright."

I'd heard of him. He'd a reputation for being tough and relentless.

"You'd no right to imprison me," I said.

Cartwright ignored me. He took a sheet of paper, dipped the pen.

"Name?" he barked.

"I came here to help."

"Good for you. What's your name?"

"It's there on my deposition."

"You tell me."

London coppers all start as constables. Work their way up by getting results, staying sober. That's in *Bradley's Guide to Modern London*, my first companion in the city. Superintendent Cartwright was at the top. Only the Commissioner was higher, and he wasn't a copper at all. So I had some respect for Cartwright. Knew I wouldn't get anywhere by blowing up.

"Khan," I said. "Hyder Khan."

He looked up from the sheet. "You one of them Mohammedans?"

"Muslims. They worship Allah, not Mohammed. No, I'm not."

"Hindu, then?"

I fished out a visiting card. Tossed it on the table. It read, *Dr Hyder Khan, Esq. Prince of Murshidabad, Certified and Proficient Chemist, Royal College of Chemistry*. Rule two: if you want to be treated like a gentleman, act like one.

Cartwright picked the card up. Whatever he'd expected, it wasn't a doctor or a prince. "Where's that?" he asked, "Moor-shid-a-bad."

"It's the old Moghul capital of *Bengal*," the major threw in, as if they couldn't trust a word I said. "Murshidabad's a hundred miles upriver from our capital, *Calcutta.*" He spoke from the back of his throat in a sing-song croak, like a bad ventriloquist. Let the last word ring like an order.

Cartwright looked at me. "That where you're from, Murshidabad?"

"From?" I said.

"Where you were born," he growled. "Grew up."

We stared at each other for a moment. Then he leaned forward, spoke slowly like talking to a child. "I was born in London," he said. "Grew up in London. I'm a Londoner. What about you?" The tone was threatening.

"I was born nowhere," I said. "Grew up, nowhere."

"Nowhere," he echoed, glanced at the major like he's missing something.

"Nowhere you'll find on a Company map of India," I said.

The Company – the East India Company – runs Britain's Indian Empire. A couple of hundred million Indians – I'm one of them – ruled by a Court of Directors from a private house in the City of London. They keep an army bigger than Britain's, led by men like the major. I think they find it hard to believe themselves, which is why they like making maps. Their India, with its forts and factories, imperial lands lined in red.

You won't find my people's villages on there.

"I was born in a clearing in a forest," I said. "In a valley in an unmarked range of hills somewhere in upper Bengal. I think it's labelled, Jungle-Terry."

Cartwright scribbled, 'born in the jungle'. As he wrote, he said, "Funny place for a prince to be born."

I shrugged. "It's where my mother was."

He sat back, made a hand gesture that said, *you don't look like jungle boy.*

I said, "At seven I went to the Nawab's College in Murshidabad."

Cartwright glanced at the major but I headed him off.

"Bengal used to be part of the Mughal Empire, as the major said. The Nawab's the local ruler. These days he's a British puppet, living on a stipend, doing what he's told."

While we were talking the major had been studying my deposition. I don't know what I'd written that intrigued him so much. Without looking up, he hummed, "You didn't learn chemistry in the Nawab's *College.*"

"You're right," I said. Then to Cartwright, "Murshidabad's a place of palaces and mosques. No laboratories. No test-tubes. I learnt my chemistry at the Medical College in Calcutta."

Cartwright glanced at my card. "You're a doctor," he said.

"Sort of. Blacks qualify as *native* doctors, can't treat white men."

Cartwright wrote it down. Then he sat back, folded his arms and studied me for a few seconds.

"So why're you in London?" he said. "You can't practice medicine."

I nodded at my card. "I came to study at the Royal College of Chemistry, with Professor Hofmann."

Cartwright put his forearms on the table and leaned in my face. "What's an Indian want with chemistry, eh?"

I was fed up with this. I didn't like it that the sergeant had tricked me into coming to the City Office. Didn't like being locked up. Didn't like the fact I'd left Bea waiting on the steps of St Paul's. I liked this interrogation even less. I mirrored Cartwright so our noses are a foot apart. "We're emerging from savagery," I said. "By the benevolence of British rule."

We stared like that while the clock ticked off ten seconds. His eyebrows rose in high arcs the way artists depict birds in flight. Gave him a permanent frown. Behind me the sergeant cleared his throat. I'll swear he couldn't stand the tension. Then Cartwright sat back. I did the same. One all.

By way of being helpful, I said, "I specialise in toxicology."

13

"What's that when it's at home?"

"From the Greek, *toxikon*. Meaning arrow poison. And *logia*, a science. I study poisons."

"So you'd know how to kill a man, with cyanide."

"What's that supposed to mean?"

"Show me your hands," he said.

Which changed everything. Because I saw at once how one thing would lead to another. Knew I was in big trouble.

"I came here voluntarily," I said.

"Your hands?"

"I'm here to help–"

"HANDS! On the table."

When I didn't move, Cartwright gave a nod. Two men grabbed a wrist each, pulled my arms out and shouldered me forward. The third shoved my face into the table. I'm pinned, crucified, palms on the desk.

"That's better," Cartwright said.

He leaned over, examined my knuckles. Then he nodded again and someone hit the back of my neck with a truncheon. I'm used to being hit so I didn't pass out. Not until he hit me again, harder. This time an electric charge shot up my spine, exploded in my head. Next thing I'm sat upright, wrists shackled in a pair of Darby's behind the chair. Something warm's dribbling down my chin. I tasted blood, sucked it up.

Cartwright said, "How'd your knuckles get like that?"

I shook my head to clear it. "Like what?"

"Cut. Bruised."

The truth is I'd fought Tom Sayers in a bareknuckle exhibition match at The Castle pub. Tom's got a grudge because I won't do title fights. Can't risk the publicity. But then people say I'm better than him, so he thought he'd show them otherwise. Ended in a proper scrap. I can't tell Cartwright that.

"Chemistry's risky," I said. "Strong acids, alkalis, exploding glassware." I use that as a cover for cuts and blemishes on my face.

"What're you," he said, "the clumsiest chemist in Christendom?"

I'd have laughed if I hadn't just been assaulted. Instead I counted the buttons on his tunic. Six down. Six up.

"Turn out his pockets," Cartwright said.

A minute later there's a pocket-watch, a folding knife, a hand-kerchief, a wallet, keys, some loose change and two tickets for the Messiah on the table. Cartwright took the bill from his tunic and tossed it on top. It was made out to Mr Henry Bullock Esq, ten guineas. Unpaid.

"You were there to collect a debt, Khan. Weren't you?"

"A reminder," I said. "Henry was a friend."

"That why you confronted him with an unpaid bill in a cellar?"

"He was dead when I found him. It's there in my deposition."

"Bollocks. You'd been in Bullock's basement before, hadn't you?"

I shrugged. "He let me use the chemical apparatus."

"So you knew about his safe."

"Yes."

"Know how much was in the till upstairs?"

When I shook my head, the sergeant said, "Five pounds."

"Five pounds," Cartwright repeated. "Not enough. So you drag Bullock downstairs, tell him to open the safe. But he won't. So you punch him. Kick him. Smash up his basement. Still won't open it. So you torture him. Rip his ears, his tongue–"

"*No!*" I took a breath. "You think I'd do that ... for ten guineas?"

Cartwright leaned at me again. "I've known plenty'd do it for a farthing, for the fun of it. But with you it's instinct, Baboo, law of the jungle. You can put a white man's clothes on, but you're still a savage out for–"

"Rubbish," I said. "Whoever messed up Henry's mouth used pliers. "Where are they?" I reckoned the attackers had taken them.

"Not pliers," Cartwright said. "But you'd know that."

He pulled a white paper package from his pocket, laid it on the table. It's slim, weighty, the one from Henry's basement. Cartwright unfolded the ends, unrolled it by half turns. Brown flecks showed on the paper, larger with each turn. The flecks became blobs, then bloodstains. Inside were three objects. Not pliers. There's a pair of medical pincers with strong jaws, shaped for rapid extraction. Or slow. Between the handles lay two human teeth. Big molars. Still weeping where the blood vessels had torn away. Henry's teeth.

I felt slightly sick.

Cartwright tapped the shiny steel. "Know what they are?"

"Dental forceps." No point in pretending I didn't.

"Kind of thing a doctor might use?"

I said nothing. They knew I'd studied medicine.

Cartwright leaned closer. "Bullock's helpless. You force his mouth open. Use these on him. But he's a tough old bastard, won't tell you a damn thing. You panic. What if he goes to the police? So you use your chemistry. Kill him, with cyanide." He nodded at the bottle on the table. "That cyanide. Then you've got the bloody nerve to come here saying it's suicide, make out you're helping us."

I said, "The bottle and stopper were in *his* hands."

"*Your* hands. That's what the sergeant saw."

The sergeant began, "He was kneeling–"

"Stow it, Chrystal"

"He reckons–"

"*Stow it!* Or you can get the hell out of here," Cartwright shouted.

"Bullock killed himself," I said.

"You're a liar!" Now Cartwright looked at me like I'd shot his dog. "We know what you did in Ivy Lane," he said. "I'm going to see you hang, Khan. Prince or no bloody prince. Help bury your rotten corpse in an unmarked grave. Then you'll be forgotten. Got it?"

The hatred in his voice said he really thought I'd done it.

He took up the pen. We all watched him scratch a few lines while the clock ticked off thirty seconds. He spun the paper, pushed it across the table. It's my confession, just as he'd told it. "Sign," he said. "Juries like a confession, remorse. Let's say Bullock took a swing at you. You defended yourself, lost your temper. Maybe you'll get transportation."

"What, to the colonies?" I said, with all the sarcasm I could find. "I'm signing nothing. Not saying another word till I've talked to a lawyer."

I could see I'd rattled Cartwright. He thought he'd had me on the run, ready to confess. By demanding a lawyer I'd tripped him, broken his charge. But then the major set my deposition carefully on the table.

"You'll talk to *me*," he said. Then to Cartwright, *"Alone."*

The Superintendent glared. He'd been dismissed from his own office in front of his own men. In front of the prisoner. For a moment I thought he'd tell the major to go to hell. But he stood, beckoned the others. They trooped out as they'd trooped in, Cartwright last. As he left, he said, "You've got fifteen minutes, Major. That's it."

I almost called him back. Cartwright was brutal but he wanted justice. He thought I'd killed Henry Bullock, but sooner or later I'd persuade him otherwise, that's what I felt.

Now I'm alone with a man who's dismissed the law, wants no witnesses to whatever he's got in mind. Like being back in Jungle-Terry where Company soldiers can rape and murder as they please. I'm wondering how a major can dismiss a superintendent, what he's got to say that no one else must hear. Why he cares about a dead druggist in a London backstreet.

I didn't have long to wait for an answer.

Three

THE MAJOR SHIFTED to Cartwright's chair. One side of his belt he wore a revolver, an Adams' Dragoon. The other side's a bayonet from a Pattern Rifle. Looked as if he'd just stepped off a battlefield on the Punjab plains. Not that I've been to the Punjab, but I know the East India Company fought two wars there back in the '40s, extended the Company's Empire all the way to Afghanistan.

The major had both Punjab medals on his tunic: solid silver etched with the Queen's head, hung on dark blue ribbons, one striped with crimson, one with yellow. What you get for grabbing a piece of India twice the size of England.

When the silence had settled, he said, "You're for the drop, Khan."

"Let's see what a lawyer says."

"There's no *law-yer*," he sang. "We're dealing with high treason."

"I thought we're dealing with Henry Bullock's death?"

The Major pulled a document from his tunic. It had a lion-and-unicorn crest with a Latin motif. A few lines of script to say Major Raikes Elphinstone was empowered to take any action he saw fit to protect the national interest. Signed by Sir George Green, the Home Secretary. Green's signature was at the bottom, next to his seal in a blob of red wax.

I knew Raikes Elphinstone. Most of Calcutta did, by reputation. Europeans called him the finest soldier in the Company army. We natives knew him as a master torturer. I'm not talking dungeons and walled prison yards. Brutality isn't hidden in Bengal. He tortured in the marketplace and village street. Have a man lifted by his ears till he wept in front of his family and neighbours.

Once he put a woman's new-born baby in a sack with a fierce cat. Said he'd whip the bag with a lathi if she didn't betray her husband's whereabouts. That way he shocked and shamed the whole tribe. Confess to insurgency and he'd hang you on the spot or put a bullet in your brain. I know, he'd done it to my people just eighteen months ago.

A burn of anger stirred in my guts.

"Any *action*," he crooned. "Heard of Colonel James *Peach?*"

"Who hasn't?"

I got home news at the East India Rooms in St Martin's Place, the gossip centre for all things oriental. The buzz in April was of mutiny in the Company's army at Barrackpore. Eighty percent of the soldiers are Indian natives – Hindus, Muslims and Sikhs – led by British officers. Sepoys, they're called, and there's no shortage of unrest in their ranks.

What made this different was that Barrackpore's only ten miles from Calcutta, the home of British rule. When you run a native army trained in modern warfare, mutiny's a terrifying thought. For a few sweaty days the British in Calcutta lived in fear. Then the mutinous regiment's commander, Colonel James Peach, was found dead, by his own hand.

"Blew his brains out in the Garrison Church," I said. "They found his body on the altar steps, pistol in his hand."

"Know why he died?"

I shrugged. "Papers were full of lurid stories. Eye-witness accounts of the look on his face, the gore splattered in the choir stalls."

"He was a *trait-or*," Elphinstone said. "If Britain's enemies had sat in conclave for a century they couldn't have dreamt up anything worse."

"What's that to do with me?" I said.

"Peach took his orders from London. When I put a gun to his head in the Church, know what he told me?"

"I'm listening."

"The order came in a dispatch, delivered by Henry Bullock."

I felt goose-skin on my back, like trickles of cold water.

"Henry?" I said. "Maybe ... Peach lied. To save his life."

Elphinstone shook his head. "James Peach believed in God. In Heaven and Hell, eternal damnation. The whole kit. He wasn't a man to die with a lie on his lips. When he named Bullock, he meant it. Then I shot him."

He drew the Dragoon, pointed it at me across the table.

The goose-skin turned to a burn of fear.

"I'll shoot you too," he said. "Right now. Or you can walk out a free man. Your *choice*." He tucked the paper back in his tunic.

I believed him. Except for the bit about walking out free. Inside me rage and fear sloshed about like tides in the Ganges delta. I didn't want to tell him a damned thing. But I wasn't giving him reason to call me a traitor, kill me in cold blood.

My arms gripped the chair back, "What do you want?" I said.

"A name."

"What name?"

"Who told you to kill Henry Bullock?"

I licked my dry lips, swallowed.

Elphinstone pointed the gun with both hands. A Dragoon fires a half inch diameter bullet, there's a hell of a recoil.

"We know it was Slegman, Clyde or Birdwood. Which one?" He spoke like the game's almost up so I might as well tell him. "You've got five seconds, Khan. Then you follow Peach. *One...*"

My heart's banging like a piston, making me ashamed. My people fought the British and their Sepoys to the last man, bows and arrows against Enfield rifles. Wouldn't retreat while the flutes and war drums played. Sounds like madness, but their courage was all the dignity they had left. I'm trying to look calm, tough, which isn't easy when you feel like jelly.

"*Two...*"

I'd heard of a Slegman and a Clyde, but I'd never met either man.

"*Three...*"

His finger squeezed the trigger so the hammer lifted, the cylinder began to turn. Somewhere in the mechanism a tiny ratchet clicked, like a warning. My thoughts spun like flywheels. Elphinstone wants me dead, like Peach. If I don't answer he'll shoot. If I give a name he'll know I'm involved, shoot me anyway. It's an execution.

"*Four...*"

"Who was in the basement?" I said. "You or me? Who saw the body?"

Quiet. Then, "You did."

"The Home Secretary wants the truth?"

A small nod.

"Tell him I didn't kill Bullock. What's more, you *know* I didn't."

The Major sat rigid. I'm trying not to think I could be dead in half a second. His eyebrows were the opposite of Cartwright's, ran straight above his eyes, then downward, like ticks. He gave a little backwards nod like, *tell me.*

"At least two men tortured him. Probably three. There's a hank of grey hair by the body, bruises on the cheeks. Someone held him down while his mouth was messed up. The place was wrecked, like a bomb had gone off. Took several men to do that. Where are they?"

"Ran off when Sergeant Chrystal arrived."

"But I stayed?"

"To make sure Bullock's dead."

"You trained at Addiscombe," I said. That's the East India Company's military college, south of London.

Elphinstone frowned. "What's that to do with anything?"

"You know a bit about poisons." I knew that because I'd applied for a job as chemistry lecturer at Addiscombe. "Which means you know cyanide can take five minutes to kill. So I poison Henry, wait till Sergeant Chrystal arrives ... call him down while I kneel over the body holding the bottle and stopper?"

I gave him a questioning look.

"Go on," he said.

"Bullock took that poison himself, just as I told Cartwright." I reminded him toxicology's my business, what I'd found in Ivy Lane.

"What about your knuckles, the bruises?"

I also knew Addiscombe cadets learn self-defence by sparring in the gym. And Elphinstone had scars on his face, one by his left eye, another on his right cheekbone. I'd say split by a fist. So he knew a bit about boxing.

"Take another look," I said. "A close one."

He kept the gun on me as he came around the table. Yanked up my cuffed hands so he could see the knuckles. They look like steel bolts in a leather glove.

"Not just bruised," I said. "Stained. I soak them in whisky with copperas and gunpowder. Makes them fit to punch another man's head. I had a fight, two days ago."

The Major sat down, lifted the gun. "You saying you're a boxer?"

"Train at the Cambrian Stores in Castle Street."

"Why didn't you tell Cartwright?"

"Boxers often land in gaol, which'd wreck my business. And he wasn't pointing a revolver at me."

"You've got a clean face for a boxer," he said.

"I fight fast. Slip and arch, use the knock-out punch. *Pretty dancing*, the old school call it ... but you don't earn more by getting pulped."

Elphinstone leaned back, chair creaking under his weight.

In a while, he said, "Why'd Bullock kill himself?"

"Didn't want to open the safe. Somebody hurt him till he couldn't take it anymore. But Henry's bloody minded, just as Cartwright said. Tell him it's his money or his life, he'd keep the money every time."

Elphinstone nodded. He knew about torture, what desperate people can do when they're faced with impossible decisions.

"How'd he get the poison?" he said.

"I told you, the place was wrecked. The poison cabinet lay on its side near the body. Ask Chrystal. Henry saw his chance, grabbed the bottle."

The Major nodded again. He bought some of what I said. Some. I breathed a little easier when he laid the Dragoon on the table. But the way he tapped his fingers said this wasn't over. More like just starting.

SO I STARTED first.

"What if Henry did deliver a dispatch? Doesn't mean he knew what it said. He's no saint, but treason doesn't sound right."

"He knew who sent it."

"Slegman, Clyde or Birdwood?"

The Major ignored me. Maybe he shouldn't've dropped those names. The Slegman I'd heard of was Chairman of the East India Company, a man so expert at grabbing land he wrote a book about it – *How to Colonize* – who celebrated holy profit in *Christ and Capital*. I'd read them in Calcutta Public Library. Clyde's his Deputy, owner of the biggest chemical company in London. They're two of the most powerful men on earth. If it's them.

"Bullock didn't go to Calcutta alone," he said. "He went with a man called Elijah Doyle. Know him?"

"Professor of Pharmacy at King's College on the Strand."

"Know him well?"

"I've heard him lecture, that's all."

"What's he look like, this Doyle?"

"Like a judge, or a bishop. Double chin. Got a belly fit to fire the buttons off his waistcoat. High forehead with a halo of white hair."

Elphinstone nodded. "Know why they went to India?"

"No idea. Why don't you ask Doyle?"

"Oh, I will," he said, with a glance at my deposition.

Then he stroked his moustache, picked up my card. "You're no prince," he said. "You're an Anglo-Indian, a half-caste. Not that you look it."

He means I'm too black. But I let it go. Elphinstone's got his own department collecting intelligence for the Quartermaster General at Calcutta's Fort William, the hub of British power. Which means he knows a lot about me. Or thinks he does.

"Oh yes," he said. "We've got a string of files on you, Khan." He gave me the dead-eyed stare. "How you tried to humiliate the Company, drag its name in the mud." He tossed the card on the table, picked up Henry's unpaid bill. "To the analysis of nitrogenous waste and lime," he read out. "What's that *mean?*"

I didn't reply, not right away. The grip of fear had passed.

I'd once wondered what I'd say to Elphinstone if we ever met. I certainly hated him. Two years ago, the Santal – my people – rebelled against years of misuse by the Company's native go-betweens. Thakur Jiu, our God, appeared to our leaders, declared an end to British rule, a new reign of fair trade.

The British couldn't believe it. When the peaceful Santal defeated the Sepoys sent to quell them, panic spread through Bengal. Rentiers and taxmen and corrupt policemen hid their loot and fled. The Company announced martial law and sent in Major Elphinstone. He got to work with ropes, whips, bamboo pincers, prickly pears, red ants, chilies ... every cruel device of torture.

The Santal leaders were betrayed, hunted down and killed, or caged and hanged. That's why I hated Elphinstone. Not because he's white or British. I take people as I find them, and I found Elphinstone the devil.

"First of all," I said, "I didn't drag the Company in the mud. The traders and tax collectors who cheated the Santal did that. Like the railway men who raped their women, the Sepoys who killed ten thousand of them, trampled their villages with war elephants–"

"Rebels," Elphinstone growled. "Blood thirsty *savages.*"

"Savages? People who cleared forests, planted crops ... toiled for less than nothing to make the Company rich?"

"Civilized men take their grievances to a magistrate."

"They did. He said their tally in rope-knots was inadmissible." I leaned as far forward as I could. "Called them dacoits – bandits – for trying to take back what was theirs. Imprisoned them, while the true thieves went free."

"They were misled by evil, designing men."

I laughed out loud. "From the mother's arms of Queen Victoria? Children led by rebels and false gods ... pulled by invisible strings and hidden hands?" I shook my head in disgust. "Rebellion was their last resort. Not a thunderclap of childish rage, not a contagion. They rejected you and your rule and your civilization. Even sent you the branch of a Sal tree to declare war, like gentlemen."

Now I'd raised my voice, it felt like something I'd waited all my life to say. "You tortured children, wrecked and burned our villages, left thousands wandering the jungle like ghosts. Who's the savage, Elphin–"

His fist hit the table so hard, ink splashed from the pot. He stared, searching for words to rebut me. I'd torn up his manual of stock insults. Let him know I wasn't fooled by Company histories that made us monkey tribes and heathens. Which was a pity because I hadn't just wondered what I'd say to him. I wanted to know what he'd say to me.

Elphinstone wasn't the usual Company man. No other officer had been to Rugby School and Cambridge University, spent their leisure reading the classics in Latin. None had his bravado. On the battlefield he was a one-man army, fond of charging the enemy guns on horseback with a hog-spear and revolver – sticking the gunners, "Like pigs," he'd say. He'd nearly been cashiered. When he *stuck* a native chief the Company meant to install as a friendly prince, he was told to resign or face court martial.

The Governor General stepped in. Found another use for his talents gathering intelligence. Which gave free reign to his blood-sport instinct. The Major hunted Wahhabi assassins, Muslim Jihadists, Hindu agitators in the Sepoy ranks, low caste milkmen, potters and shoemakers who dodged taxes, the peasant farmers who grew rice instead of indigo. Call it a threat to Company rule and Elphinstone was above the law.

He eased his collar, stared at the tabletop. When he looked up, I knew the expression. Like the swaggerers who think a dark-skinned man's easy meat. I trade punches for a while, then launch a fusillade. If they stay up I get that look; shock and desperation clothed in fury. He's got to hit back fast, or he's finished.

"It's like a Bengal *tiger,*" he said.

You'd think I was a junior officer who'd asked an awkward question.

I waited. Then, "What is?"

"Painted on mulberry paper."

"Mulberry paper?" I thought for a moment he'd gone mad.

"Oh yes," he said. "Fading paint, torn paper."

He looked at me as if to say, *work that out.*

I said, "Don't know what you're talking about, Elphinstone."

He sat back, wiped his mouth with the back of his hand.

"Governors who think they're gods. Generals who'd rather send memos than fight wars ... traders so greedy they don't notice what's happening under their noses. Most of them believe their own lies, think the natives welcome our rule, that we're civilizing them."

He pulled a face, *you get it now?*

"Then someone splits the paper, like those Santal you're so fond of. Shows several million Indians how fragile our rule is. I mend it, retouch the paint. Make the cost of rebellion too terrible to contemplate, *unthinkable.*"

I don't know what I'd expected him to say, but it wasn't that.

"Why you?" I said. "Why're you the Empire's keeper?"

His eyes darted. "I don't need to be ordered to do a thing. To see it needs doing is enough." He pointed across the table. "And I'd have hanged you in Calcutta, Khan. If you hadn't fled the town."

The discussion's over. Elphinstone flapped the bill at me, waiting to hear what work I'd done for Henry.

"Shit," I said. "Henry collected dog turds."

"Dog shit? You trying to be *funny?*"

"There's brown and there's white. Tanners like the white, so the street-finders chip away mortar, mix it with the brown. It's a wonder half the walls in London haven't collapsed. Henry wondered if you could use lime instead."

The Major squinted at me, not sure if I'm pulling his pisser.

"Did a lot of analysis for Bullock, did you?"

"Now and then, it's part of my business."

"What *business?* How'd you know to read the scene of Bullock's death?"

I'd hoped he might ask that. Give me a chance to play the only card that might save my life.

"In Calcutta," I said, "I was William O'Shaughnessy's assistant."

Elphinstone hadn't expected that.

"The Chemical Examiner ... Sir William?"

I rubbed it in. "Friend and physician to the Governor General."

O'Shaughnessy had a finger in most things in Calcutta. He'd trained as a doctor in Edinburgh but couldn't find a job. So he joined the East India Company, tried his luck in the colonies. Now he's famous. First man to treat cholera by saline injection, relieve the agony of tetanus and rabies with cannabis resin. He'd just laid three thousand miles of electric telegraph cable, all powered by batteries of his own invention. The man's a human locomotive.

The Major looked as if he could still smell dog shit.

"What in God's name would Sir William want with you?"

"How would you translate *carbon dioxide* into Bengali?" I said.

Native languages are tools of Elphinstone's trade. Men tend to use the vernacular when you're crushing their balls in bamboo pincers.

I shrugged. "Tricky in a language where there's only one gas. Air. How about *reagent* into Sanskrit, or Persian?"

His face made me want to laugh. The master torturer ... and here's me asking *him* questions he can't answer.

"I met O'Shaughnessy in Calcutta," I said. "On an abandoned bookshelf in the library at the Company's Orphan Boarding School. It was a black afternoon, sweating between monsoon downpours."

Now Elphinstone stared as if *I'd* gone mad.

"I'd decided to kill myself," I continued. "Which is why I was leafing the pages of *A Manual of Chemistry* looking for a fool-proof poison."

A year earlier my mother had died in such agony the sight and sound still haunted me. I was sent as the only black boy to the Military Orphan School where loneliness and daily beatings took what was left of my self-esteem. Joining her in death seemed like a good option. Then O'Shaughnessy spoke of a merciful science, that cured disease and banished pain. I decided to study the book cover to cover, like a bible. If he'd lied, I'd kill myself.

"The *Manual* didn't let me down'" I said. "It gave me back my life."

Elphinstone shook his head. "You've got an odd sense of humour, Khan."

"Oh yes? That's because it was born in sorrow, not joy."

"O'Shaughnessy?" he said, gave me the *tell-me* nod.

"Wanted someone to put chemical terms into native languages. I'd done it while mastering *The Manual* so I sent him a couple of pages in Hindi, a couple in Persian, couple in Bengali. Next thing I'm his assistant."

Elphinstone nodded. "What about Bullock's death?"

"The Examiner's job is criminal investigation. O'Shaughnessy saw it as a science, excavated every scene like an archaeologist. Rebuilt the crime from tiny details. He's way ahead of Scotland Yard. Anyway, I helped him with autopsies, chemical analyses, the lot. Then he got interested in the electric telegraph, sent me in his place. In the end it was my job."

"Uh-ha." He nodded as if he's impressed. "So we've established you're a good assistant."

I thought for a stupid moment he'd warmed a bit.

"You assist him with medical experiments?"

"Often."

"Then you know Calcutta Military Hospital, on Circular Road?"

"Opposite the Grand Gaol."

"The laboratory at the back?"

"It's more a preparation room," I said. "For apothecaries."

"Where Bullock and Doyle worked."

I pictured the little room – cool and whitewashed, simply furnished with a sink and workbench, wooden cabinets on the walls. A pleasant smell of dried medicinal herbs.

"Worked?" I said. He's leading us somewhere I don't want to go, like over a rickety bamboo bridge across a snake pit.

"The assistant surgeon told me Bullock and Doyle cleared out rather hastily, left a few things in a corner cupboard."

He took a sheet of paper from his tunic, smoothed it on the table.

"They worked," he said, "at exactly what you told them to."

When I looked, I felt the bridge give way. It's a list of instructions in my hand. That's why my deposition caught Elphinstone's eye. I learnt to write Persian and Sanskrit before English. My hand's peculiar, distinct.

"What were they doing?" he said.

"I told you, I've no idea."

He tapped the instructions. "What's this, then?"

"Standard piece of work. Henry asked me to purify a compound."

"What compound?"

"He wouldn't say."

"Don't play games with me, Khan."

I shrugged. "It's the truth."

It felt as if a bomb fizzed on the table between us. He picked up the revolver, examined it as if he's not sure himself what he'll do. "I'll give you another five *seconds*," he said. "Then I'll blow you across the room, let Cartwright clear up the *mess*."

I grabbed at the only straw I had. "You'll have a job saying this is suicide. It's hard to shoot yourself in the chest with a Dragoon."

Elphinstone pursed his lips, went on examining the gun.

"Sir William will want to know what happened," I said. "So will the Governor General."

"You've got a good point there."

He re-holstered the gun, went to the door and shouted, "Chrystal!" The two men spoke for a few seconds. A minute later the Sergeant, the wrestler and the sewer rat came in. The constables went behind me and dragged my chair from the table, swung me backwards so I'm facing the ceiling, arms crushed between the chairback and the floorboards. I lifted my head instinctively, saw the Sergeant grab my ankles, pin my legs to the chair.

The wrestler knelt, a knee each side of my head. The rat crouched to my left, Elphinstone to my right. That's when I saw the copper pipe in the Major's hand, like a long finger with a length of rubber tubing over one end. A nod from the Major and the rat pinched my nose shut, the wrestler took a firm grip of my ears and pressed down, hard. I yelped and the Major slid the rubber tube between my lips, down into my gullet.

I gagged, choked, wished I'd spat in his face when I had the chance.

Another nod and the wrestler pressed with his full weight, sent a searing shock of agony through my head. His eyes bulged, arms shook with effort, but he didn't let up. My face felt as if it was tearing in half or sinking in boiling oil. I tried to thrash my head, my body, but I couldn't move, not even scream, not even think my own thoughts, only, *stop the pain ... PLEASE ...*

Another nod and the agony faded to a burning ache. I'd have puked if the pipe hadn't blocked my throat. The Major made a fist round the copper pipe and took the cyanide bottle in his other hand. He balanced the rim on the pipe's open end, tilted it so the liquid pooled in the neck, reached the lip. I saw it slop and tremble, inches from my eyes.

"Still think I can't *explain?*" he sang. "How you grabbed the cyanide, took the easy way out, like Bullock. Proved you own guilt."

I daren't move, eyes fixed on the bottle. One slip and poison will dribble down my throat. I can see food stains and stubble, smell the fetid stink of onions and stale cigars and rotten teeth. *Feringhees* – white men, too close, like the ones in the jungle, hanging corpses, the *pish-tish, haw-haw* of the first English voices I ever heard.

A whisper, "What were Doyle and Bullock doing in Calcutta?"

My heart thumped like a beam engine.

Another nod and the scorch of pain returned. Worse this time. *"Doyle and Bullock?"* far away. I'm choking, torn between living agony and the terror of imminent death. Every pore in my skin popped sweat, every muscle jerked and flexed, but they held me down till a voice in my head screamed, "I'LL SPEAK!"

Only I couldn't. I'd nothing to say. All I had was a feeling of despair that matched the physical pain. If Elphinstone tips the bottle, I'll be the killer, the traitor, the suicide.

Then the pain faded like a wonderful release.

"Last chance," he said. "What were they doing?"

I gave a small nod. The tube slid almost from my mouth.

I looked at the three white faces in turn, caught each man's eyes.

"Murderers," I gasped, closed my own eyes and waited for the end.

It didn't come. Elphinstone yanked out the tube. "Get him up," he barked. When they dragged me upright, my head fell forward, and I choked and vomited down my frock coat.

The Major re-stoppered the bottle and set it on the table. Swept the mop of black hair back from his sweaty forehead. He stared at me for a moment, curious, like an experiment he'd just concluded.

"We'll do it legally, at dawn," he said. Then he walked out.

I COULD HEAR an argument outside, audible but unintelligible words, back and forth till they reached a decision. Then Cartwright came and gave the constables a nod. I was hit from behind, like a right hook from the Torkard Giant, went over with the chair, hitting the floorboards a second time.

They dragged me up, zig-zagged me down another set of corridors to a backyard. I'm stumbling, legs like rubber. Saw a police van with two horses on the cobblestones. They bundled me in the back door, threw me onto a wooden seat and locked one ankle in a shackle. Cartwright gave Sergeant Chrystal orders, chopped the air with his hand like he'd better do it right. Chrystal nodded, climbed in after me.

Then we're away, into the hot summer night.

Four

IT'S DARK IN the van, a small shaft of light slanting through the bars in the back door. Chrystal sat by it, face in silhouette. I slewed along the seat as we swung left into Ironmonger Lane, right onto Cheapside. My ears still burned, and I felt as if I'd tried to swallow a *Jhik* – I don't know the English word, it's like a rat with long quills.

Beyond the coach, London went its way, sellers calling, "Yarmouth bloaters!" and "Oranges, a penny a lot!" My head still buzzed from that last truncheon blow, waves or nausea and dizziness. We're heading up Newgate Street to the famous prison. Went left into Old Bailey but we didn't stop at Newgate. The prison drifted by, and we turned right down Ludgate Hill, heading west. I could smell the sour odour of puke on my frockcoat.

"Where're we going?" I croaked, felt a rasp of pain in my throat.

Nothing. Streetlamps rippled amber and black bars over Chrystal's open face. He stared down, head nodding with the motion. Those big eyes weren't so young now. More like worried, even a little afraid.

I closed mine, fighting what'd been dredged up in the City Office. Things worse than physical pain, that began with bodies hanging from a banyan tree. Black bodies with slender limbs, bound hand and foot, with faces fixed in death. Things that taught me who I was, that I'd fought ever since.

I'M WALKING WITH my mother by her bullock cart, on our way to collect silks from a factory by the river Mor. It's my first journey far from our village, from the forests and glades that are my life. I'll never go back. Under the gallows tree, two men sit on horseback in a tribal dress of red, white and black. I've no words to describe

33

their clothes.

My eyes are drawn to their ghostly faces and blue, piggy eyes. I feel danger, hear the elders speaking of the *Kampanee*. They're here, like evil spirits to hang Santal. I know it. One flicks his reins and flexes his hips so the horse walks lazily in our direction. My ears hear a *pish-tish, haw-haw* I don't understand.

"Shalani," my mother says. It's her name.

I won't say what happens next. They made me watch but I can spare you that. My mother doesn't scream or cry. When it's over, when they left us alive, she led me to Murshidabad with barely a word. Only that I mustn't speak of what I'd seen. She put me in strange clothes, took me to the Hazarduari Palace to meet the Nawab – Mubarak Ali Khan – left me to board in his school.

I knew just enough Persian to survive. She'd taught me in our village hut, drawing figures in the dirt, scuffing them out if anybody came. As if she'd always known. I was the lonely scholar, learned the *Kampanee* was the East India Company, the dress was called a uniform, the tribe the Bengal Cavalry.

Along with Persian and Sanskrit and geometry, I learned the *pish-tish, haw-haw* called English. My mother's visits kept me alive until the day I was rushed on horseback to a dingy room in a backstreet of Beherempore south of Murshidabad. There she died of cholera. Died in my arms while I tried to show the courage she'd shown me. I was fourteen years old, and I won't say *I* didn't cry. An Englishman, Mr McKay adopted me, sent to the Company's Orphan School in Calcutta to learn the true faith, that Jesus was my saviour.

But he wasn't, O'Shaughnessy was.

O'Shaughnessy gave me my book of spells. Who'd think water was made of gases – hydrogen and oxygen? That you could split them with electricity, reunite them – *Bang!* – with a spark. If that's not magic, nothing is. I kept the *Manual of Chemistry* as my charm, my Bible. There were no more beatings, not for the boy who spoke in alchemical riddles, who played with fire. I collected bits of glassware in a kitchen corner, used old hookah pipes as tubing, made the elements of creation. God's elements. Knew their smell and their colour. Not black. Not white. I knew secrets other men didn't, not even most Englishmen.

I remade my self-esteem by coming top in exams, beating white boys in the classroom and the laboratory and the morgue. The cleverer the boy, the whiter his skin. I wasn't a heathen or a monkey or a savage anymore. Not until Elphinstone put me on the floor and made me scream, "I'LL SPEAK!" Like knocking off a scab to find an old wound raw and festering. I squeezed my eyes tight, sought the smell of chlorine and copper, the rhythm of experiment. Spoke my mantra, *O'Shaughnessy made me his assistant... Me... ME!*

"JESUS, YOU'VE GOT some balls, Khan."
"What?" I opened my eyes.
Chrystal stared at me in the gloom.
"Go to hell," I said, quietly.
"Defying him like that ... thought he was going to kill you."
We sat in silence rattling down Ludgate Hill.
Then Chrystal said, "I wanted no part of that." Tapped the side of his head, "You ask me, that Major's got a screw loose."
"You helped hold me down," I croaked.
Chrystal looked away.
"It's your job to uphold the law," I said. "Not watch a man tortured."
He looked up, said angrily, "I do as I'm told by the likes of Cartwright! Know how I started life? Picking scrap-iron from the river Clyde in Glasgow. A mudlark they'd call me here." He jabbed a thumb at the stripes on his tunic. "Cost me dear to get these, I'm nae chucking 'em away for a lippy prince."
"Lippy?" I gasped, triggering a bolt of pain in my throat.
"Aye, that stuff about Allah, throwing your card at Cartwright, talking Greek. He thinks you're trying to make him look stupid."

"You know nothing," I said. "Men like him think I'm a piece of shit."

"You're well dressed, educated. Could've gone different if you hadn't got his back up." He turned back to the window.

I thought about that down Fleet Street to Temple Bar. Maybe I *was* aloof. Putting up a front's a way of life with me, like pretending insults don't hurt. I hadn't thought Chrystal saw me as educated, better placed than him to deal with Cartwright. It shook me up, gave me some fight back. By Charing Cross I was thinking more clearly. I need information and Chrystal's my only source.

"What about the Commissioner," I said. "What's he going to say when he finds out Elphinstone's been torturing people in the City Office?"

"He knows," Chrystal said, like I'm an idiot. "Gave the orders."

"The Commissioner?"

"Aye."

"And what the hell's Elphinstone doing there?"

Chrystal shook the back of his head, like, *don't ask.*

The coach swung sharp left, sliding me along the seat. I saw Nelson's Column come into view in the rear window, knew we're going down Whitehall into Westminster.

"Cartwright seemed very sure I killed Bullock," I said.

Chrystal gave me the *don't ask* shake again.

"Come on, Chrystal," I said. "I reckon you convinced him."

He turned sharply from the window.

"Ah did-ne!" he snapped, which I think meant he didn't.

He wiped his mouth with his fingers, gave a look like, *what the hell.*

"I told him what I'd seen," he said. "Started on your theory about suicide. But Bullock's name startled him. He runs off to the Commissioner's office. Five minutes later he comes out like there's hot steam up his arse, starts tapping messages on the electric telegraph. A bit later, private carriages are pulling up like it's the Lord

Mayor's banquet. Out gets a dandy with a fancy 'tache, looks like the laughing cavalier. Then another gent, then the Major. They're all into Wilberforce's room for half an hour."

"Cartwright too?"

"Na, he's called later. Then he come out with the Major. Gets me and the other two into his office. The Major says you killed Bullock, you're a rebel. What to do in the investigation room."

"When Cartwright gives the nod?"

"Aye. He wasn't happy, but the Major's calling the shots. Later the Major called me again. Told me to fetch that pipe from the museum, how we're to hold you down. Cartwright kept out of it."

I gave him a filthy glare.

He waved me away and turned back to the window. We'd gone into Millbank Street on the north bank of the river. Millbank Prison, that's where we're going, something else I knew from *Bradley's Guide*. Away from the City.

Outside the coach it's pitch black. Just the iron wheels rattling on the cobbles and the horses' willing trot. All I could see were a few lights out across the river. The horses slowed to a walk, stopped. Now the world's deadly quiet. The coach creaked and swayed as the driver climbed down. He crunched over the gravel and thumped hard on a wooden door ... voices, more crunching. Then the back door swung open, and two warders peered inside.

They're wearing caps and tunics a bit like the City police. One's tall and thick set, with a beard; a bear of a man. The other's clean shaven, shorter but solidly built. The shorter man held a lantern.

"Mr Khan?" the bear said.

Chrystal hopped out, pointed back at me.

The warder got in, forcing his broad shoulders through the door. The coach springs squealed. He undid the shackle and nodded me out. The riverside's chilly, smelt of sewage and stagnant water. The prison wall stretched into the darkness in both directions. We're in front of a gatehouse. The bear took my arm, marched me through two sets of gates into a gravel yard, on between two huge towers, down a narrowing avenue of high brick walls. The walls vanished into a black void, like the end of the world. Then a gleam of lamplight appeared, like hellfire. A turnkey had opened a small door to the porter's room.

Inside there's no more 'Mr Khan'. With my hands cuffed behind, it was easy for the shorter man to hook an arm through mine, wrench my head back by the hair. The bear put his pale greasy face up close to mine. He'd a crooked eye staring blankly to one side. The other eye did the expression. It was small and spiteful.

"Jesus, you stink," he said. Without warning he thumped me hard in the stomach. I gasped, fell to my knees. "You won't be no trouble, will you?"

It's the briefest summary of house rules I've ever had.

The other warder pulled my head back, said, "Answer the man."

I twisted to look at Chrystal.

Between gasps, I said. "The savages aren't very friendly round here."

The bear lifted a boot to kick me in the face.

"Let him up!" Chrystal said. "He's a Prince."

"You heard what he said," the bear retorted. "He's got it coming."

"Under my protection," Chrystal said

"You've got no say here."

The Sergeant shoved his way between me and the bear's boot. He'd what they call physical confidence. "He's nae bin convicted yet."

The bear gave a one-eyed glare, but Chrystal didn't move. I'm thinking there's about to be a serious barney, wishing they'd get these cuffs off.

"Don't push your luck, Jock," the bear said. There's an evil look in that resentful eye, but he saw Chrystal wasn't backing down. The bear nodded to his pal, *let him up.*

They took my arms and shoved me like a wheelbarrow. The turnkey led the way with the lantern, down black corridors, up and down stone stairs. The place stank like an ill kept zoo. The turnkey opened doors, slammed and bolted them behind us. Each corridor smelt different, and the same. Like going from the monkey house to the lions' den. Eventually we climbed a half-circle of stone steps, came to my cell. The turnkey cranked the lock.

Inside he lit a stub of candle on a shelf. The bear locked my ankles in leg irons on the back wall and gave the chains a yank. The warders left. Chrystal came in while the turnkey hovered in the doorway.

"I'm staying," Chrystal said.

The turnkey shrugged, slammed and locked the door behind him.

THE CELL'S LONG and narrow, six paces front to back. All freshly whitewashed a century ago. There's a window in the back wall; it's small and barred, black as night. There're two iron bunks head-to-toe along one wall. Both with stained mattresses. No sheets. No pillows. The privy's a bucket. The leg-irons mean I can't move more than couple of paces from the back wall.

A clock in Westminster struck half past something.

"What're you doing here, Chrystal?" I said.

"Minding you. Cartwright's orders."

"From what?"

"You saw them screws. The savages of Millbank, like you said."

I wrenched my arms to one side. "How about getting these cuffs off?"

He shook his head, "Major's orders."

I nodded at the bucket. "What if I need a piss?"

Chrystal shook his head, sat on the bed by the door. I fell on my side on the other bunk, feet near the back wall. If I tilted my head, I could just see Chrystal unbuttoning his tunic, settling down for the night. He gave me a sideways glance. Something's on his mind.

"What's that about Bullock and Doyle?" he asked, matter of fact.

I stared at the grimy brickwork, felt my heart sink further. I'd warmed a bit to Chrystal. He'd done what he could. And he'd begun life grubbing for scrap in the Clydeside mud, just as I had weeding mulberry bushes in the jungle. Both of us *ryot*s – peasants – who'd fought our way up.

"Who told you to ask that?" I said. "Cartwright or the Major?"

Chrystal was quiet.

"Like that guff about wanting no part in torture, the charade in the porter's room, protecting me."

It's so obvious I couldn't believe I'd missed it. This was the Sergeant's chance to prove himself, get the next promotion he's champing for.

He untied his boots.

"You can piss off home," I said. "You'll get no more from me."

I was on my own, as I'd been since the day Shalani died.

I WATCHED THE cell wall float in the candlelight. Thought about something else. What the hell had Henry got me into? I'd learned he was a sly old bastard, but I'd never imagined anything like this. What had he tricked me into purifying, left evidence of in a cupboard in Calcutta?

When I came to London, I'd banked on Professor Hofmann hiring me as an assistant. O'Shaughnessy wrote me a good character, said the Prof's bound to have something for me. Not a chance. All the students wanted to assist the great Hofmann.

But the character's worth something because the Prof. told me of a druggist name of Bullock who gets chemical work done at the College. So I went to see him. He told me right off he didn't like blacks. And I wasn't a prince then. Anyway, I thought I'd impress him by saying I'd come top in *preparation*. Hofmann starts you off preparing pure compounds like morphine. I had a head start because O'Shaughnessy had me doing it years ago.

"Have you, now," says Henry. Fetches a jar of green sludge. "Have a go at that," says he, gives me a wink like he knows how. "Only don't tell no-one, it's one of my secrets."

I went off to the College, used one of chemistry's oldest tricks: the black art of crystallization. I shook the sludge in a solvent, evaporated it over a gentle flame to a strong solution. Let it stand, fingers crossed. If you're lucky, something reveals itself as crystals. Then you filter ... rinse and repeat.

When I took the pure compound to Henry, he slapped me on the shoulder like we're real pals, got me to write out the process, the one Elphinstone found in Calcutta. Now I know there was more to that green sludge than met the eye, something that'd put my life on the line.

I'D MANAGED TO put Chrystal and the cell out of my mind, but footsteps in the corridor fetched me back. The turnkey swung the door and two men pushed past him. It's the warders who'd met us at the gate. Now the bear's holding a constabulary carbine, a short rifle.

Chrystal sprang to attention, gawping like he's no idea what's going on. The warders made way for the third man, like royalty. He'd thick eyebrows and a bulbous nose, wore blue livery and a gold medallion. With him came a waft of powder and shaving cream. He looked about as happy to be here as I was. Chrystal hastily rebuttoned his tunic, shoved his feet into his boots.

"Hyder Khan?" the liveried man inquired. "Also known as the Prince of Murshidabad." He spoke with the full *haw-haw*, like a lawyer.

"Who're you?" I said.

"On your feet for the Sheriff," the bear grunted.

I stayed where I was.

"I'm Sir William Lawrence, Sheriff of London,"

The bear stood directly in front of Chrystal, pinning him against his bed. He cocked the gun and pointed it at my shins on the mattress. "Want to spend the night in agony," he said, "bleeding to death?"

"You'll not harm the prisoner," Chrystal said.

The bear turned, flicked one of the gold buttons on Chrystal's tunic. "You're City," he said, "You've no jurisdiction here."

He's right. London's got two police forces. The City Police look after the square mile north of the Thames: Fleet Street to the Tower of London. Money-town I call it – Bank of England, Stock Exchange and the Lord Mayor's house. They wear gold buttons. The Metropolitan Police – the Met – looks after everything else, which includes Millbank Prison. Their head office is in Scotland Yard, five minutes from here. They wear silver buttons.

"Law applies, same as anywhere," Chrystal said.

The bear jerked the gun-butt hard into Chrystal's guts. The Sergeant gasped, doubled over and fell back on his bed.

"That's enough, Crump," the Sheriff said.

I swung my legs over the bunk, sat up, then stood. Chrystal's wheezing, trying to catch his breath. Crump – the bear – pointed the carbine straight at my chest. The Sheriff held out some sheets of paper, like a proclamation.

"On this day *etc. etc*," he began, "at an extraordinary hearing in the Old Bailey *etc. etc.* you were found guilty *in absentia* of the wilful murder of Henry Bullock esquire, and of high treason. The High Court sentenced you to death by hanging *etc. etc*, to be carried out tomorrow at 6am."

He dropped his arms, glowered at me like, *what do you think of that?*

You pay £300 to be a Sheriff, so *Bradley's Guide* says. Attend sessions at the High Court. People do it because it's a step to becoming Lord Mayor. Which is why Sheriffs end up doing things nobody else at the High Court wants to. Like travel across London late at night to come into this rat hole.

"I didn't kill Henry Bullock," I said. "*Etc. ... etc.*"

He shuffled the papers, held one out. My deposition.

"Your signature?" he said.

When I nodded, he shuffled the papers again, showed me the confession Cartwright wrote. Same signature at the bottom.

"Then so's that," he said.

"It's a forgery."

Chrystal began, "He didn't sign—"

The bear slapped the gun-butt into his nose with a nasty crunch of torn gristle. "Don't contradict the Sheriff," he said, like a school mistress.

The Sheriff glanced in disgust, but he didn't reprimand Crump. Just said, "You've been informed of the sentence." He folded the papers and pushed out past the turnkey.

The smaller warder followed, till Crump said, "Stay here, Skinner." Then to the turnkey, "Take the Sheriff to the gate, come back and wait outside."

The turnkey frowned but Crump nodded, *get out!*

He did, locked the door behind him. The footsteps receded.

Crump un-cocked the carbine, leant it in a corner near the door. The warders stood side by side, facing me. Chrystal's still on the bed with a handkerchief clamped over his bleeding nose.

"What happened?" I said.

"What happened?" Crump mimicked. "What happened is you called me a savage." He angled his good eye in my direction. "Listen, dog's pizzle, I got to keep you alive for the hangman. But when I'm done, you'll wish I hadn't."

"Go on," Skinner said. "Cripple him." He's keen as a dog on a chain, waiting for his master's nod.

Chrystal shoved the bloody handkerchief in a trouser pocket and got up.

"Stay out of this," Crump barked at him. "He's a dead man anyway."

I'm helpless, again. With cuffed wrists and shackled legs, I've no options. Can't even kick. I could crawl under the bed but there's not a lot of dignity there. So I looked at Chrystal, my last contact with the living world.

"Yes," I said, "stay out of it. Tell Cartwright he had the wrong man."

Then I faced my attackers to fight them best I could.

Chrystal's looking at me like he might join Crump and Skinner, kick the shit out of me for what I'd said earlier. But then he came down the cell, muttered, "Lucky I did-nae piss off home when you told me too, eh?"

He turned to Crump. "I told you, this man's under my protection."

The bear shook his head and shot a glance at Skinner. The smaller man nodded. Seems they'd agreed something earlier, something nasty.

Crump said to Chrystal, "You've got a screw for those cuffs?"

He means mine. Chrystal said nothing.

"You get in our way," Crump said, "you're a dead man. And when we're done with the blackie, we'll take his cuffs off. Guess how we'll tell it?"

They'd tell it I got the screw from Chrystal, beat him to death. That they'd had to use a lot of violence to master me. Chrystal just stared, getting Crump's measure. Then he dug in his trouser pocket, held out the screw.

"Turn your back to me, Khan," he said, eyes still on Crump.

When I did, he stuck the key in the cuff and twisted.

Crump charged. Came straight at me, jaws clamped and teeth bared. Skinner went for Chrystal. I didn't adopt the stance, just lifted my hands with the cuff swinging like a medieval mace, stepped back to get some slack on the chain. A yard out, Crump swung a scything right, but it's much too wide.

Punching opens your guard, so I flexed back to dodge the fist, shot in with a vicious left over his right arm, *smack, in and out like a piston.* Crump's so shocked he dropped his left, letting in my trademark right, *bang!* He's gone, out on his feet. But the storm unleashed my fury, so I grabbed his lapels, yanked him onto a cracker of a headbutt, paying him back for Chrystal. Crump sank to his knees, knelt there like a choirboy. I fetched him another right, spun his head in a spray of claret. Then he keeled over.

I turned left to help Chrystal, but he didn't need me. He'd got Skinner's face rammed against the cell wall, one arm twisted hard up his back. The Sergeant's staring over his own shoulder at me, aghast.

"Gimme the cuffs," he grunted.

I found the key, undid the Darby's and helped the Sergeant cuff Skinner. Then we stood quiet, breathing hard, trying to work out what's next. Chrystal jerked Skinner off the wall and shoved him at me. "Hold him," he said. I threaded an arm through both of his, locked the other round his throat. Chrystal fetched the carbine, cocked and pointed it at Skinner. Crump groaned and tried to get up, collapsed. He's face down, blood pooling round his head.

"You tried to kill me," Chrystal said to Skinner, real anger in his voice.

"That's him," Skinner whined, nodding at Crump. "Not me."

I reckon he thought Chrystal might shoot him.

"Let him go," the Sergeant said.

I did, and Chrystal waved him to the cell door with the gun.

"Tell the turnkey to open up," he said.

Skinner called, the lock rattled and the turnkey stepped in, gawped – I'm the one supposed to be cuffed and bloody. Chrystal waved Skinner down the cell, gave me the cuff screw. "Let him loose," he said, kept the gun on him.

Then he nodded at Crump. "Get him up, both of you!"

They hauled at the bear's underarms but couldn't move him.

"Roll him over," Chrystal said. He emptied the privy bucket over Crump's face. The bear coughed. Opened his eyes. This time they got him on his feet, but he sagged back down. Next time they got his arms over their shoulders, dragged him to the door. His face was ashen, the one good eye floating around like an olive in brine.

"Now get out," Chrystal said. "Come back and I'll get the Governor, tell him what happened."

"What about the gun?" Skinner whined.

Chrystal shook his head. "Out."

They shouldered Crump through the threshold, but he struggled to turn back. Since they couldn't budge him, they swung him round. He lifted his head like a half-dead animal, gasped, "Last thing you'll see, Khan ... when that bag goes over your head ... me! ... then I'll watch you kick."

They dragged him off and the turnkey heeled the door shut.

Five

THE FIGHT HAD fired me up. Chrystal and I should've been laughing and shaking hands. But Crump's words hit me as hard as I'd hit him. Brought it all back. We sat on our beds, Chrystal with the carbine across his knees, looking as shaken as I was.

"Christ Khan," he said. "You did Crump, nae messing."

"You don't mess where I come from," I said. "Not if you're black."

"Could've killed him."

"Wish I damn well had," I said. Which wasn't true. But my blood's up. "That bastard of a Sheriff barely read the sentence. *Etc... etc!* How'd they get my signature on that confession?"

Chrystal looked away. He didn't want to think Cartwright was corrupt, that he'd conspired to send me to the gallows. But he knew.

"Jim the Penman," he said. "He's in the cells tonight."

"Who?"

"Master forger, the City's full of 'em. Jim could get a signature past the Bank of England, probably has."

When I blew my disgust at the wall, Chrystal turned angry again.

"The law doesn't apply to traitors."

"Who says I'm a traitor?"

"The Major ... you're a dangerous rebel, fled Calcutta to save your skin."

"Does he now?"

"Aye. And judging by what you did to Crump, he's right."

I'd have taken offence if Chrystal hadn't just risked his life to save me a beating.

He turned to look directly at me. "You didn't come here to study chemistry, Khan. I don't believe it ... who *are* you?"

Bell chimes drifted on the night air. Ten o'clock. I'd eight hours left on earth. Just to make the point the candle flickered, sent up a coil of smoke and guttered to a tiny orange glow.

"Bloody marvellous," Chrystal said.

I sat quiet, thinking about his question – *Who am I?*

I'd struggled with that since the bodies in the banyan tree. For a while in the Nawab's school in Murshidabad I was still the jungle boy, roaming the forests of Rajmahal. In dreams I hunted fowl, dodged rogue elephants and tigers, talked to the Bonga spirits who protected me. Until a night like this in the dormitory, whispering in darkness.

One of my fellows asked, "Who are you?"

"A Santal," I said. "Son of Hansdak, who owns a bullock and a goat. Son of Shalani who embroiders silk."

They laughed at that. Why, what a storyteller I was. I should write books when I grew up. I was eight years old.

"YOU READ THE *Illustrated London News?"* I said to Chrystal.

"What?"

"The *Illustrated.* For folk who like the news in pictures."

"Very funny," he said. "Aye, we get it at the Office."

I thought they might. The police star in scenes of murder and arrest.

"See a piece last year, on the Santal?"

"The what?"

"Santal. A native tribe of Bengal."

He thought for a bit. "Oh aye, they'd a picture of that chief ... er?"

"Sidhu. Yeah, they sketched him, then hanged him. Wanted London to see he's a proper savage. You've read the story ... you know how it happened."

"Aye, I do," he said.

"Go on then, tell me."

"Why the hell should I? You're the prisoner."

"You asked who I am," I said. "I'm telling you, my way."

Chrystal didn't like being quizzed. You could feel it in the silence. But he didn't like what'd happened in the City Office, or here in Millbank. Wanted to hear I'm a rebel, a murderer, something to justify what I'd suffered.

"Well," he said, "those Santal ... they're gypsies, sunk into ignorance, treated like vermin by the Hindus. We gave 'em land and protection."

"Why'd they rebel, then?"

"Bred too fast, then turned nasty. Went back to being sav–"

"Savages, like me? I'm a Santal, Chrystal. Except we don't call ourselves that. We're *hor hoppen*, the true men. We're *mit'leka*, like one. Not a race or colour on a map. We're where we are, who we are. Not anyone else."

"Does-nae matter who you are," he said. "We gave you a place in the world, taught you to farm your land."

"Yeah, that's what the papers said." I was quiet for a while. "Know what keeps wealthy folk awake at night?"

"Why ask me? You're the prince."

"Not lords with castles and peasants. I'm talking about the new wealthy, people with money, what they call capital."

"Wouldn't know about that either," Chrystal said, bitterly.

"Then I'll tell you ... how to keep their money safe. It's not like land, you can't fence it, plant crops or graze cattle on it. Can't keep your workers in tied cottages on charity. Money's just paper, numbers in a leger. It's only real when you make it human sweat."

"Look Khan, I know you're–"

"Shut up and listen," I said. "I was born to a Bengal ruled by the East India Company. It seemed all powerful, invincible. But it wasn't satisfying its London investors. So they decided to plant indigo for dye, mulberry bushes to feed silkworms. Which meant they needed people to farm cheaply. Well, the Hindus and Muslims wouldn't do it. But then someone remembered the Santal ... we're friendly, hard-working, lived by clearing forests to grow crops. We'd always been nomadic but what if we had a homeland, protection?

"The Company circled an area with white pillars, a hilly forest no one else wanted. Called it *Damin-i-Koh* – the skirt of the hills. Told the Santal they could live there safely as long as they grew what the Company wanted. That's where I was born. My world for seven years."

It cracked my voice to remember when my skin wasn't black, when the whole world was green forest and blue sky. When my mother was alive.

Chrystal's quiet too, but in a while, he said, "What's wrong with that?"

"Nothing. We lived off the land. Getting paid anything was a luxury. We built nice huts, collected beads and cottons, pots and pans, all kinds of manufactured stuff we'd never known before. My mother did well. She embroidered silks to sell at the Mughal Court in Murshidabad, learned the Persian language."

"That how she paid for your schooling?"

"Sort of," I said. "It was a good life. More Santal came down from the hills, thousands, then tens of thousands. Taxes soared. Profits soared. But then word got around like drips of blood in a shark pool. 'Have you heard? There're people in the *Damin* who'll work for scraps. They're illiterate, like children. Know nothing of weights and measures or money and contracts.'

"Soon the *Damin* was alive with middle-men and money lend-ers, corrupt police and tax collectors. The Company was supposed to provide protection, but it didn't. The magistrates were too far off, hadn't time for men who spoke little English, kept accounts in knots. The Santal were robbed – their goods weighed in false measures, taxes raised on huts they'd built themselves, loans given they couldn't repay. They'd sold themselves into slavery. In the end the sharks took their furniture, their animals, even their wives and daughters.

"Then the railway came with more capital hungry for labour. Santal boys joined the gangs, soon had cash in their pockets while their parents had less than nothing. It couldn't go on. When pleas to the British went unheard, the leaders Sidhu and Kanhu said our God had spoken – Company rule was over. Tens of thousands gathered with bows and axes crying *Hul!* Rebel! Went in search of their enemy. They defeated the Company soldiers in open battle, advanced on Murshidabad. Now the Company took notice ... it faced rebellion.

"A huge reinforcement of Sepoys shot down my people in their thousands. Defenceless villages were trampled by war elephants, grain stores set ablaze to spread starvation. We were made an example of – what happens if you rebel."

"We?" Chrystal said. "You were there, you fought?"

"No. I was in Calcutta, only heard rumours. The Company put out a 'proclamation of pardon' – surrender and you'll be forgiven ... it meant, if you don't, you'll be slaughtered. There were rumours of atrocities in the *Damin*. The Calcutta press approved, called for mass executions. I knew what to do. My business was forensic medicine, proving murder and torture, any kind of physical cruelty. My boss, Professor O'Shaughnessy taught me how. One trick was to photograph the scene, to capture the evidence before the weather and wild animals took it. So I packed up my tools, hired a bearer and headed up river to the heart of things. Didn't take long to find the truth. The Santal army had scattered, but the ravaged huts and villages were there.

"I saw the lynched bodies, children crushed like dolls, mutilated women left lying where they'd been used. I took the testimony of survivors. Some raged. Some wept. Some couldn't speak of what they'd seen. One woman quietly told me her story, then walked away and cut her own throat. I tracked the armies, built an irrefutable record in words and pictures. Named the regiments and the colonels, spoke to the soldiers. A few enjoyed their work, most didn't. Most were ashamed, said it was more like murder than war.

"Back in Calcutta, I took it all to the Chief Magistrate. He listened patiently, showed some sympathy. But when he saw the photographs, read my transcript, he gaped and nearly fainted. This wasn't the jargon of dispatches ... it brought the dead into his office. The stench of misery ... the reality of imperial rule. He stammered that the Governor General must see it all, at once."

"What'd he say?" Chrystal said, caught up in my story.

"Nothing. That night the Secretary of the Military Board called on me, said he'd come to fetch my evidence. I smelt a rat, told him I kept it all in a bank, I'd bring it first thing tomorrow. Soon as he'd left, I found the only Britisher I trusted, O'Shaughnessy. Went to his home in Chowringhee Road and told him the whole story. He thought awhile, then said, 'You know, to be a great chemist you should study in London with Professor Hofmann. I'll write you a character.'

"I got it. Sometimes Indians took their grievances straight to the Court of Directors. The Company had even held a Torture Commission after first-hand reports off brutality in Madras. Early next morning I packed my evidence in an air-tight trunk, drew out my savings and headed to the docks. I knew they'd be after me, so I hid on a merchant frigate bound for Ceylon.

"A week later I'm at Port Galle, a coaling station for steamers heading across the Indian Ocean. I'm a long way from home but that marine highway made me feel like nothing. I'd thought the Company *was* the British Empire till I saw one steel liner after another plough into port, disgorge voices from Burma, Malaya, China, Australia and New Zealand ... half heading west to the Imperial capital, half east to colonies I'd barely heard of. What could I do against a monster like that? And the first voyage had used all my cash, so I'd have to work my passage to London. But sailors took one look at my hands and laughed. I'd never stoked a boiler or hauled a rope. I was stranded.

"Then one day at the docks I met a *Peninsular & Oriental* captain, name of Buckle, who asked what languages I knew. Next day he invited me to lunch with a Bengali opium trader on his way from Hong

Kong to London. Buckle wanted his business, but the man's English was so comically awful I had to explain most of what he said. Over coffee, Buckle hinted I should join the ship as his English teacher. The trader agreed, said he'd buy me a ticket, third class. Six weeks later he and Buckle were partners and I'm here, trudging through my first snow. Then I did something that haunts me to this day."

I fell quiet because it still made me sick to think of it.

"Go on!" Chrystal urged, "What happened?"

I sighed. "O'Shaughnessy gave me a name, Thomas Wakley, a man who publishes a journal, *The Lancet.*"

"I've heard him speak," Chrystal said, "He's a radical Member of Parliament. And a doctor, does autopsies on unexpected deaths."

"That's him, I've got to know him well. But O'Shaughnessy knew he was aiding a fugitive, so he was cagey. Didn't spell out *why* I needed Wakley's help. Turned out he more or less lived on the road in a cab, which made him hard to find. So I went straight to East India House in the City. When I told the porter I'd important news from India, he took my name and disappeared. Imagine my joy when the Chairman himself appeared, Mr Hogg. Took me to the Director's Courtroom where we sat on chairs like thrones and drank tea.

"Hogg listened, reacted like the Magistrate in Calcutta. Told me to bring my evidence in the morning. When I did, he wasn't shocked. Just read, studied the photographs, shook his head in disgust. 'Right,' he said, 'this lot's going to the next directors' meeting.' When I asked him when that was, he slapped a palm on the table. 'This very week,' he said, 'in this very ROOM! What's more, you'll be here Khan, give your evidence in person.'

"He convinced me British justice wasn't a lie after all. Not in London, the home of Queen Victoria and Parliament. I handed him the lot. Then, nothing. In a week I went back to a cold reception. There's no Mr Hogg. The Chairman's name is Slegman. 'Photographs? Journals? We've nothing like that. I'm afraid I'll have to ask you to leave, or I'll fetch the police.'"

You could almost hear Chrystal thinking in the dark.

"They knew," he said, "from Calcutta."

"Oh yeah, ... electric telegraph to Bombay, ship to Turkey, telegraph to London. They'd got a dispatch long before I arrived, had it all worked out."

We both thought about that for a while.

Chrystal said, "What could Wakley have done? I mean ... he couldn't take on the East India Company." He tried to sound consoling. But I could hear doubt in his voice, unsure if I'm a hero or a fool ... or just a liar.

"Evidence isn't worth a fig," I said. "Not without a cause to hold it like a sword to the enemy's throat."

"Aye, you're right there," Chrystal said, bitterly. "But I'll tell *you* something. Violence solves nothing. Only sows more hatred and division."

I didn't know what that meant, whether he was praising or blaming me.

"I was naïve," I said. "Let my people down."

Was, past tense? As if I'm already dead, writing my own obituary.

"I don't think so," he said. "You risked your life, came halfway round the world to find justice."

"Didn't get any though," I said.

Then I was quiet, didn't feel like talking anymore.

Six

WHEN THE TEN-thirty chimes broke the quiet, Chrystal said, "So it's only by chance you were in Ivy Lane this evening?"

"Mm? Yes ... well, not exactly ..."

"Which?"

"I called on Henry most Wednesdays."

"Why?"

"We'd have a drink in The Ship. He'd tell me if he'd any work for me. Or just tell me his troubles. Henry wasn't what you'd call popular. I think I'm ... was, his only friend. Or acquaintance, maybe."

"He liked you?"

"Trusted me, more like. Felt he was doing me a favour, talking to me. I always got the drink."

"Who knew you'd be there?"

That made me think.

"Perhaps Bullock told someone you were coming?"

"Never. Henry was meaner with news than money, that's a fact."

Chrystal paused, then, "There's something else we both know, isn't there Khan? Something Cartwright and the Major missed."

I'd an idea what he meant, but I kept quiet.

"Those dental forceps, they're yours."

That made me think a lot more.

"Oh yeah?"

"Aye. Inside one handle, next to the makers stamp is etched, *P of M.*"

I didn't know. I'd recognized the make, but I couldn't see inside the handle. And I sure as hell wasn't asking.

"And you know what that means?" Chrystal said.

"You think I tortured and killed my friend."

"Perhaps ... maybe not."

Which was charitable, given the evidence.

"Why didn't you tell Cartwright?" I said.

"He could've looked, same as I did."

I liked that, Chrystal keeping his own counsel. Not throwing me to the lions to please his boss or Elphinstone.

"There's a back way out of Bullock's shop, right?"

"Into Newgate Market," I said. "So what?"

"So you can get down behind Ivy Lane to the Cathedral?"

"Through the market."

"Bottom of the Lane, four men were crossing Paternoster Row to the Church Yard. Shifty looking. Took one look at me and got a hoof on. That's a couple of minutes before I found you."

"That'd fit," I said. "You didn't tell Cartwright that either."

"The Major said you'd done it, pulled Cartwright the same way. Took me a while to think it through. Any idea who took the forceps, tried to sell you for Bullock's murder?"

"Doesn't matter," I said. "Not now."

"It might. When the warder comes at dawn, I'm taking this to Cartwright, tell him what I know. Then we'll find the Commissioner, stop the execution."

They wouldn't. Not in two hours. It'd take Chrystal that long to find Cartwright and the Commissioner, let alone the Home Secretary. And why would he revoke what he'd just decreed? But since Chrystal's here I might as well talk to him. Like a final confession, or the last rites; a part of me that'll survive the gallows. It's why I'd told him why I came to London.

I said, "You know what makes people poor?"

"What?"

"Same thing as makes them rich. Money."

"Oh aye?" he said, like, *here we go again.* "I thought it's *lack* of money."

"Can't lack it if there isn't any," I said. "There weren't any poor men in my village, or fat ones. Didn't see either till I went to Murshidabad and Calcutta. We looked after each other ... you see?"

Chrystal's grunted.

"Oh, you'd say we're all poor," I said. "Live like savages. But we found our wealth in the soil and rain. Our God in forest glades. Our pleasure in hunting. Joy in drinking and dancing. Until the Company came. Until they told us what to grow, paid us in things we didn't think we needed."

Another grunt. "You took to the white man's ways readily enough."

"Not really. Fate took me from the jungle to Murshidabad, then to Calcutta. When I was fourteen my mother died ... I nearly followed her to the grave. That's when I found my saviour, chemistry"

"Chemistry?" Chrystal said, curious. "A saviour?"

"Why not? I'd worshipped three Gods, learned four languages, twice lost my friends, been taken from people of my own custom and colour. I was an orphan, no one to turn to. I wanted something pure, something certain. Something to trust. That's when I found O'Shaughnessy's *Manual of Chemistry*. He'd a way of putting things, made them sound ... indisputable.

"I'd a little money from my stepfather so I bought some jars and chemicals in the bazaar. Did the experiments, learnt the jargon. Found out why we digest food and breathe air, that the body's a kind of machine working in harmony with nature. I loved the pungent smells and bright colours, the whoosh and hiss of fire and gas. Like the crucible of the world before the fall. But you know what I liked best? Atomic theory, the dance of atoms ... acid and alkali to salt and water. Like nature's chemical account books. Books no one can fake or fiddle."

Chrystal was quiet. The darkness made the silence thicker, more ominous, as if I'm talking to myself. So I said, "I know that's hard for someone like you to understand."

"Like me?" he said. "What's that mean?"

"Someone who fits, a white face in a white world."

"Maybe we've more in common than you think, Khan."

"Oh, yeah? I'm not wearing stripes, carrying a stick and a rattle. No one comes running when I'm in trouble."

"I believe in justice?" he said. "As you do chemistry."

"Huh! That why you helped torture me?" When he didn't answer, I said, "I'll bet your father's a copper, swung you a job in the family business. How else did you get to be a sergeant at your age?"

"You're right," he said, quietly. "But you're completely wrong too."

"What's that mean?"

He didn't reply at first. The evening's events had shocked us both. But my story put me in a new light, no longer just a black, a doubtful character in a dank basement. I'd a life, an explanation. I'm guessing Chrystal does too.

"My Da – my father – *was* a copper," he said. "And yes, he did get me into the force. But he didn't *swing* me any job."

"What's that give us in common?"

Chrystal was quiet, as if he's not sure what to say or where to start.

"Da started out as a cotton weaver in Glasgow ... lost his job to steam manufacture, fell to scavenging along the river Clyde."

I remembered his mudlark story, picking up scrap iron.

"The shame took him to drink, to quarrelling with Ma till she left us. Then he pulled himself together, got a job in the shipyards, then he's lamplighter, then a policeman. Worked his way back, got me some schooling. He raised me a radical, to fight for the people's Charter and the rights of working men. Wanted me to be a sort of Chartist preacher, what he'd like to have done himself."

"Like Wakley?" I said, making the connection. "Votes for all men. Anyone able to sit in Parliament, rich or poor."

"Aye, that's it."

"Doesn't sound so bad," I said. "You got an education, like I did."

I heard a rustle as Chrystal shook his head.

"There're two kinds of Chartist," he said. "Da wanted the Charter by *moral* force, by persuasion. I'd got in with the *physical* force mob, eager for revolution. Thought Da naïve to think the gentry'd give up power without a fight, reckoned him a coward. Then in forty-eight it came to a head. The famine raged in Ireland and our cotton mills were shut, food scarce. A group in Glasgow marched on the town calling for bread and revolution. I joined them on the barricades. Da was a sergeant by then, found himself on the other side trying to stop the violence. They called in the army who fired on the crowd, shot six of our number dead. I hated my father, reckoned him the enemy."

Chrystal cleared his throat, struggling to go on.

"Two days later a copper sought me out. Took me to Da's room in Kirk Street. He's barely conscious. Someone had recognized him from the barricades, smashed his skull with an iron bar. Nothing the surgeon could do. When Da saw me, he whispered, 'Justice. Not vengeance.' Took him days to die, Khan. I wanted vengeance more than anything in my life before. Da had tried to stop the killing on both sides. What did he get? Reprimanded by his own superintendent, murdered by the mob. When there's no arrest, I set out to find the killer myself, took an iron bar to deal my own justice."

"That's not what your Da wanted," I said.

"Aye, but I was angry. When I questioned old comrades, they called me a traitor, said Da got what he deserved. That got me angrier ... with the police, the radicals who preached fraternity and hid a murderer. With myself for calling Da a coward. I was like you Khan, alone.

"Eventually the anger turned to madness. One early morning I found myself at the river where we'd once collected scrap. I walked up to my calves in the ooze, fell on my knees ... knelt there shivering, ready for the flow to take me. And it would have ..."

His voice trailed off. In a whisper, I said, "But?"

"He'd pulled himself back from ruin ... for me. I sloshed back to the bank, went to Kirk Street, sat in Da's chair. On a shelf were two books ... *Police of the Metropolis* and *Principles of the Law of Scotland.*"

I waited for Chrystal to go on, but he didn't.

"A Manual of Chemistry," I said.

"Aye," says he, "Justice, not vengeance."

I didn't have an answer to that.

CHRYSTAL BROKE THE silence.

"What about you?" he said. "How'd *fate* take you from a jungle village to those palaces and mosques?"

It wasn't something I spoke about. But nor was the story of Jungle-Terry or fleeing Calcutta. And Chrystal hadn't spoken of his father before, not like that. I'd put money on it. The cell had the seal of the confessional. Not because I was a priest. Because I'd shortly be dead.

"My grandfather, Dandu," I said. "He was a tribal elder who dyed raw silk to sell in the markets of Murshidabad. His daughter – my mother – was a natural seamstress with a good eye for colour and pattern. Her work got them an invitation to the Hazarduari Palace to sell to the Nawab. Mother often stayed there, embroidering silks to order. Dandu liked to hunt and dance so he stayed in the *Damin*. He died when I was four. Since his wife was dead, my mother took over the business, spent time in the village and the Palace. She taught me Persian and how to count. Wanted me to be like Dandu, a man you could rely on."

I took a breath, braced myself as had Chrystal had a moment ago.

"One day she promised me an adventure. I'd go with her to a silk factory, then to the palace in Murshidabad ... a big day, my first journey far from our village. But near the factory we walked into an execution, a hanging. Two Company soldiers attacked her, raped her. Made me watch."

The words didn't upset me. I'd thought of it too often, had the nightmare too often. But I paused, in respect.

Chrystal said, "Oh ... I'm sorry–"

"I was too young to know what'd happened. Only that she'd been mishandled. But the mother I'd known was gone. In Murshidabad she dressed me as a prince. I wasn't Shalpu anymore, I was Hyder Khan, the lion king. I begged her to take me back to the hills. She said I had to be strong. It was my fate. For seven years I boarded at the Nawab's school. It's where I learned English."

We were quiet for a while. Then, Chrystal said, "She ... abandoned you?"

I'm sure he's thinking of his own mother.

"No," I said. "She lived nearby in Beherempore, saw me every week. But she never smiled or danced or sang again. Never called me Shalpu."

"Perhaps ... you know, unhinged her mind?"

"Perhaps ... a little. She knew our people were vulnerable, felt the tightening grip of Company rule. The rape convinced her Santal life was a luxury we couldn't afford ... she'd give me the power to fight back."

Chrystal said, "You make it sound ... almost like revenge."

"She thought I'd be safe in the Palace. But more than that, she wanted me to have an education. Learn the English language, study the Company's version of history and geography, their way of keeping accounts, their laws – the very weapons they'd used against us."

"And their science?'

"That was later, after she'd died of cholera."

In a while, Chrystal said, "But ... why'd the Nawab take–"

"–a jungle boy, in a royal school? At seven, I didn't ask ... my father was Hansdak. It took a while to learn my fellows were all children of the Court. Then it slowly dawned, what *could* be, *might* be ... *had* to be. It wasn't just my mother's silks that pleased the Nawab."

"You were his child, a royal prince?"

I nodded. "But I couldn't live in my village as a *bidhua*, a bastard of the *Dikku,* a non-Santal. So Dandu paid Hansdak a bullock and a goat to adopt me. Had the midwife name me Hansdak's son, give me his *Sept*, his clan."

"Your mother saved you from the *Hul.*"

"She did ... but for what? To die on a rope, like Sidhu? Reviled as a savage who'd murdered his friend for ten guineas?"

"Stop writing your own obituary," Chrystal said. "You're not dead yet!"

"Might as well be–"

"Listen, I recognized one of those men in the churchyard ... they call him Hydraulic Jack–"

"Hydraulic Jack... you're joking."

He wasn't. We talked about Jack until Chrystal fell quiet, his breathing became regular. I was left alone with my thoughts, hearing the clock chime the quarter hours. Sometimes I'd forget what came at dawn ... then I'd remember.

Seven

THE WARDER CAME at four o'clock – dawn – just as Chrystal said. Same one as last night. The Sergeant got up yawning, buttoned his tunic and tied his boots. Brushed his hair with his fingertips. His face was still bloody, nose blue and swollen. He clamped the carbine's butt under his arm and went to the door.

"Anything else you can tell me?" he asked.

I shook my head. No point putting his neck in the noose as well.

"I'll be back" he said.

"Chrystal! I'd forget those men in the churchyard, if you want to keep the stripes ... and your life."

As he went, he said, "I've already risked them once to save your skin."

The warder held the door. "Chaplain's here in an hour."

"What?"

"God!" he said, loudly, like people do talking to darkies who don't speak a proper language. "You want the hangman's breakfast?"

"Not unless it's a bucket of *handi,"* I said. "Rice beer."

The warder shook his head, stepped out and locked the door. The cell felt desolate with the Sergeant gone. I liked the man, wanted to know how he got from a Glasgow slum to Sergeant on the City Police force.

I meant to think a lot of things before six o'clock. I closed my eyes, thought about finding O'Shaughnessy's book ... *If a youth is taught experiment, he won't be misled by false argument or superstition. He'll esteem facts! And all this with an apparatus not worth one hundred rupees.* That Sunday our chaplain preached on the Day of Judgment. *What superstition!* Chemistry's my judge ... the power to reveal poisoners, adulterators, torturers, to banish pain and cure disease. *Only esteem the facts!* I had my earthly revelation, truth beyond race and money, beyond the wicked machinations of this world. I was free.

"It's Shalpu, mama. I'll be with you soon. We'll put on our finest silks to dance in the harvest. We'll walk by the bullock cart over the hills. In the morning I'll weed the indigo plants, then we'll draw in Persian in the dust..."

I saw a black and white jungle shimmering in a tropical storm. Thoughts of death and decay cut inside my head like knives ... a woman's face contorted under a scarlet tunic, choked by a golden epaulette. Chrystal screaming, drowning in mud. The blood swelled my neck, suffocating, making heartbeats thump in my ears, until they woke me. Until I sat bolt upright, a thought coming like a thunder-clap – *I'm about to die!*

Sweat trickled on my back. The sun warmed the cell in an orange glow, like the dawn of creation. I got up for a piss. Went to the win-dow bars. Three men had built a gallows in the prison cabbage patch. In a fenced-off square of earth nearby, two men in waistcoats dug a grave without a headstone.

At five o'clock, footsteps sounded outside – the chaplain come to make my peace with a God I don't believe in. In Murshidabad I'd paid lip-service to Allah, same with Jesus at the Orphan School. Since I'd found O'Shaughnessy, *Thakur Jiu* was more an old friend, a spirit connection to the jungle and my mother.

But it wasn't the chaplain. It was the last man on earth I wanted to see.

Eight

RAIKES ELPHINSTONE HAD had a busy night. That's how he looked. He's tired and unshaven, and there's something in his expression that's hard to read; certainly angry, probably at me. Not that I cared. He'd found time to put on a pair of cavalry jackboots, the kind reinforced with metal to fend off sabre blows.

"Leave us," he snapped at the turnkey. "And lock the door."

He glanced around, taking in the cell, noted my uncuffed wrists and the blood on the flagstones. Then he took a pace forward, poked a gloved finger like the grim reaper, telling me to look outside. The hangman had come. He was fixing the noose to a man-sized sack of grain balanced on a trapdoor in the gallows. When he'd done, he kicked the bolt, watched the sack fall, bounce, twang the rope like a bow string.

The hangman sucked hard on his clay pipe and nodded, "That'll do."

When I turned back, Elphinstone had a challenging look, as if the falling sack was some sort of bid in a poker game. He hadn't come to gloat. He wanted the stakes as high as they could go.

He tugged off his gloves a finger at a time, tossed them on Chrystal's bunk. Undid the buttons on his tunic all the way down, took off the coat, laid it on the gloves. He thumbed his red braces off, let them hang. Took off his linen shirt, hauled the braces over his bare shoulders. Stood proudly in breeches and jackboots. He'd a wiry, muscular physique, thick black hair on his pale chest, several red scars crisscrossing his breast and belly. Those gunners he'd stuck must've fought back.

When he'd let me admire him, he drew the bayonet, held it slanting upward as if he might rip me open from groin to throat. He tossed the weapon on the bed, drew the Adam's Dragoon, tossed that too. For a moment he looked me in the eye, enjoying my uncertainty. Then he rummaged in his pocket for a small bottle that he held out in the flat of his palm.

"What do they pay you to beat a man senseless?" he said.

I said nothing.

"The purse. Isn't that what it's called?"

I'd meant to ignore him, but the performance was too curious.

"Three hundred," I said. "Guineas."

He pulled a face to say that suited him well enough.

"This is for your life," he said. "But you've got to earn it."

"Earn what?"

He picked up his shirt, rolled the bottle carefully inside, laid it by the door behind him. Laid the bayonet and gun on top. Then he faced me, lifted his fists.

"Think you can get past me, jungle boy?" He nodded backwards. "Reach that knife and you can cut my throat, make yourself worth hanging."

We stood like that, eyeing each other. It slowly dawned it wasn't just me who'd left the City Office bleeding. I'd cut him too, so deeply he'd risk his life to prove I'm wrong. Wrong that our struggle isn't banditry, our Gods aren't false, we're no more superstitious than Englishmen. We could be gentlemen too, didn't deserve beatings. That was too much for a man forged in Rugby School and Cambridge University, finished at the Company's Addiscombe seminary.

Standing there in his braces, fists up, I thought he might have *Made in England* stamped on his arse. He obviously thought so too, that's the problem.

"Can't get past you in these shackles," I said.

He dug in his pocket, tossed me an iron key as big as a stopcock. I kept my eyes on him as I undid the screws. Stood, whirled my arms, flexed my legs. Normally I'd have a plan. Know a fighter's strengths and weaknesses. We'd have sparred, watched each other fight. I'm sure he's never seen me box, not in the backstreets of Blacktown Calcutta. And he's not been long in London, or he'd already have found Bullock and Doyle.

There's no room here to dance pretty, but the chance to beat Elphinstone is irresistible. I stripped to the waist, pumped my chest and took up the stance. He beckoned me down the cell, came forward to meet me.

"It can't end like this," he said. Our boots scuffed on the flagstones. Our breath hissed in the cold air. "It's not possible." The first punches echoed on the stone walls. He kept a low guard, moved with grace. But he led with his eyes, sly and mesmerising as a serpent's. "Not in the natural order of things."

He angled his body, left shoulder toward me. I drew him out, took a couple of blows to feel his counter punch. We're warming up, grunting with effort. He's using his long reach to keep me back. I can't step left or right or dance him round the ring. But he holds his head up when he jabs, asking for a reply. Too obvious. I'll go inside, use one of my best worked moves.

I lined up a lazy left cross. He'll come over the top, I'll slip it left, moving fast inside with a solid body blow. He's weak in the abdomen, untrained. And his angled stance lines up the punch. If he folds, I'll finish it fast. I moved closer with my guard tight, launched the left, then ...

* * *

Pain ... darkness. As my senses returned, I felt a numb ache in the side of my head, something pressing one side of my body. I must've been dreaming, how else to explain Elphinstone's bizarre performance? But slowly I realized I was lying on the stone floor, staring under one of the beds. From outside came an insistent thumping, someone banging on the door, calling, *"Elphinstone?"*

* * *

I looked up, prompting a sharp pain in my right side. The image lagged my turning head, then overshot like liquid in a twirled glass. When it came to rest, I saw the Major rebuttoning his tunic, looking down at me with an imperious stare. "Get up!" he ordered, reached a hand under my armpit, half dragged me to my feet.

"*Elphinstone!*" the voice outside yelled.

I heard myself say, "What happened?"

"You met a better man," the Major said. "The better breed."

The lock rattled and the door opened. A bulky man in a prison uniform stepped in and looked around. He's well built, but run to fat, probably in his fifties. By the accent I'd say he's the prison governor.

"What's this?" he said. "*What's this?*"

The Major had dressed, apart from the gun and knife still lying on the bed next to the bottle. In lieu of an answer he holstered the Dragoon, slid the bayonet smoothly into its scabbard.

In his own time, he said, "There was a fight here, last night."

The turnkey opened his mouth, thought better of it. He's holding a pewter flagon and a china mug.

"Fight ... what fight?" the Governor said.

He looked at the turnkey, who shrugged.

The Major let me go. I swayed a little, still wondering what'd happened. The last minute or two were a blank. I'd thrown a punch, then ... nothing?

"Well?" the Governor said.

"Well, what?" said Elphinstone, not liking another uniform in the room.

"I've got an execution waiting out there. An executioner wants paying."

The Major picked up the bottle, held it out to me.

"I've a job for you, Khan," he said.

I stared at the bottle.

"Take it!"

I took it. *The better man?* My head's clearing, eyes refocussing, legs feeling more solid. *What happened?*

"The bottle," Elphinstone said. "What is it?"

I stared around as if I'd lost something. Looked at the floor, the walls, the door and the window. Without a glance, I said, "It's a four-ounce, test-solution bottle. Best German glass. Sold at Griffin's in Garrick Street. Quality piece."

"Not the *bottle,*" he hummed. "The *contents.*"

Which is when I grasped why the black man ends up bleeding on the floor, the white one buttoning his tunic with an arrogant sneer. Why the British ruled Bengal. Why my mother took me to Murshidabad. All of it. Once my self-esteem would've imploded like a sparked mixture of oxygen and hydrogen, left a drop of me in the vacuum of my own skull. Now I wanted to laugh.

"The bottle!" Elphinstone said. "Or do want to be hanged?"

I swirled it and studied the oily whirlpool. Pulled the stopper, sniffed. It's sweet, a mixture of benzene and acetic ether. But that's just the solvent. There's something else dissolved in the liquid. I replaced the stopper. The action and smell of organic chemistry reminded me there's a life beyond this cell, one that's good. And I could smell ... beer, Barclay's from the Southwark brewery.

"What is it?" Elphinstone said.

"I'm not a magician. A chemist needs a laboratory."

He nodded. This wasn't his idea. He'd asked if I wanted to hang. *Wanted to?* Which meant someone else had said I might not. Which had to be Sir George Green because no one else could countermand an order with his signature and seal. Which is why Elphinstone wanted to punch my head, why I could yank his pisser as hard as I liked.

"We're executing him, then?" the Governor said.

"Shut up!" said Elphinstone.

"Now look here, Major–"

"I want to know what's in the bottle," said Elphinstone, as if the governor wasn't there. "Where it's from, who made it? How soon can you tell me?"

"A week?"

"Two days."

"There's a tinge of green ... probably chlorophyll from a plant. Can't be done in two days."

"Three then, but that's your lot."

"And?"

Elphinstone pulled out my confession and the death warrant.

"We might tear these up."

"Might?"

"Don't push it, jungle boy."

I looked at the bottle. Dissolved matter's tricky to extract, like getting sugar back from a cup of tea. Finding the maker would be harder still. But I'd a few ideas.

"Three days."

"It's off then?" the Governor said, like it's a cricket match.

Elphinstone said, "For now."

The Governor left, shaking his head at the irregularity of it all.

As I dressed, the Major said, "Two things, Khan. First, you report to me at the India Office in Whitehall. No one else. Got it?"

I buttoned my shirt, said nothing.

"Second." He came closer. "You speak a word of what passed between us in the City Office, or here, I'll kill you myself. You understand?"

I put my frockcoat on. "That Barclay's ale?"

The turnkey nodded.

"Pour us a mug," I said. "You can't put it back in the barrel."

I drank it down in one, belched.

"What time did Elijah Doyle die?" I said.

The Major blinked. "Report to me," he said. "India Office."

He pushed past the turnkey and walked out.

THE WALLS FROM the porter's room felt like the path to paradise, though it might've been the beer on an empty stomach. Crunching along the riverbank towards Westminster, I made a mental list of who knew I drank with Henry on a Wednesday evening – it's a short one. Who knew my surgical instruments were initialled, could've stolen one to sell me for Henry's murder – that's even shorter. Lists that didn't matter when I'd a few hours to live.

They did now.

Part II

Analysis

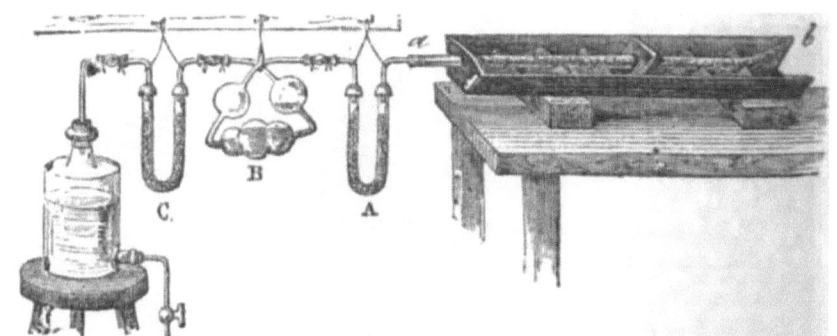

The apparatus being thus arranged, you are to heat to redness.

John Griffin, *Chemical Recreations*, 1860

Nine

THERE'S NOTHING NORMAL about my life. Nothing predictable.

A Santal boy born in a jungle should stay there. Fell trees and plough with a bullock. Dream of the prettiest girl in the village, hunt with the men and drink rice beer to feel like a king. My mother should've stayed there too, dreaming a mother's dreams ... one day her son would be the *Ojha* or the *Naike* or the *Manjhi* – the medicine man, the priest or the chief.

None of it happened. Was that because she lay with a *Dikku*, had a bastard child she smuggled into the tribe? Did *Thakur Jiu* throw us to the white men for her sin, exile me in their world? I don't believe in Gods, but I can't shake that explanation. It's too poetic. What's more, not believing in the Thakur doesn't stop me talking to him. We talk because I want my life to make sense, want a reason for my suffering.

Walking up Millbank Street I asked him why the last twelve hours had been a nightmare. There's a poetic answer, of course. One I didn't like at all. I hoped the Thakur might have an alternative, but he didn't.

When I'm depressed, I usually brew a bucket of the rice beer we call *handi*. Take a day off from life. We Santal say our tribe began with beer. In the beginning were Haram and Budhi, a brother and sister born of goose eggs. They were pure and happy until the Thakur showed them how to brew handi. They got drunk, slept together and gave birth to seven pairs of twins, each pair a boy and a girl. The twins got drunk too, slept together and begat the seven Santal clans.

That's why a Santal boy can't marry a girl of his own clan. It's a penance for original sin, born of alcohol. Why for me handi's the root of all things – of suffering and joy, of life itself.

But I can't afford a day without my wits about me. And since I'm caked in dried blood, I'll have the next best thing, a bath. Lounging in hot water's just the act of defiance I need. To hell with Elphinstone sending me off to solve his puzzles. I crossed the road, looped behind the Abbey into Great Smith Street and trotted up the steps of the Westminster Washhouse.

INSIDE IT'S TILED white and smells of chlorine disinfectant. There's a wooden counter like a shop selling everything a bather might need. Behind it stood a tall, skinny man with thinning hair and bony cheeks, wearing a full-length apron. When he caught sight of me an odd expression crossed his face.

I'm used to looks. If I'm introduced as the prince, it can be a smile, a certain curiosity. On my own and it's anything from suspicion to outright hostility. But this was something else – a look of fear, that hardened quickly to hatred. I didn't know why. Henry's death could've been reported in this morning's papers but surely not my condemnation. And even if it was, how would the man know I'm Hyder Khan?

They'd kept my wallet at the City Office, but I had a guinea piece in an inside pocket. I slapped it on the counter, said I wanted a bath.

"Can't change that," the aproned man said. "We've just opened."

I caught sight of myself in a looking glass behind him. My hair's a bird's nest, there're two days' stubble on my chin and my lower lip's split. I'd slept in my clothes. Maybe that's it, I look like a vagrant lascar, an Indian deck hand.

"I'll take a pig's-bristle toothbrush," I said, "a comb and some dentifrice."

"You deaf? I can't change it."

I took a breath, wasn't in the mood for his lip.

"I'll have these clothes laundered, too."

"What clothes?"

"The ones I'm wearing."

The man stared.

"And I want 'em back inside an hour."

He looked down, said nothing.

"What's the matter?" I said, "aren't blacks welcome here?"

"Welcome as we are in India," he mumbled.

It's an odd thing to say. Most Londoners know nothing about India, except it's far away, exotic. They see British adventurers come home with an Indian entourage, set up palatial homes. Conclude princes are easily parted from their jewels. I know a Hindu trader who says he keeps his caste in his coffers, which reminded me of a rapid cure for social inferiority.

"There's a shilling in it, for you," I said.

He weighed the odds, like an engine chewing the calculus of greed versus superiority. "Half a crown," he said.

"A bath and two towels is fourpence ... and that includes soap!"

"Take it or leave it."

I nodded, wanted the bath, He counted my change, took my order from a shelf and stood it on the counter. Then he led me down a corridor to a stall and poured a steaming bath. I half expected the jokes – *watch out it doesn't wash off* – or the opposite. The usual stuff I'd heard hundred times.

"Elsie will be along in a bit," he said.

I'd stripped and wrapped in a towel when a tubby woman with red cheeks and a bonnet tapped on the stall door. She smelt of bleach and soap.

I said, "Elsie?"

She didn't reply, but she took the bundle of clothes I was holding.

I called, "There's a tanner in it if they're back in half an hour."

She rolled her eyes and nudged the door to with the bundle.

The tubs are long, deep enough to float in. The scalding water stung the cuts but the heat soaking into my stiff muscles felt good.

Little streaks of red coiled from the dried blood on my body. I washed from head to foot, twice. Cleaned my teeth, twice. Laid back and looked up through the iron and glass roof, thought about the poetic explanation of my troubles.

I'd got no justice in London. After my evidence vanished at East India House, I put Bengal behind me, told myself I couldn't go back. What I did get – in the Imperial capital of all places – was sanctuary. I studied chemistry with Hofmann, worked with Henry, and boxed in the evenings for a good living.

Most unlikely of all I took up with Lady Beatrice Motcombe who owns what she calls an *elegant villa* in a thousand acres of farmland called Earlsacre. It's on the south bank of the Thames a dozen miles west of London. Some would call her a beauty. I dressed in nice clothes and styled myself a prince, became a celebrity in Bea's circles.

As ever, O'Shaughnessy was my savior. I took a while to pick up what London chemists call *philosophical chemistry,* but they couldn't touch me on forensic investigation. I'd a plan to use chemical rays to detect blood and poison at lightning speed. Hofmann supported me, gave me a quiet corner and bits of brass and glass. That's how I made my name, patented the *Chemiscope.* Won some real respect. Especially when Scotland Yard wanted my advice, got me going as a consulting analyst. Like I said, there's nothing normal about my life. Least of all that I'd started to enjoy it.

But the Thakur was watching. When he saw I'd lost my evidence, wasn't harrying the East India Company for justice, he put me in a basement with a dead body and a damning piece of evidence. Then I got a beating and spent a night in fear of my life. That's what happens when you cross the Gods.

I lolled to one side in the cooling water, looked at the little bottle perched on the tub. Watched it sweating in the steam, shining bright in the morning sun. Why'd Elphinstone – or more likely Sir George Green – want to know about it? *What it was. Who made it. Where it came from.* Those questions told me more than they imagined. Once

I got it in my laboratory, I'd make it speak. I felt the thrill of chemical investigation. Of opening doors shut tight to others.

The green tinge glowed in the sunlight like a spirit trapped against its will. A Bonga spirit from the jungle, sent to keep me on my toes. Once I pulled the stopper things would happen, no doubt about that. Things that were irreversible, that would probably change my life again.

I wouldn't tell Elphinstone anything. Not after that fight in the cell. I'll go straight to Sir George but not until I'm a step ahead. Just as the Major was this morning, keeping himself on top.

I climbed out of the tub and dried myself, took the comb to my mop of jet-black hair. Noticed I needed a shave. I thought about chemical analysis till Elsie tapped on the door with my clothes draped over one arm. All neatly washed and pressed and ironed dry, good as new.

When I reached out, she said, "What about me tanner?"

I gave her a shilling, which she bit and pocketed. As she was leaving, she said, "You'd best lay low for a day or two," as if the extra tip earned me some advice. She'd gone before I could ask why.

I dressed and knotted my green bow tie in the glass. There's a barber shop off the foyer which opens at eight o'clock, two minutes from now. I could see the barber inside drinking a cup of tea. A sign in the window said, 'Tom's,' and underneath, 'King of Shaves. No bleeding or pulling teeth'. A couple more customers arrived and waited in line behind me. I was first in, stepped straight back into India, back into my unpredictable life.

THE SHOP HAD chairs along one wall and a small brazier to keep the shaving water hot. There's a talking parrot that says, *"Back in forty-two."* Tom lost a leg in China in the Opium War. His stories tend to start, "Back in forty-two," as he tap-taps round the barber's chair. He calls me 'Tipu' after Tipu Sultan who saw off the Company's army with rockets. It happens to be my ring-name, not that Tom knows that.

His face told me something wasn't right. He seemed surprised to see me, frowned as if I'd a cheek coming in. I hung my jacket. Went and sat in the chair.

"Haircut and shave," I said. "Any chance of a shoeshine?"

He tapped over to the door and called out. Then without a word he started yanking a comb through my hair.

"I want it short," I said.

An urchin came and knelt at my feet with shoe polish and two brushes. Tom began a quick comb and snip, the boy a firm two-handed shine. Tom offers halfpenny shaves before nine, which is why he's busy. Normally the mood's friendly with a lot of banter. Today it's eerily quiet.

"Wasn't expecting you," Tom said.

"No? Why's that?"

"After what's happened?"

It felt like Henry's ghost following me around.

"How d'you find out?" I said.

Tom looked at me like I'm joking. "Papers of course."

Someone said, "You in the Indian army now, Peggo?"

Another said, "Watch you don't cut his ear off."

That got a laugh. Seems I'm being insulted.

Tom said, "Your lot've done it now, Tipu."

"My lot?"

"The Pandeys ... you know what I mean."

I didn't. Mangal Pandey's a Hindu Sepoy who mutinied at Barrackpore in April. The British hanged him, and *Pandey's* now a term of abuse in England.

"Done it, how?" I said.

Someone said, "You know they can't read."

More laughter.

Tom kept cutting. "Tipu here's educated," he said. "A prince."

I'm thinking about rule one, ignoring insults shows fear.

"Satan's abroad in India," said a better-spoken voice. "It's divine judgment for banning Christ's Gospel."

I could see in the mirror the speaker wore a dog collar, a vicar.

"If I was Commander in India," said another, "I'd exterminate 'em for their cruelties, raze 'em off the face of the earth."

"What's going on Tom?" I said.

"What's going on?" he said.

"Yeah, what?"

"Mutiny, that's what. You must've heard?"

"What mutiny?"

"Told you they can't read."

Now the air's thick as engine oil. No one laughing.

Tom said, "Ain't you seen the papers? It's them Sepoys, native soldiers–"

"I know what they are. What happened?"

"Back in forty-two, I fought with Sepoys in China, they're–"

"What *happened,* Tom?"

"They marched on Delhi, set it ablaze. Bastards are butchering their officers, raping and slaughtering white women in the streets."

The shoeblack boy looked up with a fearful stare.

"Satan," growled the vicar, "they've unleashed the darkest demons of h–"

"Never mind demons," Tom said, "You ask me, it's the Crimean business. British officers sent to fight the Russians ... Indians left to their own devices. What'd they think'd happen?"

"When?" I said. "When was this?"

"It's in this morning's papers."

"No ... when, in India?"

"Get on with yer work!" Tom shouted at the shoe boy.

A newspaper crackled behind me. "Report's from Bombay," a voice said. "Sent by steamer and electric telegraph on ... May 27th. Mutiny began at a place called Meerut on May 10th." The paper crackled again. "They've made Bahadur Shah king of all India."

"That figures," I muttered.

"What does?" Tom said.

"Meerut's in the north, near Delhi, the old Mughal capital. Bahadur Shah's still Emperor, but he's just a British puppet." I half turned my head. "They've really taken Delhi?"

"Oh yeah, murdered every white in the town."

I'm struggling to take it in.

"Why'd they do that?" someone said.

"The Mughal Muslims hate the British," I said. "The northern hills are warrens of Wahhabi fighters and agitators, calling for Jihad against the infidels."

"Bloody cheek," Tom said. "After what we've done for 'em."

"The Sikh Sepoys will stay loyal," I said. "They're afraid what'll happen if the British go."

"Go?" Tom said. "Back in forty-two, we thrashed the Chinese, taught 'em respect for the British. Indians will get the same, you'll see."

That got a chorus of approval. But I don't like what I'm hearing. India's not China. If a majority of Sepoys mutiny, it'll be a massacre. Might've already happened given news takes a month to reach London. And if the Company's defeated it'll make an appetite for mutiny across the British Empire.

A new voice said, "Are you a *good* Indian, Tipu?"

I couldn't see the speaker in the mirror, so I waved Tom off, twisted to look the man in the eye. It's a moustachioed lieutenant in the Bengal Artillery. "What'd you mean by that?" I said, atmosphere thick as axle grease.

As we stared, Tom said, "Tipu's a loyal subject, ain't yer?"

I lifted a hand telling him to stay out of it. After Millbank, I'd a mind to knock this cocky lieutenant round the shop. But I liked Tom and his parrot, so I turned back to the mirror. "You'll be looking for a ship," I said.

"Will I ... *Tipu?*"

"Company needs every loyal soldier."

"The Company?" the vicar scoffed, "They're worse than the natives–"

"You devil dodgers caused this," the lieutenant fired back. "With your sermons and bibles ..."

They started arguing back and forth, others throwing in comments. I'm relieved to be out of the line of fire. Tom relaxed, pulled a face to say he's baffled by the whole thing.

"Company banned missionaries from India," I said, quietly. "Didn't want religious unrest getting in the way of profits."

Tom shrugged like it's all beyond him. I sat quiet. Saw in the mirror he'd cut my hair short as the bristles on a bottle brush. Which was what I wanted, lean and hungry as Shakespeare's Cassius.

"Pomade divine? Or Rowland's macassar?"

"What?"

"On your hair," Tom said. "Or some bear fat, you won't go bald–"

"Forget the shave," I said.

I got up and took off the cape, decided to get out before the accusations started again. My shoes shone like fresh pitch. I flipped tuppence to Tom. "For you and the shoeshine."

Putting on my jacket, I searched for a parting shot. Something to show how they'd feel if I nailed up a sign at Charing Cross saying London belongs to the Santal – if you don't like it, we'll hang you. But the parrot gave me a one-eyed stare, squawked, *"Back in forty-two,"* as if it knew better.

Back on Great Smith Street I headed for my apartment. Elphinstone must've heard about the mutiny last night. That's why he wanted a fight, why a crime Briton's enemies couldn't've dreamt up in a century had become a catastrophe. What did he do? He brought me a bottle of organic liquid, one that sat in my pocket buzzing like an evil Bonga spirit. The idea chemistry's the key to a world in flames excited me. I wanted my lab, felt an urgent need to unravel this strangest of mysteries.

Ten

I KNEW BEA was in the apartment as soon as I opened the door. A whiff of scent? Her breathing? Lady Beatrice Motcombe and I might be the unlikeliest couple in London. She's educated, an English aristocrat with a sense of entitlement so inbred she doesn't know it's there. Not that she regards blacks as inferior. She regards everyone as inferior, except a handful of her own class. The rest exist to animate her world.

She'd certainly animated mine. Shortly after we met, she bought this apartment in the Adelphi Building. We looked at it together like husband and wife, and she urged me to move in on the grounds there's no point paying rent for a slum in Lambeth when I could live in style off the Strand. In reality, she'd set me up as rich men do a mistress.

It's a care-free sort of area with lots of actors and poets, artists and engineers. Some live with younger 'sisters' or even 'valets'. No one asks. I'm Bea's philosopher ... jester ... prize-fighter ... oriental lover. Above all, I'm her king of the elements, worker of vegetable miracles. I got to know another Lady Motcombe – Bea – an abandoned wife struggling to defend a way of life under threat.

When I told her I was a son of the Nawab of Bengal, she thought I must be royalty, dubbed me the Prince of Murshidabad. It's how she introduces me to her circle. She designed my *carte de visite*. When I qualified at the Royal College of Chemistry, she bought me a set of medical instruments monographed with my title, *P of M*. Which puts her second on a tiny list of people who could've sold me for Henry's murder. Not a thought I'm proud of. But there it is.

I went through the hall into the front room, where Bea stood at the picture window, staring out. It's a second-floor apartment with lovely views along the Thames. Fog and smoke permitting, you can see east to St Paul's, west to the Houses of Parliament. Bea wore a blue dress with white-lace trim, a matching ribbon in her chocolate brown hair. She's a well-rounded woman with Italian eyes, like one of Da Vinci's nudes. Gives me an itch every time I see her.

She didn't turn to greet me.

"What's that chimney across the river?" she said. "The big one."

"Bea, I ..."

"The one by Waterloo Bridge."

"It's not a chimney ... it's Lambeth shot tower. Bea, I'm sorry–"

"Gone off the Messiah, have you?" she said, still staring out.

I walked over and laid my hands softly on her shoulders.

"I called in to see Henry on the way–"

She shook me off, walked to the sofa. "Spent the night in the Ship?"

"Nope, Millbank Prison. I found Henry dead in his cellar. The police accused me of killing him, threatened to hang me."

I regretted my tone at once. The *affaire* with Bea was heaven for a year, now we never seem to miss a chance to quarrel. She spun round and stared as if I might be joking. Or maybe it's the bottle-brush haircut.

"You're such a *liar*, Hyder," she said.

I shrugged. "You've seen this morning's papers?"

"Oh yes. City of London's in uproar. Half the monied class of England are invested in India. I suppose you approve."

"Of rape and murder?"

"Huh! I thought you'd call it a *just* war."

"For God's sake, Bea." I went over and took her hands. "There're three hundred thousand Sepoys in India, most of the Company's army. All trained to fight, armed with Enfield rifles. If they mutiny, they'll crush the British. Then they'll turn on each other ... Hindu against Moslem against Sikh."

She pulled her hands free. "You think I don't know that?"

She usually mocks colonial wars. Says they're like omnibuses on the Strand – there's an occasional lull, then so many come at once you can't keep up. It's one of her signs of moral regression, like the world under siege by the manufacturing classes – men driven mad for money.

Then I remembered she's married to a Company administrator, Shapton Sands, a tax officer for the cloth trade in Gorakhpur. It's way up country in the Himalayan foothills, the kind of place the mutiny will take hold.

I said, "Didn't think you cared for your husband–"

"Shapton? I don't. My life'd be a lot easier if the Sepoys made minced meat of him." She ran her fingertips over my cuts. "What happened to your face?"

"They'd some questions in the City Police Office. Then I met the savages of Millbank prison."

She screwed up her eyes as if she'd just realized my story might be true.

"Mr Bullock, dead?"

Mr Bullock? She normally called him *that vulgar little man.*

"Beaten senseless, tortured. Took his own life, with cyanide."

Bea was shocked but trying not to show it. Then with her usual poise, she said, "Did you mention my name?"

"No."

"Why not?"

"For one thing I don't need you nannying me–"

"How dare the police arrest you? I'll speak to Wilberforce, tell him–"

"You know the Commissioner?"

"I know his superior, Sir George Green."

"You know the Home Secretary?"

She rolled her eyes. London's elite is small and intimate – they dine and dance and hunt together. Bea takes special offence at the police, their powers to question and arrest their social superiors.

Especially if it leaves her alone on the steps of St Paul's. When she found a constable on her property chasing a thief, she asked indignantly why he imagined she kept a game keeper.

"I'll write to the Commissioner in the strongest terms today," she said. "Let him know this kind of thing's completely unacceptable."

"I don't think that's a good idea, Bea."

"Why ever not?"

"For a start, there's some powerful evidence against me."

We sat on the sofa, facing each other. I took out the little bottle, stood it on the table.

"What's that?" she asked.

I told her what'd happened at Henry's shop, later at the City Office and Millbank prison. Didn't mention Elphinstone. "Just before the hanging," I said, "they brought me that bottle, said if I found out what's in it, I'd get a reprieve."

"They?"

"Seems both the British Government and the East India Company are interested. What's really damning is a policeman found my monographed forceps in the wreckage. Looks like they were used to ... hurt Henry."

Bea looked puzzled.

"Somebody took them from the Lab," I said. "Someone who knew my instruments were initialed, that I call on Henry most Wednesdays around six."

"You were *meant* to take the blame?"

"Looks like it. And who'd know my movements? My instruments?"

We stared at each over for a moment.

"You don't mean ... *huh!*" She got up and stalked to the window, looked back angrily. "You're really something, Hyder. You know that?"

"No," I said. "I didn't —"

"For all I know it *was* you," she said. "You're always complaining

Bullock sweats you for every farthing."

"I didn't mean—"

"What about that wretched driver of yours, Thorn? He knows more about your business than I do ... he'd sell you for a farthing."

Thorn's actually a *her*. No one knows it apart from her wife. She doesn't know I know. Right now, the only suspects on both my lists are Thorn and Bea. In that order. Which probably means I don't have any suspects.

I was getting up to console Bea when the telegraph machine pinged, began spooling paper-tape onto the table. Reminded me I hadn't checked my electric post. Bea bought the apartment from an engineer at the Electric Telegraph Company who'd run a spur in to test his inventions. The machine stands on an ornate table with weights dangling beneath like a cuckoo clock. Prints messages in dots and dashes. They normally spool onto the floor, but I noticed the tape was bundled up on the table like discarded paper chains.

I went over. "What's this?" I said. "Someone's torn off a message or two."

Bea sees machines as more signs of moral regression. Like the gas lighting and a hot-water geyser the engineer installed, along with a flush-out toilet that uses rainwater. She calls it a 'self-acting' apartment, full of devices doing a servant's work, stealing her way of life. Not that it stops her sending telegraphs. She's even learned to read the dots and dashes.

She said, "Oh ... a couple of the messages were for me."

"You? Who'd telegraph you here?"

"I did."

"You telegraphed *yourself* at my apartment?"

"It's *my* apartment."

I took a breath. "I live here."

She shrugged. "I sent them, they're mine."

"Once they're sent—"

"I just wanted them back, all right?"

The electric cells under the table had boiled over. I went to the kitchen to fetch a rag and distilled water. Came back and cleaned up, refilled the cells.

"I bet you telegraphed to say what you thought of me."

"I was on the steps of St Paul's for an hour, Hyder. Like some ... tart looking for trade."

I nearly laughed at the idea Bea could look like a tart.

"Worried half to death," she said. "Thought there'd been an accident. Then that you just ... didn't ..." She turned back to the window.

I went to her. "Didn't what?"

"Want to see me."

I took her waist, laid my chin on her shoulder.

Bea's older than me, wary of the world. She and Shapton married in a fog of mutual deceit – he a young Company writer, home on furlough, fancying himself lord of the manor; she a struggling landowner thinking he'd inherit his father's banking business, prop up the estate. They were both wrong.

A Scots swindler duped Shapton's father into buying worthless bonds in Poyais, a fake kingdom in Honduras. Faced with ruin he threw himself off Waterloo Bridge. When a penniless Shapton found life at Earlsacre wasn't all hunting and banqueting, he went back to tax collecting in Gorakhpur. There he bigamously married a princess, had two children, and borrowed from her father, ostensibly to pay mercenaries to fight off local warlords. Never came back.

Bea took refuge in the Marquis du Sade's *La Philosophie dans le boudoir* which her father brought from Paris in 1814. In the flyleaf he'd written, *'Revolution makes a virtue of vice!'* Bea read from it in English on our first night, short sections on du Sade's idea that animal lust far exceeds the madness of love. New in London, I assumed that's what English ladies did. When she told me about her husband, I saw du Sade as a wall around her vulnerability.

Like now. She looked thoroughly dejected.

"Well," I said. "Now you know why I wasn't there."

She nodded, turned her head so our cheeks touched.

"Let me help you, Hyder. I *know* these people. Once they realize we're acquainted they'll forget the whole thing, find some other lackey."

I don't underestimate Bea. She runs her own estate. But she's not realistic about my place in London society. Just because I amuse her friends doesn't mean I'm accepted. She can laugh at respectability among her own class, among the Adelphi crowd, but scandal's only a gnat's wing away. The likes of Commissioner Wilberforce would love to take her down a peg or two. Bengalis say the fun of secret love, matches the pain of its exposure. So I don't want her firing off high-handed letters, getting herself embroiled with men like Elphinstone.

"Let me handle this, Bea. Please. I know what they want."

"They'll let it drop?"

"I think so."

"But, if you need me ..." She twisted to catch my eye, lost for words. Then, in a whisper, "I care for you ... *so much.*"

Which left me quiet, left me on the spot.

BEA WASN'T AFFECTIONATE, not like that.

A week after the de Sade reading, a scene occurred that nearly ended our *affaire.* Arriving at Earlsacre for dinner one evening, I was led to an upper floor and directed down a corridor to a suite at the back of the house. Bea stood waiting in a fine drawing room with mirrored walls and a leather-upholstered ottoman in the middle She gave me a haughty glance, then rang for Jane Muckalt, her maid and confidante. Jane arrived in a black, ankle-length dress, kid boots and a starched white apron.

We stood for a while in a triangular tableau that felt familiar, not that I could place it. Then Bea began scalding Jane for neglecting some duty earlier in the day. She didn't reply, just stood defiantly, returning her mistress's glare.

"You'll apologize, Jane," Bea said. "Or take the consequences."

When she didn't, Bea ordered her to take off the apron. To my surprise, she did. I thought it was a quaint English ceremony, like ripping the epaulettes from a disgraced officer's tunic, though the taut air felt like something else. Jane dropped the apron on the carpet, stared at her mistress. Jane made me think of a mischievous pixie. She'd short brown hair, green, almond eyes with brows plucked high and thin. Full lips, turned up at the edges to little dimples.

"Take off the dress, Jane," Bea said.

She did. Unbuttoned down the back with one hand till it slid to the carpet in a crumpled ring around her boots. Now she stood in a white blouse and matching silk drawers. I'm getting uncomfortable. Jane wasn't a beauty, but I couldn't help admiring the swell of her bosom and the press of her dark nipples through the blouse. Her legs were a little plump, but she carried it well.

"Take off your blouse," Bea ordered.

At which point I glanced at Bea, but her eyes were fixed on Jane's.

Jane unbuttoned, shrugged the blouse from her shoulders. Stood defiant as ever, naked to the waist. Did I say she *wasn't* a beauty? Forget that. All I knew was that whatever I'd thought was happening, wasn't. Bea waited, nodded at the drawers. Jane eased the silk over her hips, her bottom, her thighs, wiggled them down to the dress below. Then she stepped out of the fabric circle, stood proud in nothing but her kid boots.

Bea strode to an oak sideboard, came back with a riding crop – a short horsewhip – and a bundle of black silk scarves. Stood facing Jane's left flank, admiring her delicious nudity in profile. The crop ended in a soft tongue of black leather. Bea ran it in a caress from Jane's throat, over the curve of her breast, down the flat of her white belly, patted the fine black hair on her quim.

"Well?" she said. "Will you apologize?"

Jane glared. Bea slapped the leather tongue on her bottom, hard, like geeing up a horse. I saw a flash of green jungle, a red tunic riding a black stallion. Blinked and shook my head to chase away the image.

Jane spread her shins, pressed them tight against one side of the ottoman. Bea tied her ankles to the couch's stubby legs with scarves. Stood, slapped again as an order to bend over. Jane resisted, long enough to cast me a glance, one as coy as it was wanton. Then she bent double and grasped the ottoman's far legs. Bea tied her wrists, stood up. Looked me in the eye as she unhooked her own dress, right down to her waist. Wriggled free to stand as naked as her maid.

Bea caressed Jane's back, said, "What shall we do with her?"

I saw the rawness of it, the breasts and faces and bottoms ... caught in the angled mirrors hung on picture wire. It's from de Sade. The reading ... "*All must be on view, just as many delectable tableaux, inflaming their lust, bringing it to a conclusion.*" I knew what we could do, every act. Bea stood behind, teased Jane's buttocks with soft strokes and slaps. Nothing left to the imagination, not even the moles and birthmark.

Bea said, "She's powerless to resist, won't ever tell."

Don't tell! Shalani's voice. The soldiers slide from their horses, drag her to the ground, roughly slap her, pull her saree up and down. I can see bare flesh, a birthmark, the fear in her eyes. Fear for me, at what I'm seeing. My throat tightened and the room melted.

I walked out. Went down the corridor, the stairs, no idea where I'm going, except away from here. Went out through some French doors onto a lawn where I found a garden seat. Sat at one end in the soft evening, listening to a blackbird sing, staring out across the placid Thames.

In a while, Bea came and sat at the other end. We didn't look at each other. After five minutes, she said, "It's too lovely an evening to fight."

I nodded.

In another five, she said, "I'm sorry, Hyder."

"So am I." Not that I knew why. Maybe in London a pretty maid's supposed to play the lover, or the whore. Part of the job.

Bea said, "I've given Jane the night off."

"Oh?"

"Will you stay for dinner?"

I nodded. Never saw de Sade's book again. Never saw Bea and Jane behave other than good mistress and maid, as if none of it happened. But a day or two later, Jane met me at the villa door, glanced around to make sure we're alone.

"Thank you," she whispered.

"For what?"

"You know ..."

I shrugged. "You mean–"

"Your kindness ... I'd have lost my situation."

"She'd have let you go?"

Jane took my hat and gloves.

After that, Bea was more familiar. Easier in my company. But there's a hole between our friendship and the boudoir, the place her love should be. Mine's there. But she'll go from amiable chitchat to rutting like an animal, then cry, push me away. Get up abruptly and come back my friend.

Doesn't show affection or need.

NOW SHE LOOKS as needy as a soap bubble in a thorn tree.

"You know I care for you, too," I said. "Listen, I'll be busy with that bottle today, but I could cook this evening, see what's in the market?"

"Adam and Eve?" she said. "Not today, thanks."

Which I understood. My first night here I made her a Santal meal on plates folded from dock leaves I picked by the Thames. Told her it's customary to sit cross-legged on the floor and eat with your fingers, which wasn't strictly true. I wanted to see how seriously she'd take my world.

"Smoke a pipe, then? Drink some beer?"

She shook her head. Which I didn't understand. At that first meal we smoked *gunjah*. She wouldn't touch till I said it aroused intense aphrodisiac desire. I took the stuff with O'Shaughnessy – *Cannabis Indica*, he called it – in the cause of medical experiment. Anyway, that night we stumbled off to bed laughing like kettles. She'd never missed a chance since.

"You all right, Bea?" When she shrugged, I said, "What about a drink at the Hotel, dinner at the Shades?"

The Adelphi Hotel is one corner of the Adelphi building, the Shades is in one of the archway cellars nearby. We often breakfast or lunch in the Hotel, dine in the Shades. The people know us, leave us alone.

Bea turned away. "I'm meeting O'Connell at the villa this afternoon."

She says "O'Connell" as if he's a skin rash I've given her. Finn O'Connell's a reforming estate manager, still in his twenties. I found him through Hofmann over a year ago, saved Bea's arable land from death by exhaustion.

"What about?"

"Hedgerows and galvanized fences," she said. "Might drag on."

"Wire fences?"

"Newest thing, apparently. God knows how you can galvanize a fence."

"With zinc."

"What?"

"Galvani ... he's an Italian. Discovered electricity ... sort of."

Bea looked at me as if I'm pulling her leg. It's a vestige of our first meeting, part of what keeps us together.

"I'll explain at dinner," I said. Seven o'clock, the Hotel?"

She turned so our noses touched. "Shall I stay tonight?"

"I'd like that." I pecked a kiss on her lips. "No letters to Wilberforce?"

She shook her head, looked around to change the subject. "The place is a mess," she said. "I'll get Jane to tidy up."

"She's here?"

"Around the corner, in the Hotel."

Jane's never far off. Bea needs servants like I do test-tubes. That first night, before we lit the *gunjah* pipe, Bea waved from the window to her carriage below. A minute later, Jane arrived to tidy up while we smoked. In the morning she served coffee with warm rolls and marmalade from the Hotel, dressed her mistress for a meeting in town. Later I helped Jane carry the silverware back to the Hotel, put her on a train to Earlsacre. She liked being treated as an equal. In our own ways we're both servants to Lady Motcombe. We've that in common.

No pipes this evening. I went over to the telegraph, ran pieces of paper-tape through my fingers. I said, "It's raining in Liverpool."

"Bea rolled her eyes. "We're not in Liverpool."

I gather weather news. If I can predict storms in port towns, I can sell the intelligence to shipping lines. It's the sort of thing O'Shaughnessy would do. Bea thinks I make it up to impress her.

"What about the opium?" she said, as if she hadn't read my electric post. I've a chain of chemists tracking adulterated drugs across the country, in this case opium that's mainly poppy capsules.

"Reached Birmingham," I said.

The message that'd just pinged in, read: <<*Khan. Be at the London and Imperial Bank, High Holborn, 10am. Sgt Chrystal*>> My electric address was on the card I'd left at the City Office. But I wondered how he knew I'm out of gaol. I glanced at the clock. Gone half past nine. I punched a reply on the finger-pedal perforator, sent a transmit request to the Charing Cross office. When the bell rang, I started the clockwork feeder, fed in the tape. As the message tick-tocked off to the City Office I went over the Bea.

"What if my meeting goes on?" she said.

"Then I'll wait. Seven o'clock?"

She nodded, a little blank.

I took her hands, looked at her. "What did those messages say?"

She pursed her lips. "Oh ... just sending you ..."

"To hell?"

"Something like that."

"I don't believe in hell."

"Doesn't mean you won't go there." She looked me up and down. "You don't look as if you spent the night in a prison cell."

"I got cleaned up, for you."

"Really?"

"King of shaves, Westminster."

I pulled her close and we hugged, tight. Looking over her shoulder I saw why I'd known she was here. She'd bought some bunches of colourful pansies, arranged two vases on the mantlepiece It melted my heart.

"Sorry I was such a bitch earlier," she whispered.

"Tonight, my love." I kissed her forehead, picked up the bottle and went into the hall. On the way I collected a few business cards and some cash. "I'll take the Lab," I called, "if Thorn's there. See you at seven. Don't forget to lock up." Bea's used to servants, not bolting doors.

"Hyder!" she called back.

I stuck my head into the front room. "Yes?"

"What is a *shot tower*?"

"You rain molten lead from the top. By the bottom it's frozen lead-shot."

She gave me another quizzical stare. "But–"

I ducked out, then back in. "Ever hear of a man called Hydraulic Jack?"

"Who?"

"That's what I thought."

I slammed the front door and trotted down the stairs.

THE ADELPHI STANDS on a labyrinth of brick passages that meander down to arcades and jetties on the Thames. It's a subterranean village of storage vaults, busy with tradesmen by day, a Hades of vagrants and vagabonds at night.

Sometimes when I wake, Bea breathing gently beside me, I wonder what powers order this world. We lie in silk sheets, made from mulberry leaves paid for in Santal blood. Fifty feet below us, wretches lie shivering and hopeless amid filth and animal dung. I've got no answers.

I rent one of the vaults to keep my mobile laboratory – the Lab. Got the idea from Thomas Wakley who edits the *Lancet* while he's riding between coroner's courts. If I get results at the scene – *Poison? Blood? Rape?* – I have an edge. So I bought an old Clarence – a *growler* they call it – with my first purse. Went to see John Griffin in Garrick Street, asked him to design a chemistry set to fit a cab. There's a library shelf, a fold-away table and a basic kit of chemicals and apparatus. But only room for one passenger inside.

Just before that, I met Thorn, a buck working as a long-night cabdriver. Bucks drive licenced cabs while their owners sleep or drink, split the fares. If I was called out at night, I'd find Thorn dozing on the Strand. She'd take me to the scene, drive me home again afterwards, all for a few pence. When I suggested getting my own vehicle, she took me to a yard off Waterloo Road, helped me haggle, then fix up the Lab.

Thorn didn't say much, barely a word. But I found she'd a strong stomach for violent crime. Wasn't shocked by what one human could do to another. She'd a peculiar sympathy for the slayer and the slain, saw both as victims of circumstance. I found that interesting, often revealing. So we struck a deal: I pay a wage and train her as an assistant; she drives and washes up. What's more, she came with a nag called Bessie who pulls us. Unless I say otherwise, the Lab's stocked and Bessie in harness by nine o'clock each morning.

Today's no exception. Thorn's sitting in the vault in a billycock hat and a high-collar jacket, smoking a clay pipe. It's part of the disguise, like talking about her wife and child, or shaving with a cut-throat. Took me a while to see through it. More to the point, she's munching a bacon sandwich, which reminded me I'm ravenous, hadn't eaten since lunch yesterday.

Seeing my hungry gaze, Thorn nodded at a burner and tripod she'd used to fry the bacon. "Breakfast?" she said. She'd left two rashers, half a loaf and a knob of butter. I slapped a sandwich together, climbed up next to her and took a big bite. I'd meant to analyse the bottle's contents before we left, but I didn't want to be late for Chrystal. I'd a feeling the Bank was important.

"Enjoy the concert?" Thorn asked.

I took an omnibus last night. Bea won't use the Lab, won't ride on top with Thorn or sit inside; says it stinks – which it does, like a chemistry lab.

"Not exactly," I munched.

Thorn nodded. "Where to, Boss?"

"High Holborn, London and Imperial Bank."

She locked the Cell and drove us up the passage to the bright morning in John Street, left up Adam Street to the Strand.

"Thought we're due in Mayfair?" she said.

I bit off another chunk of bacon sandwich. "Change of plan."

Thorn packs my instruments, runs the day like clockwork. Mostly she's the clock. That's why she's top of the list. But why'd she sell me out? I gave her a new life, a trade. Without me she'd be back sleeping in a cab.

Not that I know much about her. She's literate, knows arithmetic. She's grasped chemistry's first principle – cleanliness. Every bit of glassware's spotless, every reagent pure, every item fastened in its place. Lately I've been teaching her organic analysis, how to identify an unknown substance and find its formula. She's good, becoming indispensable.

TRUTH IS, I trust Thorn more than anyone, even Bea. A while back we took a day out, shared a bucket of handi on Hampstead

Heath. Watched the day roll over the smoky pall of London town. When we're both ragged as kite tails, I started on the story of Bea and her maid, floated why they'd treated me to such a spectacle. Didn't expect an answer, not a serious one.

Thorn filled a pipe, lit it and puffed awhile.

"Not going there," she said.

"Why not?"

She gave me one of her looks, *where the hell're you from?*

"You've no idea," I said.

"You think?"

"What?"

"All right ... they're in it together, lovers."

When that soaked through the alcohol, I laughed out loud. Nearly gave the game away by saying, *yeah, you wish ...*

"Never," I said.

Thorn shrugged, *suit yourself.*

I was oiled enough to say, "Lady M worries I'll find someone else."

"You reckon?"

"She told me ... someone *more suitable.*"

"What ... blacker?"

Thorn speaks her mind, doesn't know any other way. Which makes her a good native guide in London, one reason I like her. But I'm never quite sure if it's wisdom or humour, or just insolence. Could be all three.

"No," I said, *younger."*

Thorn gave me the look. "Your mistress provides a mistress?"

"*Un-huh* ... younger ... but *not* suitable."

"She's a maid ... you're royalty?"

"Exactly. So I get my fun, Bea keeps her prince."

"Why'd Jane play along, then?"

"Lady M threatened to dismiss her."

"Best of both worlds ... for you."

"I left in disgust, never touched her."

"Against your religion is it ... two women?"

I'd have baulked at that if it hadn't stung. Jane's undressing left me stiff as the Queen's footmen, imagining an evening with two randy white women. But I wasn't quite drunk enough to tell Thorn the real reason I'd left.

"She thanked me," I said, "Jane did ... for acting like a gent."

Thorn puffed her pipe. "I wouldn't sleep with a woman treats a maid like a blowen."

"Blowen?"

"Tart ... stone thumper?" She shook her head. *"Prostitute?"*

"Look here, Thorn–"

She smiled, punched me playfully on the shoulder.

"And neither would you," she said.

Which left me wondering until she tapped out her pipe.

"Pass the handi," she said. "Got any of that *gunjah* with you?

GOING UP ST MARTIN'S Lane, I told Thorn what I'd told Bea about last night. Mentioned the forceps, gave her the same quizzical look. Thorn turned back to the road, weaved us round Seven Dials and chewed her pipe.

In a while, she said, "You believed Chrystal, then?"

I could've kicked myself. Heard O'Shaughnessy's Irish brogue say, *"Never Assume. Check the facts."*

"Stop the coach," I said.

I climbed down and got inside, tapped for Thorn to drive on. The forceps were in their place. I fetched my Oxford bag from under the seat. It's a writing case I've made into a forensic kit, a microcosm of the Lab. Checking the contents, I thought about the forceps. Had someone initialled an identical pair? Or had Chrystal lied in the hope I'd confess? I didn't want to believe that, but it made me wonder why he'd called me to the Bank.

Eleven

THE LONDON AND Imperial's the modernest bank in London. The builders used every security device shown at the Great Exhibition of '51, which earned it a full page in the *Illustrated News*. Safer than the Bank of England they say. Only select investors get to see these wonders, so I'm curious. Outside it's a castle with a portcullis door a naval broadside would bounce off. Inside it's comfortable and efficient, lots of carved rosewood and busy cashiers.

Before I could inquire, a clerk appeared from a coffered door beside the busy counter, asked my name and beckoned me inside. When he shut the door the buzz of trade fell to a velvety quiet worthy of the riches below. We're in a cozy vestibule made by a wall and two more doors. The clerk half opened the one to our left, announced my arrival. The intrusion ended a row between a well-spoken man and a better-spoken woman. Then Sergeant Chrystal appeared.

"Give us a moment," he said, nodded the clerk into the room.

We hadn't thought we'd meet again after last night's confessions. The hangman should've seen to that. Chrystal stared, a question in his eyes.

"The *Doyle* mentioned last night," he said. "Elijah Doyle?"

"Why am I here, Chrystal?"

"He's a colleague, a fellow chemist ... Doyle?"

I shook to my head to say we're not going anywhere like this.

"I want to know who he is."

"Why?"

Chrystal took a breath, getting irritated.

"I can arrest you, Khan. Question you at the–"

"You can do what you damn well like," I said. Turned to open the door I'd just come through.

"Wait!" He lifted his hands, managed an apologetic look.

I said, "Doyle's professor of pharmacy at King's College on the Strand. But you didn't need me to tell you that."

We stood in silence again, my hand on the doorknob.

"All right," Chrystal said. "I found Cartwright, told him what'd happened at Millbank. We got the Commissioner out of bed. But while Cartwright's explaining, a message arrives. Commissioner reads it, says you've been released. That's that. Only I think Cartwright read the message upside down, 'cos outside he told me to get over to the London and Imperial Bank, see what's what."

"And what was what?"

Chrystal's face said he wasn't sure where to start.

"Early this morning that clerk you just met found a body in the vaults."

"Doyle's dead?"

I knew Doyle was dead. I'd said it to Elphinstone to test the idea he'd got the little bottle from the same Calcutta cupboard as my instructions. Last night he'd have found Doyle as a matter of urgency. But then he wouldn't've needed my help. Which means Doyle can't speak.

Chrystal nodded. "Shot."

I tried to look surprised. "When?"

"Middle of the night."

"Bank's open at night?"

"Round the clock, to select customers."

"Why call me?"

"There're ... complications."

"Not what I meant. Why me?"

"You're the best."

"Don't pull my pisser, Chrystal." I twisted the doorknob.

"Wait! Look, you asked how I made sergeant so fast. I'll tell you – by being damned good at my job. Well, last night the Major asked you about Bullock *and* Doyle. Both dead. So maybe you know something I don't."

"Does Elphinstone know I'm here? Or Cartwright?"

"Nope."

I believed him; he wants my help.

"We work together, that it?"

"Sort of," Chrystal said.

"I explain the *complications,* you take the credit?"

"You'll want to know what happened too."

I let go of the door handle. Chrystal doesn't know why they released me, which means we can both play this game.

"What're these, complications?"

"Rather you saw for yourself."

"All right, let's go look."

When I reached for the door Chrystal snatched my wrist.

"Not yet," he said.

I tightened up, looked him in the eyes. "Hands off," I said.

He slowly let go, but he'd nearly told me to mind my place.

"The manager," he said. "He's half out of his mind with worry. If it gets out there's been a murder in the vaults–"

"Murder?"

"You'll see. If it gets out, the bank could be ruined."

"Got it," I said, reached for the door.

"There's more! Doyle kept a locker in the vaults. Just now his daughter arrived, wants the body and the locker's contents."

"Know what's in it?"

"Oh aye ... nothing. But he didn't die by the locker. He died at a table in a consultation room. On it's a sheet of paper and a silver cigar case. By his chair on the floor, there's a Colt revolver, 36-calibre. That's it."

"The Colt killed him?"

"Maybe. That's why you're here."

"Does the daughter have a right to his possessions?"

"Not yet, but she's ... formidable."

"Hmm. That all?"

"Not quite. She doesn't know how he died."

"Right."

I turned the knob and we stepped inside.

THE ROOM WAS a picture – *a woman stands one side, two men the other, like lovers after a tiff.* All three of them turned together to form another picture – *two men, surprised; a woman studies the artist.* Chrystal must've said I'm Indian, it's how the clerk knew me. But my appearance still unsettled them. I returned the stare with one that said, *I'm here, I'm black, get used to it.* I do it all the time.

Chrystal said, "This is Dr Khan. Also known as the prince."

The manager looked at Chrystal. "It's not Mumbo Jumbo we need–"

"You wanted the best," Chrystal said. "He's it." Then to me, "This is the manager, Mr Eatwell."

Eatwell looked as if he did – eat well – often. He also looked like a man with a corpse in his impregnable vault and ruin staring him in the face. He's holding an eleven-shilling box of *Pritchard's Aromatic Steel Pills* – guaranteed to cure nervous debility – the white man's Mumbo Jumbo. I know Prichard's shop at Charing Cross. You'd as well suck on a ball bearing.

Eatwell, threw a pill in his mouth, shook his head. "It's not like your land here," he said to me. "This is the most advanced bank–"

"Mumbo Jumbo's from Africa," I said. "I'm from India."

"Dr Khan regularly acts for Scotland Yard," Chrystal said.

We stood quiet till the clerk offered me his hand. "John Noad," he said, "Senior Clerk." We shook.

"Adelaide Doyle," the young woman said. "Professor Doyle's daughter."

Miss Doyle had been crying but didn't want to show it. In one hand she clutched a crimson handkerchief that might've been a turkey-red bandana. In the other a small, sequined bag, closed with a button. A silk headscarf was tied in a floppy bow under her chin, worn far enough back to show a sharp parting above a high forehead. The hair's white-blond, nose angular and thin. Her eyes were glazed in gold-rimmed glasses with circular lenses, tinted green. Which made her look slightly demonic, like a youthful witch.

She wasn't pretty but I'd call her attractive. It's her seriousness, the piercing intensity of the emerald gaze. She didn't shake my hand.

Eatwell turned on her. "You, Madam, can leave my bank, immediately."

"I'll do no such thing," she retorted. "What's more, you'll take me to my father's locker, *immediately.*" She spoke precisely, like an elocution lesson.

"You'll leave," Eatwell said, "or be put out, by force"

"While you ransack his–"

"Madam!" Eatwell said. "How dare you–"

"I do dare," she said. "Touch me and you'll answer to Sir Reginald."

Eatwell looked as if an apparition had just stepped through the wall.

"Sir Reginald Clyde?" I said.

"My Mama's brother. Director of this bank."

That's the Clyde of Slegman, Clyde or Birdwood, named by Elphinstone. The one I'd worked for but never met. He's London's biggest importer of Peruvian cinchona bark. Extracts the quinine, mixes it with carbonated water to make *Clyde's Seltzer*. Sells it by the gallon to the Company to treat malaria.

"A director of the East India Company?" I asked.

"Director and Deputy Chairman," Miss Doyle said.

"I'm very sorry for your loss, Miss Doyle," I said. "But I'm here because you father didn't die of ... natural causes."

If Eatwell wanted to keep her from her father's corpse, I agreed.

"I beg your pardon?" She glared at Eatwell.

"Shot," he said, afraid not to answer.

"*Shot?* By whom?" She'd turned white.

"We don't know," I said. "Perhaps if you wait here while–"

"Don't treat me like a child," she said. "You're no prince. You're the bastard son of a depraved Company officer and an Indian whore."

Boxers learn to keep their temper, no matter the pain or the low fouls referees ignore. But I wanted to slap her. Two things stopped me. First off, hitting Clyde's niece would end my London career. Second off, she'd told the truth. The others stared. The senior clerk, Noad, said, "It's the mutiny, doctor ... put everyone on edge." I appreciated that, should've realized the London and Imperial probably has millions invested in India.

I said to Miss Doyle, "Professionally, I advise you to stay here, remember your father as he was in life. But if you insist on coming, please don't touch anything. If you feel faint or likely to vomit, move away from the scene."

She blanched further at my blunt words, as did Eatwell who'd yet to see the body. Miss Doyle looked defiantly at the manager, who looked at me. When I shrugged, he said, "Very well. But you're coming with Doctor Khan's permission, against his advice. That's what I'll tell Sir Reginald."

Eatwell had found a use for me – his whipping boy.

"Who found the body?" I said.

"Me," said Noad. "Doyle arrived about ten last night, asked me to open his locker. You need two keys, you see? Customer keeps one, bank the other. Professor Doyle often worked here late at night."

"Worked, downstairs?"

"You'll see," Chrystal said.

"Then, around five," the clerk continued, "a man turned up asking for him, Doyle–"

"At five in the morning?"

"Yes. I thought Doyle'd gone. But you have to ring an electric bell to come up, so I thought perhaps it's broken, went down–"

"This *man,*"Chrystal said, "who asked for Doyle. Have a name?"

"Wouldn't give one. I was so shocked when I came back I just said, 'He's dead,' went to telegraph Mr Eatwell. When I came back, the man's gone."

"I informed Sir Reginald," Eatwell said.

"Explains how your Commissioner knew," I said to Chrystal. Then, to Miss Doyle, "I suppose your uncle told you?"

She gave me a startled stare, said nothing.

"What's this man look like?" Chrystal said.

"Military, square shoulders." Noad shut his eyes. "Black hair, dark, deep-set eyes. Pug nose, small mouth. Short." He put a hand at chin level. "So high. He's wearing an army tunic with the insignia cut off. Smart."

"Old?" Chrystal said, "Young?"

"Middle aged, forties maybe."

The Sergeant gave me a glance.

"Then Sergeant Chrystal arrived," Eatwell said.

I lifted a finger. "Anyone else down in the vault last night?"

"No. Doyle worked alone, all night"

"Could someone hide down there?"

"No," Chrystal said. "Noad guarded the door while I examined the body, searched the whole place. Nothing."

The last exchange upset Miss Doyle. I saw the muscles in her face tighten, pain cloud her eyes. She said, "But if–"

Chrystal raised a hand. "We don't know what happened yet."

"Then the Major arrived," Noad said.

"Elphinstone?"

"That's him," said Eatwell. "Didn't want to let him in but he'd a warrant from the Home Secretary, signed and sealed."

"I went down with him," Chrystal said. "He saw the body, barked, *'Damn it!'* and left."

Which is when he came to find me in Millbank this morning.

I said to Noad. "How'd you describe Doyle's mood when he

arrived?"

"Tense ... upset. Barely spoke, waved me away when I'd used my key."

"You didn't see inside the locker?"

"No."

I nodded. "Now I'd like to see the vaults."

NOAD LED US back into the vestibule, unlocked a door that led out behind the counter. We snaked past rows of clerks and cashiers to the rear of the bank.

Taking the lead, Eatwell said, "The Imperial's a brand-new bank, doesn't have the seal of time, only the newest machines ... mechanical ciphers, things moving by electro-magnetic force. If they fail, the bank fails. That's why I *must* know how Professor Doyle died."

He went into an alcove to work a mechanism that *click-clicked* then *clunked* then *whirred*. We followed, going from a regency drawing-room into a shiny locomotive. He'd opened an iron door to a sharply descending steel tunnel. The door had dials with pointers, each circled with numerals, 0 to 9. It's a cipher-lock. You *click-click* the pointers to release electro-mechanical bolts, *clunk*. The dials are *whirred* to hide the number. They say dials are safer because there's no keyhole. Can't be picked or drilled or blown with gunpowder.

Eatwell pulled a lever that lit the stairs in blazing silver. Along the top were electric arc lights, fizzing on the mirror surface.

"No gas, no fire," Eatwell said.

I followed him into a subterranean London I'd never dreamed of. Miss Doyle came behind me, then Chrystal with John Noad at the rear.

As we descended, I said, "Who knows the numbers to that door?"

"Me and the chief clerk."

Our voices echoed metallically in the long stairway. Behind me I heard another *clunk* as Noad relocked the door.

I said, "You read George Price's book on thief-proof safes?"

"No," Eatwell said.

"You should. Dial makers say their locks are safer than keys."

"Oh, they are, much."

"Price disagrees, tells you how to pick one. You wedge in a bit of wire bent like a shackle. It's just a matter of touch to find the numbers."

Eatwell turned. "You think you could break in here?"

I shrugged. "Make yourself safer one way, you're more vulnerable another. It's like a law of nature." O'Shaughnessy taught me that. Like Henry hoarding cash in a Price's Double Door. What happens? Gets his teeth torn out for the keys. Same with dial locks.

At the bottom the tube levelled to a circular passage barred by another door, this one fitted with a Chubb tumbler-bolt lock. Through that we came to another door, this time fitted with a Hobbs Protector lock. It opened into bright sunlight. We emerged, squinting, in the middle of a long room, hushed like pilgrims in the ultra-modern citadel of riches.

The wall in front's a solid bank of wrought-iron lockers, some like pigeonholes, others big as walk-in pantries. All the other surfaces were concrete, apart from windows the size of dustbin-lids in the roof. Each was a huge lens, inches thick, focusing light on conical glass contraptions that shone like sun-burner chandeliers. As Noad relocked the final door, Eatwell pointed up. "Sunlight from the roof," – his voice rang in the stone ravine – "All done with clockwork and mirrors." The place had an odd, unearthly smell.

"No gas, no fire?" I said. "What happens at night?"

"Arc lamps on the roof." He pointed at an array of pipework. "Temperature and humidity control."

I tracked the lockers up fifteen feet to the roof. There had to be five hundred. Way off on the right, there's a library-type stepladder on wheels to reach the higher ones. All that spoilt the lattice symmetry of doors and keyholes was a single, open box.

I nodded to it. "That Doyle's?"

"Empty," Chrystal said.

"Nevertheless." I walked over, footsteps ringing.

It's at chest height, the size of a goodly letterbox. When we'd gathered in a semicircle, I gestured to Miss Doyle to look first. She peered in, stood back and shook her head. Whispered, "Emptied." Some of her resolve had gone.

"Not by us, Madam," Eatwell said.

"Your father emptied it himself," Chrystal added.

I set down the Oxford bag, crouched to a level with the box. Didn't look empty to me. I angled my head, put a hand inside and ran my fingers over the metal. Gave them a sniff. There'd been at least three items inside. I'd a good idea about two of them. I checked the door – two locks: one Chubb, one Hobbs.

"Unpickable," Eatwell said.

Noad began, "John Chubb and the American locksmith, Alfred Hobbs–"

"Said they could pick each other's locks," I finished. "So you fitted both. It's all in Price's book."

Neither lock had been forced.

I stood up, nodded. "Where's the body?"

Eatwell led us to the middle of the room, turned our backs to the lockers. He explained the room spanned the whole façade above, that the rest of the basement was cut in two by the steel tube we'd come down. On our right were the vaults. On the left, consultation rooms. We went left.

I pointed to one of the big lockers. "What would you keep in there?"

"Whatever you like," said Eatwell. "We don't ask."

"Could you hide in it?"

He shook his head. "Customers are signed in and out."

Another door led us from the mausoleum to a drawing room. On one side's a clerk's desk and a library of maps and reference books. On the other, six doors. Here the sunlight's piped through frosted windows with fake curtains, giving a warm, afternoon feel. Not what I'd expected.

Looking around, I said, "What's this place for?"

"Business transactions," Eatwell said, surprised I had to ask.

"People buy and sell ... bullion? Things in those lockers?"

"Not exactly," he said.

"It's a matter of security," Miss Doyle said.

We all turned to look at her.

"The wealth's held on paper," she said. "Bonds, certificates, deeds of land ownership." When I frowned, she added, "Think of loans, insurance ... rent, taxes, mines, commodities like rice, tea, indigo, salt, iron, opium ... jute."

"We hold deeds to land across the globe," Eatwell said.

I said, "You can buy an indigo plantation in Bengal, right here?"

"Certainly," said Noad. "The documents never leave the vaults."

"I wouldn't advise it," said Miss Doyle.

"Oh, wouldn't you, *Madam?*" scoffed Eatwell.

"No, *Sir.* The market's too volatile."

He gave her a doubtful stare. "What would you ... *recommend?*"

"In India, now? Nothing. If peace is restored, perhaps the roads or railways or canals. Something guaranteed by the Indian taxpayer."

Eatwell leaned close to her, hissed, "If Sir Reginald discusses such—"

"He certainly doesn't." The bureau ambience had restored her mood.

She found a roll of paper tape in her bag, the kind used by printing telegraphs. Tore off a few inches for Eatwell. When I raised an eyebrow, she tore off the same for me. In pale blue electrotype, it read <<*ADELAIDE DOYLE - CONSULTING INTELLIGENCER - TELEGRAPHIC AND BIBLIOGRAPHIC NEWS SUPPLIED TO ORDER - B2 ROYAL EXCHANGE BUILDINGS LONDON*>> I'd never seen anything like it.

Eatwell's face said he hadn't either.

"Wealth on paper's my business," she said.

I gave her my card, said absently, "It's absurd."

"What is?" She gave me the emerald stare.

"That a signature here changes life in Bengal. As if a sheet of paper acted across vast space like ... the force of gravity."

Eatwell began, "I assure you it's quite legal, we're–"

"A paper ticket takes you to Edinburgh," Miss Doyle cut in. "By steam and steel, by brick buttress and tunneled rock. So capital goes its ways."

We all looked. What woman spoke like that? Words that rattled my head, make me turn, gawp at the fake office in the fake sunshine – a world hidden from most Londoners, beyond the Santal imagination. You couldn't ride a ticket, but it let you ride the great machine of railway. Here a paper slip piped your interest through dispatches and telegraphs, the mechanism of Empire, from steel vaults to the steel tip of a Sepoy bayonet.

I turned, heard my mother sing – *O mother wealth, where was your birth? I was born in the soil, I was born in the splash of rain.* Saw what she sent me to see. Wealth's grave, here in this devil's storehouse beneath London where the earth's cultivators are made the slaves of loans and taxes.

When I'd gone a full circle, all eyes were on me. It wasn't coincidence two men had died violently within hours of each other, both guarding their locked and bolted secrets. Did Doyle die like Henry?

"Where's the body?" I said.

Eatwell slid Miss Doyle's paper tape into a waistcoat pocket.

"This way," he said.

EATWELL OPENED ONE of the six doors, waved Chrystal and me through. There's a round table, four chairs. On each table stood a pile of headed paper, a silver inkstand, a rack of quill pens, a candle and a bar of sealing wax. The curtained windows glowed sunlight.

Doyle sat with his back to us, as if he's fallen asleep on the table. I turned to Eatwell. "What're these rooms for?"

"Private legal work," he said, eyes fixed on me to avoid the corpse.

Miss Doyle craned over his shoulder, trying to see what's on the table.

I nodded Chrystal in, half closed the door telling the others to wait outside. I put my bag on the table. Close up he didn't look asleep. His head lay on its left side, eyes squinting right, left arm on the table cradling his head. The right hand dangled by his calf, the revolver beneath it on the floor. There wasn't much blood; a single jet had spurted over the floor to his right. The dark pool under his head had left a rusty stain on his wing collar and shirt.

Over my shoulder, I called, "Your father right-handed, Miss Doyle?"

"Yes," she said. Sight of the body had quieted her again.

I stood behind the chair, felt the rigidity in the arms and neck, studied the lividity of the hands and ankles. "Help me sit him up," I said. Opened the coat and shirt, wedged a thermometer in the right armpit. Then I sat, took a sheet of bank notepaper, dipped a pen and began my report – names, places, times.

"Let's look at the wound," I said to Chrystal. "Entry's on the right ... no exit wound ... bullet still inside." I took a pouch of metal probes and a magnifying glass from my bag, parted the matted hair. "Bullet smashed the skull ... bits have floated back in place." In another minute I found the complication. "Ah," I said, "two shots."

He nodded, whispered, *"Murder."*

"Maybe." I pressed a probe to the wound, angling till it slid inside. "Consistent with a .36-calibre ball." More probing. "Other hole slants ..." – I felt the rod hit something solid – "upwards, bullet's still there."

Then I studied the scalp.

"What're you looking for?" Chrystal murmured.

"Evidence," I said, picking up the revolver. "Two shots fired, no question." I carefully examined the fired-chambers and the cylinder. Then I pulled out the thermometer from his underarm, checked the reading.

"Eatwell," I called. "What's the temperature in here?"

His pushed the door open. "Sixty-eight ... always."

I sat down, wrote for a minute. The others shuffled in the open door, stood waiting. "Well?" Eatwell said. "What'd you make of it?"

"Died about six hours ago ... around four o'clock this morning ... sitting in that chair, by a gunshot to the head, probably from that revolver."

"Suicide," Noad said. "That's what I thought."

"Never!" Miss Doyle exclaimed. "Papa would *never* take his own life."

Chrystal glared, waiting for me to contradict Noad.

"It's suicide," said Eatwell, popping another Prichard's pill. "Can't be murder when there's no one else here."

On the table sat a silver cigar case and a sheet of bank notepaper. A single line on the paper read – *Between the devil and the deep sea!* I picked it, up. *Verso* it's covered in scribble in the same hand, random words in English, more in gibberish, like nonsense words.

I picked up the cigar case. It's weighty, a fine piece. Popped it open, gave a sniff – no trace of tobacco. Inside the lid's engraved, *Property of the East India Company, A reward of £50 will be paid if presented at a Company Station.* Same in Hindi and Persian. On the back it said, *John Arnold, 84 Strand.* He's a clockmaker, I pass his shop every day. I held the sheet of paper to the light, rubbed it between finger and thumb, gave them a sniff.

I knew how Doyle died. I knew who killed him. I knew he'd been robbed. And I knew another reason Chrystal wanted me on his side. But I'm not saying anything, not yet. Miss Doyle wouldn't hear of suicide. The very idea horrified her. Eatwell won't hear of anything else. Can't have a murder in his vaults, let alone a robbery. Which gave me an idea.

"When you came down," I asked Noad, "what was on the table?"

"I ... I don't know. The sight was so awful I just backed out."

I took the sheet and cigar case over to Miss Doyle.

"Did your father own a revolver?"

"Don't think so, I've never seen one. He abhorred violence."

I held out the cigar case.

She shook her head. "He didn't smoke."

I pointed to the sentence on the devil and deep sea.

"That your father's hand?"

She nodded.

"Any idea what he meant?"

"No." Her voice was suddenly brittle.

I flipped the sheet. "What about this?"

She shook her head, lips tightly pressed as if afraid what she might say. She wiped away tears, took a deep breath regaining control. "Is that all?" she croaked. Then, more surely, "You searched my father's person?"

"Aye," Chrystal said. "Nothing else of interest."

"What were you expecting, Miss Doyle?" I said.

"Nothing ... in particular," she said.

"He was certainly robbed," I said. "Why come to the bank for an empty cigar case and a page of scribble?"

She began, "There, just as I–"

"Robbed!" Eatwell exploded. Wagging a finger at me, he said, "How in God's name could he be robbed?"

Chrystal jutted his chin at the body, glared at me. When I just shrugged, he said, "He was shot twice." Then to me, "I say the first shot killed him."

"So do I."

"Then ... it *is* murder," Noad said.

"Oh aye," said Chrystal. "And the killer must've robbed him."

"No, no ... NO!" Eatwell shouted. "It's not possible." He shook another Prichard's into his sweaty palm.

To Miss Doyle, I said, "Why're you so sure it wasn't suicide?"

"It's a terrible sin," she said, "he believed in hellfire." As I thought on that, she added, "He often said life's agonies are nothing to eternal bliss with Jesus."

Chrystal shook his head like he'd never heard such nonsense.

Miss Doyle turned abruptly to John Noad, fixed him with a stare as if she's squaring a dozen circles.

"You!" she exclaimed. *"You killed him!"*

"Me?" Noad said, *"You're mad!"*

She lunged at him, but I moved smartly between them, lifted my arms to fend her off. Eatwell's face had frozen, mid suck on a Prichard's pill, eyes dancing back and forth between Noad and his accuser. He looked ready to throw his clerk to the lions if it'd save his own skin.

"No," I said. "Mr Noad didn't harm your father." But I'm impressed she's found the logical solution – Noad either let the killer in or shot Doyle himself.

"How do you know?" she hissed. "You weren't there."

"It's my business, Madam. My profession."

Eatwell said, "You know how this happened?"

"Doyle's robber walked past your clerks and your security doors, back out the same way."

"But how? Tell us, man!"

"Afraid I can't."

"Why ever not? It's what we're paying you for."

"I'm on Her Majesty's business." Which was almost true. Green wants to know about the bottle. I'd be amazed if Doyle and Bullock's deaths weren't involved. "You'll get my report," I said. "Soon as Sir George clears it."

Eatwell threw up his hands.

Miss Doyle said, "It could've been the military man, with the pug nose."

I shrugged. "Could've."

She squinted, thinking. Chrystal's furious. He'd saved me a beating last night, found the Commissioner this morning,. He'd told me about Doyle, got me into the bank. But he had his reasons, as I did.

"I'll take those things," Miss Doyle said, "They're mine now."

Eatwell looked at Chrystal who shrugged to say it's fine with him.

"What about my father's body?" she said.

"King's Hospital morgue," said Chrystal. "Collect it after the autopsy."

She snatched her things from me, looked at her father's back. I think she wanted to get closer, maybe stroke his hair. I touched her arm and shook my head. She recoiled, then strutted out of the room.

"Who else d'you tell, apart from Sir Reginald?" I asked Eatwell.

"No one," he said.

FIVE MINUTES LATER, I stood outside the bank with Chrystal and Miss Doyle on High Holborn. She stood at the curb a little way off, scouring the street for a carriage, I thought.

Chrystal's sour. "Funny that," he said, flatly.

"What?"

"You ... working for the man who signed your death warrant last night."

I got close, spoke quietly so Miss Doyle wouldn't hear. "Why d'you think they let me out? Seems the Home Secretary needs my services."

"For what?"

"Better you don't know, trust me."

"To hell with you, Khan!"

He turned away but I grabbed his arm, yanked him close.

"How'd you like to take a look in Bullock's safe tonight?"

He glared, as angry as I was when he grabbed me. "Price is in Birmingham," he said. "We've checked. Who else can crack it?"

"I can."

"*Pah!*" He pulled away, took a few fast paces into the road to jump on the bottom step of a city-bound omnibus. Leaning back on the stair rails, he called, "Telegraph me. If you're serious." The bus weaved into the traffic.

I beckoned to Thorn across the road. Miss Doyle turned abruptly, took a pace closer to me. The bank's image danced in her glasses amid flashes of green sunlight. I'm ready for more abuse.

"I'm sorry," she said. "What I said about your mother–"

"Save your breath," I said. "I hear worse every day."

"But–"

"You're upset, angry ... I understand."

"But Sir ... if you know how my father died, I beg you ..."

Now wasn't the time. "I know *how*," I said. "I don't know *why*. If you'd talk to me about him, perhaps ..."

She didn't reply. Thorn swung the Lab across the road, forced her way through two streams of cursing cab and cart drivers to draw up at the curb.

"May I offer you a ride somewhere?" I asked Miss Doyle. Then, quickly, "We're taking an early lunch ... like to join us?"

It's not chivalry. That cigar case is too weighty for its size, too light in silver for a fifty-pound reward. And I think there's order in the crazy scribble.

She crinkled her nose. "You *lunch* with your cab driver?"

"My assistant. He's prepared to be seen with me in company."

She hesitated. Was I joking? I didn't know myself. But the corners of her mouth turned up a little, I felt a tiny ray of warmth.

"This your carriage?" she said.

"Oh yes, I call it the Lab. Looks smart from the outside."

I opened the door. She stared at the cave of bottles and glassware, the books, the wicker-clad demijohns of distilled water, the acids and alkalis, the snakes of rubber tubing, the little sink and fold-away table.

"Chemistry goes its ways," she said.

I stowed the Oxford bag. "Like railways ... and capital?"

"Like a snail, carrying its home."

I'd never thought of it like that, travelling inside my own chemistry set. That I'd made a caravan of O'Shaughnessy's *Manual* a home.

"This where you discover murderers?" she said.

"The evidence ... a black flake might be a bloodstain, the last meal a deadly weapon."

"And your report ... a death warrant?"

We stared at each other for a moment. "You're welcome to ride inside," I said. "Bit smelly, I'm afraid." She looked doubtful. "Or you can ride on the box seat, with Thorn. I'll finish my report on the way."

I felt a pang she might walk off. Adelaide Doyle interested me, despite the insult. I wanted to talk about her father, know what a *consulting intelligencer* was. Take a better look at the world through her jade spectacles.

"I'll join you for lunch." she said, tucking in her skirts and hoisting herself expertly up next to the driver. She was slim, almost bony, as if she rarely ate.

"We'll work on the Terrace this afternoon," I called to Thorn. "But first, Fountain's penny-pies?"

Thorn nodded to Miss Doyle, said, "Simpson's Tavern on the Strand?"

"That's what I meant," I said.

Twelve

OVER LUNCH I learned a lot about Adelaide Doyle.

For one thing, Elijah wasn't her real father. She's the daughter of Captain John Ochterlony who was shot dead by accident on a Buckinghamshire farm when she was twelve. Her Uncle Reginald introduced his bereaved sister, Adelaide's mother, to Elijah Doyle. For another, being slender didn't stop her putting away mock turtle soup, roast beef and Yorkshire pudding, broccoli and potatoes – washed down with a bottle of Rioja – plum pudding and custard.

We'd have had a cheese board if Thorn hadn't reminded me to catch the sun's chemical rays at noon.

Miss Doyle wanted to talk. Tell me how her stepfather raised her as the son he'd really wanted. After a posse of governesses, she went to Bedford Ladies' College in London where she shone at mathematics and political economy. Fell in with radicals, fell out with her father, rejected Christ and cultivated – in her words – "a masculine kind of excellence" that made her unmarriageable. Instead, she'd go into business, a pipedream for a less determined woman.

She stared out as a jobbing clerk in the London Library. For six months she skivvied for bookmen, grub-street hacks and vanity authors, checked a million facts and swatted off wandering hands. It paid a pittance, but she learned the secrets of a world on paper.

One evening, ready to settle for the job of governess, she and her parents dined with Uncle Reginald. Over dessert he mentioned a London druggist who'd set up a rival quinine business. "I'd like to know more about that gentleman," he said. Three days later Miss Doyle gave her Uncle a ten-page biography – a *portfolio*, she called it – on his rival. Among other things, it reported he'd plagiarized results from the *Pharmaceutical Journal*, been accused in the *Lancet* of adulterating drugs, and that his father died in a debtor's prison.

Sir Reginald hounded him out of business.

Miss Doyle got five guineas, more than she'd earned in last six months. She asked her uncle to recommend her services, which he did, with pleasure. In the next year she made bibliographic cross-referencing a profitable science, a business. She went on about a man called Panizzi who'd made up ninety-one rules to catalogue every book in the British Museum. All the obvious ones – author, title, subject, year – and eighty-seven others! She'd adapted them to catalogue people, companies, commodities, anything anyone'd pay for.

Most of her early clients taught her more than she did them. What did a banker or insurance agent or company director or capitalist want to know? How to find out? She soon learned financial intelligence was worth more than its weight in gold. It also blinded men to doing business with a woman. The portfolios had found their market.

Then she met Paul Reuter. He'd opened a telegram office in the Royal Exchange buildings, sold European news to the London press. Through a couple of commissions, he learned of Miss Doyle's rare gift for collating data, sifting fact from gossip, the likely from the fanciful. He offered her a job as a télégraphiste – a female telegraph operator – one of the few jobs for a woman in a man's business. Really, she'd be his international intelligencer.

Miss Doyle wasn't making Paul Reuter rich. Once she'd learned to gather Europe's telegraphic news, she tracked share prices, marine cargoes docked or sunk, bubble and bust in the commodity markets. Quietly sold the portfolios to City clients. When Reuter found out, he made the mistake of accusing her in public, demanded she hand over the fees.

Miss Doyle acted out the sequel for us, wine glass in hand:

Reuter, "You've abused my trust!"

Miss Doyle, *"Teutonic swindler!"*

"Freebooter!"

"You insult me, Sir! I'll have satisfaction."

"What?"

"You'll meet me on Hampstead Heath at dawn tomorrow. Or be known in all of London as a coward!"

Which silenced the restaurant. The way she spat each word left no one in doubt the extraordinary story was true.

Reuter, "Don't be ridiculous."

"You'll die where Lady Braddock fought Mrs Edmonson. My father taught me to deal with scoundrels like you."

Her offer to bring the guns told Reuter she knew how to use one. In fact, a drunken Captain Ochterlony made his daughter fight mock duels with farm animals ready for slaughter. She could hit a sheep or pig between the eyes with a duelling pistol at twelve paces. Reuter told her to keep the money and get out. She set up as a private intelligencer, renting a line in the Bank of England's Central Telegraph Office. Opened business quarters next to Reuter's.

At which point I learned the scale of Miss Doyle's ambition. Last year she helped raise £350,000 for the Atlantic Telegraph Company. Went to Glasgow to consult Britain's sage of physical science, William Thomson, who told her a submarine cable to New York was feasible, and how to calculate the rate of dots and dashes. A week later she'd drawn up a prospectus detailing the financial return per message.

"But here's the trick," she said, waving a fork at me, "there's no money in electric post. We'll trade instant stock and commodity prices between London and New York. What's more, I'm raising funds for a World-Girdle Telegraph from London via Europe and Russia, under the Bering Sea, across Canada to join the transatlantic line in Newfoundland."

She drew it with a fingertip in a film of custard on her dessert plate, lines hanging down like suspenders to California and India.

"Only problem," she mused, "is Indian savages on the plains of the United States. But they'll soon get pushed aside."

Thorn and I shared a glance. Miss Doyle's vision was staggering, but her life story didn't hold water. Not that I didn't believe it. I did. But she'd left something out, like a fairytale without the witch, like me saying I came to London to admire the Crystal Palace – not untrue, just not the point.

"What's the problem?" I said, "with the ... *savages.*"

"They pull up the poles, cut the lines," she said, indignantly.

"I expect they cross their hunting grounds ... or crops?"

She took off the green glasses, set them carefully on the linen tablecloth.

"My dear, Sir," she said. "Our trade's gone up more in the last five years than ever in the nation's history. Primitive hunters can't block progress."

Her unglazed eyes were brilliant blue, deep set, large and nervous like a rodent's. It was unnerving, almost as if she'd undressed.

"And when the world's girdled all about," I said. "Tied up like a ball of string ... what then?"

We stared eye to eye for a moment. Then she slipped her glasses on, vanished behind the glaze. I'd startled a rare bird, made it fly away. She took a sip of wine, explained how the World Girdle would let her control the price of whale oil from Sydney to San Francisco.

I let her talk. She'd put the page of scribble and the cigar case on the table. I'd idly picked them up. As we ate, I saw the beginnings of a pattern in the nonsense. Turning the cigar case, I noted the hinges had score marks as if they slid, not that I could budge them. What's more, when I laid it on the tablecloth, something odd happened. My steel steak-knife twitched, like a compass needle.

I was poking it for an encore when Thorn mentioned the time and chemical rays. I called for the bill, even though Miss Doyle must earn my annual income in ten minutes. As we waited, I set the bottle Elphinstone gave me on the tablecloth. She frowned, curious as I'd hoped.

"I think it's what you stepfather died for," I said.

The frown deepened. "Why? What is it?"

"I'm about to find out. Want to come along?"

If anyone could link a small bottle to an empire's fate, she could.

ADELPHI TERRACE FACES south. It's like a boulevard on the Thames, lined with elegant lamps, a hundred miles from the tunnels twenty feet below. All they've in common is the Thames' bubbling stench. Every time I strike a match, I half expect to ignite an inferno from Richmond to Gravesend.

Thorn parked the Lab beneath my apartment's front windows, put a nosebag on Bessie. The noon sun burned down, sounds from the wharf drifted up. Miss Doyle stayed on the box seat, staring out across the river. Her lunchtime chatter had been in response to the terrible shock, the corpse. Now she'd gone quiet, a little sullen.

I hung my frock coat, rolled up my sleeves. Set to work in the coach doorway on the fold-away table. I passed Thorn the Chemiscope, pipetted some mystery liquid onto a watch-glass on a tripod. Crystals won't be hurried. But I took a chance, lit a gentle burner under the glass. Then I took the scope, set the levers and adjusted the screws, popped a drip of liquid in the holder. Raised the scope like a ship's navigator shooting the sun.

"You'll be blinded!" Miss Doyle climbed down from the box seat.

"It's *not* a telescope," Thorn said. She doesn't like amateurs.

Miss Doyle, to me, "Oh ... what then?"

I told Thorn to fetch a drop of quinine sulphate in solution.

"It's a Chemiscope," I said, "identifies molecules by chemical rays."

Miss Doyle looked at the brass tube. *"What* rays?"

I took another shot at the sun. "You know what the solar spectrum is?"

"Rainbow colours ... red to violet."

"Uh-huh. The ones we can see. After violet, come *chemical* rays."

"How do you know, if they're invisible?"

"Come here." She took a wary pace closer. I moved to her left and slightly behind, put my arms round her torso to lift the scope to her right eye. She tensed, looked down at my arms, then me. "Come on," I said, "look in the eyepiece." I could smell her Lavender and Jasmine perfume, the starch in her blouse. She hiked her specs onto her forehead. When I'd got the scope in place I had her in a firm grip, cheek by cheek trying to see what she can.

"What do you see?"

"Nothing. Just a sort of murky disc."

I told Thorn to put a drop of quinine sulphate where the mystery liquid had been. Embraced Miss Doyle again.

She said, *"Oh!* ... that's ... *lovely."*

"Quinine turns the chemical rays to brilliant violet. It's a test for quinine, my own invention."

She turned in my arms. "So your liquid ... isn't quinine."

"Correct." Which so spoiled my pet hypothesis I wouldn't quite believe it.

Then she noticed the embrace, me squeezing her bosom. Took the opportunity to take a good sideways look at me. I tentatively opened my arms, let her go. She didn't move, just dropped her specs back on her nose. I reset the scope's screws and levers, popped in another drop of mystery. Shot the sun.

"Chlorophyll," I said, confirming my earlier suspicion.

"How's chlorophyll of value?"

"It's not. But it's in all green plants, often leaves a tinge in herbal decoctions. Suggests whatever's in here came from a plant."

"That ... thingy-scope's useful." she mused, as if it smelt like money.

"Patented."

Thorn said, "Crystals!"

The evaporating pool had left a crusty, white ring on the watch-glass. I unclipped a test-tube, scraped some in with a spatula, handed it to Thorn.

"Nitrogen test?" she said.

"Indispensable," I said. Thorn mixed and heated.

To Miss Doyle: "Your stepfather worked for the East India Company, their chief magician at turning plants into country houses."

She ignored the gibe. "He advised on economic botany."

"Recently went to India with Henry Bullock. Know why?"

"No. Why?"

I wanted her on the trail. She'd a personal interest in knowing why her stepfather died, could open doors shut tight to me. Which meant I had to give those ninety-one rules a scent to chase.

"They worked in the Calcutta Military Hospital," I said. "Testing a new medicine, that's my guess."

"Like what?"

"A febrifuge, a fever cure. Quinine, I thought."

"Quinine's not new. Uncle Reginald sells the Company all it needs."

"But he gets it from Peruvian cinchona trees–"

"Which they hoard to hike the price, then wildly over harvest." She nodded. "Papa's told the Company for years to get cinchona trees to India."

"Steal them from Peru?"

She ignored that. "Papa's a Christian, wanted the Company to farm the trees at cost, offer quinine at a rupee a dose to the natives."

"What's Uncle Reginald think of that?"

"He's ..." – she made an attractive flick of her eyebrows – "... sceptical. Prefers to take his chances with Peru."

"I'll bet he does," I said.

Clyde has his own world-girdle. He traffics Chinese coolies over the Pacific to cut and load cinchona in Peru, to crew ships through the staggering seas around Cape Horn to London where the yellow bark yields the crystal sugar known as quinine sulphate. Via Alexandria and the Indian ocean, *Clyde's Seltzer* finds its way to Calcutta. The final hop: Bengal opium to Hong Kong – *vile dirt* the Chinese call it – sowing misery that drives the young across the Pacific.

"Surely," she said, "you're not suggesting–"

"Your uncle killed your stepfather to save his business?" I shrugged. "Quinine's from a family of drugs, the *alkaloids*. Another's caffeine from tea and coffee and cacao ... lots of plants. What if another plant made quinine, one that grows in Asia?"

"But it's not quinine, your ... thingy-scope proved it."

"Hmm. Another alkaloid, then ... morphine or nicotine–"

A crack and sucking howl said Thorn had shattered a red-hot test-tube in cold water. She filtered, acidified, held it to the light. We all looked up.

"No blue, no green," Thorn said. "No nitrogen. Forget the alkaloids."

"Damn!" Clyde had been the perfect fit.

A movement caught my eye, a shadow in my apartment above. It's Bea. I thought she'd left for Earlsacre. Annoyed at my carelessness, I said, "What've we got? Two druggists go to Calcutta, work in the Military Hospital. Both've died violently in the last day. We've a mystery liquid from a plant. Company's so worried it sets its finest soldier on the case, with the right to go anywhere, kill anyone in Her Majesty's name."

If I thought I'd shock Miss Doyle, I was wrong.

She said, "You're on the case too."

"Just chemistry, they want to know what's–"

"In the bottle? All you've told us is what isn't ... or your assistant has. Maybe the Queen should hire *him!*"

I'd have felt bad if a door hadn't slammed, and a bustled Bea come swooshing over the paving slabs. I'm ready for some earache but Bea's smiling, at least she's got a sort of grin fixed on her face.

"Take the Lab down to the Cell," I said to Thorn. "I want the formula for those crystals. And get out the big magnet. I'll be down in a bit."

"Gotcha boss," she said, began clearing up.

The other two women and I stood in an even triangle. I made the introductions. "I'm afraid Miss Doyle's father was found dead at the London and Imperial Bank this morning."

Bea said, "Suicide?"

"Bea!"

Miss Doyle said, "No."

Bea said, "Does the light hurt your eyes, my dear?"

"Bea!"

"Are we acquainted?" Miss Doyle said.

"We have several ... mutual acquaintances."

"I doubt that."

"Oh, we do," Bea said. She kissed my cheek, quietly hummed, "Careful with *that one*, Hyder," and walked off.

I called, "Tonight, seven-thirty at the Hotel?"

She flourished a wave over her shoulder. It was an odd performance, half hysterical, as if she'd been close to tears. Thorn slammed the Lab's door, climbed on the box seat and geed Bessie along the Terrace. I was wondering if I should apologize to Miss Doyle, when she said, "Henry Bullock's dead?"

"Last night, in the basement of his shop in Ivy Lane."

"And who's this Company soldier?"

"A name's dangerous," I said.

"Pah! Trading secrets is my business, Sir. I could shame or gaol half the aristocracy in England."

I shrugged. "Raikes Elphinstone, the Home Secretary's agent." She'd got the scent, so she might as well have the full stench. "Talked about Britain's enemies. High treason. Gave me three names ... Slegman, Clyde or Birdwood."

"Or?"

"Apparently."

She made a far-away stare. I'm guessing a lot's going on in that educated head, dozens of rules sifting through a warehouse of data.

I said, "You know who they are?"

She said, "Not *who... what.*"

"*What?*"

"Tell me how my stepfather died."

"Meet me this afternoon at five o'clock, I'll tell you then."

"Why–"

"I need to find an Indian plant. Then I talk to Sir George Green, then I'll tell you what I know ... if you'll tell me *what* those men are."

"You know the new Reading-room at the British Museum?"

"No, but I'll find it. What's there?"

"I'll be there, five o'clock."

I walked her up Adam Street to the Strand, found a respectable looking cab. "May I keep the cigar case and sheet of paper, till we meet?"

She unbuttoned her bag, hesitated; handed them over. I helped her into the cab and held the door. "About my parentage," I said. "You know Panizzi's ninety-second rule?" She's as puzzled as a missionary asked about the Eleventh Commandment. "It says, don't believe everything you read in catalogues."

I slammed the door and the coach pulled out into the traffic.

MY 'CELL' IN the Adelphi cellars is a semicircular brick tunnel with an iron door on the front ... like a prison cell. The Lab stands in the middle with a stall for Bessie one side and a chemical work-bench the other. The bench's lit by three oil lamps, giving a yellow, evening-by-streetlight effect. At the back's a heavy punch-bag-on-a-chain and some weights.

Thorn and I worked side by side at the bench. She's stoking a little furnace to bring the crystals to redness. Their vapour is piped through glass bulbs and U's of tubing that suck out the elements one by one. The Cell's hot. I'm messing around with the cigar case and a big magnet, thinking about the twitching knife, how magnetism's involved. I turned the case over, touched the magnet – *Click!*

I said, "What'd you make of Miss Doyle?"

129

Click? I opened the case, touched the top again – *Click!* Something releasing in the lid.

"She asked about divorce."

I found a smaller magnet, ran it over the lid, searching, till ... *Click!*

"The Act?"

"Matrimonial Act, yeah."

The case's hinges are all that's moveable. I touched the magnet, squeezed the hinges together. The lid's inner surface fell open to reveal a brass plate with two rows of six dial-counters across the middle. They showed a jumble of letters.

"What about the Act?" I said.

"Did I approve?"

"Of making divorce legal? Do you?"

Thorn studied the furnace, tapped the glassware.

The teeth of six cogwheels protruded from the brass plate, one beneath each pair of counters. I thumbed a cog round, making the two counters above cycle through the alphabet, one forwards, one backwards.

Thorn said, "What do *you* think ... about the Act?"

"A lot of dirty linen's going to get washed in public."

Reformists have pushed for years for an Act of Parliament to legalize divorce. The whole thing's going nowhere till Lord Palmerston's liberals won a big majority back in April. Now the Matrimonial Act will be law in a matter of months. And divorce in civil courts means anyone can watch, including the press. Bea's circle talks about little else.

"Why'd Miss Doyle care?" I said. "She's not married."

"Matter of principle. Like voting, or owning property, or working." She gave me a sideways glance. "I'll bet Lady M's not in favour."

Thorn's nosy about Lady Motcombe and me. All I've told her is the episode with the maid, so you can see why.

"She's ... undecided."

Actually, Bea's torn. By birth she sees marriage as a cornerstone of society – ordained by God, indissoluble by man, least of all a grubby clerk in a civil court. But real life's different. She's the one with a title, with money and property, yet her husband cleared off, lives openly with another woman. Nothing Bea can do about it. That's not right, either.

"Maybe she wants a divorce?" Thorn ventured.

"Who says Lady Motcombe's married?"

"Miss Doyle."

That made me think.

"You'd quite a chat on the way to lunch."

"She talked, I listened."

Thorn's apparatus hissed and bubbled, doing the magic of analysis. As she weighed the residues, I looked at the mystery crystals under a microscope – long and spindly, silky white. The ones I'd made for Henry more than a year ago, identical. Thorn worked on the numbers: grams of this, atomic weights of that, all in neat columns. I turned the cigar-case counters back to the setting left by Doyle, set it down next to his page from the bank.

"'Between the Devil and the deep sea,'" I read. "What's that mean?"

I flipped the page to the scribble.

"Caught between impossible choices," Thorn said. "No way out."

"Except death? Like Henry Bullock."

Thorn underlined something at the bottom of her sheet, brought it over. She looked at the page of scribble, then the cigar case. "What's that?" she said.

"Each line's written in six-letter groups. He writes twelve or so letters, stops, then starts again below. Same pattern, different gibberish."

"And?"

"And if you look at the final six letters of the last line ..."

"Same as the letters on the top row of counters. Which means?"

"It's some kind of ... deciphering machine."

Thorn read the inscription, saw the case was Company property, worth a huge reward. "That thing's as dangerous as a gallon of prussic acid," she said.

I shrugged. "What've you got?"

She'd underlined, $C_{30}H_{44}O_{10}$ – the molecules are made of thirty atoms of carbon, forty-four of hydrogen, ten of oxygen.

"Plus or minus a hydrogen or two," she said. "Useful?"

"Not really, but a formula impresses people. What we've got's an organic compound from a plant. If it's valuable enough for the Home Secretary to care about, it's got to be a dye or a drug, probably from India. Probably a drug if Henry's using it in a hospital. In which case it's not British because–"

"Herbalists here would know about it."

"Uh-ha. And the plants must be growing nearby, in London."

"Why? Might've been shipped, from abroad."

"No," I said. "The sludge Henry gave me was green, decocted from fresh leaves. And active principles – drugs – degrade once plants are dead. It's here somewhere, probably in a botanic garden, a hot-house ..."

"Kew Gardens?"

I almost said, *"No. Too big, too public."* But then I remembered a dinner at O'Shaughnessy's home in Calcutta and a book I'd bought last year.

Thorn said, "Don't you know the Director at Kew?"

"Deputy Director ... Joseph Hooker. O'Shaughnessy introduced us."

I met two Hookers at that dinner. The first had a peppery temper, complained about amateur botanists. The second waddled round the dinner table, flapping his elbows, talking like an Indian peafowl. I think he'd upset his host by asking how he got the East India Company to fund his schemes, kept dropping names of Royal Society fellows he knew in London. O'Shaughnessy lit a *gunjah* pipe, talked about the medical powers of cannabis as it went around.

Hooker had a smoke, curious. When O'Shaughnessy tapped the pipe, and said, "Aphrodisiac," Hooker laughed out loud, kept saying, *"Aphro-dizzy-ak,"* like it's the funniest thing he's ever heard. O'Shaughnessy said, "The bird game," which is where you're assigned a bird and have to speak in its call. Wasn't long before it's impossible – in O'Shaughnessy's words – to preserve seriousness. The next morning, Hooker vanished up country, wouldn't show his face after the peafowl performance in front of the natives.

I was still grinning as I walked to a shadowy bookshelf at the back of the Cell, called out, "He was *botanizing* in the Himalayas, also known as stealing any Indian plant worth a bob or two." I brought the book to Thorn. *"Flora Indica,"* I said, "first thorough compendium of Indian plants."

"By Joseph Hooker." She flipped the pages. "Says he consulted a hundred and twenty authors, over a thousand volumes of botanical books."

"And his own botanizing in India. Which means?"

"If anyone'd know of a new vegetable drug or dye, it's him."

"Except he can't," I said. "You've met Henry, would you let him loose on valuable chemical work?"

Thorn's pained look answered the question.

"Exactly. Hooker would've taken it to Hofmann."

"Maybe it's like Shiva," Thorn said.

That made me think. Last year a German chemist announced a new alkaloid from a Brazilian plant, *Erythroxylum*. Hofmann was doubtful, told me to redo the experiments. Turned out Hooker grew the plant in Kew, so Thorn and I went thieving. Gave the shrubs a rapid prune and hared off in the Lab. Not exactly ethical but the British collector in Rio Negro didn't ask the natives either.

I made the crystals ... alkaloid all right, therefore medically active, like morphine and quinine ... but also like strychnine, so I tried some on a frog I found hopping by the Thames. Delicate skin makes frogs martyrs to organic chemistry. You can tell one poison from another by the way they croak their last. This one went numb, then recovered, which suggested an anesthetic. So Thorn and I tried it ourselves, smelt money. Didn't say a word to Hofmann.

I said, "You mean Henry did the same, didn't tell Hooker it's valuable?"

"Not necessarily Bullock who found it."

"Huh! Then let's go see Hooker."

"Kew Gardens?"

I opened my mouth, but nothing came out. Stood there, catching flies.

"Something on you mind, boss?"

It's the fight with Elphinstone. It cycled in my head like the galloping horse in a kid's Zoetrope toy – *I move, he moves, nothing, I move, he moves, nothing* – over and over again. But it's not the image, it's the feeling. Like a call from my past, like some kind of tribal instinct. The rule before rule one: *the zero rule.* When I told Sergeant Chrystal the *Manual of Chemistry* saved my life, I wasn't lying. But it wasn't the whole story, not by a long chalk.

"We'll go via Castle Street," I said. "I need to break someone's nose."

Thorn glanced up from the sink where she's washing glassware.

"What happened to violence solves nothing?"

I'd told her about Chrystal's maxim on the way to the bank.

"It doesn't," I said. "Except when it does."

While she cleaned up and readied the Lab, I worked the punch-bag. Ended with a flurry of blows that rattled the chains, made Bessie stamp her feet nervously. I wasn't walking into another ambush.

Thirteen

THE CAMBRIAN STORES in Castle Street is Nat Langham's pub, the heart of London boxing. It once saved my life. The day Hofmann told me he wanted £30 in fees rather than an assistant, I was in trouble. I'd come a long way, been duped by the East India Company. Now my studies at the Royal College looked sunk. I spent a couple of days drowned in handi, feeling sorry for myself, then I sobered up and faced the truth.

I needed a job. One that paid well, that'd leave me free to work in Hofmann's lab all day. One a black man could do. One I could start that week.

I'd an idea but it'd take some pluck. After a couple of hours in the pages of *Bell's Sporting Life*, I squared my shoulders and strode up Castle Street into the Cambrian Stores. I'd read about Nat, knew he'd never lost a fight, had a deadly left called the 'pick-axe'. When I told him I'd worked my fists in Calcutta, he leaned on the bar, looked me up and down, nodded to a back room.

Without a word he chucked a pair of sparring gloves at me.

"Hit me," he said.

I danced around, sparred a bit.

He said, "Hit me, or I'll hit you."

So I did, gave it all I'd got. Nat stands his ground, soaks up punches, old school. Called me the *pretty dancer* till I rocked him with a left, till he couldn't land a decent punch. That's when he put up his gloves and gave me a hard stare. "Who taught you to fight like that?" he said.

"Life. And a woman called Shalani."

"Come and have drink," he said. "You should meet Mungo."

YOU COULD SAY O'Shaughnessy made me a champion boxer.

But like so much else, it began with my mother. Her plans for me didn't include serving a puppet prince, so at fourteen she found me a job with Captain Robert McKay, a Company officer in Beherempore. He's more clerk than soldier, wanted a trusty scribe and translator. But days before I began, my mother died of cholera. McKay took me in, gave me a job and a home.

Wasn't long before I found his interest in me went beyond copperplate. As his obituarists quaintly hinted, 'he never married'. His unwelcome attentions left me numb, but within months McKay too died of cholera. To save his reputation, he claimed on his deathbed to be my father, which meant I was officially Anglo-Indian, entitled to board at the Upper Orphan School in Calcutta.

The School attached no shame to pupils born out of wedlock, none to being Anglo-Indian, a half caste. But children ape the world around them. Our teachers were all British, all Christian. Every pupil was at least half white, except for me. With a Mughal father and Santal mother, I was the blackest of the blacks, had to wait on older white boys, like a fag at an English public school.

One, Duncan Gloag, made me his slave. It wasn't hard. I was awash with grief, had no friends, nowhere to hide. Gloag was a bereaved bully, whose comfort was making me more miserable than he was. I polished his boots, did his schoolwork, even took beatings for things he'd done. Since his father died a decorated captain, the masters wouldn't hear a word against a hero's son. If I complained, I was a filthy, envious liar.

Then I found O'Shaughnessy's book. I wouldn't take the library copy, so I dug into a small legacy from McKay to buy my own. Bought it second hand from a dealer who didn't notice – or didn't care – O'Shaughnessy had signed it on the flyleaf. In my mind it was fate, meant for me.

I collected tubes and jars, until the morning Gloag and his crony Douglas Muir found me in the refectory kitchen trying an experiment. Gloag snatched the book. When it fell open at 'deadly poisons', he said I meant to kill him, went crazy. Kicked and stamped my makeshift chemistry set to pieces. Shoved the book in my face. "You won't see this again!" he said, stood glaring, like, *what're you going to do about it?* – hoping to provoke me, give him cause for a beating.

Chemistry was my hope. Which made me the worm ready to turn – or rather, the horse. The Nawab in Murshidabad liked to bet on animal fights in the palace zoo. He'd match species that didn't naturally fight so you'd no idea who'd win. Bear versus leopard? Alligator versus three wild dogs? I remembered a horse, a mare called Mahua set to fight a tiger. I'd ridden her, didn't want to watch. But she kicked the tiger to death inside two minutes, confounded the whole court. I remembered.

Gloag held my book above his head to make me jump for it. Instead, I ducked down and punched him in the guts. When he doubled over, I thumped him on the nose drawing blood. Muir grabbed me by the elbows from behind so his friend could punch at will. I used the grip to lift my legs, kick Gloag in the chest. He shot backwards, grabbed my feet, pulled me from Muir's grasp so I crashed onto the floor. I twisted away, scrambled up to face them.

They're furious I'd fought back, had put me in my place. But when they charged, I pelted them with broken porcelain and glass, bits of tubing, iron, anything I could find. They lifted their hands and backed off. When the missiles ran out, I charged at them, shouting like a warrior, punching and kicking anywhere I could. We writhed and grunted, them grabbing my limbs, me wrenching free, renewing my attack. I couldn't win, not with two strong boys against a smaller one. Except, like Mahua, I did.

"STAND TO ATTENION!" barked a parade-ground voice.

We jumped up, stared ahead, panting. It's Skirving, our drillmaster. He's always to attention, probably slept to attention. Now he's surveying the scene. He picked the book off the floor, opened the title page.

"Chemistry? This yours, Gloag?"

"Yes, Sir!" he lied.

Skirving gave him the book, nodded at the wreckage. "Who did this?"

"Khan, Sir!" Gloag lied, again.

Skirving gave me his parade-ground stare. "That true, Khan?"

"No, Sir!" You answered him like a soldier, or else.

He turned to Muir, raised an eyebrow.

Muir glanced at Gloag, then said, "Khan, Sir!"

The drillmaster looked at me again. I'd given my answer, stared ahead.

Skirving's a former sergeant in the Bengal Infantry, proud of his enlisted rank. Proud to have led soldiers in the toughest fighting against the Gurkhas on the northern frontier. "Worthy enemies," he called them, his yardstick of men. He hated a sneak as much as a liar.

"Very well," he said. "Line up, touch your toes. All of you."

Skirving carried a swagger stick, used it to whack six burning blows to each backside. Then he sent us for brooms to clear up. While we swept, he stepped outside to smoke. Gloag buttoned my book inside his shirt. He thinks the caning's my fault, that I should've taken the blame. When we passed, he hissed, *"You'll pay for this, Khan. Just you wait."*

When we'd done, Skirving inspected the work, then said, "Get about your business, Khan." I was halfway to the library when he called me back to the centre of the yard. I thought I was in for more punishment, but what I got was a curious stare as if it's the first time he's really noticed me.

"You earned that caning, boy. Know why?"

I stared ahead. "No, Sir!" I didn't.

"You let Gloag take what's yours."

He'd obviously seen what happened through the open door.

"That book's your rifle. Never let anyone take it."

You didn't query Skirving, certainly not on parade. But my blood's up and the criticism hurt.

"They surprized me, Sir!"

He shook his head. "They're always on the prowl. Be vigilant."

"I tried ... to get it back, Sir."

"And failed. If I hadn't stepped in you'd be in the sick room."

"There're two of them, bigger than me ... Sir."

"A rabble. You let them choose the place, the time, the order of battle."

He stood quiet, letting me take it in, think about his words. Then he said, "Think they'll let it go?"

"No ... Sir."

"You want your book back?"

"Yes, Sir!"

"Be in the gymnasium, ninety minutes before morning Chapel."

That's how I joined the boxing club. 'Punch' Skirving was a former bareknuckle champion in need of a body to make up his 'side'. I'd impressed him, not that he'd admit it.

Four mornings a week, ten of us ran two miles, lifted dumbbells, pressed and squatted, sparred and worked the bag. I was strong with a good reach, fast and aggressive but in control. I liked physical contact, the noise of the crowd. What's more, if you picked a fight with one of Punch's side you picked a fight with us all. Gloag and Muir kept their distance.

The club was like a military unit. Punch was a father to his orphans, his martial wisdom our code. Colour didn't matter. What counted was effort and loyalty. I held my own against tougher boys than Gloag, learned to shudder the punch bag with a left or right. My tattered spirit healed, grew.

One day Punch took me aside, said, "Got your book back?' I shook my head. "You need to," he said.

Next day I tackled Gloag at morning break. My time. My place.

My order of battle. "Gloag! I want my book." He gave me a superior sneer, turned back to his friends. I said, "Then it's theft." Everyone knew he had it. "Bring it here at break this afternoon. Or we settle it in the gym."

His group fell quiet. Honour was decided in the ring, before the whole school. Gloag's on the spot. The quiet spread, more boys drifting over at the prospect of a fight. A few of our side stood nearby.

"I ought to thrash you here and now," he said.

"Fetch the book, then. We'll call it the purse."

Gloag's on his own, the side would see to that.

"Huh!" he sniffed. "Then it's the gym, like gentlemen."

We never met. Muir brought me the book next day, said Gloag wouldn't fight a half-caste. The *Manual* was torn, smelt of piss. I didn't care. Gloag was damaged too, smelt of cowardice. I cleaned the book, made it a token of my new self – the boy who played with fire, whose fists *were* fire. Not everyone liked me. I'd never be white. I'd have to fight Gloags all my life, but I'd learned there're greater things than skin colour – like loyalty and justice and courage.

I kept fighting after I left school, made money in Calcutta's Blacktown. When O'Shaughnessy found out I thought he'd fire me. Instead he made science of pugilism. We spent hours on trajectories and momentum, a rational defence, how to use medical knowledge – in his words – *to render a man insensible by percussion.* I found the 'knockout' punch, how to dance pretty. Put that with Punch's zero rule – *choose the place, the time, the order of battle* – and I was a champion.

Until I let Elphinstone outfox me. I had to put that right.

THE CAMBRIAN STORES is quiet in the afternoon. Nat's behind the counter drying and hanging pewter pots. I waded through the tables to the bar.

I said, "There's a soldier in here last night."

"Good day to you too," Nat said. Went on drying.

"Sorry Nat, I'm in a hurry."

"Soldiers in here every night."

"A Major, Company Army."

Nat nodded. "Elphinstone?"

"You know him?"

"Not really. Saw him fight at Woolwich a few years back."

"Any good?"

"Oh yeah, called himself the British Bulldog."

"Strike me lucky!" a voice said, "Elphinstone's in London?"

It's Mungo Walsh, my manager.

Nat nodded. "In here last night. Asking about Tipu."

Mungo dubbed me 'Tipu,' to wind up a British crowd.

"Asking what?" I said.

"Your style."

"And?"

"I told him the Imperial Stout packs a punch."

Mungo looked at me.

"Someone tipped the odds," I said, touched a cut on my face.

Nat said, "He's chatting to Mick–" A table skittered across the floor, a chair fell and a man shot out the back door. "–Fahey," Nat finished, staring after the man who'd fled. "That's him."

Tom Sayers came over, the British champion. "What's up with Fahey?"

"Tipu's face," Nat said. "Seems Fahey had a chat with Elphinstone."

I told them about the arrest, the challenge, the *I move, he moves, nothing.* Didn't mention the sleepless night or the narrow cell or the pool of Crump's blood I slipped in.

"They were sparring, upstairs," Tom said.

"My moves?"

"Now you mention it."

Had to be Fahey. He was in line to join Mungo's stable, but Nat said I was better. Fahey kicked up hell, being pipped by a nigger. We settled it in the ring. I'd have gone easy except he'd insulted me, and I needed the money. It was brutal, ended with the knock-out punch. Fahey's never got over it.

"Why're you boxing Elphinstone in a prison cell?" Mungo said.

"His call, something to prove."

"He fixed the odds," Nat said.

Mungo smacked his newspaper on the bar, pointed at 'Sepoy Mutiny in India.' "Anything to do with that?" he said.

"Oh yeah," I said. "His time, his place, his order of battle."

Mungo stared at me. He'd never heard that before, but he got the idea.

"Sounds like you need a rematch."

I'd hoped he'd say that. I don't care who Elphinstone is, or who he knows, or whose crest he's got on a piece of paper. I want him in the ring, no tricks. I hadn't forgotten how the Company spirited away my evidence or the sword you need at the enemy's throat.

Mungo's my sword. He came into boxing to earn quick money, wanted his own tavern. Turned out his talent wasn't fighting, but charming the 'fancy' – the toffs who patronize boxing. They pay the purse and cast the glamour. Now he's an impresario with a stable of fighters. I thought of him when Miss Doyle was on about the World Girdle – same agile mind, same eye for a prize.

"Reckon you could set it up?" I said.

"Be easier with a title."

I shook my head. There's always an edge with title fights. They're the big money, the big crowd, the big cut for Mungo. But they attract the law. Strictly speaking, bareknuckle isn't illegal but they get you for assault and disturbing the peace. I can't afford that, not while I'm working for Scotland Yard.

Mungo gave me a thoughtful stare. "Give us a few minutes," he said. Went upstairs to what they call the Rum-Pum-Pas club. Down here's for ordinary folk, mainly boxing. Up there's for the fancy. For lavish dinners with cock fights, gambling, sparring between topless women.

"Melrose is upstairs," Nat said. "Know what that means?"

"Yeah," I said. "Why don't you show me how Elphinstone boxes?"

The Duke of Melrose is king of the fancy, what they call an 'exquisite' – all frills and sulphur-coloured gloves. He's made an art of snobbery, as if being alive's beneath him – eyes half closed, pained expression. Starts a sentence with "Em ... ah ... eh ..." like a boiler getting up steam. Then he lisps and says 'w' for 'r'. But he's the one makes challenges, especially titles.

For fifteen minutes, Nat had Tom mimic the Major's style, me attacking, defending, trying moves. Then Mungo trotted down looking a bit smug.

"What if the law couldn't get involved?" he said.

"But how–"

"I said, *if?* Would you do a title?"

"Well, if ..."

He nodded me upstairs. The Duke sat at a table with a white linen cloth, smoking. He took the cigar from his lips with a flourish, blew a stream of blue smoke at the ceiling and waved us to sit.

"Ah ... eh ... you wish to ... em ... challenge Major Elphinstone ... but you're wowied ... eh ... about the law?"

"That's right, Duke," I said.

"Your Gwace," he corrected, which irritated me. Titles should be earned, not inherited. It's something Bea and I argue about.

Mungo's busy sketching with a charcoal stick on a big sheet of butcher's paper. "The Duke's got a plan," he said, without looking up.

"What about bweckfast?" said Melrose.

"Breakfast? It's a bit late for–"

The Duke gave Mungo a languid wave.

Mungo looked up. "The fight ... breakfast tomorrow, here."

I almost laughed. "Here? *Tomorrow?*"

Fights are normally in isolated fields a good train ride from London.

"Saturday's ideal," said Mungo, "Coppers can't tumble us that fast. Never suspect we'd try it in London." He kept my gaze. "In any case, the Duke pointed out the law can't touch soldiers. They call it *defensive exercises,* say they're having a *field day.* Which means we're in the clear, instructing the army."

Before I could say a word, Mungo spun the butcher's paper to Melrose. He'd sketched me holding the stance in front of a crowd. On a union flag hiding my face it read, 'Imperial Championship!' The headline was, 'Match of the Century' and below, 'The BRITISH LION will fight TIPU the Bengal Tiger'.

Which is when I saw their angle – the mutiny, the imperial championship, a black fighter. The home bets on Elphinstone would be massive. I win, Melrose and Mungo clean up.

His Grace gave it a haughty glance, nodded. "Vewy good, Mungo!"

The flyer *was* good, Mungo-magic.

Mungo, to me, "Five hundred?"

"Guineas?" I said, felt a tingle of excitement. Talking money means I've agreed, more or less. A year's salary for a morning's work.

"For the champion," said Melrose. "We'll deliver your challenge to Major Elphinstone this afternoon."

"Can't refuse," chimed Mungo. "Not a soldier in the Honorable Company army. And with the mutiny ... well ... national pride."

I felt my guts churn, my heart pump faster. But it's no use pretending it's not what I'd come for. Melrose tilted his head back, nodding at an engraving hung behind the bar. It's a white-haired English gent in a major-general's uniform, complete with dress sword, staring serenely from the Bengal countryside.

"Know who that is, Tipu?" he said, making 'Tipu' sound a bit like 'boy.'

I knew all right, learned about Robert Clive in the Nawab's college. The very Nawab whose dynasty Clive installed for betraying their predecessors at the Battle of Plassey. Not that it earned Clive any loyalty in Murshidabad.

"The orginal's in Government House in Calcutta," I said, putting Melrose back in his exquisite box. "It's Lord Clive."

"Conqwer-er of Bengal," he mocked. "Chance for a return match, Tipu?"

I wasn't having that. The Duke affects wealth but all he's really got is a title and debts, lives purse by purse off men like me.

"Hardly," I said. "The man's a scoundrel."

Melrose sat up, gave me an indignant stare. "A Bwitish herwo!"

I got close enough to make him lean back, remind him who'll be bloodying his fists tomorrow. "Clive's a reckless vagabond," I said, "an office boy turned soldier who tried and failed to shoot himself, twice ... so loathed by his fellow Englishmen he cut his own throat with a penknife."

I stood back, eased my collar.

Melrose took a moment to regain his exquisite poise.

"Do you know who I am?" he said.

I nodded, said nothing.

"Your fwend's forgotten his place," he said to Mungo. Before either of us could reply, he added, "Clive's a bwilliant militawy tactician."

I forced a smile. "If you mean bribery," I said, "fake alliances, sailing the Nawab's exchequer down to Calcutta as his personal fortune ... I'd agree."

The Duke stared. Mungo stopped sketching. For a minute I thought the fight's off, I'm about to get barred from the Rum-Pum-Pas. Melrose took a draw on his cigar, puffed at the ceiling. Gave me a poke with the fingers holding his cigar. "I like you, Tipu," he said. "You've got pwide, nerve. But vagabond or not, the mob here'll be with Clive, so mind you don't let us down, eh?"

"Course he won't," said Mungo, shading his sketch. "You alert the fancy, Nat does the venue, I'll whip up a crowd."

Melrose nodded, gave the languid wave dismissing us.

BACK AT THE bar, Mungo said, "Take care with the Duke, Tipu ... it's just his way. None of us blames you for hating Clive."

I looked at the white faces. "I don't hate Clive," I said. "The Company hated him ... so did half of Britain. To me he's ... interesting."

Mungo, Tom and Nat looked baffled.

"A feted soldier," I said, "with no military training? An office boy who's twice Governor of Bengal? Sprung from nowhere to riches and fancy clothes?"

"But he conquered your country," Mungo said. "Looted the place."

"He took what he could," I said. "Wouldn't you? Others envied him, hated him because he rubbed their noses in the filth of their ill-gotten wealth. A scapegoat for their own greed and incompetence."

Mungo stared as if he'd just pegged me for an uncivilized black, beyond his comprehension ... possibly dangerous. I slapped his shoulder, said, "Don't worry, Mungo. I'm going to make you rich." He shook his head. Then he gabbled the plan to Nat and Tom, showed the flyer. Rolling it up, he said, "I'll get a few dozen of these printed up," hurried towards the door.

"What time's his Grace call breakfast?" I shouted.

"Let's say ... ten o'clock," he replied, vanished through the door.

Nat gave me a long stare. "Every boxer in London will be here," he said. "You'll be in *Bell's Life*, news across the Empire."

"Want us in your corner?" Tom said.

"Oh yeah."

"Warm up, early? Give you a massage."

I nodded, croaked, "Thanks."

On Castle Street I up got up next to Thorn. "All right, boss?" I nodded, sat thinking. "Drop me at Waterloo Road Station," I said. As we turned south, I felt my hands tremble. Fighters spend years building up to a match like this. I'd less than a day. Nat's right, it'll be in *Bell's Life*, read by every sporting gent from here to Sydney Australia. If I go down it won't be *Pandey-the-traitor*, it'll be *Khan-the-loser*.

Fourteen

KEW GARDENS IS ten miles from the City, a half hour train ride from Waterloo Road station. I bought a sixpenny *Guide to Kew Gardens* and a second-class ticket to Kew Bridge.

Ten minutes later I'm sailing out on a viaduct, level with nearby rooftops and church spires, south of the river. We rumbled through rows of back-to-back houses, into the green fields of Surrey. It's a sunny day, patches of grey and white cloud coasting on the summer breeze.

Then we swung north over the Thames into Kew Bridge station. *Bradley's Guide* says the line was built by the Great Western Railway to serve their new docks at nearby Brentford. Tons of timber and coal and grain are shipped by canal from the north of England to London wharfs.

Or they were. Now the Great Western waylays the cargo at Brentford, like a pirate, loads it onto trains to send direct to London wholesalers. Kew and Brentford were quiet villages for centuries, far from the City. Steam changed that. Now they ring to hammers and singing navvies, new buildings, new shops, new residents. Locals complain, locals make fortunes selling land. I hear it all the time from Bea.

I paid a halfpenny toll to go south over Kew Bridge, pulled out the *Guide*, thumbed it as I walked. It's by William Hooker – Joseph's papa – with felicitations to the Christian God and anyone who'll give money. Joseph told O'Shaughnessy his father's Director of Kew Gardens. Since Joseph's now Deputy Director, I'm guessing William swung his boy a job.

The *Guide* lists rarities imperial travelers are urged to send with all haste – especially the Chinese rice-paper plant and the camphor tree of Sumatra. Visitors should dress respectably, stay on the gravel paths, and remember plants are often moved daily from one 'house' to another to let in new arrivals. The world's botany is heading for Kew like exhibits to the Great Exhibition.

I WAS STILL on the bridge when I felt something wasn't right. Folk coming the other way looked glum or irate. A few snatched words said they'd been turned away from the Gardens. The main gates are on the far side of Kew Green, a big meadow with a church and a dozen ancient trees. I walked over, swinging my Oxford bag, soaking up the sun, avoiding glances.

Blacks get scarcer west of London docks. By Kew, it's just me.

The ornate iron gates were chained shut, guarded by a police sergeant. A thin pall of smoke dimmed the sunlight in the Gardens behind. The air smelt of charred wood. More policemen stood in front of the houses backing onto the Gardens, more visitors milled aimlessly on the Green.

"What's happening?" I asked the sergeant, nodding at the chains.

"Garden's shut," he said, blankly, which was obvious. He went on staring expectantly in case I needed directions back to India. I didn't push it.

Some folk had settled to picnic on the Green, others crossed Richmond Road for tea at the Coach and Horses. I went that way but there's no room. So I stood alone by the road scratching my head, looking back over Kew Bridge. I'd expected more hostility after this morning's abuse. Maybe news of an Indian mutiny hadn't got to Kew. Or the shock had faded. Or they didn't care.

Either way, two thoughts sparred in my head. One said I'm out of steam. I was so sure Hooker and his Gardens had answers for Sir George that I'd stopped worrying about execution. Now I felt the drop, the nameless grave in a cabbage-patch in Millbank yard. The other thought said it's a damned odd thing the Gardens are shut just as I turn up for answers.

All the while I'm half watching a black and white parasol bobbing this way, the owner's walking fast, weaving past gaggles of people. A woman, obviously, with a carpet bag. Miss Doyle? She saw me, jabbed the parasol to pin me in place till she got here.

"Thank heaven!" she puffed, threaded an arm through mine and led me to a quiet spot on under a tree.

"For what?"

"I found you," she said. "I want the cigar case back."

"Said I'd bring it at six."

"I realized it's Company property, not mine to lend."

I didn't believe it. Like didn't believe she only learned my name this morning. That insult on my parentage came from a portfolio. She hadn't *just realized* the cigar case was Company property. Someone'd told her. But I still wanted her talking to me, maybe more so.

I said, "How'd you find me?"

"An Indian plant? Who else but Hooker? The man who names foreign weeds with barbarous binomials." When I looked skeptical, she said, *"Flora Indica?"* Which was plausible.

"Don't have the cigar case with me," I lied.

She stared at me, or rather, studied me, as if there's a lot more than a cigar case on her mind. I responded in kind, took out the little bottle, shook it.

"This is more important," I said. "Matter of life and death."

"Whose?"

"Mine."

"They nearly hanged you for killing Henry Bullock."

A blunt question and an accusation in one. "Who told you that?"

She rolled her eyes as if I'm a fool – *knowing's* her business, so's *confidentiality*. But she wanted an answer. I felt like yanking off those green glasses and slinging them in the road. They gave her a stare you couldn't bounce back.

"Henry Bullock killed himself," I said.

That surprised her, intrigued her too. Which led me to tell it from the start because someone else obviously had. I told it fast, like a burst from a volley gun, including the fact Henry was my friend. At the end, I said, "Put that in your portfolio."

She looked blank, cogs spinning like a calculating engine – *whirr, crunch, whirr* – till I got the balance, "Why'd they ask *you* investigate the bottle?"

I'd thought about that. "Home Secretary wants the best ... which means Hofmann at the Royal College. Mention chemistry and India, he'll send you to Doctor Khan. And there's me waiting for a rope at Her Majesty's pleasure. You can almost see the smile on Green's face. He's got me by the balls."

"The throat?" she suggested.

"Enough to assure my best services. I find the *what*, the *where* and the *who* of this liquid, they tear up my death warrant." I nodded at Kew Green. "So I need to know how it's tied to those Gardens. It's why I'm here."

"And you think it's to do with my father's death?"

"Sure of it," I said. Which wasn't entirely true.

"Let's speak to Hooker, then."

I nodded again. "Gardens are closed. Copper told me to hook it."

"I thought you're working for the Home Secretary?"

"Yeah ... well, there're limits."

"What if *I* got us in?"

"*You?* Pile up the portfolios," I mocked, "clamber over the wall?"

She looked at me as I imagine she did Reuter while challenging him to a duel. "You'd rather be hanged than accept a woman's help?" she said. "Or spend your life fleeing the law?"

I'd seen myself in rags, a stowaway to the arse-end of empire, dodging the likes of Elphinstone. Didn't fancy it. I like my lives in London – boxing, Thorn and the Lab, my *affaire* with Bea. No one's driving me out of town.

I said, *"What* if you could get us in?"

"You'd tell me how my father died."

"And you'd tell me *what* Slegman, Clyde and Birdwood are?"

She nodded, gave me a businesslike handshake, all before I'd time to say, *"Whoa... what's the plan?"* She stood the parasol and bag by the tree, peeled off the green specs and passed them to me.

"Guard my things," she said.

"Miss Doyle–"

"Call me Addie ... now we're partners."

"Partners?"

In lieu of an explanation she puffed up like an actress heading for an entrance and walked off. I looked at the carpet bag. They're usually made of old carpet, cheap and handy for the train. Not hers. This one's new carpet, stylish. I'd half a mind to look inside. If I had, I'd have been dead within the hour and world history might be otherwise.

THE ADDIE WALKING away wasn't the one I knew. This one's a Victorian lady – taller, straighter, all bosom and bustle, aloof with a touch of vulnerability. Going in a wide arc past circles of pic-nickers, losing all trace of me. I watched her bottom sway, remembered our chaste hug round the Chemiscope, her perfume. Wondered if that's what Bea calls *suitable.*

That's until she turned towards the gate and the sergeant. He smiled openly, touched his hat and leaned an obliging ear to her inquiry. They talked, pointed across the Green. Then Addie feigned a small curtsy and took the same path back, regaining her stride and stare with every step.

"Well?" I said. "The sergeant seems to have warmed up,"

She pulled on the green glasses. "God, men are so ridiculous!"

I'd like to think she means white men. "We're in?" I said.

She pointed to a Georgian house a few doors up Kew Green from the main gates. "Hunter House," she said, "it's the library and her-barium. Sergeant Smollett said I'd find Hooker there."

I'd assumed he worked inside the Gardens. "Don't suppose he said why they're shut?"

"Fire in plant 'ouse fifteen, Ma'am," she aped. "Seems several adjacent houses are unsafe."

"You said you'd get us in."

"To see Hooker."

"I wanted to see the botany before the botanist," I said. "Find something specific to tackle him with."

"Like what?"

"An Indian plant that'd make a decoction of the right hue. Hooker won't like questions from a woman and a black man, especially after the fire. He's got a prickly temper, reckons Indians are mean and miserable, not to mention killing whites in the Northwest Provinces. Then there's the bird game."

"The *what?*"

I told her about cannabis and the Indian peafowl, gave little flap with my elbows, a squawk. She coughed an unexpected laugh, tried to look aloof. "Don't you take anything seriously?" she said. But she couldn't help smiling.

"How about finding a way into Hooker's study?" I said.

Then we talked business. She rattled off the Hooker portfolio and asked what I knew about Imperial politics.

"Pretty simple," I said, "control the natives, make money."

Addie shook her head. "No wonder they nearly hanged you."

"Growing up in India under British rule there didn't seem much more to know ... Company's like a Roman legion, the military arm of British capital."

She thought awhile, then said, "There're two tribes here – more or less – the Tories and the Whigs."

"Like Hindus and Muslims?"

"Not exactly. The Tories are conservative, fear the wrath of an Anglican God, think the Queen should run the country. They dominate the Company's Court of Directors, give it a powerful voice in

Parliament. In return, Company patronage gives jobs to their way-ward sons."

I thought about that. "And the Whigs?"

"Rule by Parliament, peace and progress through free trade, reform ... civilizing the heathen natives throughout the Empire. Point is, they hate the Company, see it as Tory jobbery, been chipping away at its power for years."

"But ... if there's no Company, there's no Indian empire to rule."

Addie shook her head. "The Company runs India for the British Government. Shut the Company and Parliament's in charge, which is a *coup d'état* for the Whigs. They'll call it reform ... progress."

"Because it's a Whig Parliament ... at the moment."

She nodded. Now she'd laid it out so clearly, it's a revelation. Made sense of things I'd read in the London papers. "So some of the locals hate the Company as much as the Wahhabists do in India."

"There're a few ifs and buts," she said, "but that's the gist of it. Sir George Green wants the Company gone, abolished."

"And Raikes Elphinstone's a Company servant."

"Right ... so which side's he really on?"

I looked quizzical. When she didn't go on, I pitched in my two-penn'orth and found Plant House 15 in the *Guide to Kew Gardens*. Ten minutes later we'd a story, a plan to get in by bluff. Which means heads or tails, no half measures.

HUNTER HOUSE IS a dull, Georgian affair. There's a flight of stone stairs to a columned doorway, which lends a little class to a brick box. I knocked and waited. When a man name of Black answered the door, I showed a police warrant-card I use to access scenes of crime, gave him a *carte de visite*.

"Khan ... from the Home Office," I said. He looked at Addie and her carpet bag. "My assistant. She sketches findings, for the records"

"Ah." He waved us into an airy hall and walked off. Which surprised me as I hadn't told him our business. Inside, Hunter House

couldn't decide whether it's homely or institutional, like an art gallery. But an odd smell says it's stuffed with moldy books and desiccated plants.

I recognized Doctor Joseph Hooker at once – tall, slightly stooped and a little sullen, still with the sharp parting and side whiskers. Studying my card.

He looked up, *"You?"*

I'd half a mind to do the elbows, squark, *"You!"* like a peafowl. What I said was, "Calcutta, fifty-one, O'Shaughnessy's chemical assistant."

"Prince?" he queried.

"Didn't use the title then."

He'd aged, put on weight, gained a dimple in his chin. It suited him, being older, less wiry. I'd say handsome.

"You're early," he said.

"Early?"

"Efficient," Addie said. "Dr Khan's a busy man."

"Should've gone to the main entrance," Hooker said.

"I ... thought–"

"Sergeant Smollett directed us here," Addie said.

Which was irritatingly quick-witted but gave me time to work up some gravity for a heads-or-tails line. "The Home Secretary isn't satisfied with the Major's account of the fire."

Heads says Elphinstone remembered what I'd said in Millbank – *a tinge of green ... from a plant.* Now the Gardens are shut, guarded, on fire. He'd got here first. Addie agreed.

"Sir George sent you?" Hooker said, looking a little baffled.

"He did," I replied. I'm baffled too. Hooker isn't surprised we're here, only that Sir George sent us.

"But the Home Secretary sent Elphinstone. I saw the letter."

Which was heads *and* tails. Elphinstone's been here but *I* don't have a letter with Green's signature and seal. I needed some authority, even at the risk of offending Hooker, so I said, "Is Sir William here, the Director?"

"Gone to Whitehall, to complain about this outrage."

"Outrage?"

Hooker waved me off with a condescending glare, couldn't believe they'd sent a darky. I'd a feeling he's about to throw us out, which meant I had to up the stakes. "Sir George sent him. But Elphinstone's a major in the East India Company army. Runs their intelligence department in Calcutta, in fact."

Hooker's eyes narrowed.

"Missed any *Erythroxylum* plants recently?" I said.

That got his attention.

"Yes," he said, which sounded like, *how the hell d'you know that?*

I knew because Thorn and I took them, but I nodded as if it's no more than I'd expected. "Any in Plant House 15?" The *Guide* says there are.

"Yes, but what's that–"

"To do with the fire? They might be of medical value."

Hooker screwed up his face to say he's lost. And suspicious.

"He might've misled you," I said. "For the Company's sake." Before he'd a chance to reply I took out the little bottle, shook it. "He wanted to know which plant this came from?"

Hooker nodded. "You're suggesting he lied?"

"Not for me to *suggest* anything," I said. "Sir George asked me to investigate the fire, report the facts. He's concerned by certain ... irregularities in Calcutta's Military Hospital. This liquid's involved."

"I see. So why the interest in *Erythroxylum?*"

"It creates a kind of martial euphoria, could be of military use." I made up *martial euphoria* on the way over. Addie liked it. "The Company might want to establish plantations in India."

"Good God," Hooker said. "You mean Elphinstone's playing a double game, took the plants? That's no less than theft."

I nodded. "Which means there's a ... political dimension."

"Political?"

"Delicate," I said. "Sir George has to be sure of his ground before taking it to the Prime Minister."

"Delicate, *how?*" He'd forgotten all about throwing us out.

I sucked a breath through my teeth. "You've read the papers," I said, like I'm hinting. "The Company's lost control of the Northern Provinces, Delhi."

Hooker shook his head to say he didn't follow.

"The Company will say it's not their fault, but a theft ... a scandal."

"India could fall," Addie said, as if he's a fool not to see it.

I shot her an angry glance. Politics was her realm, and she didn't like hearing me deliver the clever lines. But Hooker wouldn't be lectured by a young woman.

She said, "If it does, the rest of the Empire—"

"Keep out of this Miss Doyle!" I said. "Remember your place."

She glared, furious, about to put me in mine.

"Doyle?" Hooker said. "Elijah Doyle's daughter?"

"Yes," I cut in, worrying the game's up.

"But he was—"

"Found dead this morning in the London and Imperial Bank. Just like Henry Bullock in his shop in Ivy Lane last evening."

We stood in silence, Addie glaring at me with a look I hadn't seen before, like I should know she won't forget what I'd said. Hooker's looking at me too, patting is lips with his fingers, wondering how the deaths are related to the fire.

"I investigated Doyle's death this morning," I said. "At the Home Secretary's request."

"And?"

"Confidential, but he was recently in Calcutta with Bullock, at the Military Hospital." I shrugged as if the connection was obvious.

Hooker pulled a face to say it wasn't to him. Nor to me. But I kept to the script, tried to look as if I'm weighing up what I'm allowed to say. How to tickle Hooker's prejudice while sounding like an Indian chemist.

Addie told me the Company wouldn't fund his botanizing in India. The Admiralty stumped up, which means the British Government, the likes of Sir George Green. Then the Company refused to fund the publication of *Flora Indica*. Hooker'd love to see them face down in the mud, get his boot on the back of their necks.

"Well, I'm playing blinders here," I said, "but India's fall could incite rebellion worldwide." Then, more cautiously, "Couple that with scandal in London ... Parliament might decide–"

"To rule India directly," Hooker said, "abolish the Company."

"As an Indian subject I'm bound to agree rule by–"

"The end of Tory patronage in India!"

Hooker licked his lips like a kid at a sweetshop window.

"Progress and prosperity through free trade," I said. "And science."

Hooker almost smiled. "What do you need?" he said.

Huzzah! I nearly said, *"Directions to Plant House 15,"* but Hooker wanted to help, knew more about botany in British India than anyone on earth. So I shook the little bottle, made a foam of dancing green bubbles. "Did Elphinstone explain his interest in this?"

"Blasted cheek!" Hooker said. I thought at first he meant me, but then he said, "Had the damned nerve to bar me and Sir William from our own garden, waved some letter from Green. We'd a hell of row, I can tell you."

I looked sympathetic, repeated my question.

Hooker shook his head. "He asked if I knew what plant it might've come from. As it happened, I'd seen something similar in House 16. Yashoda makes it as a decoction from the leaves."

"Yashoda?" It's an Indian name, Hindu.

"Native Bengali. Brought her here in fifty-one. Her late father was an Ayurvedic healer. She assisted him, had a wide knowledge of medicinal herbs. I thought she'd be useful while I compiled *Flora Indica*. She runs a sort of dispensary for the poor. It's behind the Post

Office in Brentford Market Place, number five, I think."

"Know what plant she uses?"

"That's the odd thing. It's sweet wormwood, a common daisy."

"British?"

"No, Asian. Came in a Ward's case from the Apothecaries' Garden at Chelsea, supposedly a miracle cure for fever. The apothecaries didn't agree, sent it here. Yashoda grew it in the Museum Stove with other medicinal herbs. That's that, till Major Elphinstone turned up this morning."

I said, "Stove?"

"Hot house, also known as Plant House 15, south side of the Museum."

Addie said, "What's a Ward's case?"

"A doll's greenhouse," he said. "You sow the plants inside, sealed under glass. As they grow, they make their own oxygen, cycle the water. You can roll them on the high seas for months, long as they're tied under awning. Don't get seasick, or homesick. Most of our live specimens arrive like that, growing in Ward's cases."

"Where're these from?" I said.

Hooker's mouth opened, closed. Then he beckoned with a long, bony finger. We followed him into a high, airy room full of cabinets filled with dried herbs, lined with bookshelves holding every one of those thousand volumes he'd consulted for *Flora Indica*. There's a table by a picture window. On it's a microscope, some herbs and a notebook. A pen lay on the page with a spatter of ink as if he'd thrown it down in irritation.

Hooker found a quarto volume, thumbed the pages, ran a finger down the index, flicked to a cross-reference, tapped the page. Then he fetched a folio volume, so heavy it took two hands to heft it down. Same procedure with the book laying in the crook of his elbow. I could see it's an alphabetical list of species in the Gardens, entries glued on oblongs of paper. The big pages crackled as they turned. Hooker took out two sheets of paper and offered them to me.

It's a letter written from Shanghai in the autumn of 1853. I read:

My dear Moore, I am honoured to furnish you with plants which, at first sight, may seem no more than common Wormwood. I too would have come to that conclusion had it not been for the following, singular occurrence.

Shortly after taking up quarters in a Buddhist temple at Tein-tung, I suffered a violent attack of fever. So severe was the illness that my good friend the priest – with whom I was staying – insisted on fetching a Chinese doctor from nearby Tein-tung-ka. I was reluctant to place myself in his hands, but a drowning man "will catch at a straw." When the doctor arrived, I was delirious with a burning fever, but he questioned me closely about my symptoms and habits. He then used his knuckles (dipped in hot tea) to massage me under the ribs – with such violence I almost cried out – and bid me swallow about a hundred small pills washed down with herbal tea. After a similar treatment three days later, the fever left me, and I was completely cured!

The jealous doctor refused to answer any questions about the pills, but my friend told me the principal ingredient was a species of plant that grows abundantly in the hills of Ningpo. It is these plants – known locally as Tsing'hwa – you will find growing in the case. Medical men will probably smile as they read these statements, but there was no mistaking the results. Indeed, from an intimate knowledge of the Chinese, I am inclined to think more highly of their skill than people generally give them credit for. Being an ancient nation and comparatively civilized, they have carefully handed down many remedies from father to son. Some may be equal if not superior to our own, and well worth investigation by Europeans.

I have, & c, Robert Fortune.

I said, "Who's Moore?"

"Curator of the Apothecaries' Garden in Chelsea," Hooker said. "And Robert Fortune is–"

"I know him," I said. "We met in Calcutta Botanic Garden in fifty-one."

I recalled thick side-whiskers and a sullen stare.

"Fortune's more gardener than botanist," Hooker said. "Went plant hunting in China after the peace of Nanking in forty-three."

"After the Company forced China open for British trade," I said, as if for Addie's benefit. "Dressed himself as a native, smuggled valuable plants to the Horticultural Society in London."

"His use of the Ward's case changed botany," Hooker retorted. "So much so, the Company had him fetch Chinese tea, to plant in Assam and Darjeeling."

"Fetch?" I wanted to laugh at that, but we weren't here to debate economic botany. At least, not tea. "That's when I met him," I said. "On his way up country from Calcutta. But you don't believe him, about the drug?"

"Know how Fortune lives now?"

I shook my head.

"Books. Sensational stories of his travels in China – forbidden cities, battles with pirates ... the man's got nine lives. A miraculous fever-cure's just another tale. Anyway, the apothecaries didn't believe him. Nor did Yashoda, and she knows the medicinal plants in that part of the world."

"Why'd she make a decoction, then?"

"Experiment? Curiosity? I don't know." When I just stared, he said, "Fortune was *delirious,* by his own admission!"

He checked a reference and hefted the volume back on the shelf. Went to a cupboard, ran his fingers up a pile of card and eased out a paper folder. Inside's a spray of dried leaves. They were fern-like, feathery-green with tiny yellow flowers at the tips. I caught a sweet, aromatic scent, like camphor. A hand-written label dated 1854 read, *Artemisia Chinenesis (Tsing'hwa).*

"Could this grow in India?" I asked.

Hooker went back to the cupboard, found similar folder; inside's the same plant. This time the label's dated 1844. It read: *Artemisia Annua*, from Mr Wade's garden in the Punjab, the foothills of the Himalayas.

I said, "You showed the Major all this?"

"Certainly not."

"The letter?"

"Nope. Didn't like his manner or his tone."

"What *did* you tell him?"

"What I'd seen in the Museum Stove, said I'd walk him there. That's when he produced Sir George's letter, told me he'd go alone. A while later I heard a crack, a small explosion. Before I could investigate, the Major came back, smoke drifting behind him. Told me the Gardens are shut, no one's allowed in till he says so. Shortly after he left, a police guard appeared on the gates. Then came a Company soldier saying you'd come in the late afternoon to collect the evidence. I thought the Major sent you, now I know otherwise."

I glanced at Addie. We had to get on before whoever Hooker'd confused us for turned up. I waved the letter, said, "I'll hang on to this, for Sir George."

"Can't do that," Hooker said. "Part of the record, we have to–"

"Green's a lawyer by training," I said, "likes to see the evidence. I'll mention your generosity." Addie told me about Green. And that the Hookers rely on Government grants to keep the Gardens running.

Hooker said, "You'll mention my name?"

I nodded, felt a spike of excitement. If the liquid in the Museum Stove's the same as in my bottle, I've got my answers – where it came from, the chemical formula, and I'm fairly sure Henry made it. Which lets me off the hook. Or out of the noose. Fortune's letter's an extra, like a double bonus. Solid evidence for Sir George and one up on Elphinstone. But I reckoned I could do better yet.

"Certainly, I'll mention your name," I said. "But it'll sound a lot sweeter if you can throw light on something that's troubling Sir George."

Hooker's shrug said he'd do what he could.

"Suppose for the sake of argument," I said, "Fortune's story about this plant's true ... or partly true ... or someone *believes* it's true. Why would a Company director risk his position and good name for it? Why risk having a hound like Elphinstone, a Company servant, hunt him down?"

Hooker bowed his head, thinking. He looked up a couple of times as if he'd speak, then he lifted the bony finger again and beckoned us to follow. "To hell with Elphinstone," he said. "There's something I want to show you."

Fifteen

WE LEFT HUNTER House at the back, along a winding trail in sunlight dappled through trees and bushes, till we came to an ancient door in an ancienter brick wall. Hooker forced the rusty iron bolts, creaked the door past a mat of cobwebs. Nobody had been this way since the Battle of Waterloo.

We emerged in bright sunshine at the Gardens' northeast edge. Ahead a gravel path ran straight to a far-off lake and a tall pagoda. Not a soul to be seen.

Hooker waved an arm in a grand gesture. "What do you see?"

We stood, quiet, taking in the clipped lawns and finely pruned trees, the earthy islands of shrubs and bushes. I hated the place. Took me back to the day my mother brought me to Murshidabad, the first time I saw a building bigger than a hut, or nature laid out by human hands. It looked shorn, bald. A plantation with martialed ranks of identical flowers, like battalions in the Nawab's service. Or Hooker's.

"A beautiful garden on a beautiful day," Addie said.

"I prefer nature's arrangement," I said.

Hooker ignored me. "A garden," he echoed. "That's what most folk see."

"Except Elphinstone's scared off your visitors," I said.

"I don't give a damn," Hooker growled. "You think it's my job to hawk exotic plants, line the nursery man's pocket in the suburbs?"

"Isn't it?" I said, thinking I'd get more if I tightened his spring.

Hooker led us on down the gravel path.

"Our work," he said, "could solve the greatest mystery of philo-sophical botany, perhaps of our age."

Addie and I shared a glance, stared at him, all ears. Now we're walking three abreast, one each side of Hooker.

"Is a species descended from an originally created pair?" he said. "Or are they mutable, advancing from a primeval germ by a general law of nature?"

"Why, the latter," said Addie. "Surely a man of science can't believe in the Christian myth of creation? *Species* are the myth, the *creation* of systematists."

I admired her nerve, expected Hooker to blow up.

"It's a curious fact," he said, as if she hadn't spoken, "that as species migrate over vast areas, they don't grow where they like best, but where they can best find room. You see, plants in a state of nature are always warring, contending for monopoly of the soil, the stronger ejecting the weaker, the more vigorous killing the more delicate. Although," – he looked at Addie – "unheeded by the *common* observer, this constant war varies a plant's character. But only the most *superficial* naturalist mistakes this for ... *mutability.*"

Which left as both quiet. Cynicism's part of my defence, my self-esteem, but I couldn't've made that up. Couldn't help wondering if local blooms looked down on the coloureds from overseas, the kind Fortune sends in Ward's cases.

"Doesn't say that in the visitor's *Guide*," I said.

"Say what?"

"Battalions of Indian primulas and rhododendrons are waging imperial war across London's suburbs, toughening their character."

Hooker gave me the look Elphinstone had – *you've got an odd sense of humour*. Then, he said, "You mentioned the Chinese War, the Opium War as some call it. Why'd that start?"

"I told you," I said. "To open the country for British–"

"Because the Chinese seized the Company's opium in Canton," Addie interrupted, "tried to ban the trade."

"The drug's a contagion," Hooker said. "Raging through China like a deadly plague. But why?"

"Silver bullion," Addie said.

"Because?"

"Tea," she finished, like turning a trick.

Hooker looked smug, content a white woman, Elijah Doyle's daughter, could outwit a native Indian. I gave her the look she'd given me – *I won't forget that.* Hooker wheeled us sharp left, round half a horseshoe-shaped path, on towards a circular medical garden. He pointed off to the left at a cluster of glazed plant houses, reeled off nations and rarities from around the globe.

Then, he said, "Tea's the Company's biggest Chinese import. But the Chinese wouldn't exchange it for Company goods, wanted silver."

"A crime against free trade," I said, chasing the cynical high ground.

"Indeed ... so the Company did a deal the Chinese couldn't refuse. Sold Indian opium to British smugglers, gave them access to Chinese ports. Which more than balanced the silver trade. Brought chaos to China and huge fortunes to the Company. Then they had an even better idea–"

"Robert Fortune smuggles tea plants to India," said Addie.

"Company makes the profit on Indian tea."

"No more silver to China."

"Only cash from opium."

"And when the Chinese impound the drug in Canton?"

"War," said Addie. "China opened by force for British commodities."

"Where does the money end up?" asked Hooker.

I looked around. "London," I said. They'd given me the trick.

I knew all this, sort of. I saw Robert Fortune load Ward's cases and Chinese tea workers onto a steam ship in Calcutta. Cargoes of opium going the other way. Tom the barber's leg gone in the Opium War. But I hadn't seen it with a botanist's worldwide eye. Or a trader's, like Addie. Hadn't seen how it fit together, the strings pulled from London.

"Now what do you see?" said Hooker.

"A stockyard of useful products."

He nodded at a weed-less flowerbed. "No warring here," he said. "We preserve each species as it was created."

"Like freshly minted coins," Addie said.

"The devil's Eden," I said.

"Huh!" said Hooker. "There's a nice coin in the Museum Stove, *Cinchona calisaya*, the Peruvian fever tree. Fortune took a Ward's case of seedlings to India. Sadly, they didn't make it to Darjeeling, not this time. But if another plant made quinine, or a similar drug, one that grew freely in India–"

"Worth a tidy sum," I said.

"Several," said Addie. "Like jute?"

"Jute?"

"A good's a good, but they're all shipped in jute sacks."

I felt like a child at the adult's table. "And quinine?"

"India's a living hell to whites without it," Hooker said. "Keeps soldiers fit to fight. Africa's worse, and that's the next imperial prize."

We walked into a hamlet of sheds and wheelbarrows, stacks of flowerpots and sieves, piles of compost. The gardeners' busy routine had frozen when the Gardens shut. I'm thinking of Addie's uncle Reginald. If Henry'd found a quinine substitute, Clyde would have to get it or face ruin. He's back on my list.

The path went sharp right, snick-snacked back on itself through a grove of tall trees. Hooker pointed to a copse of conifers ahead.

"The plant houses are behind those," he said, quietly.

His tone made me cautious. I edged us off the gravel onto the grass. We moved slowly, quietly. "I'll tell you this," Hooker whispered, "the Major found more in the Museum Stove than he bargained for."

"Why's that?" I hissed over my shoulder.

"His manner. First, he's cock-sure, ordering us about like subalterns. But when he came back, you'd think he'd charged the Russian guns at Balaclava. Shaken, in a foul temper."

I led with my arms wide to keep the others back. At the trees I stopped to peer through the foliage. The plant houses are across a wide lawn, built against the sunny side of the brick Museum. They're sixty yards off, angled towards us at about thirty degrees. The largest, the Museum Stove, is a black skeleton, partly collapsed, still smouldering.

Two things struck me. First, the adjacent houses looked secure. The brick walls had held the fire. Not even a broken windowpane. This wasn't about safety. Second, there's a sentry, a young sepoy in a scarlet uniform, off guard in the dreamy afternoon. He's at ease, rifle leant on his thigh, smoking a pipe.

"That's the one," whispered Hooker, "told me you'd be coming."

"If that's how he stands guard I'll have him court martialled," I said.

Hooker mouthed, "Think I'll get back to the Herbarium. Lots to do." He didn't want it getting back he'd disobeyed orders. "You'll let me know what you find?"

I nodded, and his steps faded, leaving birdsong and the buzz of insects in the heat. I leaned to Addie. "We brazen it out ... don't see any other way."

She nodded, but her face said she hadn't forgotten me telling her to remember her place.

"Together, then," I said. "Quick and professional."

We went briskly across the lawn, swinging our bags, me whistling.

THE MANUAL SAYS a sentry challenges at thirty yards. This one didn't. The grass muted our steps and he's not watching. When he did notice us, he tapped out his pipe and picked up his rifle. Didn't cock or shoulder it.

At twenty-five yards, I shouted in Bengali, "Where's the challenge, soldier?"

"Who comes–"

"Friend, lucky for you."

I put down my bag, opened it so he could see the rows of instruments and bottles. Handed him my card, continued in Bengali, "What's your name?" He hesitated. "Want me to tell Major Elphinstone you're lounging like a limp prick instead of challenging us?"

"No ... Sepoy Basak, Sir."

I switched to English. "We're here to collect the evidence."

"Where's the cart?" he asked.

He's no more than a boy, English heavily accented.

"On its way," Addie said.

I took my bag, pointed to a spot ten paces away, out of earshot. "Stand there, Basak," I said. "Keep guard!"

I faced the Stove. It's like a conservatory: twelve paces long, five deep, twice a man's height where the canted roof meets the brickwork at the back. Bits of charred doorframe said I'm in front of what'd been an entrance.

Inside it's laid out in three strips. At the front's a knee-high flowerbed, at the back a terrace of wooden shelves rising to chest height, like a wide staircase. A flagstone pathway separates the two. At one end's a boiler sprouting hot-water pipes. At the other's a small work area with jars, a case of books and a large bench holding some chemical apparatus.

The fire began in the middle, in front of me. All that's left here is brickwork and the big iron frame that held the flowerpots on wooden shelves. The frame's blackened and bowed, littered with broken pots and fallen windowpanes. The damage is less serious towards each end, mainly scorching. A few roof panes are still intact.

I sensed Addie move next to me.

"You'll get nothing from that wreckage," she said.

Which sounded like a challenge. She'd got us in. She and Hooker had shown me the world from the high mountain of London, like the temptation of Christ. Except the Company's directors weren't telling

Satan to get hence, quite the reverse. Now it's my turn.

I said, "Even in chaos nature proceeds with regularity and order."

"Immanuel Kant," she said, which took the breeze from my sails. I thought O'Shaughnessy made it up.

But I nodded. Then I looked and listened, tasted the air. The first odd thing's the smell. I expected wood smoke, maybe a whiff of nutmeg and cloves. The house is full of tropical spices. What I got was fish and something that jolted me up country to a trampled village in Bengal. Not gunpowder. Not rotting flesh. I stepped over what'd been the threshold, now just a line between the gravel path and flagstone floor.

Addie came closer, pointed down. "There, a broken lamp. Elphinstone must've dropped it."

I shook my head.

"It's plain enough," she said, "What's your explanation, then?"

Quietly, I said, "Why light a lamp on a sunny afternoon?"

I crouched, leaned down to sniff the wreckage by a lump of fused metal. "Drop a lamp," I said, "it breaks. But the glass chimney and oil holder are there on the flagstones, intact." I pointed at the mis-shapen lump. "That's the burner that joined them, stinks of whale oil. Elphinstone took it apart, tossed oil on the planking, then the lit burner. It went up like matchwood."

"He did it deliberately?"

I moved left down the pathway, shoving aside the remains of roof timbers, stepping over tub-sized flowerpots, coughing in a swirl of ash.

Addie followed me outside, watching intently. At the bench I found what I'd come for. By the end-wall was a cluster of plants like the ones Hooker'd shown us, except these had bright green leaves; feathery fronds that reached waist high. I pinched a leaf, smelt a flood of eucalyptus and camphor so pure and sharp it made me giddy, a scent from the heart of nature.

"Artemisia Annua ... Tsin'hwa?" Addie said.

"Grown by Yashoda. There's the Ward's case they came in, by the wall." Addie nodded. I crouched by a patch of green stems that'd been cut off near the ground, traced the arc of the cut. "Twelve-inch blade."

"A scythe?"

"Bayonet, more like. The kind Elphinstone carries on his belt."

I cut a sprig, put it in my bag and went to the workbench. It wasn't difficult to read. I told it out loud, tracing a finger over the apparatus.

"Yashoda strips the leaves, grinds them with pestle and mortar, soaks them in," – I took a sniff – "smells like piss. Strains it through muslin and" – I pointed to the floor by the Ward's case – "stores the liquid in those demijohns." I hoisted one up to the light. "Same as in my bottle. Watch this."

I pulled the stopper and poured some on the hot iron frame. It spluttered and hissed but I poured till it cooled enough to pool.

"Not good chemical practice," I said, "but look, see where it's evaporated? Same needles. Same colour. Same crystals." I stoppered the demijohn and put it back on the floor.

That's when I found what I hadn't come for.

IT BEGAN WITH an old friend on a low shelf, a shrub with pairs of deep-green leaves. On each stalk, near the stem, were pairs of tinier leaves that visibly moved, gyrated in slow circles.

Some say they're dancing, some say signalling, which is why it's called the Bengal telegraph plant. My mother told me they're waving, had me wave back. After she died, I always had one in a pot to wave at, to remind me. I murmured: *hello, fancy seeing you here, so far from home.* The little leaves twitched and moved in reply, made me smile despite it all.

Then I read the signal, recalled the smell, up country in Bengal. Let it mingle with other thoughts. Why light a lamp on a sunny afternoon? Why burn the Stove's centre when the evidence is at one end?

Why'd Hooker hear a small explosion? What shook Elphinstone like a suicidal charge? I went back to the middle of the stove, Addie tracking me again outside.

She said, "What?"

I said, "Watch."

I took a palm-sized mirror from my Oxford bag, crouched and bounced sunlight into the dark under the ironwork, right to the back. Let it slant and flicker over blackened brick, charcoal, earth, fragments of terracotta pot, until it lit something else. Something like the pelt of a dead rat.

Addie said "What?"

The ironwork is like a twisted cage, keeping me out. Too hot to touch. I went back to the end, cleared the bench and turned it over. Dragged it bumping and scraping to the entrance where I stood it on end, legs facing the former range of shelves. Then I tipped it forward so the legs fell into the hot iron, gave me a solid surface to scramble over.

Addie said, "Be careful!"

The table crunched into the debris as I crawled forward. It ended a couple of feet short of the rear wall. I could've slipped round the back near the telegraph plant. Maybe that's what it tried to tell me. But Addie's watching, so I slowly stood, arms out, set a foot on what looked like a solid piece of angle-iron. I tested my weight, then took a step and planted a hand on the hot bricks at the back.

I jumped, slid and scuffed my way down to the flagstones behind the iron frame. Addie shrieked. I called, "It's all right, I'm fine." I crouched sideways, accustomed my eyes to the gloom. Heat from the debris baked my face, making me squint. But I found the pelt from the back.

Not a rat. It's a small white dog, lying with its back arched in an unnatural bow. I saw a buckle and a brass nameplate, the remains of a collar. Which led to the ashes of a lead. Which led to something worse. A human body, small and huddled. It was barely a corpse.

More like an outline in lumps and patches, a sort of fossil you might brush and trowel to picture the original in relief.

The outline of a child with cramped limbs. The skull appeared crushed by falling flowerpots, but as I peered from left and right, I saw the injury's not due to heat or debris. There's a hole in the forehead and a ragged chunk of bone hanging off the back. Which left little doubt about the cause. I moved back to survey the scene, to find the regularity and order.

Addie called, "What've you found?"

Boy scurries into the metal framework. To hide? Elphinstone lights the lamp, looks under the shelves, crouches, levels the gun. I copied, turned, pointed my fingers at the bricks in line with the boy's head. Found a half-inch ball from an Adam's Dragoon buried in the mortar. I turned back, studied the shapes. The boy falls, traps the lead beneath him. Elphinstone starts the fire, the dog throttles itself trying to escape the flames. I whispered, *"Why kill the child?"*

Except I must've spoken aloud because Addie said, "What's that?"

I reached for the dog's nameplate. Blew on it. Buffed it. Read, *"Skipper," 50 Market Place, Brentford.* Then I shuffled down the bricks to the telegraph plant, turned to come down the flagstones.

A voice outside shouted, *"Who goes there?"*

What happened next probably took two minutes but to me it could've been forever, or the blink of an eye. I couldn't say because I don't recall it in time. Only in actions and voices and growing horror.

THREE MEN WERE walking quickly across the grass, maybe thirty yards away, fanning out to confuse Barak. He shouldered his rifle, aimed at the centre man. He should've fired, but the man's in an army tunic, moving like a soldier. Like most Indians, Sepoys are seasoned to fear whites. Their business might be killing, but not white soldiers. That's a court martial offence.

I nearly ducked behind the flowerbed, out of sight. But Addie's outside, watching, so I kept going, stepped out next to her.

She's got her carpet bag in one hand, the other clasped to her mouth as if seeing what'll happen next. The man on the right raises his arm like a crane jib, aiming a revolver at Basak. When the heavy Enfield swings his way, the man on the far left, shoulders a cavalry carbine, fires. A ragged hole and a spray of blood pop in the back of Basak's tunic, followed by a chime of falling glass. Basak drops his rifle and falls on his back, slightly propped on his elbows. He stares in shock at the dark patch creeping over the front of his tunic.

The man in the middle draws a revolver, walks within a couple of paces of Basak's prone body, points the gun at the Sepoy's head.

I shout, *"No!"*

A mistake. It says I care; the man can make a point. He aims, like dispatching an injured horse. I'm thinking, *no insignia, square shoulders, the hair, the eyes, the pug nose* – it's the man who inquired after Elijah Doyle at the Bank.

Basak looked up confused, then terrified. He opens his mouth to speak or scream but nothing comes because the shooter fires. The sentry's head kicks back, falls heavily on the grass. His body jerks, heels hammer on the turf as he's marching double-time to heaven. Then he's still forever, a brown cheek resting in the green blades. The shot echoes, birds squawk. The gun points at me.

The two men with revolvers regrouped: the killer in front of me the other behind. The latter shoved me a few paces from Addie, thumped the back of my legs to I dropped to my knees. He pushed the gun into the nape of my neck. The killer crouched, shoved a gun barrel under my chin, lifting my gaze up to his. I've lost control of the situation, no idea what to do. My heart pumped harder.

"This is simple, Pandy," the man in front of me said. "I get the paper from Doyle's locker, you stay alive. Got it ... *bojha?*"

I swallowed, didn't want my voice cracking. "No idea what you're talking about," I said. Which isn't true. I know what he wants, and I know who's got it. I might even have told him if I didn't think he'd kill me anyway, because I might already have read the paper.

"Tch, tch!" he sighed. "Shoot him in the calf, Jack."

The revolver eased from the back of my neck.

"Wait!" I said. "You were at Henry Bullock's place, you killed him."

"Me?" He laughed. "Bastard killed himself!"

Which means these're the men Chrystal saw last night. The killer nodded at Jack to fire. I couldn't think what to do so I shut my eyes to wait for the blast.

"Let him alone, Meigs!" Addie called. "He doesn't have it."

"Stay out of this, Miss Doyle" said Meigs. "You had your chance at the Bank. Do it, Jack!"

"I've got the paper!" Addie yelled.

Which must be a lie.

"You?" Meigs said. "But–"

"Take it," Addie said. She walked forward, opening her bag, rummaging inside. "Trouble with you Khan, you're too free with your fists."

Which my fists seemed to understand before I did, because they balled up and my shoulders tensed. The rest happened in two acts.

First act: Meigs gawped at Addie; an explosion punched my left ear; I fetched Meigs a hard right that sent him spinning backwards so his gun flew in the air; a body and revolver thumped to the ground on my right.

I said, *"What happened?"*

After a dazed second, I saw Addie had pulled a pistol and shot Jack dead.

Second act: Meigs crabbed away in a supine skitter towards his revolver; Addie grabbed Jack's revolver and aimed it two-handed at Meigs.

"Stop!" she said, "Or I fire."

Meigs stopped. The way she stood, feet planted, arms outstretched and easy like a marksman, said the only question was which eye she'd put the bullet through. The third man dropped his discharged carbine, slid a hand towards a revolver on his belt.

Addie flicked her eyes at him, shook her head. Meigs did the same. "Fetch their guns, Khan," she said.

Meigs said, "Hiding behind the memsahib's skirts, Pandy?"

Can't say that didn't sting, but it's no time for heroics. So I collected the guns, put them in her carpet bag, picked up my bag too. I'd noticed we're only fifty yards from a wooden door in the high brick wall flanking Richmond Road.

As we backed away, Addie said, "Doctor Khan doesn't have the paper you want. Nor do I."

I'm wondering how to get through the wooden door – fire at the bolt, maybe? Climb over? But the problem solved itself because a key scraped in the lock from the other side. The door opened and two Sepoys shoved a barrow in.

"Major Elphinstone send you for the evidence?" I said.

They nodded, confused. I hiked a thumb over my shoulder. "Back there." We pushed past, turned left and hurried up Richmond Road. After about fifty yards, we tossed the guns over the wall, headed for Kew Bridge.

Sixteen

WE WALKED IN silence past Kew Green. The questions and anger boiling in my head left me speechless ... till I heard myself say, "No more shows at East India Dock, then."

Addie glanced at me, fearful the violence had turned my brain.

"You shot Hydraulic Jack."

"What?"

"Best hydraulic crane-driver in England," I said, "so Chrystal says. Does roundabout rides for the kids, juggles rum barrels to amuse their parents."

"He'd have given you a ride to the morgue if I hadn't saved your skin."

"There's that," I said. Which is why I hadn't ditched her already. Just as if I'd seen that pistol in her bag I'd have taken or unloaded it.

In another minute, I said, "You know Meigs, then?"

"Know *of* him. I've seen him around East India House, that's all."

"What business d'you have there?"

She just looked at me as if I'm an idiot, as usual.

On Kew Bridge the dam burst. A lot louder than I'd intended, I said, "You *knew* that paper was missing, *knew* they'd come looking for it. Good God, Addie, there're two dead men back there, I was nearly one of them!"

"I *didn't* know."

We stopped to face each other.

"So what's that about you having your chance at the Bank?"

"I just ... didn't know–"

"You're a damn liar!"

"I'm not!"

"Explain it then, *go on!*"

"*Explain what?*"

"Why you want the cigar case back, feigned tears at your father's death when you're really after a damning document? If you'd been straight with me that young Sepoy might still be alive!"

"I *was* straight–"

"Or is it *you* the paper condemns, your guilt about your father's–"

"*No!*" She glared, furious. "You've no idea what you're saying."

"You're pretty cold for someone who just shot a man dead."

"*How dare you criticize me!*" she shouted.

We fell quiet. Her lip trembled and tears rolled down her cheeks, but she still stared defiantly, as if the emotion's a side-show. Folk were watching and giving us a wide birth, so I took her arm, tried to pull her to the stone balustrade. She yanked it away, stood beside me looking upriver. We pretended to study the sunny greens and blues, the distant stacks of timber and brick in the new Brentford dockyard. Both wondering who'll speak.

She turned, said, "Tell me something about *you*. A secret burning in your heart. That won't let you go. One you've never told, never will again."

It wasn't a question. More like a sentry shouting, *"Who goes there?"* Like the singular wait while a flipped coin spins on its edge.

Still looking upriver, I said, "I'm not the bastard son of a Company officer. I'm the bastard son of Mubarak Ali Khan, the late Nawab of Bengal."

A shadow of sadness crossed her face. Was that the best I could do? Tell her a lie, or something Bea already knew. I'd failed. She stood a little hunched, hugging herself, as if I'd wounded her. I said, "She wasn't a whore, my mother. She was a native Santal, a business-woman, a trader, an artist in dyed silk whose exquisite coats and saris pleased the Nawab."

Addie looked at me, flashed a brief, sarcastic smile. *So what?*

"He paid her well, but ... like any courtier she had to serve his wishes."

"You mean ... but the *Bengal Obituary* says–"

"I'm Captain McKay's son? My mother put me in his service. He claimed paternity to get me an English education at the Orphan School."

Addie was surprised, as much by the error in her paper world as that my princely title wasn't just a lie. I could've told her a lot more about McKay she'd never find on paper. But I'm circling what I want to say, trying to ease my toe into an icy bath. "My life's a before and after," I said, "Like BC and AD."

"Before and after what?" she said, curious now.

I told her about my village, the walk to the silk factory, the hanging bodies and the rape. Our sullen march to Murshidabad. The Nawab's school. "I lost my mother twice. She died of cholera, but the soldiers took her spirit. Took her from me." Now I turned to look in her eyes. "Seven years in a garden of Eden, that's how seems. Then we're driven out, reborn in misery, to ..."

"To what?"

"I don't know ... an unlikely journey, one a Santal boy couldn't imagine. It makes sense for a while, then ..." – I shrugged – "it doesn't. I think my mother knew ... at least, that's what I tell myself, because it makes her feel close, as if she's watching. But ..." I shrugged again.

Addie looked concerned, as if she's about to throw some light in my darkness, might unpick the puzzle. She said, 'Did you find them?"

"Them?"

"The soldiers! The ones who raped your mother?"

"Well, no ... I never ..."

"Whyever not?" She spat the words, as if I should be ashamed.

"I was seven ... by the time I left the orphan school, joined Calcutta society, it seemed ... an age ago, like a myth or some other life. They were devils ... demons from another world."

"You know their regiment, their rank."

I nodded, told her.

"How old?"

"Men ... but ..." She'd staggered me, crashed my past into my present, upturned my world more than the shooting with Meigs. I shut my eyes, saw the awful scene as I hadn't before. Not a vivid horror, but as O'Shaughnessy might see it ... forensically. "They were ... around thirty, certainly under forty."

She nodded. Didn't need to say, *twenty years, more or less ... still alive, living where? Perhaps in London?* Which made me shiver, wonder why it took a stranger on this bridge to make me think of it. Like Chrystal saying my mother wanted revenge. Was that it ... I'm supposed to slaughter her attackers like rabid dogs?

"No," I said. "She wanted ... better." And then, "My people are beaten and swindled every hour of every day. God knows, the Company killed enough of them in the Hul. Burned whole villages. What's a woman's fate to that?"

"Your *mother*, Doctor?" She came closer. "You make scopes to catch criminals, but not your mother's rapists ... the men who took the life from her eyes?"

She looked back upriver. I nearly hurled her own words at her – *How dare you criticize me!* – except I'm not sure who I'm angry with. In any case, she cut me off, said in a matter-of-fact way, "My mama shot my papa dead, with his own flintlock rifle."

"An accident?" I said, though it obviously wasn't.

"Oh no ... he'd showed her how to do it."

I didn't think the dare was just for me. I'd partly told my story because I hoped she'd tell me hers, about the witch in the fairytale.

"Captain Ochterlony?" I said.

"Mama said he was a good man until the last Maratha war. But he wasn't. Handsome, yes. Witty, certainly. A good dancer. But John Ochterlony was crazy from the start, bent on making his mark and his fortune. It's why he joined the Company and went to India. Came back a cripple. Worse, he came back an embittered drunk on a stingy pension, wanting someone to blame."

"Embittered?"

"Led the Bombay Infantry at the Battle of Koregaon–"

I whistled. "That was bloody, but a hell of a victory for the Company. Gave it most of India."

"Company got India. Other white officers got gold and a leg up to senior ranks ... governorships. Even the native soldiers were made grenadiers–"

"Even?" I said, "They did most of the fighting."

"I ... I meant, that's how he saw it. He got a walking stick and a withered arm. Couldn't aim a rifle, so he taught me and mama to shoot, in case of dacoits."

"Dacoits?" I nearly laughed. "On a farm in Buckinghamshire?"

"He had ... irrational fears. Some days he thought he was in India, couldn't defend his family as a man should. Everybody round about knew it. Anyway, the drink destroyed his wife's love. When he'd bruised her once too often, they took to separate beds, and in his ... loneliness, he lay with me, as a wife. I was twelve."

She looked at me, wanting a reaction.

I said, *"Huh!"* because I couldn't think of anything else. I thought about McKay, but I wouldn't tell her that, even though I felt I should ... not that.

"Huh?" she echoed looking back upriver.

"So, your mother shot him?"

"Not right away. She tried pity, reason, shame ... when nothing moved him, she acted. The Captain – so we called him – kept the house locked and bolted, said we'd the right to shoot anyone who tried to break in. Well, each year he went to Company dinners in London – military reunions – went by railway from Banbury."

"Thought he loathed the army."

"Oh, he did. That's why he paraded his injuries, what he called his impoverishment ... rubbed their noses in it and drank at their expense. So Mama wrote a fake invitation on Company paper. The

Captain went off expecting to be away overnight but when he found no reunion, no room booked, he came back on a late train in a foul temper. Started thumping on the front door threatening murder. Mama'd done the geometry ... fired a shot through the door and the Captain's heart ... just as he'd always told her to."

After a respectful pause, I said, "Fooled the coroner?"

"Of course. She burnt the invitation. Played the distraught widow so well it even fooled me for a while. Folk pitied her – a mad, crippled husband who'd taught her to fear intruders, put a deadly weapon in her hands. Anyway, she's Sir Reginald Clyde's sister, my father's social superior."

I thought it over for a while, from a forensic point of view.

"When did she burn the invitation?"

"Before he left. She jotted a memorandum in his hand on a scrap as if he'd made the thing up himself, stuck it in his pocket. The coroner believed it."

I nodded. It's pretty much foolproof, even if you had suspicions.

"And so you learned to deal with men who threaten you?"

"Me ... or mine. Quite so."

WE STOOD QUIET. I knew she hadn't told me the whole truth about Meigs or the Bank. But she'd saved my life. It was Meigs who'd driven Henry to suicide, who I should've shoved face down in the Palm House pool till he told me who'd sent him: Slegman, Clyde or Birdwood? Instead, I'd picked on a brave woman.

Addie still had tears on her cheeks. I passed her a handkerchief. She nodded, took off her glasses and dried her eyes. Looked more like the woman I'd glimpsed behind the calculating engine in Simpson's Tavern.

She said, "I haven't risked your life. Nor anyone else's. There're things I can't tell you, but it's better if we work together." She turned. "You see, I loved my stepfather, very much. I *must* know who killed him. And why."

I'd touched a nerve earlier. "You feel you're somehow to blame?"

She gave me a searching look, judging if I'm worth an explanation. Then, "I told you he wanted a son, but it's not so. I tell folk that, to ... explain myself. Truth is my education was a sort of experiment."

"Women can learn as well as men?"

"More ... all rational beings, *even* women, will recognize Christianity as the true religion?"

"I've tried three," I said. "Seemed much the same to me."

"Oh, yes. But he thought God revealed himself by the order in creation."

"You mean science?"

"Natural law."

"Like gravity–"

"Yes ... but more like, animals, living machines. They must've been designed and made ... by God."

"Hmm ... but, why the Christian God?"

"I think ... that's assumed," she said.

"God the father... the Son and Holy Ghost ... I never understood that."

"Well, it's ..." She didn't like things she couldn't explain. "Anyway, I had to study everything as a child ... materialism, atheism, socialism, the free association of the sexes ... but *reason* was supposed to bring me to Christianity."

"Only it didn't." I said, with more sarcasm than I'd meant."

"I'm my own woman. Mama and the Captain saw to that."

"A free spirit with a pistol and a deadly aim?"

She ignored me, said, "My circle at Bedford College rejected the *Bible*. We learned Anna Wheeler's *Pretensions of Men to Retain Women in Slavery*, by heart." She raised her head, declaimed to the river, "'*Women of England! Degraded, Awake! Contemplate the happiness that awaits you when all your faculties shall be fully cultivated.*' But a woman can't *Awake!* if she marries, relies on a man." She shook her head. "My stepfather meant well, paid for my education. But in the end, I disappointed him. He was ashamed, humiliated by what I became."

"Should've been proud," I said, rather limply.

"*Pah!* Men loathe women in business. Especially the successful, educated ones, who make them feel stupid. Believe me."

"We've that in common, then. Aliens in a white man's land."

She gave me a curious look as if she'd never thought about 'white' and 'man' like that. She nodded slowly to say she'd need to give it some thought. I used the pause to fish out the brass nameplate, held it in the flat of my hand.

"Found this among the flowerpots," I said.

"Fifty, Market Place," she read. "Isn't that near where Yashoda lives?"

"She's number five. We need to call, find out who else knew about Artemisia. On the way I'll tell you what I found in the Museum Stove, on one condition. You tell me *what* Slegman, Clyde and Birdwood are."

"And my stepfather?"

"Soon as I've seen Sir George this evening. I promise."

I got the calculating stare. She nodded, picked up her bag and walked with me over the bridge. "By the way," I said, "if you're Addie, I'm Hyder."

"Pleased to meet you, Hyder," she said, as if we're starting again.

"Likewise, Addie."

"Still partners?"

"We're a good team," I said. "Still need each other's help."

I wasn't sure what to make of Adelaide Doyle. She wants my trust. That's for sure. It's why we'd traded solemn secrets, why she'd told me about her fathers. Finding out how Elijah died clearly means more to her than loyalty to Uncle Reginald. I can trust her while I've information she wants – like the European balance of power, or the Company and the Mughal princes it's pensioned off in India. A matter of mutual self-interest.

But it felt like more than that. I liked her, shared her sense of alienation from the world, her need to fight prejudice every day to stay alive. It made her forthright, an acute analyst of the world – sharp in observation, blunt in expression ... like me. Or is that just what I want to believe? Will she betray me when she's got what she wants? I'll stay alert for a change of wind, see what happens.

I'D HAVE THOUGHT a lot more about meeting Yashoda if I'd known exactly where she lived. But I didn't, so walking up Kew Road I told Addie what I'd found in the Gardens. By the time we turned left down the High Street, I was struggling to follow *what* Slegman, Clyde and Birdwood are. Her explanation was so full of charters and acts – *vide* statute this, *Victorii* that, sentences beginning 'Whereas'– that I stopped her and said, "Can you explain it for a man you're making feel stupid?"

She rolled her eyes. "The Company runs India *for* the British Parliament. But since the Company appoints the civil and military officers, *it* rules India, *de facto.*" She paused. "Too *technical* for you?" I rolled mine. "However," she continued, "Parliament *alone* can make war or peace or annex Indian land and suchlike. In which case it still acts via the Company. But." She raised a finger like an altar bell for a sacred rite. "Parliament won't make *all* the Company's eighteen directors privy to its plans."

"Because it'd be all over the newspapers in no time?"

"Partly. But foreknowledge of Imperial action's a valuable commodity. Which is why Parliament deals with just three directors, all bound by a solemn oath of secrecy. Namely the Chairman, the deputy Chairman and the Senior Director ... known together as the Secret Committee, which is currently–"

"Slegman, Clyde and Birdwood?"

"That's right. It's a political capillary, a tight channel of power."

"Whose dispatches have the dual authority of Parliament *and* Company?"

She nodded, and I whistled like a winter gale. No wonder Uncle Reginald was useful to her business, that she spent time at East India House.

"Mind you," she said, turning abruptly to go north over the High Street, "it's a miracle they agree on anything long enough to draft a dispatch."

"How so?" I called, nodding apologies to a veering cabby.

"Religion. Poles apart. Take Hastings Birdwood ... he's a retired Company colonel and Senior Director, fat, over seventy, used to be an atheist. Then he's caught having a threepenny-upright with a dollymop in Leadenhall Market. My stepfather *saved* him, for Christ. Now their creed's Matthew 24."

"Matthew 24?" I'm thinking: *why Leadenhall Market?* Admiring how Addie lets every phrase sing in its own vernacular.

"Evangelicals," she said. "'*Preach the gospel in all the world; then shall the end come.*' Their business is converting natives, the fast line to eternal bliss. Which makes the Company–"

"Jesus ... unlimited, whatever it costs."

"Just so. But the natives have to see the flyer before HE comes with HIS flaming sword to save subscribers. It's why they fund legions of missionaries, like salesmen hawking carpet bags. Then there's Nathanial Slegman, the Chairman. Ugly, but well dressed. His Christ is the moving spirit of capital, his God the great magistrate in the sky – all seeing, all knowing, sending all from captain to cabin boy to hell if they don't serve progress and profit. He'd prefer the natives Christian, English speaking, but not if it brews mutiny."

I loved the vignettes, even though it irked me her wit was sharper than mine. It's worth it to hear the Company titans stripped bare.

"And Clyde," I said, "your uncle?"

"*Pah!* Uncle Reginald? He's tall and lean, handsome, they say. Sees high Anglicanism as his private club – strictly for gentlemen, ideally from Eton and Oxford. Doesn't give a damn what natives believe as long as the Company buys his quinine. Can't abide worship with the lower orders, let alone blacks." She glanced at me. "Well, you asked!"

"Not fond of missionaries, then?"

"Scoundrels, out for themselves. The three go hammer and tongs at Court meetings, especially over quinine. My stepfather sends end-less memos on shipping cinchona plants from Peru to India, which sets them arguing over the Company's duty to the natives."

I pondered all that as I looked out for Brentford market. The High Street crosses its south side. We ought to see it shortly.

I said, "What if one of them forged a dispatch?"

She looked at me as if I'd asked her to waltz the rest of the way.

"I'm serious," I said. "What if?"

"Impossible. Even if they faked the signature and seal, the admin-istration in Calcutta would reply, reveal the forgery."

I wasn't so sure. "At the very least it could take months."

"Yes, but it'd be ... treason–"

"Elphinstone's words – *treason, dispatch*. Almost in the same sentence."

She wasn't convinced. But she squinted, the way she does. Gave me a resentful stare, as if I shouldn't've put that thought in her mind. All the while she twiddled a gold ring on her right hand. I might've pushed it further if we hadn't reached the Red Lion Inn at the corner of the market square.

THE MARKET PLACE is a square, edged by brick houses with a central villa that looks like a new town hall. Probably packed twice a week on market days, but now it's baking quietly in the sun. Next to the Inn going north is a Post Office, just as Hooker said. We stood in front, eyeing a dark alley down one side. I looked round the square for number fifty, where the dead boy had lived. Where a mother's life's about to be broken. Should I tell her? Once the Sepoys took away the evidence in the cart there'd be no trace of the child or the dog.

"Let's try the alley," I said.

Addie nodded. She's still pensive, still wondering about a forged dispatch. "The alley," she said, as if it's the last place she'd like to go in a white-cotton dress and a pair of kidskin ankle-boots. It led us to a cobbled yard of workshops and what Bea would call *slum dwellings*. There're carts and barrows standing on the stones, a strong smell of malt in the air. A distant hammer tink-tinked on something iron.

Addie pointed to a door with peeling maroon paint. The exposed wood was grainy, weathered by the decades. It's number 5A, which made a *ring-a-ding* in my head. Painted below in yellow letters was, Yashoda's Florist and Herbalist, under that a hand-written card, OPEN.

A dark staircase went left to a first-floor landing where the bolted doors seemed to murmur, *Piss off!* Up another staircase we found another door that opened into an airy room. Inside, light streamed from a glass roof into a half-florist, half herbalist's shop.

The walls were shelved with jars of herbs whose fragrance made me giddy for Bengal. Potted plants grew on tables under the glass roof. At the back were watering cans and the metal apparatus you'd find in an apothecary's shop. An Indian woman emerged from a back room, went behind a counter in front of a leaded-glass bookcase. She's wearing a red and cream saree with matching head scarf. A myrrh-scented bamboo stick smouldered on the counter.

"How may I help you?" The heavy accent sang with crystal diction. It was masculine, like her gaze, compassionate and tough.

"Yashoda?"

"As it says on the door."

She's slender, late in middle age. The scarf cast a shadow that made her eyes seem black. Her face was hollow, weather-beaten as her front door. I went to the counter, pressed my palms to make the Hindu greeting, *"Namaste."* Then, London style, offered my card. Her fingers were artistic, roughened by work.

"I wasn't expecting anyone today," she said.

In Hindi, I said, "Because of the uprising?"

She just looked me up and own, replied in Hindi, "What brings you here, son of Mubarak Ali Khan?" She thinks I'm a Muslim baboo, either an idle prince, or a native clerk, aping the whites, taking pay for a cheap seat at the Imperial table. If she knew I'm a Santal she'd likely throw me out. To a high caste Hindu, we're untouchables, savages.

"What brought *you*, Yashoda ji?"

She hesitated, then, "I've no beard or moustache."

"Women can't practice medicine here either."

"I sell flowers." She looked at Addie, standing uneasily by the door. Slums and peeling paint aren't her world. "This woman needs my help?" Yashoda said.

Why else would a black prince bring a smart white woman here?

"We need your help," I said.

"What're you saying?" Addie asked.

In English, Yashoda said, "You need my help?"

Addie said, "What on earth do you mean by that?"

Which is when I saw two things: a china bowl on the floor and a broomstick with a horse's head – a hobby horse. I heard *ring-a-ding* and felt sick in my stomach. I dug in my pocket, cupped the dog nameplate in my palm, rubbed it – not *5o*, it's *5a*. I held my forehead, turned away and said, *"Ahw!"*

Both women stared. I went to Addie, held out my palm, murmured, "It's here." She said, *"Ah,"* and shut her eyes. Yashoda said, "What?"

I opened my mouth, but the words stuck in my throat, too brutal to utter. I went and held out the blackened nameplate. Yashoda looked at it, then at me. She's confused ... then clinging to scraps of doubt. But as she took the plate in her long fingers the wrinkles in her face deepened.

"A fire," I said, "in the Museum Stove. We investigated–"

"Rosie?"

Our eyes met ... hers pleading ... mine full of sympathy. For some reason I'd assumed the dead child was a boy. I nodded. "I'm afraid, Rosie's ... that is, she didn't ... survive."

Yashoda stared as if I'd spoken in Chinese, not because she didn't understand, because she didn't want to. Didn't want this news. "What do you mean?" she said. "Coming here, *with this nonsense!*" She covered her face.

I couldn't say the girl was murdered. Not then. But I didn't want to say she'd burnt to death either. "She died instantly," I said. "Didn't suffer."

"In a *fire?*"

"She was shot."

"Shot?"

Then she believed it. Gasped as if I'd slapped her. She folded her arms tight round her body and staggered back against the bookcase. The leaded glass rattled, and I hurried round the counter thinking she'd faint. Addie did the same the other side. But Yashoda found her feet, put out her palms to keep us at bay. We stood like that for half a minute, her breathing deeply, finding her poise. Then she lifted her chin, pushed past me and hurried to the door.

I chased her. "Where're you going? *Yashoda!*"

I caught her by the wrist on the landing.

"Let go! I'm going to my child."

"You won't get in! The Gardens are shut, guarded."

She pulled, glared at me furious and accusing, as if it's my fault. Which I understood, because in a way it was. If I hadn't told Elphinstone about the chlorophyll – *probably from a plant* – he'd never have come. She yanked her wrist away, looked down at my card. This time she read it more carefully.

"Who *are* you?" she said. "The police? You don't look like police."

"I'm a doctor and a chemist. There was a fire this morning in the Museum Stove. I was told to investigate." When she looked at Addie, unconvinced, I said, "My assistant, an artist."

"Why'd you come here, to me?"

"You had to be told." It's a decent lie.

Yashoda gave me a pitiful stare. I'd brought such dreadful news, but she's grateful I'd bothered. She went back into the shop, led us to a parlour at the rear. The room's a jumble of Indian items she'd found in London. As we sat at a small table, Addie's eyes lit on a shrine with a woodcut of the goddess Kali – eyes fierce, tongue red, holding a severed head. Addie reached out, then clasped her hands and sat down. Mindful of her abrupt words earlier, she said, "I ... we're very sorry to bring the news your daughter's dead."

"My child," Yashoda said, "Not my daughter."

"Your child?"

"I took her in. Gave her Skipper as a friend, taught her to tend plants in the Stove. She felt safe there, in her own world."

I said, "If she'd heard a stranger coming, would–"

"Rosie heard nothing. She was deaf. 'Daft Rosie,' they called her because she barely spoke ... easily led into foolishness, or worse. No lullabies sang her to sleep." Yashoda looked to the shrine where she seemed to find comfort. "Rosie was blameless, of good Kama. Her atman – what you'd call her spirit – is one with Brahman, the infinite atman." She held the nameplate tight. "Kali Ma sent her to me. Now she's taken her, as fire becomes fire."

We sat quiet, Addie and I exchanging glances. *Do we leave? Stay?* I had questions, but I didn't want to intrude on Yashoda's grief, as if we'd only come for information. But then she looked straight at me.

"Why?" she said. "Why would someone kill a child?"

I didn't know. Rosie could've identified Elphinstone, but Hooker knew he'd been to the Stove. What else could she have seen? I took out a sprig of Artemisia, put it on the table. "I think they came for this," I said.

"A plant? My child died ... for a plant?"

"It's said to cure malaria."

Yashoda rubbed the leaves in her palm, smelt the scent. "It's good for *vishama jwara*, the wrath of Rudra, which Shiva commanded to become fever. It restores the doshas."

Addie looked lost, so I said, "Rudra's the Hindoo God of storm. In Ayurvedic medicine the doshas are a bit like humours, have to be balanced." Then, to Yashoda, "Joseph Hooker said you didn't believe in its power."

"I didn't know the plant then, gave no opinion. I've used it since for indigestion, some fevers."

"What if it contains a powerful drug, as cinchona does quinine? Something equally effective for malaria."

"Then it'll be of benefit in India."

"Papa tried to grow Cinchona there," Addie said, "hoped to provide quinine for the natives at a rupee a dose."

"Natives?" Yashoda said. "Was your ... *Papa* a Company–"

"If there *was* a cure," I said, changing direction, "how might you test it in London?" I'd thought of that in Hunter House. Calcutta's a long way from here, and Henry never left the City unless he really had to. He must've had reason to think Artemisia worked, smelt money. Lots.

Yashoda wouldn't be deflected, "Company servant? Your ... Papa?"

"What's wrong with that? He believed it his Christian–"

"*Pah!* Quinine steadies the Company sword. You British stirred up fever, digging up the land for crops and roads, for railways, driving the holy Ganges through canals. No wonder the Gods visit distemper on the land–"

"They're works of progress, of civilization–"

"Yours, not ours! The uprising will drive you from our land!"

Addie looked away, literally bit her tongue. She got up, said, "I'm sorry for your loss, Yashoda." Then, to me, "I'll wait for you outside, Hyder." She left the shop, quietly closed the outer door.

Yashoda glared, defying me to take a side. I didn't disagree. The Company *had* dug up the land, might've disturbed all kinds of vile miasma. But insulting Addie wouldn't change that. "Miss Doyle meant no disrespect," I said. "Her stepfather died violently this morning. She's upset."

Yashoda looked down. She regretted her sharp words, felt her own grief returning. I said, "I know it's an awful time, you don't feel like talking. But the man who killed Rosie ordered all trace removed. There'll be nothing but ashes. My report, my word's all we'll have. If you'd answer a couple of questions, it might help bring him to justice."

She looked up. *"Ordered?* What kind of man can give such orders?"

Which left me with nothing more plausible, less likely to catch me in a lie, than the truth. I said, "Major Raikes Elphinstone–"

"Elphinstone, that devil! I thought he hunted in Bengal?"

"Right now, he's doing someone's bidding in London."

"You'll bring *him* to justice?" she said, scorn turning to anger, "a Company major, the Governor General's bulldog? You? A native, a black? You're getting way above your station, doctor. Or are you just a liar?" Without letting me answer, she shouted, *"Get out!* And take that woman with you." Then, to herself, "No one cares about Rosie, they'll say she ran away."

I didn't get out. Couldn't let her dismiss me. Not like that. But she's right, no court in this land will bring Elphinstone to justice. My card lay in front of her on the table. I reached for it, wrote two sentences in Sanskrit on the back, slid it over. "Read," I said. She stared at me. *"Read!"* I commanded.

She read. Looked up, confused.

"It's the truth," I said. "I swear it."

She read again. Looked up and studied my eyes for what seemed an age. Then, she said, "What is it I can tell you?"

"Who knew about your work with Artemisia ... that it might cure fever?"

She thought. Shook her head. "No one apart from Rosie. But she couldn't ... oh, and there's Billy."

"Billy? Who's he?"

"A trainee gardener at Loddiges nurseries in Hackney. He wrote to the Director last year saying he's interested in medicinal herbs. Sir William agreed I'd train him in return for work in the Gardens. Billy stayed ... oh, three months. A serious character, hard worker."

"Did you mention Robert Fortune's letter, the miracle cure?"

"Yes ... but I told Billy I didn't believe it."

"Didn't Loddiges close last year? Sell off their stock?"

Yashoda nodded. "I've no idea where he is now."

"Hmm ... what's his surname?"

She closed her eyes. "Impey ... William Impey. But I can't see him and Elphinstone–"

"Neither can I. But could Billy have taken some plants?"

"No. I'd have noticed. Rosie certainly would. She knew every plant in the Stove, didn't like harvesting them even when we had to. But ..." She got up and went into the shop, came back with an air-tight jar. "The seeds," – she popped the lid – "they're tiny, you'd never miss a spoonful."

As I examined the jar, Yashoda went to dig in a sideboard drawer.

"A spoonful would be plenty," I said. "Are they hard to grow?"

"Sowing and watering require some care, so does temperature control. Otherwise, it's easy enough. They grow in a season, produce a lot of seed."

She came and stood next to me. I was wondering what else to ask when she took my hand and placed a coin in my palm. "For Miss Doyle," she said, closing my fingers. "Please give her my condolences." Then she sat in her chair and closed her eyes. I got up to leave. Quietly, I said, *"Phir milenge,"* – till next time – and walked across the shop. I'd opened the outer door when a voice said, "The Dreadnought."

I turned back. "The what?"

"The Dreadnought hospital ship," Yashoda said, "moored off Greenwich. That's where you'll find malaria. Where they quarantine sailors, sick and dying of tropical diseases. Ask for Henry Rooke, the apothecary. He's consulted me often enough on Asian remedies."

"Henry Rooke. Thank you–"

"Doctor Khan ... I have your word? You'll avenge my child."

"It's as I've written. No more. No less."

I left, closing the door behind me.

D OWNSTAIRS, ADDIE SAID, "Do you often do that?"

"Do what?"

"Make promises you can't keep."

"What like?"

"Bringing Elphinstone to book."

"Not me, *us*. We're partners, remember?"

"But–"

I lifted a hand to say, *quiet, let me think.* I've got the answers for Sir George. The problem is, I've got religion too as the American missionaries say, like you get a cold. Nothing I can do about it. The Thakur expects me to do more than dodge the gallows, so I've made a plan to get my trunk of evidence back. Not a complete plan ... more like a sketch for a flying machine: I've got the steam engine, the wings and the propeller. I'm just not sure where all the coupling rods and levers go. Or if it'll fly.

It certainly won't without Addie's help, no question about that.

She said, "But–"

I raised the hand again.

She said, "You're *very* annoying, Hyder. Do you know that?"

"That story we told Hooker, about a Whig Parliament hating the Company, a scandal in London tipping the balance. Is it true?"

"Well ... perhaps. Does it matter?"

"Oh yes. Because there's not one mystery here, Addie. There're two. The first's the liquid Elphinstone gave me. That's solved, except for an important question – does the drug work? With a bit of luck, I'll have an answer to that this evening." She made to object, but

I held up my hand up again. "The second's the sheet of paper you came to collect this–"

"I didn't! I came for the cigar case–"

"What did Meigs mean, then?"

She sighed. "All right. It didn't take long for East India House to hear of my stepfather's death. By nine o'clock, I'd a condolence note from the Company which included an urgent request that I empty his locker and return any confidential Company papers. That's all I knew."

"And the cigar case?"

"Didn't see it as confidential–"

"Until?"

"I left you after lunch. I mentioned the case to a Company director."

"Who?"

"Un-hah. That's my business."

"It's the key to you stepfather's death."

"Oh, please," she said. "Don't take me for a fool."

"I'm banking on the fact you're not," I said.

Seventeen

WE WALKED IN silence up Brentford High Street, looking south over the river at the trees in Kew Gardens. Both weighing things up, weighing up each other. Outside the telegraph office at Kew Bridge Station, I said, "Don't suppose you know the Home Secretary's electric address?" She gave me a look to say this crossed a line, then scribbled on a corner of notepaper, tore it off.

I sent three telegraphs: one to a doctor at Greenwich Hospital, including the cost of a messenger and a reply; one summoning Chrystal to the Old Coffeepot at Newgate Market at six o'clock; the last telling Sir George to expect me at the Home Office at eight thirty.

Outside Addie's reading the *Evening News.* We had a brief spat when the London train pulled in. She'd bought a first-class ticket, wouldn't sit with me in second. We settled on an empty, first-class compartment, sat opposite each other on finely upholstered settees by windows with little curtains.

I looked out. She read the paper.

When I'd done my weighing up, I took a magnet and the cigar case from my bag. Addie hadn't seen inside the case. I opened it, pointed to the Company's inscription and offer of fifty pounds reward. "See that?"

She looked over the paper. "Why, it's the cigar case. You said–"

"I lied. See the inscription? Why's it worth all that?"

She just frowned and slowly shook her head.

"Watch." I touched the magnet, pinched the hinges to let the false lid drop.

"Oh!" she said, as with the Chemiscope. She's genuinely surprised or she missed her vocation as an actress.

"Now what d'you say?"

She took the case and thumbed a cogwheel, watched the counters above cycle the letters. "It's a sort of ... alphabetical calculator," she said.

I put the page of scribble on my knee. "Your stepfather was working on this when he died. Now, the machine has two rows of six counters." I tapped the groups of words on the sheet in turn. "Four groups of three words. Each word, six letters long. Each group has one word above, two below, like a pyramid. The top words are legible, the two below, nonsense. I'd say he was–"

"Deciphering a message. Or trying to."

"Trying to ... that's what I thought. The message Meigs wanted."

"That's a guess."

"Inference ... but the message must've been on the table in the Bank vault. So where is it now?"

"Someone must've taken it."

"*Uh-ha.* Elphinstone spoke of a *treasonable* dispatch, worse than anything Britain's enemies could dream up. *Worse than.* Which means it wasn't an enemy, it was–"

"A Company Servant," she said, eyes widening like a rabbit spotting a fox. Or like a woman who's just realized a forged dispatch isn't a flight of fancy. "One of the Secret Committee."

"Does the Company encipher dispatches?"

"Yes, often. But I've never seen anything like this."

"What if your stepfather held on to the dispatch, kept it in his locker?"

She leafed through the newspaper, turned it to me, scrunching the page to mark a Stop-Press with her thumb. It read: *Chief Clerk Dragged From the River.* Beneath it said John Noad's body was found in the mud on Limehouse Reach at one o'clock. The writer suggested an accident or suicide and assumed lacerations on the corpse were due to a steamer paddle or propeller.

"Suicide?" I said, with a shiver. I'd likely have been dumped in the river myself but for Addie. "Meigs thought Noad took the dispatch?"

She nodded. "But you know who did, don't you?"

I nodded back. "That's why I'm going to open Henry Bullock's safe."

"A Double Door? Impossible. In any case, how could it be in there?"

I tapped my nose. "Suppose it was, eh? How could we read it?"

"Read it? A government document of the utmost–"

"Not if it's a forgery. And I bet it'll tell you why your stepfather died."

She looked as if the anchors of her life were pulling loose, letting her drift into a perilous sea. It's a feeling I know well. Then she shook her head, trying to concentrate.

"Well," she said, "we'd need to know the cipher they're using. She looked at the cigar case, turned it this way and that. "The mechanism's a clue, so are the groups of words."

"Yeah, I'd got that far."

"I use secret writing for confidential messages," she murmured. "I *think* this is a Vigenère cipher. And six cogs, suggests a six-letter keyword–"

"Keyword?

"To encipher and decipher the message."

I shook my head, none the wiser. She twisted her mouth, thinking.

"Imagine," she said, "each letter of the alphabet has a number, where A is naught, B is one, right through to Z is twenty-five. You chose a keyword, say, six letters long with no repeats. Write it under the first six letters of the message. Then each keyword-letter pushes the message-letter above, down the alphabet by its own numerical value." I must've looked blank because she said, "Suppose the first letter of a message is ... 'C.'"

"All right."

"And the first letter of the keyword is ... 'D'."

"With you so far."

"The letter 'D' has the number '3' in our scheme, therefore it pushes 'C' three letters down the alphabet to?"

"That'd be ... 'F'?"

"Right."

"What happens when you reach the end of the keyword?"

"You just repeat it, all the way to the end of the message."

"*Huh*, sounds simple when you put it like that."

"But effective ... unreadable without the keyword. You normally do it on paper with an alphabet square, but this machine makes it mechanical. Nothing written down." She peered, said, "*Ah!*" Slid a tiny knob in the brass plate. It hinged up, lifting the front six cogs from the back six. "Now all twelve counters can be set to any letter."

She studied the case and the scribble all the way from Barnes to Putney. At Putney Station she slid across the carriage, sat next to me. Laid the scribble in her lap and held the case so we could both see it.

"Let's start with the words," she said. "These legible ones," – she tapped *BENGAL, CHRIST, FATHER, JUDGES* – "are guesses at the keyword. Beneath each he deciphers twelve letters in groups of six. He gets nonsense, tries another keyword. Which means–"

"We know how the cipher works?"

"More than that. Because if this," – she dialed BENGAL into the front six counters – "is the first keyword, and this," – she dialed the six nonsense letters below into the back six – "is the deciphered message, then this," – she closed the brass plate reengaging the cogs, turned the front six counters back to 'A – "is the original'. The back six now read *USBEJP*.

Her nimble fingers worked like a weaving machine as she did the second six letters, repeated the process for the other groups, always getting the same result – *USBEJP DWIPEE*.

"It's nonsense," I said.

"It's in cipher. We'd need the actual keyword."

"Can you find it?"

"Find it? It's not a misplaced latch-key! Keywords protect the greatest secrets of the Empire. It's impossible."

"They said that about cracking dial-locks, then George Price did it with a bit of bent wire. Safer one way, more vulnerable another. Law of nature."

She sank into the upholstery. "You can't *crack* a cipher with bent wire."

I thought about that. "The Company sends dispatches to commanders all over the Empire. How many are there?"

"Dozens, perhaps hundreds."

"How long are they overseas?"

"Months ... years."

"Perhaps they're given a keyword before they leave."

"No. Each is unique to a message, never written down."

"Christ, father, judges," I said. "Your stepfather tried bible words."

She slowly nodded, touched her forehead and squeezed her eyes shut as if in pain. "You couldn't put a clue in the message itself," she whispered, "too risky. Can't rely on commanders recalling great lists of words, too unreliable. It must be ... methodical, systematic."

"Like a formula?"

"... but I can't see how."

She gave me a curious stare, then looked out at the fields of Battersea Park racing by the window. As if still absorbed by the scene, she said, "What exactly, will you tell Sir George this evening?"

Guessing a woman with her Company connections wouldn't want the dispatch mentioned, I said, "What he wants to hear."

"But surely you don't think," – she looked straight at me – "Green gives a damn about bottles or plants or malaria cures?"

"That's what Elphinstone asked–"

"Green thinks whoever ordered Bullock's torture also gave him the dispatch. That if you found the bottle's history, you'd find the traitor."

She raised her eyebrows, inviting me to agree.

"I want my death warrant torn up, that's all."

"You can do better than that. *If* we find the dispatch, *if* we can read it, I'd say we have a valuable commodity."

"To whom?"

"Whoever pays the most, of course."

"It's not money I want, it's a trunk."

"A trunk? What on earth–"

I told her briefly why I'd come to London, how I was tricked out of my trunk. She'd made me realize Sir George might pay well for anything damaging to the Company. Now I could see us fighting over this dispatch, arguing about who to sell it to. I said, "Surely you don't want the Company abolished, Addie?"

"Why not? They take the lion's share from India, throw me the scraps. Shut the Company it'll be a free for all, hordes of speculators, all chasing investment advice."

"Portfolios?"

She nodded. "We could work together, partners in India."

"Mutual self-interest? But we're a bit ahead of ourselves, no closer to finding this keyword."

"Not at all. You've got me thinking, but I'll work better in a library."

"A *library?*"

"Books ... words. It's how I navigate the world ... by alphabet and atlas, gazetteer and concordance. By title, by daily and weekly–"

"Yeah, I get it," I said, before we got to rule ninety-one. "Reading-room in the British Museum?"

She shook her head. "Closes at six. I prefer the London Library in St James Square. Open all hours, to subscribers."

"In all those books," I said, "can you find out who Henry Bullock's sister married? I think her name's Ethel or Enid. Something like that."

Addie nodded. "I'll try."

The train slowed, rumbled over the viaduct into Waterloo. Sooty brickwork and filthy windows coasted by the carriage. Addie packed the scribble and cigar case in her bag, which was fine by me. They're no use without the dispatch. Then a blur of passengers swathed in smoke and steam announced the platform. We got up, gathered our things.

"In March," I said, "I tried joining the East India Club. Got a letter saying my birth and nationality weren't *homogeneous* with other members."

"Well ... they're not."

"Being an East Indian isn't enough?"

"Being an English *woman* isn't enough for any London club. But what's that to do with anything?"

"Isn't the Club right next door to the London Library?"

"Is that *significant?*" she said, in a way that made it obvious it was.

I WENT STRAIGHT to the station telegraph office. It's just possible I'd have a reply from Greenwich. The clerk looked at me as if I'd inquired whether the mutineers had taken Calcutta yet, but he flicked through a box marked 'received,' shook his head. As I turned away, Addie tapped the glass, got the attention of a young télégraphiste at the back of the office. The young woman grinned, mouthed *"Adelaide!"* and came to an empty window at the counter.

They smiled, chatted, and I saw a different Addie. Someone younger and more girlish, not the hard-nosed intelligencer she'd become. The télégraphiste looked my way. "Can you read Bain's telegraphic code?" she mouthed. I nodded.

She went in turn to the clerks working the receivers until one tore off a paper strip. Cutting out the transcription saved ten minutes. The télégraphiste passed it to the clerk I'd spoken to. He checked the prepayment, gave me the tape. It's from the Dreadnought via Greenwich Hospital. I read it, laughed out loud. "Oh Henry," I said, "you old rascal."

Addie said, "What so amusing?"

Walking out of the station, I said, "'Bullock's Remedy.' Modesty wasn't Henry's strong suit. You read Bain's telegraphic–"

She plucked it from me, read as we walked: <<*Bullock enquired Dreadnought March '56 about malaria cases. African cabin boy close to death, too ill to swallow quinine. Treated by hypodermic syringe with 'Bullock's Remedy.' Sipping broth in hours, fever gone in 3 days. Prof. Doyle came to witness subsequent cases. Bullock then ceased contact. Rooke*>>

On Waterloo Bridge Road, I said, "That's how they knew, how they tested a malaria cure in London."

"But who paid for the trial in Calcutta Military Hospital?"

"Who indeed? That's the nub of it, the key to the whole business."

And I thought, *better do right by Yashoda.*

WE PUSHED OUR way along the busy pavement, round handcarts selling coffee and fruit, and said hello to Thorn who's waiting in the Lab, as instructed. She took a big bite from an apple, nodded back. I offered Addie a ride but said she'd hire her own carriage.

"How long," I said, "at the library?"

"An hour's enough."

"Then we talk, in confidence. You too, Thorn. And Chrystal."

"Why them?" Addie said.

"Thrums S?" said Thorn. "Secrets are safe there. Food's good too."

Addie said, "What's the thrums S?"

"Sans Souci Saloon, in St James Street," said Thorn. "It's a favourite with bishops and politicians. Some sirs and lords."

"Huh, never heard of it," Addie said. "Food *better* be good, I'm starving."

"Very select," said Thorn.

I nearly choked at that. But she's right, it's perfect for privacy. I waved an arm to attract a passing carriage.

"Meet me outside, Addie," I said. "A lady needs an escort. It's five minutes from the London Library."

I held the carriage door while she settled inside.

"The dispatch," she said. "You'll share it with me, no one else?"

I nodded, went to close the door. Addie held it open, said in a casual tone, "How do you know Lady Beatrice Motcombe?"

I smiled. "We made experiments together."

"No!" she gasped, as if it's a euphemism for some vulgar tryst.

"Really. She's interested in philosophical chemistry. We got as far as making hydrogen and oxygen."

Addie searched my face for a sign to say I'm joking. I pushed the door.

She pushed back, said quietly, "Only ... I wouldn't take her too seriously. She's a frightful gossip, you see?"

I remembered their exchange on Adelphi Terrace.

"Not with me," I said, pushed harder.

Addie resisted harder. She grasped the door's open window frame, drew herself nearer. "Not *with* you, perhaps ... but certainly, *about* you."

Which so astonished me, I said, *"What?"*

"You know her husband's planning to divorce her in the new year?"

I just stared, dumbfounded.

"You'll be cited, as co-respondent."

"As what?"

"Her adulterous lover. Just thought ... you should know."

She slammed the door making a face that said, *there, you think about that.* But as they pulled off, the face let in some worry. The bombshell dazed me so much I couldn't face Thorn. Instead, I ordered two mugs of milky coffee from a cart, gave myself a couple of minutes to find some calm. Then I climbed up next to her, passed a mug.

"All right, Boss?" She'd noticed.

I said, "You brought the jars and electric battery?"

"Inside, packed as you said. Wire too. Find anything useful at Kew?"

I took a breath, pushed Addie's poisonous words away. Then I told Thorn what'd happened at the Stove House and Yashoda's shop. Asked her to take us to Ivy Lane."

"What's there?" she said.

"I'm going to shift a mighty power."

Thorn threw the apple core in the gutter, passed me her mug.

"Like Archimedes, with his lever?" She flicked the reins.

"Nope. Weigh it against an equal power. Then a feather-weight shifts the balance."

"What featherweight?" she said, easing us into the traffic heading north.

"Bit of paper. It's why I need the chemical key to a Double Door safe."

At Waterloo Bridge, she pointed at the Feathers Tavern on the other side of the road, said, "Been seeing those all afternoon."

"What, pubs? You got a thirst on?"

"I'd say you've got a fight on." she said. "Match of the century?"

It's Mungo's flyer, pasted on the brickwork. Must be on hundreds of walls across London by now. Which brought back my promise to Yashoda. Made my guts churn.

"Just want my honour back," I said.

"Break someone's nose?"

"People die in prize fights."

Thorn glanced, a little anxious.

I said, "Mungo and Melrose made it a battle of the races, for money. Now it's a vendetta for a murdered child."

"You're the judge and jury?"

"Mainly executioner."

I'd told myself it's for Rosie. For Yashoda. But it's not. Not just for them. It's been coming since the gallows tree by the river Mor. Since I saw what Company soldiers did to my people's villages. Since

Elphinstone tortured me in the City Police Office, threatened to kill me. When Yashoda called me a liar, it was a challenge, one I had to accept or think myself a fraud.

"No sweat," I said. "The British Bulldog's an old man."

"I'll be there."

"You won't. You'll be outside the milliner's shop in St Martin's Lane, with a fast carriage and a strong pair raring to go. That's if I'm Imperial Champion."

"What if you're not, Boss?"

"You and Mungo can scrape me off the boards in the Rum-Pum-Pah club."

Part III

Crystallization

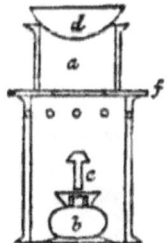

The figure exhibits a mode of slow evaporation :
b is the lamp, *c* the wick-holder, *f* the perforated
plate resting on the lamp cylinder and supporting
cylinder *a*. The solution to be evaporated is
marked *d*.

John Griffin, *Chemical Recreations*, 1860

Eighteen

NEWGATE'S THE BIGGEST meat market in London, filled with people and noise. The stalls are stylish, like long pavilions. Traders hurl their beasts into the basements, leave them crippled till it's time to slit their throats. You can hear them braying and whimpering and squealing. Upstairs the gutters run with blood, hundreds of carcasses hanging from steel hooks.

The place smells like a butcher's shop, which it is.

When I arrived a little after six it was closing up. People crowding into the pie shops and taverns to spend their earnings. The Old Coffee Pot's a favourite, already rammed. I didn't fancy shoving my way among county farmers and town butchers, so I flipped an urchin a halfpenny to fetch Chrystal for me. It took a while because the sergeant's off duty, wearing mufti.

When he finally came out, he grunted in his native burr, "I've answered yer summons, Khan, but I'm nae happy aboot it." He looked ridiculous. The rifle butt last night had broken his nose. It's taped with plaster, a purple bruise that paled to yellow at the edges spreading under his eyes and across his cheeks. I'd have made a joke if he hadn't got it defending me.

I led us to the wall on the market's east side. Behind it's a long row of terraced houses, one of which was Henry's. We stood between the wall and an empty wagon that smelt of straw and dung. Chrystal's still angry I'm acting for the Home Secretary, that I wouldn't share my findings this morning. Feels betrayed. But I haven't the time or patience to argue.

I said, "The ringleader in Henry's shop last night – man called Meigs, also inquired at the bank this morning."

Chrystal stared off to the south at the dome of St Paul's. "Aye. I thought I recognized him, along with Jack. How the hell'd you know about Meigs?"

"We had a chat in Kew Gardens this afternoon."

He gave me a severe stare – *don't get funny with me Khan.*

"Nearly blew my brains out," I said.

"You're lucky to be alive. Cap'n Meigs is ex-Bengal Army. A gang-master for East India House ... oversees the muscle at the Company's docks and warehouses. Sorts out thieves, smugglers, anyone the Directors call trouble. Half his trade's violence. Thinks he's above the law."

"Sounds like he is."

"Company protects him from above, fear from below–"

"What if you could nail him? Nail the man who gives him orders?"

Chrystal shook his head. "Don't know why I'm even talking to you, Khan."

"You want to know who killed Elijah Doyle," I said. "I can do better than that. What if you could nab England's worst traitor since Guy Fawkes? What if it might just save your life?"

"You're a crank, a madman." He turned and headed back into the market. "I'll find Doyle's killer," he called.

The dismissal fired my anger. I chased him, shoved in front so we're chest to chest, eye to eye. "I'm deadly serious, Chrystal."

"Get out of my way!"

"Or what?" I still fancied decking him for locking me up last night.

"You're a liar," he said. "Don't tell me you got the better of Meigs."

"I didn't. Turns out Adelaide Doyle's handy with a cavalry carbine."

He just gawped, wondering if it's some bizarre joke.

"Listen," I said, "last night you said we'd more in common that I thought. Now I'm telling *you* the same. I'm doing Sir George Green's bidding because I've no choice. No other reason. You don't like it that Meigs is above the law of your land, same for me with Elphinstone. We can bring them both down, Chrystal. Together."

He frowned as if mulling the idea over. But then, he said, "You're telling me Adelaide Doyle outwitted Meigs, with a carbine?"

I took a pace back. "And two of his crew."

"Jesus Christ," he said, laughed out loud. "Talk about petticoat rebellion."

I laughed too, said, "We need to look in Bullock's safe."

Which killed the laughter.

"George Price's in Birmingham," Chrystal said, "we checked. No one else can do it without a key. And I'm not shop-breaking, risking my job."

I beckoned him, said, "No break in, I promise."

WE WALKED ALONG the wall past gates and alleys till we came to Henry's place. I pushed on the wooden gate, swinging it open. "See," I said. "Not locked. When I went in the front last night, Meigs and Co. came out here."

We crossed a yard to the back of the house. There's a backdoor to the shop, stone stairs down to the cellar. We went down, into a backroom where I'd often worked with Henry drying and soaking plants. There's a pleasant, aromatic smell. I led the way to the door through the dividing wall, into the front room where I'd met Chrystal last night. The body's gone but the air still smelt of dog shit. Still a mess, except someone's cleared a path to the safe.

I crouched by the safe's doors, set down my bag. There's just enough daylight from the windows above to work by. Chrystal crouched next to me. Each door's got a sturdy T-handle and its own lock. The wrought iron's like armour, Price's name and the patent number stamped on the front like talismans. Chrystal looked at me, raised his brows to say: *you're kidding, right?*

I gently lifted a wide-mouthed jar of grey paste from my bag.

Eased the stopper. "Hold these," I whispered, passing the jar like an overfull teacup. I used a spatula to spoon the paste into the nearest keyhole. Did it as if my life depended on not spilling a drop. Which it did.

"What's that, acid? We can't damage–"

"*Shhh!* It's liquid destruction, stable as a starving fox in a henhouse."

"Dangerous?"

"Put it this way, you jog the jar we won't need burying."

Chrystal's Adam's apple bobbed like a shuttle. "What ... death?"

"Instant ... painless." I looked up, gave him smile. "But still death, eh? I call it 'pyromite,' because 'pyro' means fire and ... chemists like ending words with '-ite.' The 'm' makes it, well, mighty." Talking calms my nerves. "Discovered by an Italian ... so dangerous he tried to hush it up. The Prof. had me make some hoping it'd have a medical use. I mixed it with diatomaceous earth, made the explosive stable ... more or less."

"More or less?"

"Didn't tell the Prof. He'd sell it to Woolwich Arsenal, blast a lot more blacks to Kingdom come."

Chrystal kept quiet, so I said, "Keep talking. Stops my hand shaking"

"All right. Tell me who killed Elijah Doyle."

"You first."

"What?"

"Come on, Chrystal."

"I've nae idea what you're–"

"You got two men killed, you know that? Nearly three."

"Rubbish!"

"All right. What's Doyle doing, sitting at that table?"

Silence.

"In the locker, he kept a well-oiled revolver that left a film on the bottom. I saw the shape of the cigar case and an envelope. Where's the envelope?"

More silence.

"You've heard about Noad ... tortured, dumped off the Isle of Dogs. That was Meigs after the envelope. Then he killed a young soldier in Kew Gardens, getting to me. Would've killed me too but for Miss Doyle. Which means you're next, because one of us must've taken it."

He hadn't thought it through. Licked his lips, swallowed as he took it in. But he kept quiet, watched me fill the keyhole. Both of us had sheens of sweat on our foreheads, and I could feel it trickling from my armpits.

"You don't know much about revolvers," I said.

"Never used one."

"Neither had Doyle. Didn't know how to load it."

"So what?" he said, pleased to change the subject.

"You've to fit the ball snugly in the chamber, stick a blob of grease on top. Otherwise sparks jump from one chamber to the next, fire that too. One pull on the trigger, two shots. The powder burn on the frame was plain to see."

"You're saying ... but there's no suicide note."

"'Between the devil and the deep sea.' That's it."

"And what the hell's that mean?"

I gave him a glance, like I knew. Which I didn't, not for sure.

"He was trying to read a dispatch," I said. "The one in the envelope you took from the table."

I'd done filling the first keyhole. We waddled a step to the left, and I began filling the second. "Why'd you take it?"

Chrystal blew a breath, shook his head. No point denying it. "Looked important," he said, "thought it might ..."

"Lead you to Doyle's killer?"

"And Bullock's."

"Show me."

"You're kidding? It's evidence, a confidential document by the highest authorities in Britain, why'd I show it to some ..."

"Foreign native ... Indian?"

He ignored that.

"First off," I said, "you can't read it. But I can."

"Oh aye," he scoffed.

"I'll spell you the first two words ... U S B E J P and D W I P E E."

He frowned, slid a hand in his jacket and drew out the prince of envelopes: weighty, vanilla, addressed in a penman's hand to Colonel James Peach, Chairman of the Military Board, Calcutta. Above stood the Company Crest and 'PRIVATE AND CONFIDENTIAL.' The flap had been closed with the wax seals of the Company and the House of Commons.

Chrystal gently set the jar down, took out the dispatch. He scanned the first two words, creasing his face as if he's watching the world's cleverest card trick, something truly uncanny. He looked up, said, "What is it ... Russian?"

"Vigenère cipher ... I mentioned Guy Fawkes, that dispatch is like a ton of gunpowder under East India House, if someone lights a match ..."

Chrystal stared down as if he'd suddenly noticed he's holding a venomous snake. Folding it quickly into the envelope, he said, "I'll mail it anonymously to East India House ... get shot of it." He slipped it inside his tunic.

The second keyhole was full. I repacked the jar, pushed a percussion cap into each keyhole. Two wires ran from each cap, then twisted into a single wire platted in silk thread. We backed across the room unspooling the wires, Chrystal carrying my bag.

"Home Secretary'd give a lot for that dispatch," I said. "Especially if we could read it for him."

"Oh no, I'm nae getting involved in–"

"Wouldn't you like to be *detective* sergeant?"

Chrystal hesitated. "What if I would?"

We settled behind the wall in the back room, closed the door. I set a battery on the floor and wound the earth wires to the negative terminal. Holding the others by the positive, I said, "Who's your boss?"

"Cartwright."

"Above him?"

"The Commissioner ... Wilberforce."

"Higher!"

"Er ... suppose it's the Home Secretary."

"Exactly, not the East India Company. Cover your ears."

"What?"

"Just do it."

I closed the electric circuit.

YOU GET A sort of *Woof!* with gunpowder, a violent burning. We chemists call it *deflagration.*

Pyromite's different. Shock waves from the caps turn it straight to hot gas. I call that *detonation.* Which is why a thunderbolt split the air, and the room leapt like an earthquake. The doors flew open. The windows splintered. I felt pain in both ears as I watched Chrystal mime, "JESUS CHRIST!" eyes bulging, his hands clamped tight to his head.

Then I led us back the way we'd come, choking on dust and falling plaster.

The safe's an iron cripple: twisted, the locks just ragged holes. One door's open, the other hanging on a single hinge. The fireproofing mixture in the double skin trickled onto the floor like powdered blood. A dying Double-Door. The seeing's better now because the filthy half-lights are nothing but evening breeze.

I shoved a hand in the safe, ran it over the shelves, yanked open the deposit boxes. Nothing. I checked the floor for paper or ash. Nothing. We bolted upstairs, waited panting by the shop's front door. Then we calmly stepped out, looked up at the building as if to say: *what on earth was that?* The Lab pulled up. I got inside. Chrystal climbed up next to Thorn. Dogs barked and gulls wheeled above. Jolting off down Ivy Lane the sun was a lemon moon in a mass of bubbling cloud, a storm brewing in the west.

THE SANS SOUCI Saloon's more a small hotel than a boozer. You can live there, rent rooms for an hour, eat in the restaurant or drink in one of the bars by day or night. The *Yokel's Preceptor* – which flaunts 'knocking shops' and 'introducing houses' in mock disgust – calls it a 'flash crib'. I've been twice with Thorn as recompense for evenings of gunjah and handi. It's the most respectable house in London where no one respectable would be seen dead.

Four of us sat at a table in a quiet recess, though you could see into a barroom through an open doorway. I'm opposite Chrystal, next to Addie who's opposite Thorn. Chrystal's staring doubtfully at a gaggle of noisy drinkers across the way.

"Complete waste of time," he muttered.

"What is?" said Addie.

"Khan just blew up Ivy Lane to open an empty safe–"

"Empty!" Addie said to me, "but you–"

I held up a finger, said, "Patience."

"What's she doing here, anyways?" Chrystal said.

"I'm wondering the same about you," Addie retorted.

I gave Chrystal a look. I'd told him not to mention Henry's shop, especially not the suicide story. Outside we'd had a serious barney, almost came to blows. He thought I'd risked his job and the general public, not least when the half-light windows blew across the Lane like a Shrapnel shell. I thought a bit of flying glass was nothing to what the Sepoys did to my people's villages in Bengal. We'd have gone on if Addie hadn't turned up the road from King Street.

"This place is full of marjories and tribads," Chrystal groaned.

I glanced at Thorn. "Poofs," she said, "men and women. Not to mention stone-thumpers and blowens."

I didn't ask. Addie did. Looking around in fascination, she said,

"Is this what they call a female hell?"

"Sort of," Thorn said, lighting her pipe, "there's all sorts here."

"Not me," Chrystal said, getting up. "I'm not being seen–"

"Sit down, Sergeant," I said. "We're here to talk business."

"That's the point," Addie said. She got it.

Chrystal didn't like it, but he sat. Liked it even less when an effeminate waiter greeted Thorn, warmly welcomed her strange crew. Thorn ordered a jug of ale, some jellied eels and a large dish of kedgeree to share. Addie wanted a glass of champagne. Chrystal asked for coffee.

When the waiter left, I said, "We – the four of us – have a common interest in finding out why Henry Bullock and Elijah Doyle died."

Chrystal nodded at Thorn. "Who's he, then?"

"My friend and confidant," I said. "You'll find out why he's here." I wasn't sure what that meant, but Thorn rarely let me down.

"Let's start with Henry Bullock–"

"Hang on," said Chrystal. "I'm not sharing info–"

"Just listen," I said, "then decide. Henry told me there's money in that safe, and something else, important. Somebody else thought so too because they tried to make him open it. Now it's empty. Henry wouldn't hide a key anywhere you'd find it. So, what happened?"

At first, no one spoke. Then Addie remarked the torturers mightn't have wanted the safe open. Which led Thorn to speculate the safe's a blind, never held anything. Or Henry'd emptied it himself. Which goaded Chrystal to give a professional's opinion, as I'd hoped. It's obvious to him Henry'd given up the key in agony, killed himself in despair while the safe was ransacked. Then Meigs relocked it. It's plausible, but I didn't believe it.

"Why kill yourself," I said, "when the safe's already open?"

We talked about that till the food arrived. The waiter poured ale for Thorn and me, set down coffee and a lively glass of champagne. We helped ourselves to eels and kedgeree. I took it easy as I'm meeting Bea in half an hour. I'd been looking forward to a quiet drink but given what Addie had told me it seemed likely our meeting would become a quarrel.

Thorn sipped her ale, squinted into the distance as she puffed her pipe. The walls and pillars are lined with mirrors, which means you can discreetly watch anyone who takes your fancy in another room. Thorn laid her pipe on the linen tablecloth.

"Put yourself in Bullock's place," she said. "You're in agony, can't stand it. But you'd rather die than give up the key. Why? What's worth more than life?"

It sounded more a challenge than a question. We sat chewing, thinking, until Addie said, "You mean he thought his life worth less than the consequence of someone opening the safe." She helped herself to more kedgeree.

"Exactly" Thorn said. "There's only one thing I'd die to protect."

"Family," said Chrystal.

"And who's the only person Bullock might've entrusted with a key?"

"Family," I said, "maybe his sister?"

Addie snapped her fingers. "What if–" She looked at Chrystal, wondering if she should put anything his way.

"Go on," I said, fanning the flicker of trust.

"What if I told you Ethel Bullock married Oliver Impey in eighteen forty-two. Which makes Billy–"

"Henry's nephew," I finished.

"What?" said Chrystal. "What's that mean?"

I pulled a face to say, *we need each other here.* Then I explained what we'd learned at Kew, and from Yashoda. "So it's Billy," I said. "Told his uncle about *Artemisia Chinensis*, took the seeds. But where'd they grow the plants under–"

"Loddiges nurseries," Addie said, "where Billy was a trainee gardener. They closed eighteen months ago but at least one hot house is still there."

"Yeah," I said. "That makes sense. Henry extracts the liquor, gets me to crystalize the drug ... tries it on the Dreadnought. And then–"

"Convinces my stepfather," said Addie. "Who persuaded some-one at the Company to fund a trial in India."

Chrystal's thinking, struggling to keep up. But then he made an interesting leap. "So this Billy Impey," he said, "knew about the key. Emptied the safe sometime today. I need to find him, get the rest of the story."

I gave Addie an encouraging nod. She understood, took out her notebook. "Fifteen Vinegar Lane, off the Commercial Road in Stepney."

"Thank you," Chrystal said, made to get up.

"Not yet," I said. "That's only *half* the story."

I pointed at Chrystal. "You've got the evidence to nail the man behind this." Still looking at him, I pointed to Addie. "She's the one can read it."

"Hold on, Khan," Chrystal said. "That's between you–"

"He took it?" Addie said, glaring at Chrystal. "Stole the dispatch?"

"It's police evidence–"

"My uncle Reginald's a Company Director! A word from me and you'll be shovelling horse dung on the Strand, if you're lucky–"

"Whoa, Addie," I said, "We're on the–"

"Jesus, Khan," Chrystal said. "You'll cost me my bloody–"

"Unless," Addie intervened, "the Sergeant will work with us."

CHRYSTAL STARED AT her, then at me. I don't know what's in his mind. Not even sure what's in mine. I'd put him on the spot but he *did* take the dispatch. Now he's got a chance to give it back, put things right. I don't know if Addie can read the cipher, but I'd like her to try.

Chrystal must've thought the same because he slipped a hand in his jacket and tossed the envelope towards Addie. "Take it," he said, "it's no use to me."

"Not so hasty," I said, catching it in mid-air.

"That's mine!" Addie shrieked.

"Un-hah," I said. "Ours." Then, "Can you read it?"

She folded her arms, staring at me angrily. Then she looked away, tapping a boot absently on the carpet. When she turned back, mouth twisted to one side, she said, "There're three possibilities ... but I'll need to see it."

I took out the letter, unfolded and smoothed it on the table. Kept it firmly pinned it under my fingers. Same quality paper. Same crests. Same heading. Beneath the crests, it read, 'Secret Committee Dispatch: Strictly Confidential, for the attention of Colonel James Peach, Chairman of the Military Board, Calcutta. It was sent from East India House, dated 1st December 1856. It read:

USBEJP DWIPEE QWETWL BEYAZL QDRBPP BGVLMU IZUOCW MXFRQP LATAPE ZARLW EWHLT XPZKVC VPKQJT SAEWTO RQQJDN IHMFWI IWLURR XCQVXE WWCTII GLBWUW MEPTVE JLVVDU XEWFWA XDBGGS PPOERN

The signature read, James C. Melvill, Secretary, on behalf of the Secret Committee and the India Board of Control.

Addie said, "You've a magnifying glass?"

I took one from my bag. She took off the green glasses, bent close to the paper. Thorn brought a candle closer, and Addie went line by line through the text. She studied the margins, nodded for me to the flip the sheet. She studied the blank verso then told me to hold it up in front of the candle. Finally, she sat upright, passed me back the glass and put on her spectacles.

"You speak it, Vigenère?" Chrystal said.

Addie gave him dismissive frown and coughed a blank laugh.

"It's not a language," I said. "It's a cipher, secret writing."

She said, "Is that a clergyman, in the bar-room?"

We all stared at a man lounging in clerical vestments, holding court as if giving an impromptu sermon.

Thorn said, "What, the Arse Bishop, he's–"

"I beg your pardon?" Addie said.

"What he's called," said Thorn. "Because of his—"

"Yeah, we get the idea, Thorn," I said.

Addie grinned at catching the church in rank hypocrisy. She went into the barroom. The Bishop's in his sixties, portly with a craggy face and a drinker's nose. Addie used the unctuous greeting she'd given Smollet at Kew, got a similarly obliging reply. The Bishop looked surprised then curious, took a thick book from a portmanteau. Addie riffled the leaves, ran down and across a page. She asked for another book. I recognized the King James Bible. More riffling. She curtsied, returned the book, then came and sat back down.

I kept the dispatch pinned to the table. She took out the cigar case, glanced back and forth at the cipher as she wove the dials, flipped the plate.

At first, she looked satisfied, nodding as if it's what she expected. But then she went, *"Oh!"* as if she'd pricked a finger. A moment later she stopped dead, staring down at the line she'd just deciphered, which none of us could see. The case slid from her fingers, clattered onto the table, the floor. She ignored it, lost in concern about the words she'd read.

"So ... what does it say?" Chrystal asked.

Addie turned to me. "You're seeing the Home Secretary at eight thirty?"

"That's the plan." I put the dispatch in its envelope, stowed it securely in my bag. I reached for the cigar case, but Addie grabbed it first, twiddled the dials back to a row of A's. Then she closed it, put it in her carpet bag.

"I want you to meet me in the London Library at nine," she said. "I need to speak to you, alone."

"What about working together?" Chrystal said.

Addie looked down the table at Chrystal and me. "I think you both know how my stepfather died. *I* don't. I know what the dispatch says. *You* don't. I'll trade with Doctor Khan at nine. That'll conclude our *collaboration.*" She turned to me. "I wouldn't mention the dispatch to the Home Secretary, Hyder. Not if you know what's good for you."

With that she put a stack of coins on the table, picked up her bag and left.

Chrystal didn't seem bothered. He got up, said, "Dispatches are above my station. I'm going to find this Billy Impey, see if I can lay hands on Meigs and his mob. That'll do me."

I almost asked him to stay. Wanted to explain he's an important rod in my flying machine. Same as I'd thought about telling Addie how her stepfather died in return for deciphering the dispatch. Not the right time or place.

"You'll let me know what you find out, Chrystal?"

"Not if you're playing games with the likes of Sir George Green."

He rummaged in his pocket. Thorn began to say Miss Doyle had covered the bill, but Chrystal flipped her a coin and walked away. I had Thorn read out the dispatch's particulars while I jotted them down. That way I can study the message with the original hidden away. Then we left too.

GOING ALONG PALL Mall past St James Park, the sky had clouded over. The air was growing thick and humid ready for a storm.

Thorn said, "Miss Doyle put that kedgeree away."

"Active mind," I said. "Uses a lot of nervous force."

Thorn nodded. "You reckon she actually read that dispatch?"

"Yeah ... well, she looked pretty shocked at what it said."

"Looked," she said. "I mean, that business with the magnifying glass, begging books from the Arse Bishop, twiddling the dials ..."

I hate it when Thorn makes me feel stupid; or worse, inferior. If some sapper or baboo in Calcutta said he'd cracked the Company cipher, I'd kick his arse. But an educated white, fools me every time; even a woman, even though I'd swear they wouldn't.

"If it's a blind, it's damned clever," I said.

"Need a lot of nervous force?"

I felt like spitting. Addie could ransom the facts, spin me a line on what the message says. Feels like she's been bleeding me all along, filling in details of her stepfather's life, tracing the dispatch. I'll want to know how she solved the puzzle of the keyword before I trust another word she says.

"The Bishop fetched a Bible from his bag," I said. "But before that another book ... thick with a brown leather binding. Any ideas?"

"A hymnal?"

"All Things Bright and Beautiful in the Thrums S? I remember The Parson's Clerk's Upright followed by Kitty's What D'ye Call It."

Thorn smiled. "All right, a concordance, then."

"What the hell's that?"

"Like a vicar's crib ... you want to preach on anything from Adultery to Zion, it tells you where to find it in the *Bible*."

"*Huh* ... that's more like it. A theme leads you to a specific verse?"

"Yep. Then there's the *Book of Common Prayer*."

"You like making me feel stupid, Thorn. Don't you?"

"Everything liturgical?" She grinned. "Services, daily readings through the year, like a manual for the Church of England."

"And the colonies?"

"Glue of the Empire. Binds us together around the globe."

"Hmph. They really call him that, the Arse Bishop?"

"Matter of fact, he married us," Thorn said.

Which left me quiet, thinking all the way to the Adelphi Hotel.

Nineteen

WALKING INTO THE dining room I'm wondering how to play it with Bea. I could ignore what Addie said, assume it's spiteful lies meant to cause trouble. Which it might be. On the other hand, I'm upset, angry in a way that'll be hard to hide. It's not Bea's fault if her husband wants a divorce, nor if I'm what they apparently call the *co-respondent.*

But gossiping with friends while keeping me in the dark about an imminent scandal's another matter. Infuriating. I've got to know.

When I spotted Bea at a table by the wall, I knew something's wrong. She looks despondent, miserable. I'm five minutes late, but there's no carafe of wine or bread and butter. Normally she'd wave, pour me a glass to fire-up the evening. The Adelphi dining room's one of the finest in London, all golds and yellows with a big chandelier, polished floorboards and plaster cornicing. Like a stately drawing room.

Today it left me cold. I drew out the chair opposite Bea. Began to worry more when I wasn't scolded for being late. "How's the meeting," I said, "the galvanized fences?"

"Cancelled." She obviously didn't want to talk about it.

I'm guessing she's not interested in shot towers either, but nor am I this evening. I said, "You all right?"

"Yes ... well, not really. I've been feeling ... a bit odd. If it wasn't for Jane, I don't know what I'd do."

That stung. "Jane? I'm a doctor, you know?"

"Yes, but–"

"A *native* doctor? Listen, just tell me what's wrong with you."

"Oh, I don't know ... my heart sort of flutters, my fingers tingle.

Sometimes I feel a bit sick."

"You're working too hard, worrying about galvanized fences–"

"It's nothing! Jane makes a soothing mint tea. It'll pass."

I wasn't soothed. The thought's growing that our affaire's been tied up with divorce from the start. I nodded upwards. Somewhere above, on the other side of the building sat our apartment. "Where's Jane, *tidying up?*"

"She came on the train with me, from Earlsacre. Since we're dining here, I gave her the evening off."

A waiter brought me a tankard of Barclay's ale, my usual. I indicated for him to stay. "Let's eat here," I said, "I'm due at the Home Office at eight thirty."

"Oh?" Bea said, glancing indifferently at the menu.

"I know what's in the little bottle."

She wasn't interested, so I ordered roast lamb followed by cherry tart and custard. Bea asked for Julienne soup and a bread roll, inquired about mint tea.

I said, "What happened to curried lobster and a glass of Riesling?"

She grimaced at the thought. I'd meant to bring up Addie by asking why Bea'd been so short with her earlier. But she said, "Why's that woman on the Terrace this morning?"

"Miss Doyle? I met her at the Bank. Her stepfather was found dead in the vaults."

"Dead? Was it ... his heart? Apoplexy, I shouldn't wonder."

I bunched my eyebrows, curious. "Apoplexy?"

Bea waved the question away.

"Matter of fact," I said, "he shot himself."

If I thought I'd shock her, I should've known better.

"Huh!" she said. "Not surprised."

I took a gulp of ale. "Apoplexy?"

"Nasty piece of work, that Adelaide."

"Oh? Didn't strike me–"

"A Jezebel!" Bea glared. "A bookish, bespectacled, devious

minx."

I frowned. I'd never heard Bea speak of another woman with such venom. I laid my chin on my fist, said skeptically, "Really?"

"Oh yes. Still, what can you expect ... father a drunk, mother a complete fool ... you know she shot her husband, by mistake? Anyway, we'd a mutual friend. *Had!* Lucy Ocklynge."

Lucy has a mansion in Fitzroy Square. They're fast friends, with an edge. Lucy's genteel, new money – lawyers – well below a count-ess. *"A sweetheart, none the less,"* Bea says. They've got a circle, that lunches.

"Married to a big-wig in the City?" I said, to keep it moving.

"Nathaniel. Well!" as if that's the unspeakable nub of it.

"Well ... what?"

"Happily married for twenty years, until Nathanial hired the Doyle girl to advise on something ... oh, I don't know, electrical ... a corset?"

I frowned, then, "The World-Girdle Telegraph?"

"That's it. Anyway, Lucy's a wonderful artist, paints street urchins and suchlike ..."

Two waiters arrived. One to set out the cutlery and crockery, the other set down dishes of hot food. As they left, Bea called, "I'll take a carafe of Riesling," went on, "Well, last year Nathaniel gave Lucy a special birthday present, art classes with a brilliant young painter, in Clapham of all places. He studies the female form, taken from life–"

"Nudes?"

"Nature's masterpieces," – she leaned closer – "adorned the most where least adorned! He's a very advanced notion of aesthetics. You must remember when Lucy wanted to sketch us ... you know?"

"Naked ... after you told her about the *Kama Sutra.*"

"Cupid's scripture, exactly."

I'd countered the Marquis de Sade with half-remembered lines from the Hindoo art of love. Bea's circle was intrigued – "Bedroom instructions, like a drill manual? The very idea!" I didn't mind gossip in that department.

"Next thing we hear," she said, "Nathaniel's produced sworn affidavits of Lucy's adultery with her teacher, in Clapham–"

"She didn't *have* to sleep with–"

"Oh, you haven't seen him ... an Adonis! Anyway, the whole thing was calculated. Nathaniel paid the boy to paint her naked, make love to her. But then came the bombshell – Nathaniel's divorcing Lucy in the new year ... for Adelaide Doyle. Poor Lucy's mortified, went straight to one of her lawyers saying she's proof of Nathaniel's adultery with the Doyle girl–"

"Adelaide's the *co-respondent?*"

"Proud of it.

"But a woman can't divorce on grounds of adultery alone?"

The wine arrived. Bea took a long sip, shut her eyes and sighed with relief.

"Oh, don't we know it!" she said.

We'd argued about the fact a woman had to prove bigamy or rape or cruelty. Bea thinks the vows should apply equally, goose and gander, that kind of thing. I don't. A man's got to know his children are his own.

"But it'll be in open court," she said, "before the public's gaze, the press! Lucy thought it'd put Nathaniel off, but he swears he'll go ahead. That slut, Miss Doyle wants a cause. Thinks she'll undermine marriage, martyr herself to the free association of the sexes. Doesn't care tuppence for her stepfather!"

"The evangelist–"

"The moralist ... the professor! The principal at King's College wouldn't risk a scandal. Doyle would be pilloried, a laughing stock."

"Lose his job." I'm thinking of the devil and the deep sea.

"The companies won't like it much, either."

"Companies?"

"Nathaniel's a former director of the New Zealand Company, still on the board. Presently Chairman of the East India–"

"East India! Lucy's husband's Nathaniel *Slegman?*"

"Yes, I thought you knew."

I laid my knife and fork on my meal, sat back. "Why the hell didn't you tell me this morning?"

She made a wide-eyed face, mimicked, *"Don't want you nannying me!"*

I blew a long sigh. "Did Lucy know about the initialled instruments?"

"Why, yes I ... but she wouldn't tell, it's understood."

I put my head in my hands. "You told her, while she was still on speaking terms with Adelaide Doyle, with Nathaniel Slegman?"

"Hyder! She's my closest friend, my confidant. At least Nathaniel had the decency to leave. Lives more or less at the East India Club."

"But ... Miss Doyle spoke as if she loathed him–"

"You idiot! It's not his good looks she wants. Really, Hyder!"

"And what do you want me for?" I said, anger starting to boil.

"What the hell's that mean?"

"How about divorce?"

"What divorce?"

"Yours! Miss Doyle told me. ... the gossip, how I'm a co-respondent?"

Bea's stunned, dropped her spoon, splashing soup on the tablecloth, leaving orange slivers of carrot on the front of her dress. She stared as if I'd just said I hated her. Then her mien toughened from Bea to Lady Motcombe, the peer, mistress of the Earlsacre estate.

"I see," she said, as if I'd reported a drop in agricultural prices.

She tried to wave off an approaching waiter, but he bowed and slipped a folded sheet of hotel notepaper in front of me. I'd told the Home Office to reply here, so I opened it at once. It said, succinctly, that Sir George Green would see me at eight o'clock, or not till further notice, which by the mantel clock gave me twelve minutes. As I read, Bea dabbed her dress clean with her napkin.

She looked up. "There's something we need to talk about. I'm sorry if—"

"If you think Lucy and Nathaniel will be a scandal," I said, "wait till they hear about Lady Motcombe and the Black Prince! Probably spice it up with quotations from the *Kama Sutra!*" I got up, tossed my napkin on the table.

"Hyder! Where're you going?"

"Sir George just brought the meeting forward by half an hour."

"What meeting?"

I caught sight of her silver evening-bag on the table. It's pretty, sewn with coloured beads, my first gift to her. It reminded me I shouldn't take the dispatch to the meeting in case Sir George has me searched. I sat down, took the envelope from my bag, slid it over the table.

"Take this, Bea," I whispered. "Tell no one. No one!"

"Yes, but ..." She stared apprehensively at the fancy script, the double seals of Company and Parliament. "What's this?" she murmured.

"Drop it in our mailbox at the Adelphi. Understand?"

"Yes, but—"

"No!" I hissed, as she opened the flap. I made a grab for the envelope.

She drew back "I want to see a thing," – she unfolded it – "before I go smuggling ... *huh!*" Her eyes grew wide. "Good God," she said, folding it hastily away. "You realize this is—"

"I *know* what it is," I said, rising to her condescension. "I mean to get more than exoneration from Sir George-bloody-Green!"

"How?"

I leaned forward, told her the gist in terse whispers.

She laughed at me. "You'll force the Home Secretary's hand, blackmail the East India Company—"

"To get justice for my people? *Yes!*"

"Justice? They'll throw you to the dogs, you fool—"

"*Fool* am I now?" I got up, grabbed up my bag. "Just do as I ask!"

"Well THANK YOU!" she said. "I'll dine alone, then?" As I walked away, she called, "As a matter of fact, Shapton–"

"Not now!" I called back.

On the way out, I caught myself in an oval looking-glass. It's slightly convex, showing the whole room in a bulged instant – me, angry; Bea staring after me, hurt. It's a dreamy picture that'll haunt me for the rest of my life.

OUT ON JOHN Street I gave Thorn the night off. Told her to be ready at nine with a flash cab – a Clarence or a Brou'm – and a fast pair. I'm not arriving at the Cambrian Stores in the Lab, and I'll need some speed later.

Then I'm alone, hurrying down the dark alleys of Hungerford Market, feeling my confidence drain like a cold bath. I should be working out how to play the dispatch with Sir George. *Damn Bea!* The last thing I needed was an English aristocrat, my lover, treating me like a damned native.

A black in a white world moves like a tightrope dancer, just a slip from the vertigo of inferiority. I'm on my way to meet a 'Sir,' a 'baronet,' one of Britain's highest ministers. I need to look him in the eye, never blink.

I went faster in Craven Street and Scotland Yard, charging my foe, building my nerve. Then I turned down Whitehall towards the Houses of Parliament. The sun's low, a red-gold ball lighting the charcoal cloud a holy crimson. The white-stone buildings glow pink, aping the grandeur of imperial Rome.

I imagined the colonnades of Calcutta's Public Library, the place I met a librarian called Peary Chand Mitra. His lectures were an earthquake in my mental landscape. If O'Shaughnessy's my white uncle, Mitra's my black one. His father got rich as a Company go-be-tween, sent his son to the new Hindoo College. In a short-lived bub-ble of free thought, Peary's generation – the Young Bengal – breathed the fire of natural rights and free markets.

I met the Middle-Aged Bengal. Still glowing. Still speaking English better than most Englishmen. Still railing against the hypocrisy of empire. Chand's lectures made the races equal, taught us India had astronomy and philosophy while the British were still savages enslaved by foreign invaders.

By the Treasury Building I'd enough steam to step into the ring.

I showed Sir George's note to a commissionaire who sent a messenger boy. In a while the boy led me up a stone stairway, along a carpeted corridor, through airy rooms of state, till we came to a cosy office overlooking Horse Guards Parade – the bullseye of British power, if such a thing exists.

Sir George sat behind a surprisingly small desk, more like a table. But big enough to sign a death warrant. He's in latter middle age, balding with white, mutton-chop side whiskers. Wearing a limp bow tie over a wing collar and a shabby, miss-buttoned jacket I wouldn't shovel dung in. He offered an aloof stare rather than his hand. Let me stand like a schoolboy in front of the headmaster.

"You've got some nerve," he said, "demanding an audience. I won't ask how you came by my electric address."

He didn't ask, I didn't answer. But I noted the Eton-Oxford *haw-haw*.

"You were told to report to Major Elphinstone."

"I've news you mightn't want him to hear."

Sir George sat back, knitted his fingers – *pray tell*. I took out the little bottle and Fortune's letter, stood them side by side on the desk.

"You asked three questions," I said. "In 1853, Robert Fortune sent a case of plants, *Artemisia Chinensis*, to Kew Gardens via Chelsea. He claimed they held a cure for malaria. The plants fell into the hands of Henry Bullock, who extracted the drug and tested it on the Dreadnought Hospital ship. He persuaded Elijah Doyle it was of interest to the East India Company. The Company sent Bullock and Doyle to try the drug at the Military Hospital in Calcutta."

"*Hmph!*" he grunted, reading Fortune's letter. "That all?"

"All? It's what you asked."

He got up and went to the open window. Stood in the last ray of sun, staring at the parade ground, at Buckingham Palace across St James's Park. I took advantage of the lull to ask a direct question.

"It wasn't you staged my arrest?"

"Certainly not."

"Your name's on my death warrant."

"Which saved your life. You can thank Hofmann for that."

Sir George's mission stopped Cartwright hanging me. Since the lull went on, I said, "You wanted to know who ordered Bullock's murder. Except it was suicide. Four men tortured him, led by a man called Meigs. Whoever sent them, sold me for the crime."

"And who's that?" he said, as if I hadn't a clue.

"Slegman, Clyde or Birdwood."

He turned abruptly from the window, squinted at me.

I headed him off with, "Elphinstone, when he thought I was a dead man."

Sir George took two documents from a drawer – my confession and death warrant. Handing them over, he said, "You've been useful, Khan. But our business is done. I advise you never to utter a word of this affair."

I didn't like the lofty tone or the dismissal. "What about the dispatch?"

His face went cold as the national interest. "You realize," he said, "I can send you straight to the Tower, no warrant of execution required?"

"Elijah Doyle," I said, "took his own life."

"Suicide? Murder, surely?"

"Two shots? Gun misfired. But there's a page of scribble says he's trying to crack a Vigenère cipher." I let the words hang, picked up an official envelope from a tray on the desk. "An oil film in his locker says there's an envelope, like this. Doyle's stepdaughter took the scribble."

"And the envelope?"

"The attending sergeant."

"Then I'll contact–"

"But ... I acquired it. Thought you'd prefer it in your hands?"

"You're saying the dispatch exists ... that you have it?"

I nodded. "It's safe."

Sir George sat, waved at me to do the same. For a minute he softly tapped the blotter. Then, he said, "Doyle can't've read it. The Company boasts the method's utterly secure, known only to the Secret Committee and select senior officers abroad. The dispatch is no use if I don't know what it says."

"What if I could read it?"

"*You?* Get out, Khan!" he barked. "Before I lose patience. I thought for a foolish moment you'd be useful to me."

I stared back, angrily, racking my brain for a counter.

"I'm serious," I said, struggling to keep the calm he'd lost. "Doyle's scribblings told me there's a keyword, six letters, biblical. He knew that much. I'm meeting someone later this evening who'll tell me the rest."

More cautiously: "And who might that be?"

I outlined what'd happened at the bank, why Adelaide Doyle was prepared to do business with me ... hoping all the while I'm right. I'm counting on that worried look at the last phrase. If Thorn's doubts are justified, I'm for the Tower.

Sir George clearly knew Miss Doyle. "Well, well," he said. "Perhaps you *are* useful. But you're in a deadly game." He tugged a bellpull by the chimney breast. Rummaged in a drawer, passed me a document fit for a king's investiture. A uniformed boy came in. "Fetch Vernon Smith," Sir George said.

I'm reading the 'Oath of Solemn Allegiance.' The legal jargon felt like thumb screws. All I remember is, *'I solemnly swear on pain of death to defend Queen Victoria against all conspiracies and attempts made against her Person, Crown or Dignity.'* In brief, I'm her agent, who'll be executed for any disloyal act, like divulging this chat with Sir George.

A cherub-faced man with a mop of black, curly hair came in. The twirled moustache says he's Chrystal's laughing Cavalier, from last night.

Sir George said, "It's the famed Doctor Khan." Then, to me, "Vernon Smith, President of the Board of Control for India."

I'd no idea I'm *famed*. We nodded to each other. The Board is Parliament's watchdog on the Company, there to stop it hogging markets, going bankrupt, invading principalities ... bribery ... brutality ... you name it. Things greedy people do when no one's watching. The Board's job is to watch.

"We need you to swear and sign the Oath," Sir George said.

I nearly baulked at that, until I realized it cut both ways.

"One condition," I said. "Two copies. One for you, one for me." Being Her Majesty's sworn protector might come in useful.

He grunted at the gall, but he did it. I swore and signed two copies. They witnessed. We sat. Sir George repeated my story to Vernon Smith. Then, to me, "We *know* who wrote the dispatch, *know* its content, *know* the writer's named in the text. What we need, is proof. So, you fetch the envelope—"

I'd lifted a finger. "There's something else," I said.

"Ah, thought there might be."

I told them why I'd come to London, about the stolen trunk. All the while, I waited for the protest, the fury at me holding the Home Office to ransom. But they listened in silence, more and more intent as the story ran. When I'd done, Vernon Smith turned to Sir George. "Sounds like the Torture—"

"Un-hah!" said Sir George, quieting his junior. Then, to me, "You have photographs, documented admissions by serving officers?" When I nodded, he continued, "You think they still exist?"

"Oh, I'm betting there're tucked away East India House."

It's what I'd call *the imperial frame of mind*. Mapping and collecting, displaying trophies – like dogs licking their own vomit. The trunk's there somewhere, with a thousand other native curiosities.

"You'd like the evidence in return for the dispatch?" said Sir George.

"Partly. Mainly I'd like you to petition Parliament, grant the Santal people protection from tyranny. Give them their own land, mark it in capitals on Company maps."

Silence. Then, "You're serious?" Sir George said.

"Yes." Then I laughed out loud. Maybe it's the Oath, a joke in the Queen Victoria club. Vernon Smith joined in, then Sir George did too. Like three officers howling at a filthy story in the Bengal Club. I'm not sure if we're laughing at my audacity or the fact I'm about to be kicked out.

When the laughter faded, I said, "I toyed with Santalia."

Vernon Smith said, "The Santal Parganas."

Typical. The last imperial invaders, the Mughals, carved India into revenue districts they called parganas.

"Sounds like a tax district," I said.

"A place of protection?" Sir George suggested.

Still, a name – which surprised me, until I recalled Addie's story. The dispatch concerns one man, my evidence the whole Company. Like the Torture Commission: it pinned the blame on the brutish, native police; but not before the Whigs used it to shame the Directors. With a full-scale mutiny in progress, my evidence might topple Company rule.

"In the morning," Sir George went on, "I want the dispatch, with its contents in plain English, on this desk. Then we'll meet at East India House at ...?"

"The Directors' meeting is at four o'clock," said Vernon Smith.

"Three, then," said Sir George. "With the dispatch."

"You'll trade it for the trunk?"

"We'll start negotiations. You'll probably find Miss Doyle there too. The Court's considering Company support for her World-Girdle

Telegraph."

"Which Director is it?" I asked. "Slegman, Clyde or Birdwood?"

"Read the dispatch," said Sir George.

I got up, made a small bow. "Till tomorrow, then."

As I left, Sir George called, "Doctor Khan. Going over Elphinstone's head is a dangerous move. I'd keep out of his way if I were you."

"I'll square it with him," I said. "First thing tomorrow."

I left them to think about that.

I WANTED TO jump the last few steps onto Whitehall, punch my fists in the air and shout, *"Way-hay!"* I tore up the confession and warrant, scattered them into the gutter. I'd boxed Sir George like an exhibition match. That's how it felt. Got what I wanted. I'd show Bea what a damned native can do.

Now for Addie at the London Library. She's hard to dislike, despite what Bea says. Got her own game, but I wouldn't've got this far without her. Now it's the last round – I say how her father died; she explains the Company cipher. Then the wind probably changes and the pact's over.

That's what I was thinking round Charing Cross into Cockspur Street, when I sensed someone behind me. I'm used to that. Idiots who think I'm a clown or a freak, who tail me, mutter insults and menaces, or just gawp.

Or maybe Sir George had me followed.

On Pall Mall I glanced back in the lamplight, saw two men catching up, both well-built, looking business-like. Pall Mall's a broad avenue through elegant squares and statues, not a place to dodge into alleys. Past Regent Street I went to cross the road to St James Square. A fancy carriage veered into the curb blocking my way. I stopped, turned so I could see the cab and the men behind.

When the door swung open, I knew they'd come for me, balled up my fists for a fight. The door blazed the Company crest, and when

Captain Meigs leaned out it felt like a reckoning – like he'd come to collect. Miss Doyle might've pulled the trigger on Jack, but her uncle and her lover make her untouchable. The black takes the beating, as usual.

Only it wasn't a gun Meigs pointed at me. It's a gold-embossed card.

"Your lucky night, Pandy," he said. "Get in."

"Lucky?"

"Dinner at the East India Club. Seems they'll let a black in these days."

"About time," I said. "We pay for it."

"Oh, you'll pay for Jack," he said. "Soon as this is over."

I looked at the men five paces away, waiting for Meigs' orders. He nodded them away. I took the card – a handsome, unsigned invitation, like a rider-less stallion come for the weary traveller.

"Dinner with whom?" I said.

"*Whom?* Jesus Christ, Pandy, where'd you learn to talk that?"

"Slegman, Clyde or Birdwood?"

"Just get in!"

"I'll walk." The Club's five minutes away.

Meigs' slammed the carriage door and fell in next to me. We walked in silence. Billows of cloud to the north flared with lightning, far-off thunder grumbled in the night. Heading towards the Square's north-west corner, Meigs said, "Want to know how to use a knife and fork?"

"Like you used forceps on Henry Bullock?"

"He's a stubborn cove." Meigs gave me a sideways grin. "Squealed enough though," he said, in case I imagined he'd any pity.

"Didn't give you a turd," I said, taking the smile off his face.

"We got what we wanted, Pandy."

Nearing the Club, I saw a light in the London Library next door. I'm due to meet Addie in fifteen minutes so I'm not intending to get past the soup course. We went in the Club door, through the entrance and staircase halls to the dining room. The air's heavy with the smell of fat and stewed cabbage. I felt a trill of excitement and curiosity at who I'm here to meet, why they've sent for me.

When a butler arrived, Meigs said, "Prince of Murshidabad," and I showed the invitation. The butler told us to wait, vanished among the candlelit tables. I pulled back my shoulders, ... I needed my dander up, as they say.

Meigs said, "I've got a few sovereigns say you'll get the shit knocked out of you tomorrow morning."

"I've got something says I won't."

"Yeah?"

I set down my bag, poked a playful left at his chin then hooked a vicious right under his breastbone. Meigs sank to his knees with a strangled groan.

"See what I mean?"

Now I'm ready. The butler signalled me over with, "This way, your highness." Meigs was on all-fours, heaving for breath. "Must be something he ate," I said, as the butler led me to a quiet nook.

DINNER HAD BEGUN without me. My host sat at a carved oak-table in a matching chair upholstered in red. He'd a bald, domed head, with a rim of grey hair, curled up at the ends like fishhooks. Face old, jowly, looking annoyed. "The mackerel's tougher'n rubber," he chewed.

"Hyder Khan," I said, with manners he evidently lacked.

"Slegman," he grunted, gestured to the chair opposite.

I sat, sizing up the man I'd been told was Addie's consort; I won't believe lover. She's right about ugly ... but well dressed? He's wearing brown corduroys and a red jacket with a yellow cravat. Could've come from a fox hunt. Made me feel like an undertaker.

"What business had you with Sir George Green?" he growled.

"Private business."

He looked up. His face is a bit like Henry's, warts and all. Except there's something ill proportioned about Slegman's. Not that I'm sure what – a lack of humanity perhaps? A face I wished I hadn't seen, that'll cling like a nasty smell or a scene from a nightmare.

"Don't get clever with me, Khan," he said. "Or you'll regret it."

Which sounded more like a fact than a threat.

"You gave Green the dispatch?"

Now I knew the answer to Slegman, Clyde or Birdwood. Knew why I was invited to dinner.

"Dispatch?" I inquired.

"From Doyle's locker," he sighed. "You took it from Sergeant Chrystal in the *Sans Souci Saloon* an hour ago."

My dander suddenly felt less up. Only Addie knew about Chrystal. What else had she told? To trade punches, I said, "What about the trunk of evidence I brought to East India House?"

"That what you want?" he said. "Your price?"

I didn't reply at once. Didn't want to queer my deal with Sir George. But if I could get the trunk back sooner, under my own steam, so much the better.

In the lull, Slegman said, "That's what Green wanted, the dispatch?"

I shook my head. 'Wanted to know where Bullock's Remedy came from."

"Then you still have it, the dispatch?"

"It's safe," I said, taking a breath, trying to stare him down. "But if you try dealing with me as you did Bullock, it'll be in Sir George's hands damned fast."

Which wasn't true, but he nodded as if he granted me that much wit.

"Bullock's Remedy," he mused, forking in more mackerel. "So that's what took you to Kew Gardens. You realize you led Meigs there? As for Bullock, he more or less *dealt* with himself."

"That's a new one," I said.

He pointed his fork at me. "I put a lot in that drug, offered Bullock a good price. Know what he wanted? A patent and fifty percent of profits, in perpetuity! Wouldn't budge. Wouldn't part with the plant or the process." He shrugged, "Might as well've tied himself on the rack."

I beckoned a waiter. "I'll have coffee," I said, "with cream."

When the waiter left, Slegman said, "Suppose you get the trunk? What happens to those statements, photographs?"

I told him, even suggested naming a territory the Santal Parganas.

He nodded. "What if I give you my word the Company will do as you ask? No need for that trunk to leave East India House."

"And the dispatch?"

"Oh, I'll need that, tonight."

I'd have walked out then but for the nagging doubt the trunk's already gone, my deal with Sir George worthless. So I called Slegman's bluff.

"I'm surprised," I said, "you entrusted Bullock with the dispatch."

"Bullock? Don't play tricks with me—"

"I know for a fact Bullock delivered it to Colonel Peach."

"That what Bullock told you?" he said, with a sneer.

"Raikes Elphinstone, in the City Police Office, when he thought I'd shortly be on the gallows ... thanks to you."

Slegman stopped mid chew, mouth open. I saw a ball of sticky mackerel lying in his leathery tongue. I'd landed a punch.

With a fake frown, he said, "And how might the Major know that?"

"Peach told him. Shortly before Elphinstone blew his brains out."

Slegman reached for a bottle of Sancerre sweating in an ice bucket. The tremble in his hand as he topped his glass said I'd rattled him. He took a gulp of wine, fixed me with his jet-black eyes. "My, my," he said, "you *are* well-informed. What else did the Major tell you?"

I held the stare. "That we're dealing with a crime Britain's worst enemies couldn't've cooked up in a century."

The black eyes gleamed shock, which turned to fear, which turned to hatred. *How much had Peach blurted out with a gun pressed to his head?* Slegman stood, abruptly, threw his napkin on the table.

"Wait!" he said. "I'll be back."

My coffee arrived. I coiled in the cream, feeling pleased with myself. I'd put the Chairman in his place. Left him in no doubt the Home Secretary and I knew the scale of his crime, whatever it was. Made sure he'd part with anything to get that dispatch back.

Who'd have thought it? A boy from Jungle Terry. Maybe Slegman felt a sudden need for the privy? He's no cleverer or stronger than I am. It's just a toss of the cosmic dice; him born to a London drawing room, me to a bamboo hut. Just as fate brought us here and put me on top. I smiled.

SLEGMAN WAS GONE ten minutes. He came back with a book he laid on the tablecloth to his right. The spine read, *Nautical Almanac, 1857.*

I nodded at it, said, "Afraid you'll miss a lunar eclipse?"

"You think you're clever, Khan?" No tremble, except perhaps of irritation. "You put on a frock coat, get a chit from a German chemist ... think you can sit eye-to-eye with me? Back in India I'd have whipped your damned arse."

I leaned forward. "You want to know who killed Elijah Doyle?"

No one but Chrystal and I knew that.

Slegman leaned forward too. "Want to know what'll happen if that dispatch isn't in my hands in ninety minutes?"

"You'll destroy the trunk? Then what'll you trade?"

"How about your child's life," he said.

"Pah!" I sat back. "You're miss-informed, Slegman. I've no child."

The black eyes showed surprise, then a spiteful gleam.

I don't know what he means. But it's no bluff, that's for sure. I stared back, turning it in my mind. *Child?* Does he mean my work? The fruit of a youthful dalliance in Bengal? I could think of none.

My thoughts came back to Bea, the restaurant – *something we need to talk about.* She wasn't well, but they weren't the signs of carrying a child. In any case, she told me she's barren because she never had a child with Shapton.

Slegman grinned like a marsh crocodile. "You didn't know ... Shalpu?"

That name: like lightning. Only Bea knew my mother called me Shalpu. *Bea – Lucy Ocklynge – Adelaide Doyle.* How else could Slegman know?

"Oh yes," he said, "I know about you and Beatrice Motcombe, your adulterous affaire ... how you humiliated Shapton Sands, a man I'd known since Haileybury, went to Calcutta with as writers."

Haileybury's the Company college for civil servants, *writers* they're called.

"The most dissolute school in England," I said. "Where you learn to tax the daily bread, cull the *redundant* population by famine–"

"Your vile tongue'll have you hanged–"

"Your vile deeds'll see you damned!"

He poked the fork at me again. "You want to see Beatrice Motcombe again, let alone your bastard child, you'll do ... *exactly* as I say."

"Liar! You wouldn't dare–"

"Dare?" He nearly laughed. "She lives with a native, drinks in hells ... duped Shapton into a childless marriage for money, scorned him like a tenant pauper–"

"His father gambled the family fortune on a mad–"

"Cheated ... by a scheming Scot who preyed on his civilizing–"

"Bollocks! He was blinded by greed–"

"Who gives a damn what happens to that Motcombe woman? Except her husband ... who'd rather see her dead. She's wilful, headstrong ... who'll weep when she's washed up with the sewage on the Isle of Dogs–"

"I would!"

"You? If you're her champion, God help her!"

I got up, fury rushing like a tide. Blood pulsing so hard in my ears it made Slegman's voice far off.

"Take a boat from Adelphi Warf," he said, "to the steam pier on Hungerford Bridge. Arrive at exactly ten o'clock. There you'll hand me the dispatch and I'll tell you where to find your whore. Got it?"

I glared down, incensed.

"If you fail," he said, "they're gone with the tide."

I gripped my side of the table, tipped it into his lap with a furious roar. The crockery and cutlery clattered into his midriff, splashing his shirt with coffee and gravy and wine, shocking him with wave of icy water from the bucket.

"If they go, you'll go too," I hissed. "I swear it!" I added my weight to the table's, forced the top into his gut till he wheezed, eyes bulging, arms flailing like an upturned turtle. "And you'll bring my trunk of evidence, or you'll get nothing from me. You understand? NOTHING!"

Two men slipped from the shadows, grabbed me one each side like bears. It took three goes to pull me off. The table rocked back onto its feet. Slegman sat panting and furious, covered in his dinner. Our eyes locked in mutual hatred. I balled my fists again, ready to battle for my life.

"Leave him!" Slegman gasped. Then, more quietly, "Let him go." The bears eased their grip. The wine bottle lay on its side on the tablecloth, quietly glug-glugging a pool of Sancerre. "You'll get your evidence," he said.

Neither Slegman nor I said a word, but our eyes did – we're enemies, at war, no mercy given or expected.

I levelled my tie, smoothed my coat, picked up my bag and strode out.

Twenty

IF I'D HAD my wits, I'd have gone next door to the Library to wring the dispatch's message from Adelaide Doyle.

But my mind is on Bea. I'd demanded the trunk because I cared about my people, didn't think Slegman would murder an aristocrat. *It's a threat.* But running the half mile to Adelphi Terrace, I'm not so sure. *I shouldn't've provoked him.* Like poking a wasps' nest, but the swarm went buzzing after Bea. Slegman probably knew I'd met her. Thought I'd given her the dispatch.

I ran upstairs. Found the front door open, gaslights on and hall silent. A wisp of hope said Bea's still at the hotel draining the carafe. In the front room the wisp evaporated. There's a quiet, like wreckage after a storm: a trail of broken ornaments from the sideboard to the table to the fireplace; fireirons in the hearth; tongs nearby on the rug in a spatter of fresh blood.

A pace away, Bea's handbag lay open. Huddled on the sofa sat Jane Muckalt hugging her midriff, staring at the picture window as if I wasn't there.

"Where is she?" I said. "What happened?"

Jane flashed me an accusing stare, turned away. I went over, saw scratches on her left cheek – red, ragged lines, gouged from her eye to her jawline. The cheek's pink too, swelling from a blow. I crouched, took her shoulders. More softly, I said, "Where is she, Jane? Tell me."

"Gone," she said, blankly.

I shook her. "There's blood ... is she hurt?"

"They took her."

"They?"

"Two men."

"When?"

She shrugged. "Ten ... fifteen minutes ago. I don't know."

"What *men?* What'd they look like?"

"Look like?" She glared. "What the hell does it matter? Men! They took her ... she's gone. It's finished!"

"Finished? What're you talking about?" I squeezed her shoulders harder. "Tell me *exactly* what happened."

"Where were you?" she said, angrily. "Why'd you abandon her in the hotel? If you'd been here—"

"She said that ... *abandoned?*"

"Yes ... *ABANDONED!* Never seen her so hurt."

"For God's sake, Jane. Tell me—"

"Oh, I'll tell you! My Lady came in, upset, asking for tea. I was in the kitchen when there's a knock at the door. Lady Beatrice said to answer. When I lifted the latch two men barged in wanting a letter or some such. My Lady said she knew nothing of it. They threatened her. She told them to go to hell ... they tried to grab her ... she dodged round the sofa. They chased her, and she caught one of them a crack on the head with the fire tongs."

She nodded at the red patch on the rug. "That's his blood, not hers. Then they were angry, called her horrible names, twisted her arms. They slapped her. But she wouldn't tell so they hauled her out of the apartment."

I tracked the debris ... the ornaments and fireirons, the open front door ... it fit her story. Which made it my fault. I'd told Bea to tell no one, should've realized she'd honour the promise whatever it took. I'd thrown her to the dogs.

"Hauled her where?" I said.

"How the hell do I know?"

"Didn't you try to stop—"

"Look at me!" Jane cried, getting to her feet. "What do you *think* I did?"

I lifted my hands. "I'm sorry. If I just had an idea where they'd ..."

"If only you'd *been* here!"

"I wish to God I had–"

The dispatch. I grabbed my bag and ran out of the apartment, down the stairs two at a time. I didn't doubt Bea but I'd a rising sense of panic till I rattled open the mailbox, found the envelope with the dispatch inside. I slid the envelope into a pouch in my bag, closed it up. Blew a long breath.

Upstairs I expected Jane to pile on the scorn, but she'd turned needy. She wrung her hands, made imploring eyes that drew me over. She came closer too, pressing into my chest. I held her, tried to hug some reassurance ... which felt pleasant, but wrong in the circumstances.

I won't deny I've had what Bea'd call unwholesome thoughts about Jane. She's comely, alluring in looks and manner. Younger. I don't feel guilty. It's Bea who undressed her for me, offered her like a toy. I can't help seeing Jane naked, as if we're already intimate ... lovers of sorts. Like now. Bea's confidants, alone and worried what's happening to her, how we'd live without her.

Moist eyed, Jane said, "Oh, what're we to do, Doctor Khan?"

"I'll get her back."

"You know where–"

"No ... but I know who's taken your mistress. I've–"

"My mistress!" She took a pace back. "She's *our* life, *our* home, *our* position in the world ..."

I should've been more considerate. When we met, Bea and Jane were more like friends than mistress and maid; shared glances and giggles over secrets they wouldn't share with me. The ottoman affair ended that, put them back upstairs and downstairs. But Earlsacre is Jane's life too, one she'll never replace.

"I know," I said. "They want the letter ...we've agreed to exchange–"

"Agreed? You had it all the time?" She clasped a hand to her throat.

248

"Yes ... no! Look, they'll get it at ten this evening." I nodded at the window towards Hungerford Bridge. "At the steam pier."

"It's about those dead men, isn't it ... why they put you in gaol?"

"Listen, Jane–"

"Oh God ... it's the Company!" Her lower lip trembled. Then her eyes fluttered, and she toppled against me sinking limp in my arms. The evening had been too much. I laid her on the sofa, went into the kitchen to rummage in a cupboard for the cooking brandy. I wondered how much Bea'd told her.

As I rinsed a glass, a half empty cup of herbal tea caught my eye. It smelt faintly of peppermint, tasted bitter. I threw it in the sink. In the front room, Jane was shivering. Her hands fiddled with nothing like a child in a nightmare. She wouldn't take the brandy, just shut her eyes and shook her head. I'd have pressed it if the telegraph hadn't struck up its clockwork chatter. I went over and tore off the tape.

<<*Impey went to Ivy Lane last night. Not seen since. Chrystal*>>

I put my hands together, fingers to lips; a pose I got from O'Shaughnessy. It conjured his presence, let him work through me. *What would he do?* I sat at the finger-pedal and typed:

<<*Hackney station 12 noon tomorrow. Come armed. Khan*>>

The message tick-tocked away. Would Chrystal wait or go to the nursery on his own? I'd no idea. Even less if I'd make it myself. When I got up, Jane had picked up the glass and gone to the picture window. Looking out she tossed the brandy back in one. I picked up my bag, went and stood next to her.

She nodded into the darkness, said, "That where you'll meet?"

The Bridge starts a little west of the Adelphi, runs a quarter mile over the Thames to Lambeth. *Bradley's Guide* says it's a 'marvel of modern mechanical ingenuity,' which it is – a roadway on chains, strung between red-brick towers on concrete piers. The south pier doubles as a landing stage.

"Yep, ten o'clock sharp. We'll be safely back by a quarter past. I'll need a rowing boat."

The Thames is like black velvet. Bolts of lightning lit the scene in metallic arc-light, bright as day. Jane pointed down and to the east. Beyond the Terrace is a wooden jetty outside a ramshackle tavern called the Fox Under the Hill.

"You'll find a waterman there," she said. "Anytime."

I knew it. Thorn and I had danced there with the coalheavers and ragtags who live in the tunnels under the Adelphi. A clump of rowing boats nosed the jetty, owners sipping ale in a lantern light, nodding along with a concertina.

"You can watch from here," I said, trying to be reassuring. "See us coming back."

Not that I felt reassured. In a rowing boat I'd be unstable, two feet below the pier. Slegman will be on solid concrete above. He'll call the shots, be gone before I can scramble ashore. I glanced at the mantelpiece clock, then checked the envelope in its pouch. Buckled the bag shut.

Sensing my departure, Jane turned and took my lapels. "But if you don't find her ... you won't leave me alone, will you?" The neediness again, now mixed with fear. "Say you won't, Hyder ... please."

"We'll be back," I said. "Stay here, don't open the door to anyone but me."

I left her there, watching the lightning crackle.

CROSSING ST JAMES Square, the London Library looked closed for the night. But as I got closer, I saw a figure sitting in a bay window, a candle burning on the table. It's Adelaide Doyle. When I tapped the glass, she got up to unlock the front door like the privileged subscriber she was.

We sat at a floral tablecloth facing each another. Around us the shadowy room was rammed with books: floor to ceiling, wall to wall. In front of the books are more books on trolleys and free-standing cases, like a literary jungle.

In lieu of a greeting, I said, "Place needs a stiff comb with Panizzi's ninety-one rules."

"Don't try to be funny, Hyder."

"I wasn't."

"You've seen the Home Secretary?"

"Yep."

"Tell me who killed my stepfather."

I sat my bag on the table, took the copy of the dispatch I'd made from my pocket, smoothed it on the cloth. "First you'll tell me what this says."

She shook her head. "After you."

I thought she'd try that. I'd been to the Library to read Liebig's *Agricultural Chemistry,* knew how the books are shelved. I got up, went into an even gloomier room to a run of books marked *Liturgies &c.* In a while I found the *Book of Common Prayer.* In another while I found the *King James Bible* on the shelf above. Back at the table, I laid both books facing Miss Doyle.

"You saw me in the Saloon," she said. "It's a bluff."

I opened the *Book of Common Prayer,* ran a finger down the page. Then I found a cross-reference in the *Bible.* Laid the open books before her. We stared at each other but before either of us spoke, a lanky, well-dressed figure crossed the window outside and knocked on the door.

Miss Doyle got up, let in a man in his latter fifties who some would call good looking for his age. They sat together facing me, the man glaring, cold faced as a father confronting his daughter's jilter.

Sir Reginald Clyde?" I suggested.

Must be. For one thing he fit Miss Doyle sketch on Brentford High Street. For another there're family traits – deep-set eyes, high cheek bones. And the man looks calculating, aloof. I could see him studying Bryce's *Treatise on Double-entry Bookkeeping,* fondling the key to his private pew in High Church.

"My uncle," Miss Doyle said.

It wasn't planned, but I said, "If I had fever, it's what I'd take!"

"Your meaning, Sir?" Clyde said.

"*Clyde's Seltzer,* you put it on the label."

"What if I did?"

"Cost me my job at the Sanitary Commission."

The job was testing medicines, *incognito*. The scale of adulteration in London snuffed out the embers of my belief it's the hub of civilization. Give a sick man poppy cases for opium or chalk for quinine, it's murder. But *Clyde's Seltzer* came up trumps, so I ended my report with a flourish – *If I had fever, it's what I'd take!* Somehow Clyde got hold of it, probably for a price.

"Your words," he said. "You deny them?"

"Written in confidence, not an endorsement."

"The public should know."

"I agree. But the Commissioners thought you'd paid me to use their good name ... gave me a verbal kick up the arse ... fired me."

I wasn't feeling polite. I was wondering why Sir Reginald Clyde's here. Is Miss Doyle worried Bea's told me who fed my private life to Nathaniel Slegman? More likely it's family loyalty: Clyde wants to know about malaria cures, about a dispatch that could bring down the Company.

He looked at my copy of the enciphered text, then the two open books. Propped an elbow on the table, squeezed the bridge of his nose and shook his head. Seems the Company needs a new cipher. I'd worked it out while riding with Thorn. Miss Doyle's study of the dispatch told me there's nothing hidden: no watermark or secret insignia, no cryptic motto on the back. The keyword clue had to be in plain sight on the front – something unique that'd change regular as clockwork. Now I know I'm right, I know the keyword.

Miss Doyle's stare was inscrutable ... bloody irritating.

Which is why I said, "You run a deadly business, Miss Doyle."

"What happened to Addie?"

"She nearly got me hanged. Could yet murder my child."

I still think Slegman might be bluffing, but I'm not sure.

Miss Doyle squinted, thinking. I'm remembering her uncle's competitor ruined in a few lines, the Indian savages run off the American plains.

"What you call *intelligence,*" I said, "is nothing but a trade in gossip; a fee to you, life or death to your victims."

"It's the facts," she said. "Undeniable–"

"Well, here's a fact ... Elijah Doyle shot himself. Suicide."

"Liar!" she fired back. "He was shot twice."

"By his own hand–"

"Impossible!"

"Between the devil and the deep sea," I added, spitefully. "Why not?"

She gulped, darted her eyes like a cornered squirrel. With no other way out, she grabbed her carpet bag and ran from the room. Clyde called, "Adelaide!" but the response was a front door slammed so hard it rattled on its hinges. We saw her go past the window, holding her skirts, walking fast. For an odd, fleeting moment I wondered why she'd left so abruptly.

His NIECE'S EXIT ruffled Clyde. I thought he might chase her or leave himself. Instead, he said, loftily, "Did you have to be so abrupt? Suicide's a damnable sin. She's afraid that wicked dispatch condemned Elijah to eternal hell."

I wasn't being treated like a fool – It's Rule Three, or maybe Four. "She doesn't believe in damnation," I said. "It's her affaire with Nathanial Slegman troubles her ... that the spectre of divorce drove her stepfather to suicide."

Clyde sat more upright as if raising himself above the mire. Now I thought he'd leave. But he didn't. He took a breath, murmured, *"Suicide?"* Then, "If any man deserves an eternity in hell, it's Nathanial Slegman."

"Harsh words," I said, hoping to goad him.

"You've read the dispatch."

I nodded at the books to say, *I know the keyword, what do you think?* "Your niece told you what it says?"

"That's why I'm here."

"It's not for sale."

"I'm not buying," he said.

"You know Doyle tried deciphering it before he died?" Clyde's face said he didn't. "His final words ... between the devil and the deep sea? What do you think he meant?"

Silence. Clyde thinking, eyes shining in the candlelight.

I know the keyword, but I can't use it without an alphabet square. What's more, a few cryptic lines mightn't mean much. Clyde's just the man to explain, so I pictured Miss Doyle's face as she'd read in the Saloon.

"First part of the dispatch was predictable," I said, off hand.

"Really? You surprise me."

I shrugged, hoping he's not calling my bluff.

"Slegman ... taken in so easily?" he said. "Can't understand it." The mystery seemed to trouble him. He clasped hands and laid them on the tablecloth. Looking straight at me, he said, "I need your word this goes no further, Khan."

I shouldn't've, but I said, "You'd trust the word of a savage?"

"I *trust* your clever enough to know your own self-interest."

Ouch! Rather meekly, I replied, "All right. I agree."

He gave a sharp nod, like a handshake. I did the same.

"Last year," he said, "I'd a visit from Henry Bullock. He told me he'd discovered a miraculous cure for fever. Said he'd come as a favour, so's not to put me out of business."

That figured. Henry fancied himself as the Sir Reginald of Ivy Lane. The *Illustrated News* did a sketch of Clyde, made him a chemical celebrity – the handsomest, richest, pharmacist in town.

Clyde rolled his eyes. "I don't need to tell you about the crackbrains and fraudsters who peddle wonder cures."

"Hence the Sanitary Commission," I said.

"Exactly. Well, he wouldn't say more. Only that he wanted a pile of my money to finish his work." His voice tightened. "Must think I'm a damned fool. I threw him out, threatened to set the dogs on him. But then Slegman ordered a secret trial in Calcutta Military Hospital." He lifted his hands, gave me the shining candle-eyes. "My niece thought you might throw some light on the matter."

"You didn't know about the trial ... until the dispatch?"

Clyde shook his head. "Couple of hours ago, from Adelaide."

I believed him. Which meant I could drop a bombshell. But gently, like a petal fluttering through his brain.

"Bullock thought he'd found a febrifuge," I said. "A native Asian plant."

"He actually believed it?"

I nodded. "Your harsh words taught him it'd be hard finding a backer. So he let me use his lab in return for crystalizing the active principle. I didn't know, of course. Then he tested it on malaria cases on the Greenwich hospital ship."

"Good God–"

"Oh yeah ... we all underestimated Henry. Then he got cleverer still, invited Elijah Doyle to witness the cure. Wasn't Bullock who went to Slegman, it was Doyle, the honest Christian."

Clyde nodded. "So *that's* why Slegman–"

"Funded the trial? Yeah, didn't want anyone to know, least of all you–"

"And?"

"Success, apparently ... better than quinine."

Clyde bit his bottom lip, muttered, "Christ almighty."

"But then Henry wasn't so clever ..."

"Yes? Go on–"

"He got greedy ... wanted the lion's share."

Clyde snapped his fingers. "Slegman tried to beat it out of him ... Bullock took his own life ... takes the secret with him?"

"Not quite."

"For God's sake Khan ... I could be ruined!"

I sat back, mirroring the candle-eyes. "The second bit of the dispatch surprised me."

He licked his lips. "The rifles?"

"Why so secret?"

Clyde shook his head. "Can't discuss that, not even for a miracle cure."

"State secret, is it ... matter of national security?"

"Something like that."

I dug in my coat, showed him the Oath I'd signed two hours ago. Clyde read, studied the signatures, crinkled his brow with a snort of astonishment.

I said, "I won't blab any secrets–"

"Except to Green."

"He knows ... all of it."

"What? But how–"

"Raikes Elphinstone ... put a gun to James Peach's head, got the whole story ... pulled the trigger–"

"My God! Clyde took a moment to think it through. Then, he said, "Huh! Didn't think Peach was the sort to blow his own brains out ... but how did Elphinstone *know* about the dispatch?"

"No idea. But he's in London chasing evidence. That's how I got involved ... Green thought I'd murdered Henry Bullock to shut him up, wanted my testimony that Slegman put me up to it."

"And he got you to sign the Oath because ...?"

I took out the little bottle, shook it. Explained how Bullock and Doyle had left it in the Calcutta General Hospital. "Green wanted me to track down the source, hoped it'd lead to Slegman."

Clyde nodded absently, his thoughts elsewhere. "Peach deserved a bullet in the head, for his treachery." He nodded to the ciphered text. "Green's got the dispatch, the original?"

"Nope."

You'll sell it ... to Slegman?"

I nodded, wasn't mentioning the trunk of evidence.

"I'd buy it myself," said Clyde, "just to bring him down, but more scandal's the last thing the Company needs right now."

"So what about the rifles?"

"The cartridges, the fat."

I shrugged. "You forget, I haven't been in India for eighteen months."

He stared like his niece, cogwheels spinning in silent calculation. The balance: "I want the plant, the chemistry, the drug ..."

"For a price."

"How much?"

"It's not money I want."

Clyde said, "How'd Bullock *stumble* on a febrifuge?"

"Robert Fortune via the Apothecaries' Garden in Chelsea." I want to convince him, not give too much away.

"Tropical?"

"Semi."

"How'd he grow enough for the Calcutta trial?"

"A private nursery and Slegman's money."

"Name of the plant?"

"Un-huh... that's all, on account."

He poked a finger at me "You know I could ruin you, as a chemist?"

"Or you could set up plantations in the Himalayan foothills. Assam. Darjeeling. No worries about Peruvian bark or perilous seas."

He stared across St James Square, nibbling a nail on his left hand. Then, he said, "Sepoys, mainly Hindu or Muslim, the one won't eat beef, the other pork. Know how to load an Enfield P53 rifle?"

"Nope."

"Bite the paper tip off the cartridge. Last year Doyle warned the Company some of the P53 cartridges might've been greased with beef or pork fat. Seems no action was taken until ..." He nodded at the dispatch copy.

"Slegman warned the Chairman of Calcutta's Military Board," I said, as if I knew. "James Peach."

"Not warned ... illegally informed. We'd already reprimanded Peach for handing out Bibles in Bengali and Sanskrit, preaching on parade. Now he told his Sepoys they'd defiled their religions by eating beef and pork, said he'd baptise them as Christians, which we strictly forbid. So, we relived him of command. When he wouldn't recant, we threatened court-martial ... seems Elphinstone saved us the trouble."

"Slegman *meant* Peach to tell his Sepoys?"

"Why else fake a ciphered dispatch?"

"But ... what'd they gain–"

"Salvation. Doing the Lord's work." I must've looked lost because Clyde said, "Think like an evangelical ... how likely is it a tiny nation conquers and rules so much of the world?" He didn't wait for an answer. "For them, *impossible* ... unless it's ordained by God, which means the Company rules by heavenly decree, has a sacred duty. You know, Matthew 24–"

"Gospel to all nations, then the end comes ... the day of judgment?"

"Precisely. We banned missionaries because they stir up religious unrest, disrupt trade. But with the Whigs in power, there're liberal Directors like Slegman who see Hindus and Muslims as forces of Satan ... want the gospels taught. Slegman confirmed the cartridge story to stir up unrest."

"Like Mangal Pandey, the mutiny at Barrackpore."

Clyde nodded. "Says they're evidence of God's anger, that we must raise Christ's banner from one end of India to the other or lose the Empire. But the story got out of hand, convinced the Sepoys we're planning forced conversions. Went up country like a thunderbolt ... ignited a bonfire of grievances."

"Surely Doyle couldn't've intended–"

"Good God, no. He was a moderate, peace loving, thought a

cheap malaria cure would bring the natives to Christ." He leaned ominously from the shadows. "It's bad, Khan, the slaughter's horrendous. In Calcutta we damn near lost Fort William. If we don't act fast our colonies will go like dominoes."

"If Britain's enemies had sat in conclave for a century, they couldn't have dreamt up anything worse?"

"Well put. The Whigs've waited years for something like this. They'll blame us for the mutiny, rule India directly through Parliament."

"No wonder Doyle killed himself," I said.

"Oh yes ... he warns about the grease to *avert* unrest, Slegman does exactly the opposite. Doyle must've suspected, managed to keep the dispatch. Then he hears about the mutiny and has to know the truth ... if he delivered the fatal message. When he couldn't decipher it, killed himself in despair."

"But why'd a man of peace keep a revolver at his bank?"

"Standard issue," said Clyde, "to Company servants on business in India. He didn't want to keep it at home."

That made sense. "Well," I said, "you've told me about the devil ... what about the deep sea?"

Clyde nodded thoughtfully, blew a sigh that nearly guttered the candle.

I said, "What does your niece see in Nathanial Slegman?"

He stared out at the Square while the candle settled to a gentle lick.

"Life's hard for Adelaide," he said. "Father died violently, mother in childbirth. Both fathers raised her like a boy, encouraged her independence and free thinking. She's a brilliant mind for business ... imagination and a flair for mining facts. Men don't want a woman like that. Has her father's strength, some'd say ruthlessness, finds men *like* him ... alluring."

"She admires Slegman's brutality," I said, "his commercial empire?"

Clyde gazed outside again, then at the floral tablecloth, then me.

"Truth is, Khan, I partly blame myself."

I listened. Folk often make me a confessor. Maybe it's the native in a frockcoat, like a priest's fancy dress. Or that blacks know pain; what's a bit more to a whipping boy? Maybe they just think I've no one to tell.

"Adelaide did well selling intelligence," he said. "But she resented making duller wits rich for a fee. Then she'd a vision, like the spirit of the age – an electric telegraph round the globe ... a nervous system to annihilate space and time. To make the whole world a London suburb. But the capital cost's colossal, and she wanted to own a share. When she asked me for a loan, I refused."

"Why ... if you'd such faith in her?"

He shrugged. "The prejudice of most men. Seemed contrary to the natural order to entrust so much capital to a young woman. And so ..."

"She went to Slegman. But why'd he agree?"

"Didn't at first. Took him a while to recognize Adelaide's brilliance. Then he saw himself as the spider at the centre of a worldwide web, king of the globe's intelligence."

"A Zeus as rich as Croesus?"

"Quite so. They struck a deal. Even he hadn't the money to buy a controlling interest, so he helped Adelaide raise the capital for a share ... just enough to give them a joint holding over fifty percent. Then they worked together."

"That's how they became lovers?"

"Hmph! Partners, more like. They'll control the World-Girdle telegraph, keep each other close. Adelaide loves a man who admires her mind. He sees a talent for business, knows a wife can't testify against her husband."

"Well," I said, "devil or deep sea ... it's Slegman to blame. It's his divorce threatens scandal at home, his dispatch sparked an uprising in India."

260

"My poor niece," Clyde said. "I fear for her, really I do."

A dial-clock high on the wall says it's nearly nine thirty. I need to go.

"Elphinstone," I said. "Why would a Company soldier work for Green–"

"Elphinstone!" he spat, like a bad oyster. "Earl Canning's creature, the Governor General of India."

"But ... isn't the Governor a Company appointee?"

"Officially, yes. But a Whig Parliament means we're told who to nominate. Canning and Green are hand in glove, both'd like to see the Company abolished, run India between them. The last Governor saved Elphinstone from court martial, put him in charge of intelligence ... he's not on our side now."

"Told me he doesn't need orders ... just knows."

Clyde liked that. "Chapel and playing field," he said. "Rugby, Cambridge, a trained hound chases a fox ... doesn't even know why."

"Doesn't bother you ... the Company could be abolished."

He thought about that. Then he sighed and said, "It's familiar, like a comfy pair of shoes ... I'd like to keep it that way. But Parliamentary rule means free trade ... no Company telling me where I can and can't establish plantations ... a big advantage if you've got the capital ... *Plus ça change,* as Karr sagely put it."

I pocketed the dispatch copy, thanked him for the lecture on imperial politics. Then I told him what I really wanted for *Artemisia Chinensis.* He nodded at the two open books I'd left on the table.

"They should be reshelved," he said.

"I expect they will ... the librarian?"

With a look of distaste, he said, "We're privileged subscribers." He closed the books and took them into the gloomy room to reshelve.

I left, jogged back to the jetty at Adelphi wharf. It's hot, thick as dal, raindrops oozing like lentils from the air, plopping on the pavement. The storm's about to break.

Twenty-One

TIME ISN'T A stream. It's a thicket with small clearings for memories. Like walking by the bullock cart with my mother to the river Mor. Like the fateful ride from Adelphi Wharf to the Hungerford steam pier. One-way. No return to the life I'd had, the one I'd thought was mine. Until it wasn't.

* * *

A waterborne beer-seller called Pennyfeather rowed me into the night. An old man with a leather coat and broad shoulders, biting a clay pipe: a shilling, there and back. The Thames flows north by the Houses of Parliament, swings west and wide under Hungerford Bridge, smells of engine oil and sewage.

Like my first day in England, trudging down Commercial Road from East India Dock in search of the model metropolis: the gardened palaces of Murshidabad blended with the neo-classical splendour of Calcutta's White Town. Happy, well-dressed people, enjoying the civilization they're foisting on the rest of us. What I saw were the grim-faced poor, rows of their poky hovels, black with soot and smoke – noisy factories, a smutted sun – always the gagging stench of shit drifting off the murky Thames.

That's when it dawned: I was there. London was all around me.

It's around me now, a scatter of lights through the falling rain. Slegman's out there, waiting, listening for the same chimes. Bea too. I'd put her from my mind after I'd left Jane, got absorbed with Clyde. But as the riverbank slid away, I lost my bearings, sought calm in Pennyfeather's firm pulls: the rhythmic groan of the rowlocks; water hissing on the bow. I felt chilly, adrift on the high tide.

The rain fell harder, heavy drops bouncing off the river, kicking up a foam. Pennyfeather wedged the oars, turned up his collar and pulled on a sou'wester. We veered and tacked, dodging skiffs and steamers that slipped in and out of the night. I'm astern, facing my ferryman. Stabs of lightning lit his weathered face a ghostly white, thunder tore the sky louder with every pull of the oars.

The journey felt aimless until Pennyfeather slowed and stirred the oars. We turned a sharp ninety degrees to see the southerly tower fifty yards upriver, eerie by storm light. A door on the walkway leads down inside the tower to a ledge on the concrete pier: the landing stage. That's where we meet. I'd told Pennyfeather to listen for the chimes at ten, but he'd never hear them over the storm. Instead, he dug in a pocket and pulled out a watch.

The rain came harder still, sticking my hair to my forehead, dribbling cold down my back. The Thames is always moody, tempered by gale and tide and the rain it drains from England's heart. Now it's a boiling flood. Poised for the seaward ebb, for the drama on Hungerford Bridge.

We wait.

The Bridge is a high footway joining Hungerford Market to the labouring masses in Southwark south of the river. The market's closed, the Bridge empty. Slegman chose well. I'd called him Guy Fawkes, said he'd never harm Lady Beatrice, but Clyde's words changed that. He'd massacre the whole nobility to get that dispatch back. Otherwise, he'll be a bigger traitor than Fawkes, burned in effigy every End-of-Empire Day.

I want to see Bea, pull her into the boat, pull her close. I swear we'll never quarrel again, not after this. I opened the bag, protecting it from the rain with my body, saw the envelope. I shut the bag and held it tight.

We wait.

BEA AND I met through desperation and poverty. She was desperate. I was broke. A few days after Prof. Hofmann mentioned Henry Bullock, he called me to his private room, asked if I'd heard of a Lady Beatrice Motcombe. When I said I hadn't, he twirled his Prussian moustache.

"An original donor," he said. "College wouldn't be here without their generosity. She's reading Miss Marcet's *Conversations on Chemistry*. Wants someone to show the experiments."

"An Indian?"

Hofmann shrugged. "Tell her you're descended from a Mughal prince."

"Like the boy king of the Punjab?"

It's fashionable to dote on the young Maharaja of the fallen Sikh Empire. He's held in captive luxury in London, beyond his scheming mother, while the Company makes the Punjab a tenant farm for British adventurers.

"Queen's very taken with him," he said.

"The obedient courtier?"

Hofmann's face darkened. "Pays well, wouldn't hurt."

I smiled. "Of course, for the College." I respected Hofmann.

The Earlsacre estate hugs the river Thames not far from Kingston. Covers a lot more than an acre. When I arrived on foot from the station on a bright morning, frost crunching underfoot, it put a spell on me. Like the longing I'd heard from Brits in Calcutta for hedgerows and lanes, robins and cottages.

My first taste of England's jungle-terry. But there's a shabbiness, just beyond the charm of weathered age. I was jogging my confidence up the steps of the villa's portico when Lady Motcombe opened the door. Nothing shabby about her. She caught my eye at once, not that I'd show it.

In India, white women are taboo to the likes of me; a lynch job, if you're lucky. She knew who I was from the hour, the case of apparatus I'd lugged from the station. I'd brought glassware to match the illustrations in Miss Marcet's book. If Lady Motcombe had misgivings about a native tutor, I quelled them by introducing myself as Prince Hyder, chemist, son of the Nawab of Bengal. She was flattered, felt Hofmann had made an effort.

We sat at a table in a bright bay-window, overlooking a lawn. Don't think she'd read a word of the *Conversations*, but since she mentioned *chemical philosophy* I began with the *elements*, set up some apparatus to make hydrogen and oxygen – transparent, odourless gasses.

Here's how it went:

"This is oxygen. Relights a glowing splint. Like ... this."

Lady Beatrice: "Oh."

"This is hydrogen. Pops when it burns. Like ... this."

"Mm." She gave me a look – *burns, pops ... you call that philosophy?*

"An element's a simple substance," I said. "Can't be subdivided by chopping or grinding or pounding ..."

Disdainfully: "And how's that useful?"

"Useful?"

"To the soil. Phosphorus?"

"Ah," I said. "Like Nitrogen?"

She nodded. A few queries and false starts later, I found her farm manager had gone three years ago. She'd taken charge out of pride. Crop yields dwindled. Eventually someone told her chemistry restored tired soils. Dismantling my apparatus – which Jane took to wash up – I said I'd analyze the fields, revive them with scientific nutrients. She was delighted.

I took my samples, went off to read about lime, saltpeter, dung, bones, guano, super phosphates and the business of artificial manures. Armed myself with *nitrogeno-sulphurization*. In ten days, I'd a plan for each field and crop. Regularly walked the grounds with Lady B. Three months later – mid-summer's eve – the vegetables thrived. I'm invited to dine with her.

Part of my secret's Finn O'Connell. I found Finn through one of Hofmann's farmer-benefactors, persuaded Lady B to hire him as manager. Finn's desperate to make a mark, reorganized the farm. But Lady B, wary of the lazy, Popish Irish, insists it's me who turned things around, worked my chemical magic on the soil. Now she's worth money as well as land.

Which is why at dinner we sat at opposite ends of the table like lord and lady, served by the butler. She called me her 'prince of the elements,' her 'savior,' then settled on the Prince of Murshidabad. No mention of a husband, not then. After dessert, she dismissed the butler. We strolled in the grounds by moonlight, drank champagne, talked about the beauty of the heavens. A hot evening.

She said, "Can you swim, Doctor Khan?" Took my hand, ran down to the river. Slipped off her shoes, then her gown, then her petticoat and silk drawers. Jumped into the water from the little jetty. I glimpsed her in the moonlight – naked, white – exciting as only forbidden fruit can be.

"Come on," she called. "Don't tell me you're shy?"

I caught her midstream, where we splashed and laughed to hide our desire. Swam closer. She gripped my shoulders. I felt her nipples hard against my chest, her legs wrap around mine. "Kiss me, my prince." I did. Then she shivered, said, "I'm cold." She led me into the house, into bedroom where it seemed mere courtesy to dry her. She dried me. There's the bed, big and soft, turned down with satin sheets. What better way to warm ourselves? To cuddle and rub, hide beneath the bedclothes.

Then there's no pretense, no excuse required.

When Bea fell asleep, the night was nearly gone. In the chilly dawn she stirred and mewled, curled against me and slept on. I pulled the bedclothes round us, watched the moon sink below the oaks, the sky flame red striking a new day. Felt happy. Not because I'd found my love. I wasn't such a fool. But it's a moment to savour. We'd caught the rules off duty, grabbed an unlikely moment. When we get up, she'll be my employer, trust me not to be so vulgar or tiresome as to assume.

But it wasn't so. We breakfasted together. I spend nights at Earlsacre, she does at the Adelphi. The affaire grew because I thought it wouldn't. Like an exotic weed behind the compost heap; no one seemed to notice or care. Her servants accepted me as the Prince. Bea and I spent more time together, ran the estate together, talked about politics and religion, about marriage and divorce.

Now I can't imagine life without her.

One night, after we'd made love, she told me she was married. Off hand, just like that. Before I could object, she said he'd left her, lived with a native wife in India. Why shouldn't she take a lover? It's her estate. I swallowed the deception because it suited me. I like the secret life. No question of marriage. No children. Nothing awkward.

But there're consequences. Not wanting to be kept, I told Mungo I'd do prize fights for a purse. Earnt more in a few hours than Hofmann does in a month. Then there's God. Bea's Anglican Church is like a military band keeping everyone in step, Christ waving the baton. It's assumed I hear the music, even though it's the heathen lover she wants, the endowed native with animal desire, trained in physical love. I sang Christian hymns at the Orphan School, said the prayers, knew when to kneel and say Amen. I play along.

It's a good life. Or it was. Like the weed, there's always a worry someone will notice, tear you up and chuck you on the heap.

THAT'S HOW IT felt now, sitting in Noah's flood.

I'd just learned Bea's pushing for a divorce. That she's carrying my child. The thought thrilled me. I wanted her back from that ogre. Wanted to tell her things I'd never even told myself. I didn't want to be without her, ever.

Pennyfeather glanced at the watch, rowed a few hard strokes, then turned us so the stern nosed against the pier. I turned too. High above on the walkway a coach and horses appeared, mute in the storm. Doors slammed silently. There were no footsteps in the stairway. Slegman and Meigs appeared on the ledge a yard above me. Slegman held a lantern. Meigs held my trunk.

"Show him," Slegman shouted through the gusting rain.

Meigs opened the lid, rested the trunk on the pier edge. Tilted it so I could see inside. It's all there: diaries, legers, photographs. Just as I'd packed it.

"Where is she?" I called back.

"Nearby." Slegman dangled a key on a ring fixed to an oblong of wood. The kind that floats if you drop it in the river. "The dispatch?"

"I want to see her!"

Slegman shook his head. I'd have kicked up more of a fuss if I hadn't already guessed he wouldn't bring her as a captive. I might've laid a trap. This way it's just a trunk for an envelope. Everything else is deniable.

I leaned over the bag, fetched out the envelope. Slegman's eyes widened in the flickering light. "Show me!" he barked. I hesitated, cast my eyes around the pier. No tricks. I opened the flap to find ... nothing. No dispatch. My guts clenched. I swallowed hard, struggled to keep calm. Rummaged in the pouch, all the pouches, the whole the bag. No dispatch.

I checked my pockets, checked the bottom of the boat. A hot sweat like a blush broke over the neck and shoulders. I looked up. Slegman and Meigs looked down, both soaked, their hair stuck to their foreheads as mine was.

"Where is it?" Slegman called.

I stood unsteadily, gripping the stern. Held up the envelope hoping he'd reach down ... I'd a mad idea to catch his wrist, drag him into the boat. Then Pennyfeather would row, and I'd make Slegman tell me where he'd hidden Bea.

But he kept back. "SHOW ME!" he shouted.

"He ain't got it," called Meigs. "It's a bluff."

"You gave it to George Green."

"I didn't!"

268

Slegman stared, decided Meigs was right. He gave a nod to shut the trunk, and both men walked away.

"NO!" My shout was cut off in a blinding flash and a seismic rip of thunder. Then, "For God's sake tell me—"

Slegman turned, threw the key at me. "Find her yourself! And you'd better be quick about it." Then they're gone.

I scrabbled for the key in the boat's sodden hull, tossed it in my bag, threw the bag on the pier hauling myself after it. I ran squelching up the stairs, kicked open the door to the footbridge. The coach's already twenty yards away, heading south at a gallop. No chance. I looked at the key. How many million keyholes might it fit in London?

I turned on the walkway, following the skyline with its dancing tongues of electric fire. Wind howled down the black Thames, shrieked though the steel hawsers. I felt swamped, sinking in despair. Far across the river, in a window in the Adelphi, I saw a figure in silhouette. Jane, hands clasped in front, peering out. Depending on me, like Beatrice and our unborn child. I'm only their hope.

What would O'Shaughnessy do?

Not a million keyholes. They took her from the Adelphi. She's nearby, north of the river. The maker's name is stamped on the key's bow. Same maker as my key to the Cell, from a shop off the Strand. I jogged north towards Hungerford Market. The wooden floater's stamped YS SEWER. There're sewer outlets all along the north bank, some sealed with iron gates. I ran back over the bridge.

The tidal Thames flushes the sewers twice daily. Iron gates keep out finders, men who'll risk disease and monster rats to salvage the loot of London's drains. Men who often drown. *The Nautical Almanac, 1857.* Not a lunar eclipse. It's the hightide at Waterloo Bridge. Slegman wants to blame me for letting Bea drown. *Run faster.* I shot onto the top terrace of the empty Market, skidding on the shining planks, raced down two stairways to Villiers Street, left onto the waterfront two hundred yards from Adelphi Terrace.

Slowed to a fast walk. *YS SEWER?*

Then the Thakur lent a hand. Past Buckingham Street, I came to the end of York Street. YS. Beyond the promenade, jutting into the river's a free-standing portico, like a king's mausoleum. It's a columned water gate, an ornate pier known as York Stairs. YS.

I ran through the archways onto the stone landing that juts into the river. The storm's passed its peak, fallen to occasional flickers and steady rain. By the lamps on Adelphi Terrace, I made out the brickwork on the bank west of the gate, the crown of a submerged arch. I dropped the bag, tore off my frockcoat and jumped, felt a shock as rancid, icy water closed over my head.

Bobbing up, I made couple of frog kicks to the arch, breathing hard, almost blind. Reaching down I felt the bars of an iron gate closing the sewer's mouth. I took a breath, worked my way down the grating, feeling for the lock. Underwater it's black – no up or down, only driving desperation. I ran my hands over the iron bars like a mad ape in a cage. Found the plate, the keyhole, went up the bars for air trying to ignore what's seeping into my brain.

The slack water in the sewer says the tide's up, about to turn.

I held the key ready, worked down the iron using a thumb to find the keyhole. Pushed in the key, turned clockwise, anticlockwise, wrenched the gate back and forth. Felt my hair and clothes floating on my skin like cold rags.

I forced the key till it turned with an eerie echo from the miles of tunnel beyond. *It fits, she's here!* I hung on as the gate swung out taking me into the river, legs drifting like fronds with the flow. Then I went hand over hand down the bars to the sewer's entrance. It's a yard wide, a little more in height. *What am I looking for? An air-bubble in the roof, a side chamber? How far before the tunnel rises above the water? Fifty yards? Half a mile?*

I went for a breath, braced my hands in the entrance, hauled my way inside. Moved forward, blind, poking and kicking the walls, feeling for an opening. Five yards ... ten ... the brickwork's ragged, unyielding.

Then I heard another eerie clang, felt the pressure rise. My throat's gagging for air. It's suicide to go much further but what else can I do? A pulse of colder water hit me, forcing me back. I dug in my bootheels, held out against the rising current wondering how a tide could fall so fast. The flow swelled, pushed harder. I held on, strangling my own urge to breathe.

Then something hit my chest, like a log. Heavy and fast moving, it tore my feet loose, sent us racing together in the stream ... twisting and bumping. I pushed it away, felt cloth, the squash of a body. Shoved in horror at the thought of a gnawed ratcatcher. But the cloth's silky, expensive. The flesh is plump and firm. I fumbled for a grip, felt hair, a neck, a shoulder ... grabbed an upper arm as my own shoulder hit the gate hinge, stinging with a fiery lance of pain.

I seized the ironwork with my left hand, held the body with my right as it went with the tide. The stretch crucified me, lifted my head above the water. I heaved a breath, holding on as the body turned, followed the current into the river. Then the pull returned, sliding my hand from the biceps to the elbow, to the wrist, to a final, frantic grip on the fingers.

Then it's gone.

I held the gate, gasping. *What happened?* The swell of water told part of the story. The storm drains are open, channeling a square mile of torrential rain down the sewer. Something small and sharp in my right hand told the rest. I squeezed my fist, swam to the submerged York Stairs, staggered from the river, my clothes raining water. I squelched back to the waterfront terrace, to a gas lamp. Opened my fist to see the object in my palm, the one from the fingers.

A ring. Bea's crest on the bezel, plain to see.

COSSIMBAZAR'S A TOWN near Murshidabad, once the great marketplace of Bengal. Famed for its river, its fragrant atmosphere, its silks and ivories. Then a mighty storm swelled the Ganges, gave it a climatic fit that altered its course overnight. Left the riverbed dry, the town an evil-smelling swamp, overrun by wild beasts, the air deadly with malaria. The palaces fell, the docks were dust.

That's how I felt. My solid world gone in a moment. No cold. No pain. Only an aching emptiness. Like when my mother died. Like that monsoon day in the library at the Upper Orphan School. A void.

I must've found my coat and bag, walked along the waterfront. Must've climbed the stairs to Adelphi Terrace, gone into No. 8, up to my apartment. How else did I get here? I thought I'd stood still in Cossimbazar amid the cry of wolves and the smell of death. But there's Jane Muckalt, staring at my sodden hair and clothes. My ashen face. My tears.

Her lips moved. "Where is she?"

I held the ring in the flat of my hand. Jane looked. I looked. That's when it was real. Like a fist in the face. Like the irrepressible urge to vomit.

"It was her," I said.

"Was?"

"Oh mercy, it *was* her. In the sewer, the river."

"Drowned?" Jane said.

She was now. But what if she'd been alive, what if I'd held on?

"I tried," I said. "I–"

Jane's eyes flashed panic. "Don't leave me! Say you won't."

She touched my lapels, drew back at the wet. Went to fetch a cloth. She undressed me, must've done because I'm naked on the sofa, wrapped in a towel. She held a cup to my lips, said, "Drink ... drink!"

I drank. She did too. It's handi from a fresh bucket. Strong ... the first dip from the top, like fire. I felt the burn in my throat, the heat in my stomach, then through my body. The horror drew back, just enough to make me want it further off. Another cup. The void thickened, warmed. We must've gone into the bedroom, she must've undressed because she's naked too; like Eve, everything that's love and beauty. We must've got in bed because she's soft and warm, holding me. Another cup. We're both crying, trembling ... moving like lovers. Another cup ... pretending we're other people on another day ... somewhere else.

The room turned the way a room can't turn. I flew at the ceiling as no one can – effortlessly, willing the flight in my machine, racing faster. *Oh mercy, it was her!* Faster, too fast, till the wings buckle. Till we spin crazily downward, like a shot partridge, a dead bird flapping, falling into oblivion ...

Part IV

Mechanical Operations

29. Contains Handsaw, Hammer, Mallet,
    Two Gimlets, Two Bradawls, Chisel,
    Gouge, screw. Price 9s. 6d.

John Griffin, *Chemical Handicraft,* **1866**

Twenty-Two

Saturday, 27 June, 1857

TAP-TAP. TAP-TAP.

Daylight. An instant of blank normality. My last respite.

Tap-tap. Tap-tap.

The memory soaks me like acid. Then nausea, pain thumping in my skull.

TAP-TAP.

The apartment door opened, someone came in. I held my eyes tight shut, keeping out the day. Someone's in the room.

"Boss? Doctor Khan?"

Thorn. What the hell's she doing here? I heard a rustle as she drew close, felt a hand on my right arm, a shake.

"Boss?"

I said, "What happened?"

"The fight?"

I cracked my eyes, making the room tilt, the nausea rise.

"Go away," I said. "Leave me!"

I yanked off the covers, staggered to the flush toilet to puke. Puked again. Knelt, head in the bowl feeling sicker than I'd ever felt. Someone's garrotting my skull, and my tongue's sprouted a sour fungus. As I tried to push up, my left shoulder clenched, buckling in a spasm of pain. I realized the cannonball tugging at my groin is actually my bladder. I took a long piss. Then went and sat on the bed with my head in my hands. I'm naked, don't care.

Thorn's not looking at me. She's looking at the form under the blankets on the other side of the bed, the tangled crown of brown hair on the pillow. It's Jane, sound asleep. When I caught Thorn's eye, she shrugged ... *not my business.*

"We're late," she said.

I shook my head, wished I hadn't. "Doesn't matter ... *nothing matters.*"

"You're ill?"

"Lady Beatrice ... she's gone. Drowned."

Thorn's shocked. But she rode it out keeping her gaze on me. Then she looked away, counting the odds. My assistant.

"You're not ill?" she said.

I didn't reply.

"Then you can fight."

"I've got no fight."

A pause, then she said, "Better the loser than the didn't-show-up."

"I can't ..." My voice cracked.

"Lost the martial spirit?"

"Go to hell, Thorn!"

Her face softened. "Look, I'm very sorry about Lady Motcombe, but ... it's not me who'll go to hell." She leaned over to put something like a coin on my bedside table. "Found that on the hallway floor."

It's what Yashoda gave me for Miss Doyle. Not a coin, but a brass medallion etched with the goddess Kali – *force of time, slayer of demons.* Shoving a bloody tongue at me. *As fire becomes fire.* I remembered little Rosie, the child I'd promised to avenge.

I pressed a fist to my forehead, holding in my brain. "I can't ... I've no mettle, hardly the strength to stand. And this shoulder ..."

Thorn crouched on a level, sniffed my rancid breath. "How much?"

"Don't know ... a bucket. Feels like more."

She studied me a while. "Throw yourself in the Thames ... that it?"

"Why not? It's what I deserve. At least I'd be with Bea."

Thorn sighed, a sad puff to say she'd never thought to hear that from me. I could've strangled her. Thorn's a way of holding a mirror, showing me what I can't or don't want to see. Bea's gone. It's supposed to be my fault. I even believe it. Can't see over the grief and guilt. Thorn stared at me a while, like a doctor wondering how to treat a difficult case.

Then she went into the kitchen. The tin bath clattered down and the gas *whoofed* under the hot-water geyser. In a while she came and led me to the tub, tossed me a face cloth, a bar of soap and the pig's-bristle toothbrush I bought yesterday. "Back in ten minutes," she said, hurried out of the apartment.

THE ROUTINE OF washing let her words soak in.

If I don't fight, I really should jump in the Thames. Can't live the rest of my life as the didn't-show-up. The fraud. Not after what I wrote for Yashoda. Then there's Mungo and Melrose, banking on me, literally. If I don't show, my boxing life's over – the friends, the money, the elation. I'll be a laughingstock, confirming every insult I've spent my life rebutting. Boxing's about confidence, attitude. I should be sparring and stretching, letting Nat and Mungo talk me up. Honing my nerve, loading every sinew. If I turn up sullen and wilted, go down in the first round, they'll say it's fix. There's no way out.

I scrubbed myself twice, scoured my mouth with dentifrice. What'd Thorn said, *"lost the martial spirit?"* There's something more than truth in those words. I took a breath and slid under the hot water. Maybe I'll never have to come up.

The front door slammed. Thorn came into the kitchen with a bag from Hungerford Market. She unpacked coffee, fruit and spices on the kitchen table, set the coffeepot on the stove.

"There might be a way," she said.

"A way?"

She fetched a bottle of quinine sulphate from a cupboard, studied the label.

"To save the Championship."

"Might?"

She shrugged. "Fifty-fifty." Threw me a towel.

I'd no idea what she meant, but evens are a lot better than I had ten seconds ago. I buried my face in the towel, tried to look past the misery and the mill grinding in my head. Held on to the sincerity in Thorn's eyes ... to her sanity and sobriety, things I'd lost.

She closed the bedroom door, letting Jane sleep. Began mashing fruit and sprinkling spices. Quietly, she said, "What do you usually do before a fight?"

"I don't know, get up steam, focus my strength ... picture the victory–"

"Just the last bit–"

"Huh! Not much chance of that!"

"Imagine we're just fetching the cup," Thorn said. "You've got to look the part. The Major's an old man, remember? No sweat."

"Tipu the paper tiger?"

"If you like."

Feels like I'm stepping off a cliff because Thorn says I'll grow wings and fly away. Right now I can barely *walk* away. In a while, I said, "Better the loser?"

"Fifty-fifty."

She tipped the coffee in a pot of water, mixed in the fruit and spices, added some quinine. Handed it to me in the bath. The coffee smelt homely, comforting. I tightened my stomach and sipped, felt the pungent flavours prickle on my tongue, suffuse my insides like a bright dye dripped into water.

I said, "What's the plan, Thorn? How the hell am I going to walk off with the Imperial Championship? Or do I just take a beating? Put up a good fight, for a darkie. Let the mob enjoy my blood on the boards?"

Thorn stuffed and lit her pipe. Gave me a look – *Oh yea of little faith.*

"Reckon you can look the part? Stay up for a round, maybe two?"

"If I fight defensive, probably. Then what?"

"Then Her Majesty's constabulary arrives, breaks up the fight."

"Why would–"

"'Cos I'll tip 'em the wink."

"But–"

"Ungentlemanly? So's cribbing your moves, decking you in a prison cell."

"Melrose reckons the police can't touch soldiers for boxing."

"Defensive exercises?" Thorn snorted. "A field day? Not if you're selling tickets, taking bets. Not if it's at the Rum-Pum-Pas club. I'll speak to Inspector Adamson."

She's right. Mungo offered me a fig leaf. I took it to get Elphinstone. But the coppers can't ignore a bare-knuckle fight on their own doorstep. And Adamson's from some Christian sect that abhors violence.

Thorn said, "Half the Met will be there before you can say *knock-out!*"

"They arrest me, it's the end of forensic work for Scotland Yard."

"Like I said, fifty-fifty. But we'll be out the backway, a cab waiting in St Martin's Lane. Return match in a week." She shrugged. "You'll still be the Imperial Champion ... just a matter of time."

"Find the martial spirit?"

A spirit more than truth.

Thorn nodded. I got up, towelled myself down. I'm not happy at throwing a fight. Don't like deceiving my enemies, let alone my friends. Boxing's my religion. My saviour. Ever since I joined Punch's side in Calcutta. Not something to turn on and off like a tap.

"You're taking a risk too, Thorn. They find out you squealed–"

She shrugged. "Then we're in it together, eh?"

I tossed the towel at her, said, "All right, let's go flip the coin."

I finished the tonic, fetched my boxing suit from the bedroom along with the Kali medallion. Jane slept on. Pulling on the leather trousers, I said, "You're right about Adelaide Doyle."

"Yeah?"

"Took the dispatch in the London Library while I fetched a Bible and the *Book of Common Prayer*. Planned it, I think. Meant me to see them in the Saloon. She'd have sent me to fetch them if I hadn't gone of my own accord."

"You sure? She didn't strike me as a thief."

"Nor me." I pulled on my boots, began to lace them. "But there's a lot at stake. And listen, who knew it was in my bag? You. Chrystal. Adelaide Doyle. And I saw it, Thorn. Saw it! Right before I met her. She took it, she's partly to blame for Bea's death."

I realized Thorn didn't know what'd happened, so I told her the story from my meeting with Slegman to finding Bea's ring in my hand. Spoke coldly, as if I'm putting it together myself, like a half-remembered plot from a book. By the end I was angry, determined to confront Miss Doyle with the misery she'd caused. Let her know what her husband-to-be is capable of.

I put on a white shirt with my damp frock coat over the top. Thorn combed my hair. I tied my headgear: a turkey-red bandanna with the ends dangling down my neck. Now I'm Tipu the wild-eyed savage, the thug, the dacoit, the heathen ... whoever you'll bet against to watch a white man beat him, who makes your blood boil when he wins.

I picked up the Kali medallion, and we went down to the coach parked on the Terrace. Climbed up, side by side on the driving seat. The remains of last night's storm hung over the city, a chill of rain in the air. The river's grey, pitiless. I turned away, squeezed the medallion for luck.

Kali, destroyer of evil, consort and spirit of Shiva ...

I turned my head abruptly to Thorn, my eyes wide, mouth falling open.

She said, "What?"

I said, "What if ..."

"What if, what?"

I almost laughed. Not because it's funny, because so it's bloody perfect.

"It's what O'Shaughnessy would do," I said.

"What is?"

"Go via the Cell, Thorn. And you can forget about Scotland Yard."

I shut my eyes tight, ran my fingers into my hair and squeezed my skull. "I'm going to need your help."

"What, now you're out of bed?"

"Yeah, I know ... but I need to set the stage."

She picked up the reins, gave them a shake.

"Well, we're late. Tell me on the way."

WE WENT UP Haymarket into Orange Street, which crosses Castle Street a hundred yards south of the Cambrian Stores. I knew they'd be busy, but the scene still shook me. Castle Street's choked with abandoned carriages, men calling odds and holding up tickets, costermongers selling breakfast coffee and beer. Whores are waiting to clean up on the blood lust. The upstairs windows at the Rum-Pum-Pas club are wide open, men leaning out with clay pipes and pots of ale. It must be rammed inside.

I held on to an illusion, a kind of self-mesmerism that separated mind and body – *I'm ready, stoked, Elphinstone won't stand a chance.*

We went the back way, as arranged, up St Martin's Lane to the milliner's shop. Nat's pacing anxiously outside. I glanced at Thorn, hoping for reassurance I didn't get. She's already lost in the unfolding plan. As we rolled to a halt, I hopped down, blinked away the jolt of pain in my head, nodded to Nat and looked around like I own the place.

"Thought you'd hooked it," Nat said. "Lost your balls."

"Winding up the crowd," I said, striding past him into the shop.

Thorn fell in behind with a small chemical cabinet we'd fetched from the Cell. Nat clapped a hand on her shoulder. "Ticket?" I shoved him aside, said, "With me!" The three of us strode past racks of bonnets and top hats, out the back, across a courtyard, through a gate into the rear of the Cambrian Stores. We climbed a staircase to Nat's living room, went through a door to bedlam in a baker's oven. We're behind the bar in the Rum-Pum-Pas club.

I nearly walked straight into Mungo who's staring around like a chicken in a fox's den. "Thank Christ!" he said. "They're saying it's a sell." He got up on the counter, waved his arms for quiet. When no one noticed, he pulled me up next to him, told me to throw the stance. I lifted my fists and gave the mob a look. There's a wave of quiet.

The room's barely recognizable: yesterday it was aired, peaceful, set like a fancy dining room; today it's hot and hazy, reeking of smoke and sweat. The furniture's shoved back against the walls, floor packed so tight it's hard to think you'd get another soul inside. But folk are pushing in the door, waving tickets.

At the back they've clambered onto the tables, anything for a clear view of the roped off platform in the middle – the ring. In the centre's Elphinstone, bared to the waist, wearing the boots and trousers of his dress uniform.

"Look at him," Mungo said, "Strutting about like he's already won"

"Brought his own crowd," I said. "The moustachios."

"Soldiers ... reds and blues. No love lost with our lot." Mungo rubbed his palms. "Going to explode, soon or later."

The lull startled the Major. He stared around till he found me on the bar, tried to lock eyes. Mungo leaned closer, said, "Duke's raised more battle money ... another two hundred guineas, if you win." He hoisted my arm, like I'm the winner, baiting a storm of whistles and cheers from the floor.

Elphinstone's seconds leapt into the ring, shouting, "Coward!" and "Black-faced monkey!" Urging me down with big sweeps of their arms.

Elphinstone sneered as the whole room seemed to join the

pandemonium.

"The tiger'll bite your head off!" Mungo shouted back. "Won't you, Tipu?"

I jutted my chin. "Yeah!" But I didn't feel it.

When I turned away, I'm face to face with Robert Clive. Lord Clive – the serene stare, the white hair like a judge's wig, the gold brocade.

Yesterday I dismissed him. Not now, not amid this mayhem. He's glowering the white man's superiority, boiling away my fragile self-esteem like water off a firebox, stirring up dread – *I'm a madman with no real plan, a black-faced dog of the inferior races ... a jungle boy ...* An electric kick of panic surged through me. Paralyzing, lighting up all my fears, every scrap of self-doubt I've ever had.

"You all right, Tipu? Yeah?" Mungo's voice, far away.

I want to step into the tranquil scene behind Clive, the place of my people. Time out of time. To a quiet mulberry plantation in the Bengal jungle. To a life I might've lived if we'd never left our village, if we'd never gone to the silk factory by the river Mor ...

If.

I want to say, *"I can't do it ... let me out of here,"* but through the din, I hear Mungo say "Go wipe that damn sneer off his face, Tipu. We'll fleece this lot, get drunk for a week."

Which was a jolt. He means Elphinstone, but I'm looking at Clive. I felt a flicker of rebellion, tangible and teasing like a tiny flame of hope.

I said, "It's a ship in a bottle."

"What?"

"The portrait ... that's not Clive, the bully-boy, the crook–"

"What?"

"The reckless youth, the trickery and lies!" I let the flame grow. "Outnumbered! Outgunned! His victory dash was madness, a crazy bet against the odds."

Mungo yanked me round to face him. "What the hell're you–"

"How he won! The Battle of Plassey ... Bengal!" I grabbed his lapels. "My wager's chemistry – what happens once, must happen once again. Believe it!"

"Whatever you say, Tipu," he said, like I'm a madman talking Chinese.

"Toss the coin!" I said. "Fifty-fifty!"

Then I jumped down, blood rising, feeding off the noise.

Thorn's talking in Nat's ear. He's giving her a *who-the-hell-are-you?* look, but he nodded to a doorway. Four of us went in – Nat, Mungo, Thorn and me – crossed a kitchen to a spacious pantry. Thorn shut the doors behind us so it's suddenly cool and quiet.

She said, "Let's get these off." Took off my frockcoat and shirt. Then, to Mungo, "Left shoulder needs some work." He began kneading, turning the arm, muttering, "You're all right, Tipu. Aren't you? Yeah?"

I said, "Thorn told you how I want to do this?"

Both men nodded. Mungo kept working the shoulder, then the arm. Nat did the same on the right.

"Lot of soldiers out there," I said.

Nat said nothing, but his face did – there'll be trouble, whoever wins.

"Think Melrose'll play along?" I said.

Nat shrugged. "Don't see why not. It'll stoke the crowd."

"You'll tell Frank Dowling too? Help quiet things?"

Dowling edits *Bell's Life,* the paper that makes fights history.

"In the front row," Nat said, "Ringside."

"Yeah, I saw him. I want every blow on breakfast tables across the world in the morning." I told Yashoda she'd find justice there, for Rosie.

More nods. I rolled my shoulders, did some squats. Nat held out his huge hands for me to punch, make sure I'd a decent left despite the nagging shoulder. I'd fought with worse. I sparred till Thorn stood the chemical cabinet on a chest-high shelf between pats of butter and wedges of cheese. Then we'stood still, the others watching curiously.

Thorn opened the box, lifted out the apparatus. A quarter-pint stoppered-bottle. A large watch-glass. A metal spatula. A glass tube of quarter-inch bore. She set them carefully on the shelf.

I said, "Nat, Mungo ... outside. We need a minute."

NAT AND MUNGO led me into the crowd. Not that I needed them. I'd have leapt off the bar to get at Elphinstone and his seconds and anyone else doesn't like blacks. I think I shouted it. Nat went left, hauled me onto a steelyard where a timekeeper slid weights and called numbers. Lisping toffs prodded and poked me. Nat rubbed linament on my shoulders, cooed reassurance.

I watch my sweat sparkle, feel drops slither in my throat.

I say, "Where is he ... WHERE IS HE?"

The Duke of Melrose says, "I'm the wefewee—"

"You're the undertaker ... your Gwace!"

Thorn's saying, "Easy, take it easy Boss."

"Pay off your ... em ... er ... debts," I say, laughing in Melrose's face. "You piece of namby-pamby shit!"

Nat pulls me off the steelyard into the crowd, elbowing a path. There's a thunder of stamping as we get near the ring. Faces roll by; some nod, most hurl broadsides of every filthy slur they know, soaking me in spit. I spit back, tell them to go to hell. Mungo turns to shout, *"He fights old school ... don't let him get a hold.* Which is so damn funny I shout, *"Old man ... made in England stamped on his arse!"*

Close behind, Thorn says, "Easy. Easy!"

"Crushing a cockroach!"

I grab a rope to spring into the ring, turn a circle in the uproar. Smiling, arms aloft. No pain. No worry. Just a gorgeous euphoria that makes me wonder why I ever feared Elphinstone or the Company or the whole damned British Empire. Nat ties the colours to our corner. Mungo rubs resin on my palms for grip, tips a tablespoon of brandy down my gullet.

Nat's got my shoulders, says, "You're charging too soon, Tipu!"

I nod like a madman.

"He's used to savage warfare," says Nat.

I laugh, almost hysterical. "I'm his savage–"

"You'll beat him–"

"To death."

"Keep fly! Fib him ... tap him ... use the knockout punch."

Thorn's hanging over the ropes, calling, "THE CHALLENGE!"

Melrose is at scratch, shouting, "Get back, get back!" at the ring-side crowd as they drum their fists under the ropes for the fight to start. Elphinstone's next to him, ribbed and sleek as a racehorse. Now I meet his gaze with a look to curdle molten steel. He tries to stare me out, but there's tension in his eyes – the weight of the mob's rage and my demonic hate.

Melrose lifts his arms, pats the air for quiet. Nat and Mugo join in, so does Frank Dowling who's climbed up ringside. I'm pacing like a tiger, trying to ease off full throttle. Melrose folds his arms, taps a foot like nothing'll happen till it's quiet. The drumming slowly fades and folk at the front lower their voices, fall quiet. Silence ripples out till it's just the clamour on the stairs and hawkers in the street. Elphinstone holds out his palms like he's lost something, glares at Melrose – *what the hell's going on?*

"Print this, Dowling," I shout. "Every damn word!" Then, loud as I can, "ELPHINSTONE!" I wait, let all eyes settle on me. "ELPHINSTONE! YESTERDAY IN KEW ... YOU MURDERED A LITTLE GIRL. KILLED HER DOG."

There's a buzz of chatter, people repeating what I've said, passing it back. The eyes turn to the Major, even his own crew's.

One of his seconds points at me, shouts, "LIAR!"

"SHOT HER IN THE HEAD," I say. "BURNT THE DOG ALIVE."

Now they hear, fall quiet until a voice calls, *"Answer!"*

"Let's get on with it," says Elphinstone to Melrose.

More voices call, *"Answer!"* Then it's a chant: *"Ans-wer! Ans-wer!"*
The moustachios are silent ... not joining in but expecting a reply.
The Duke and I step back, leave the Major alone in the centre of the
ring, looking around – an officer and gentleman who won't be caught
out in a lie.

"Ans-wer! Ans-wer! ANSWER!"

Elphinstone holds up his arms for quiet. Then, "THIS MAN'S
A LIAR! I DID NOTHING BUT MY DUTY ... NO MORE!" His
seconds nod and clap theatrically, get applause from the moustachios.

But I've rattled the Major, it's written in his eyes.

"I'VE GOT THE BULLET," I shout, "THE PROOF!"

Melrose sees his moment, steps forward beckoning me to do the
same. We form a tight triangle with Elphinstone at the scratch mark.
Melrose raises an arm between us like the sword of truth.

Under it, Elphinstone hisses, "I'll teach you, boy!"

"Call me 'the Boss,' Feringhee!" I growl back.

"Shake hands," says Melrose.

We slap, except the Major grabs my wrist, pulls me onto a left jab.
I take it, use the forward drive to slant a hard blow up into his solar
plexus ... feel him cave, hear *"Urgh!"* above the crowd's roar. See him
flinch, stagger. Behind him Melrose dives from the ring.

If the crowd wants blood, they're about to get lots of it.

I lift my fists – body angled, left foot forward – follow Elphinstone
to his corner ... he's hurt, retreating, but I won't end it by putting him
down. Not yet. I rally jabs and feigns, chopping down his punches,
getting his measure ... floating and flying. Broken flywheels tick
madly in my head – *take it or dodge it he's got to move ... take a tap to give
a hammer ... hungry eyes telegraph the news* – over and over. I move
effortlessly, pop his phiz and pummel his body, crowd cheering or
sighing at every twist in the drama.

He's slow. Slogs round-punches that open his guard. Next one I
step inside, throw a hard right, follow with a left that slips my hand
behind his head. I pull him forward and down, swing a right up into

his face ... again ... again ... shout, "Call me Boss," with every punch, till I take a hard left to the body, dance back out of range, watch the claret pour from his nose.

One his eyes is half closed, nose flat and twisted. He's tiring, guard low and lazy. I jab a hard left, come forward smashing my right elbow into his head ... slip the arm over his shoulder, round his neck, pivot ... hurl him, cross-buttock. For a magic moment he's upside down, legs turning like windmill sails above us ... then he hits the ground, hard, shuddering the ring,

Round over.

Nat: "Stop playing, Tipu–"

Me: "Gonna fib him–"

Mungo: "No!" Put him down, knockout!"

Nat: "You're losing blood, wearing out."

I laugh "It's his! The Feringhee's blood, you idiot!"

Nat grabs my head with both hands, says, "Finish it, now!"

I pull free as the timekeeper calls the round, get back to scratch. The Major's crew are working the sponge and water bottle, using every second. I think it might be over, chance gone. But then he's on his feet, back to the line.

I pick up, peg away with jabs and crosses, riding his replies like a cork on an angry sea. Somewhere in the rally I draw him over the top with a weak right, take a left on the kisser to land a cracking left of my own, so brutal it shakes my arm, sends an arc of blood and sweat into the crowd

Amid crazy cheers I hook a right under his ribs, stagger him so he folds forward onto my elbow coming the other way. Then the arm's over his head and round his neck. I step in, turn. This time I clamp his head by my left thigh, elbow pinning his left arm. I fib his face, work my right like a piston, saying, "Call me Boss! Call me Boss!" Till something hits my lower back, hard and stinging – *bang, bang!* Then a sickening flood of pain blurs my vision. I'm on my knees.

Round over.

Hauling me to the corner, Nat says, "You're gonna piss blood for a week. Tipu. No more body blows!" Mungo sponges me down, says, "You had him! Stop the taunting ... playing the black master. There's a bloody fortune riding on this."

"Yeah, my blood!" I say, but there's no laughter now. I'm coughing, spitting claret in the bucket. "Where'd *that* come from?" I ask Mungo, who's sluicing my face, wiping my eyes. He's looking over my shoulder. "You let him back in with the kidney punches," he says. "Finish it, Tipu. Now!"

At scratch there's an ache in my back, a knot of nausea spoiling my dance. Elphinstone's worse – face so mashed you'd barely know him, left shoulder sunk, arm limp. I go to work in earnest, closer, no fibs or taunts, only taking risks for the big punch. Elphinstone knows it, opens up in reply. I've got the stamina, so I circle, make him follow, jabbing and ducking, our eyes locked so tight the crowd spins round us in a distant blur.

He's a hell of a fighter, makes up in guts what lacks in skill.

But he's dazed and desperate, lunging for a wrestling match. I dodge back, again and again, feeling spikes of pain in my back, till he stumbles onto big right, staggers to the ropes, trapped. Now it's *face, ribs, gut, gut, face, face, gut, ribs, ribs* ... like sparing with a bag, letting out my rage, for my people, for little Rosie for my WHOLE DAMMED LIFE ... till the crowd's yells are deafening and the Major's seconds scream, "Get him off! Get the animal off!" Till I pull back, aim a body blow that folds him forward, an uppercut that snaps his head up.

He gapes ... stares disbelieving, grabbing at his throat as he falls back over the ropes. He sags down, hanging by one hand, clawing at his Adam's apple with the other.

TOTAL UPROAR. NAT'S shouting, "It's over, it's over!" at Melrose. Mungo's in the ring, arms wide, screaming at the Major's seconds to toss in the sponge. They'll have none of it, too busy trying to shove him back on his feet. I'm holding the stance, till one of the seconds shouts, "Not down! Not out!" Then to Melrose, "End of the round ... end the round!"

If he's not down, I'll hit him harder. But I don't get there.

The air whines and whirrs with police whistles and rattles, people shouting, "Coppers! Coppers!" Men pile against the doorway, shaking fists and cudgels, ready for the lawmen storming up the stairs. Inside the crowd seethes as soldiers shout, "It's a steal!" throw punches at the fancy. Boxers step in to protect them, using the excuse – the room erupts in a mighty brawl – boxers against soldiers, everyone against the police.

Mungo grabs my arm. "You've done it, we're away–"

Elphinstone's seconds are still shouting, "He's not down!"

"Bollocks!" Mungo shouts back, "You're holding him up."

Which is true – it's the rope in the crook of his arm and the seconds outside the ring pushing his arse off the boards. Mungo pulls my arm, says, "We're away, come on Tipu!" I look at Elphinstone, who's giving me a pleading stare, pouting like a beached cod, like he's desperate to speak.

I pull away, stride over and crouch by him. Up close it's like Henry – split lips, one eye lost in a mass swollen tissue, blood everywhere. Elphinstone's hurt, breathing heavily.

Between gulps of air, he croaked, "Did ... did ... n ... n ..."

"Did, didn't ... what?" I said, with a kind of contempt.

His seconds let his arse sink to the boards, lean in to hear what he's got to say. He gasps a word like, "I's or aye's ..." till all he had was a wheeze.

Nat and Mungo appeared, and Mungo said, "Christ's sake, Tipu, lets–"

A fresh peel of shouts makes us turn to see the Met's finest bulls thrashing through the door, scything down the mob like demented harvesters. We turned to Nat, the landlord, but he's eyeing Elphinstone, looking worried.

"Needs a doctor," Nat said. "And I need him out ... all of you, gone!"

"You're a doctor," Mungo said, voice tight.

"Me?" Hadn't reckoned on helping Elphinstone. But I want to know what he's saying, so I said, "Bring him!"

"What?" said one of his seconds, "Where?"

"Out of here," says Nat. "Now!"

"Cops get him ... you're cashiered," I said. "We're all in gaol."

That did it. The Major's seconds are Company lieutenants, mid-twenties: one tall and dark, the other shorter and stocky, blue eyed with a scar on his left cheek. They took his arms, I took his feet, and we dragged and carried him from the ring, over the bar, through the living room, down the stairs.

Thorn's bumping along with us, cradling the chemical cabinet, my clothes piled on top. Across the yard, she said, "Up to Hackney?"

"Too early," I called, struggling with the Major's legs.

"We're late!" she called, which confused me.

Going through the milliner's shop, I said, "Midday?"

"Already a quarter to."

"Impossible!" I said, at the four-wheeler in St Martin's Lane.

"Fight lasted more than an hour," said Thorn.

Bundling the Major into the cab, I said, "Bollocks ... it's ten minutes, if–"

"Hour and a quarter," said the blond lieutenant, as we lay Elphinstone on the floor between the seats, propped his head on the far door.

"Shiva," called Thorn, climbing up on the box seat, "lord of time."

I caught my face in the cab window – looked like a plate of cold Rogan Josh, mashed as my opponent's. Mungo shoved in behind me clutching the Imperial trophy and a hefty bag of cash. The taller lieutenant made to follow, but Nat grabbed him in a bearhug, pinning his arms. He kicked the cab door shut and nodded to Thorn to drive on.

The blond lieutenant called, "Hey!" but we're already rolling, on our way north to Hackney.

Twenty-Three

MUNGO SETTLED IN next to me, facing forward. The blue-eyed lieutenant sat opposite. He'd wispy blond hair and pock-marked skin, looked like he could handle himself in a fight. Which is why Nat had evened the odds by making it two on two. Not that Elphinstone's likely to cause much trouble. He's lying on the floor between us, looking ill.

Mungo put an arm round me, scrubbing a dry shave, saying, "We did it, Tipu ... we *bloody did it!*"

"You bloody didn't," said the lieutenant. "Melrose never declared."

Mungo hugged the trophy. "You ain't getting this," he said. Kicking a heel on Elphinstone's chest, "Look at him!"

The lieutenant lunged forward at the insult, ready to fight. I met him with the flat of my right hand, shoved him back.

"Get your filthy hands off!" he said, shrugging away my touch.

"Shut up!" I said, "both of you."

The Major had been quiet as we carried him out, just a dead weight slowing our flight from the coppers. Now he's a veiny blue, skin slick with a film of sweat. I moved to crouch over him, hoping he'd talk.

The lieutenant's arm shot out: "What're you doing?"

"Examining him ... he's not breathing properly."

Which was true. The lieutenant's arm dropped, but his eyes shone mistrust. I knelt over the Major, waggled his chin side to side.

"Have a care," the lieutenant said.

"Tipu knows what he's doing," said Mungo, leaning in his face.

"Wake up!" I said. "Oy! Elphinstone ... can you hear me?"

I slapped his cheek – a pat, then harder. The lieutenant was hovering, ready to knock me aside. The Major's eyes opened slowly. He blinked a vacant stare which stirred my medical oath, even a little concern.

I reached for my frockcoat, slid the Major flat on the floor and bundled it under his head. The throat's swollen, windpipe crushed. That final uppercut did it. My forearm knocked his chin up, but my fist hit his throat, as intended. Lethal. Now he's a medical case ... airway tight, the swelling finishing the job.

I felt the others catch my concern. I've no instruments. The cab's jolting and sliding over the cobblestones as Thorn races us to Hackney. I called to her to stop. We slowed, veered left to the curbside in a Holborn backstreet. The Major's barely breathing, just quick, constricted hisses. I got closer, slapped his face ... again ... "Major!"

His eyes opened, stared in confusion. In dregs of residual air, he gasped, "D-o-g ... r-a-b-i-e-s." Then his back arched and legs jerked in some kind of fit.

"Do something, Tipu!" Mungo said.

The Major's face grimaced in pain and fear. His breathing became a stuttering *hic-hic-hic* ... like a steam pipe stoppered by a ball-valve. I pictured a woodcut in a treatise, a couple of lines of print ... *left thumb finds the sternum ...*

"Gimme your knife," I said.

... second finger on the cricoid cartilage ...

Mungo: "What?"

... first finger steadies the trachea ...

"Pocket-knife!"

Mungo levered out five inches of dull steel, flipped the wooden handle my way. I stretched the skin on Elphinstone's throat ... *blade vertical, an inch cut ...* pricked the tip in the textbook spot. As I tensed to make the incision, he rolled his eyes down, saw a bare-chested Indian in a headband with a knife at his throat. Instinctively he bucked and snatched at my wrists.

Which panicked the lieutenant into throwing an arm round my neck and dragging me backwards across the carriage. Which prompted Mungo to dive at the lieutenant in my defence.

For half a minute we writhed and grunted on the floor, lieutenant on top gripping my knife-hand, me trying to punch him with a left, which I couldn't because Mungo's got both arms round his neck trying to pull his head off. I caught a glimpse of Thorn, hands cupped to the cab window, shaking her head. I shouted, "Stop! Stop! I'm trying to save his bloody life!"

We stopped, a frieze of taut, mistrusting muscle. Slowly relaxed ... unwound, turned to look at the patient. If ever a man looked dead, Elphinstone did: face purple, arms limp at his sides, eyes wide and blind. I scrabbled over, felt for a pulse in his neck, listened to his chest ... nothing. I said, "He's gone."

AFTER A FEW seconds, Mungo said, "Oh ... Jeez!"

"You murdered him!" shrieked the lieutenant.

"He's the murderer!" I fired back. "You heard me at the–"

"It's a lie!" he said, "A dirty–"

"Did he deny it?" I said, scrabbling over, getting close. "Well ... did he? I saw the body, lieutenant. Dug the Dragoon bullet out of a wall ... found the lamp he used to set the lot on fire."

Mungo said to the lieutenant, "If anyone killed him, you did."

I waved the knife. "He was suffocating, I was cutting a new airway."

The lieutenant looked at it, then at the Major. Then he saw what'd happened. "You're really a doctor," he said. Hauled himself onto the front seat, head in hands. When his shoulders shook, I thought it was rage, prepared for another round. But it wasn't rage. He's crying.

Mungo and I shared a glance, pulled *what the?* ... faces. Maybe he loved his commanding officer. More like he saw how it'll go if the truth gets out.

Thorn opened the cab door, stuck in her head. "Tracheotomy?" She reads my medical books in the Cell.

"Cutthroat," I said, and shrugged.

She climbed in and slammed the door. Sat down next to the lieutenant with her back to the horses. In lieu of words I puffed a long sigh. Mungo said, "What the 'ell're we gonna do?" I folded his knife shut, handed it over. The lieutenant looked up watery eyed. "I didn't mean ... we can't ..."

"The truth? I said. "Nah, no one'd want that, least of all the Major."

"What then?" Mungo said. "Fight's gonna be all over *Bell's Life* tomorrow, you made damned sure of that, Tipu."

"Yeah ... I know. Well, he either goes in the Thames, east of Blackwall–"

"No!" said the lieutenant. "No ... he gets a Christian burial–"

"Or?" said Mungo.

"Back alley, east of Aldgate. Plenty of lascars there who'd happily beat his brains out ... or make it look like robbery. Either way he'll get a proper burial." I pointed at the lieutenant. "But we stay mum, let 'em prove otherwise ... or else it's gaol, disgrace for us all."

He nodded. Not happy but understanding his own skin's at stake.

Thorn said, "We're due in Hackney, Boss." Which meant, *the body needs dumping, fast.* "Give me a few minutes," she said, climbing out.

I pulled on my shirt and coat. Mungo stashed the trophy and cash on the seat, gave me a *"Guard it!"* look. He climbed out to wet a handkerchief in a puddle, then cleaned up my face and closed the cuts with bits of adhesive plaster.

He's worried, and I know why. We can cook up a tale about how the Major vanished but it's the lieutenant who'll be quizzed. He'll have to lie barefaced and stick to the story. What if he spins a yarn to save his own skin? His word against ours. Who'll the Company believe?

Mungo's tongue wormed around under his top lip as he gave the lieutenant an interrogating stare. "There's the matter of the Major's purse," he said.

I caught on, said, "How much?"

"Fifty ... guineas." He looked at the lieutenant. "Elphinstone earned it, might was well be yours ... it's what he'd want–"

"You mean ... the seconds–"

Mungo stared harder. "I mean ... you."

"Me? No, I ... couldn't ..." But his eyes said something else.

"You got him away," I said. "Took risks as his second, made sure he got a Christian burial ... kept his good name."

Mungo pulled the bag tight against his body, like sweets he didn't want to share. He counted out the money, held it in the flat of his hand.

"Get a man started in Bengal," I said.

"I'm not sure ..." the lieutenant said, hand hovering. His tongue licked his lips, quick and nervous, like a snake. "Well, if you think ..." He took it, stuffed the notes and guinea pieces in his pockets. Then, quickly moving on, "What'd he meant by 'dog, rabies?'"

I shrugged. "Delirious ... there're lots of rabid dogs in Bengal. A bite can cause an awful death ... hallucinations, fits of terror, agonizing muscle spasms." As I spoke, I felt an inkling of what Elphinstone wanted to say. It's a thought I tried to put away.

Then we worked out our story ... *Major comes to, gets himself dressed, insists on being dropped off in ... Cornhill? ... Bishopsgate? ... says he's got business out east.* We fixed the details, went over it. We're going over it a third time when another carriage drew up next to ours. Thorn jumped down with the other cabbie in tow, a man in his fifties with a face crabby enough to make him eighty. Thorn opened our door, letting in a pleasant smell of tobacco and beer.

She said, "Jem here'll–"

"Uh!" I said. "The lieutenant's about the leave."

The lieutenant looked at me, then at Mungo. He patted down his

299

pockets and climbed out of the carriage.

"Elphinstone went east," I called. "Keep thinking that till you believe it!"

He glanced at the corpse, looked like he was pleased to walk away.

Mungo grinned, punched me on the shoulder.

"What?"

"He took the loser's purse, which means–"

"You need to find Melrose," I said. "See what he says."

Mungo's face fell, but he nodded. Normally we'd be sharing out the winnings, drinking a tavern dry. Not today.

I said, to Thorn, "Jem'll what?"

"Take him east, for a guinea,"

Jem's bloodshot eyes swiveled round the cab. He sniffed, wiped his mouth on a filthy sleeve. "You want it proper ... nameless grave, yeah?"

"That's it," I said "We thought if–"

"Five guineas," he said. "It's done. Gone."

"Gone where?"

"That's my business. He gets a priest and a pauper's grave. No questions."

Mungo said, "Three guineas."

"Four."

"Three and half ... but I wanna know–"

"No, you don't," I said. Then, as he counted out the money, "I've got some business up in Hackney, Mungo ... find you at the Stores tomorrow, yeah?"

He took the hint. "I'll find Dowling," he said, "see what'll be in *Bell's Life* tomorrow." He eased the trophy inside the loot sack. Climbed out.

"Remember," I said, "Elphinstone went–"

"No. You remember, Tipu," – he pointed a finger – "You're the Imperial Champion!" He rattled the money bag. "That's what this bloody lot says!"

I SAT NEXT to Thorn as we rattled north up Bishopsgate, Mungo's words rattling just as hard in my head. There's too much riding on the fight to call it a draw or pretend it never happened – winnings and side-bets, bills to pay.

"Worked then," Thorn called, above the galloping hooves. "Shiva."

"Oh ... God, yeah. We need to talk about that ... but not now, eh?"

I fell quiet.

In a while, Thorn said, "Penny for 'em?"

"Penny? Ah ... Jem's stronger than he looks." He'd dumped Elphinstone, single handed inside his cab. "So what'll he do with the body?"

Thorn gave me a look – *you really want to know?*

I nodded, and she said, "He takes the dead from workhouses to the London Necropolis. Easily slip in one more. They get a grave, a Christian burial."

"Necropolis?" I said.

"A station that's also a mortuary, by Waterloo. They stack corpses in the arches under the viaduct, take 'em by train to a huge cemetery near Woking."

I thought of gliding over the viaduct to Kew, oblivious to the piles of bodies beneath. Like the vault in the London and Imperial bank, so much hidden under the great metropolis. "A manufactory for the dead?" I said.

Thorn nodded. "Probably where I'll end up."

I wasn't unhappy Elphinstone was gone to a nameless, pauper's grave in a far field, less mourned than the maimed and murdered he'd left across Bengal.

Thorn looked at me again ... *so what're you really thinking?*

We slowed for a pack of Hansom cabs weaving round us in a dash for fares at Bishopsgate railway terminus. Then we accelerated up Shoreditch Road.

"Elphinstone," I said. "Lieutenant keeps his mouth shut it'll blow over ... probably. If not, could be war with the moustachios, mainly against me. There'll be challengers for the trophy ... as many as it takes."

"Lots of prize money."

"Yeah ... I'd rather keep my job. And stay alive."

"What you wanted, isn't it ... judge and executioner? Justice for Rosie."

We drove in silence for a half mile. I'd felt increasingly odd since the fight in the cab – the ghost of too-much-handi rising like the living dead, hands trembling. I could feel my own heartbeat, heavy and irregular.

I said, "I thought so ... but Shiva threw that last punch. There's the Major smashed up, struggling to breathe ... thought it'd feel like victory but, I dunno ... fact is, I tried to save him ... failed in that farce of misunderstandings."

"He was a killer ... what about the babes in sacks?"

"Yeah ... I don't feel that bad about it ... worst is, I don't think he murdered Rosie."

"Who then?" Thorn said. "You think Meigs–"

"No, it's Elphinstone ... but I couldn't see *why*. Hooker knew what he was after ... and when he was dying, he wanted to tell me something. In the ring he said, 'eyes,' then in the cab, 'dog' and 'rabies.' I reckon in the Stove he heard the dog bark under the wooden trestles, lit the lamp to see into the gloom. Saw two glinting eyes and fired ... thought it was a rabid guard dog."

Thorn's laugh was ironic and disbelieving. "Finds he's shot a child."

"Sets the lot on fire to cover it up."

"Not exactly honorable."

"No ... it weighed on him. Not part of some Imperial scheme to civilize the natives, just ... a stupid error of judgment, a mistake ..."

I put my face in my hands. The euphoria I'd felt in the ring hadn't just drained away. It'd crashed down into Hades with an emptiness I couldn't've imagined. I'm like a photographic negative: spectral black where the white should be. And with Bea gone there wasn't much white to start with.

Over the coach's thunder, Thorn called, "So what's in Hackney?"

"We're not the only ones to work out why Henry killed himself. I think Meigs guessed he'd told a relative about the key ... came back later in the evening, waited. Billy Impey turns up and opens the safe ... they grab him, make him reveal the old Loddiges nursery in Hackney. Which means Slegman knows about the plant, where Henry grew it ... probably."

"And Billy?"

"Ah ... they'll want him alive ... only one who knows how it's done ... the growing, making the drug. After that, he's dead meat. We need to hurry."

Thorn forked right at Shoreditch Church, headed up Hackney Road. The cobbles reverse-telescoped to infinity, a nervous vertigo from the dizzying speed. I pressed into the box seat afraid I'd fly off. Felt the touch of the chemical cabinet between our thighs, the one we'd brought from the Cell.

"Stop the cab," I said.

"What? We're—"

"Pull over Thorn ... now!"

We swerved to the curb by a pond in an open field. I stumbled down with the cabinet, climbed inside and slammed the door. Felt the safety of walls, the humming silence broken only by quacking mallards on the pond. I stood the cabinet on the seat opposite, set out the watch-glass, the spatula, the glass tube ... un-stopped the jar of white powder.

Shiva. THAT'S WHAT I call it.

After the frog trial, Thorn and I each took a dab. Nice. Tried a swig. Nicer. Snorted it like snuff ... what can I say? For most of an hour we're the lords of divine energy, fuming with martial spirit. Alkaloids should end in '-ine' but 'Erythroxyline' didn't sound like a tonic to beat laudanum. Hooker tagged the plants *Erythroxylum coca*, so it could've been 'cocaine.'

I like Shiva.

Hofmann's other assistants turn chemistry into cash ... why not me? But I'd found the rub: *the Lord Shiva giveth and the Lord Shiva taketh away.* Or the reverse. He'd cheated time and pain – the handi, the punches, the insults – most of all Bea, gone with the tide. I hadn't taken it in since falling comatose in Jane's arms, since Thorn dragged me off to meet Elphinstone, since I'd snorted enough Shiva to storm Fort William single handed.

Now it's back, all of it, fermenting like a foul yeast.

Outside the pond mirrored the mottled blues and greys of the clearing sky. Beautiful ... but not to me. I'm brittle as an old gas mantle; dust to the touch. The horses snort and stamp, clink their harnesses. They're as confused as Thorn ... why've we halted the race to Hackney station?

I trailed a line over the watch-glass, used the tube to hook up. Like turning a valve on super-heated steam ... a hiss, a blast ...

Twenty-Four

WE'D MISSED THE feast. That's how it felt.

A fire drew us east from Mare Street. Angry black smoke, driven by balloons of orange flame: a chemical inferno. We chased it across watercress meadows to a field of bents and summer flowers with an iron and glass hothouse the size of small church. A nearby boiler house belched fire from its windows.

A gunshot split the air, then another, louder. Three men bolted from the boiler house with their clothes on fire, two of them armed with cavalry carbines. Caught in open ground they fired at targets behind the shed. The return fire was devastating. The two men jerked and arched, specks of tunic and flesh spitting out behind. One fell on his back, dead. The other twisted into a crawl, made it a few yards before sinking to his elbows, keeling over like a downed animal.

The unarmed man fell to the ground, rolling about to stifle the burning patchers on his clothes Then he stretched out in a submissive spreadeagle on the turf.

Next a youth staggered out, hands up. By then we'd hopped down in front of iron gates, the entrance to a former Loddiges nursery. Trains had made the village of Hackney a city suburb, hiked land prices beyond the means of botanists. The lonely patch was waiting for the builders, ringed by a wire fence on spiked iron posts. We were clambering over the gates when two Company soldiers ran from behind the engine shed, pointing revolvers.

Then came Chrystal, struggling to keep up, holding a blunderbuss that belonged in the police museum. It had the feel of a battlefield: determined men, ready to kill or be killed. Thorn and I raised our hands, stood motionless.

A soldier kicked the downed men in turn, making sure. The other shouted, "Down, down!" to the one with his hands up. He fell to his knees, hands behind his head. The first soldier went to the spreadeagled man, held a revolver an inch from the back of his neck. That's it: feast over. Except a fifth man in a tidy frockcoat walked out from behind the engine shed, flicking blades of grass from his trousers. Sir Reginald Clyde.

We all stood still, and the fire went out like turning off a gas tap.

THE VICTORS LET off steam, with, "Jesus Christ! ... like a canon .... what a bullseye! ..." and making fun of Chrystal's blunderbuss. We walked through the long grass to join them. Thorn was serious and alert. I was choking guffaws, riding Shiva's happy ... Shiva's warmth ... Shiva's numb reality.

Clyde said, "You're late, Khan!" which stifled the laughter. His white skin, together with his clothes and titles gave him immediate authority, a ruthless air I hadn't seen in the library. That was the private Clyde. This one's the Sir, the Deputy Director, the fist squeezing the globe like a money sponge.

A soldier dragged the spreadeagled man up by his collar, shoved him towards us with the revolver in his back. The other tried to push the youth our way, but he resisted, shrugged off the officer's grip with an angry, "Get off!" I thought it'd come to blows, but the younger man held out his arms to say he didn't need pushing.

We stood in a wide circle – Clyde, Chrystal, Thorn, the soldiers with their prisoners – all staring at me. I sniffed at a tickle of powder on my nose, wondered about numb lips, or eyes jumping like dragonflies. Then it dawned. I look like a clown from a storybook: boots and leather trousers, white shirt and frockcoat, a turkey-red bandana; my face a salad, speckled with plaster. Chrystal's thinking: *bareknuckle at the Cambrian Stores.* The soldiers: *who won?* Clyde's just thinking.

When he'd thought, he introduced lieutenants Chesney and Kyd, veterans of the Anglo-Sikh wars. Chesney's eyes bulged and roamed, making him seem inquisitive or simple, by turns. Kidd had receding hair and a heavy brow, looked too old to be a soldier, though he wasn't. I introduced Thorn, but no one cared.

Then we tried to work out what'd just happened.

First, who's who? Clyde nodded at the smoking bodies twenty feet away, said, "Meigs and one of his bullies."

I nodded to the man with a revolver at his head, said, "Another bully. He was at Kew yesterday when Meigs murdered a young Sepoy."

"In Bullock's basement too," said Chrystal.

Clyde got close to the bully, and Kyd pressed the revolver hard in the back of his neck. Mention of a dead Sepoy piqued the sense of a battlefield, the menace of imminent killing. "Name?" Clyde demanded.

"Sam ... Goad. I work for the Company–"

"You don't," said Clyde. "You're Meigs' creature–"

"Meigs worked for Slegman–"

"Stow it!" Kyd said, jabbing the gun barrel hard in the back of his neck.

"You tortured Henry Bullock," I said.

"Nah ... Meigs, not me."

"The initialed forceps ... where'd you get them?"

"Meigs brought 'em," Goad said.

"Where'd *he* get them ... Nathaniel Slegman, I'll bet?"

Kyd jabbed his neck again, harder. The lieutenants are stoked and restless, like a couple of apprentice boys after a brawl. Old soldiers back in action.

Goad gave me a sneering stare, like *go to hell!*

"He threatened me," said the young man. "Said if I didn't tell him how this place works, he'd cut bits off me till I did."

"Billy Impey?" I said.

"Who?" said Clyde.

"Henry Bullock's nephew."

"What if I am?" said Billy. He frowned at Clyde. "I *know* you,' he said, "Sir Reginald ... Clyde's Chemical Manufactory, I've read your book, *Quinology*, read about you in the *Illustrated News*–"

"Shut up!" said Clyde. "You'd be dead if it were not for us."

"I can look after myself," said Billy. He pointed at Chrystal. "He's the one near killed me, with that ... musketoon."

"You're right there," Kyd said, impressed at Billy's nerve.

A glance from Clyde shut Kyd up too.

I'd got Billy wrong. No doubt about that. He's not the innocent boy I'd imagined, and none of his uncle's crafty, hunted look. There's a likeness round his eyes, the shape of his head, but Billy's handsome. Nicely dressed in leather trousers and waistcoat, gypsy style. He'd closely cut blond hair, like a cap, wide eyes that're serious and intelligent.

"Listen boy," Clyde said. "You realize you're a conspirator to treason–"

"Treason! How the hell d'you work–"

"He doesn't know," I said. Then, to Billy, "There's a native uprising in India, Henry delivered a letter that might've sparked it."

"Uncle didn't–"

"No *might've* about it," said Clyde, pointing a finger. "One more word ..."

Billy nodded, kept quiet. But he didn't look afraid. More like thoughtful, working the odds. Chrystal looked worried because it feels like Clyde's got a plan, that we're being led along. I'd told Clyde to bring two armed men to meet Chrystal and me at Hackney station at midday – my price for *Artemisia Chinensis*. I'd thought Meigs and his bullies might be here with Billy.

"How'd the shooting start?" I said.

"Lieutenants came to reconnoiter," said Chrystal. "Saw–"

"Saw Billy being marched about at gun point," said Clyde. "We went down a side lane, came up behind, through the foliage. No sign of life, so Chesney came over the fence for a closer look." He nodded at the bodies. "They saw him, fired a shot to scare us off–"

"That's Meigs–" Billy couldn't keep his mouth shut.

Goad: "We thought it's kids ... playing around–"

"I saw a face at the window," Chrystal said, "took aim. When they fired, I fired back," – a pat on the blunderbuss – "with this ... just ... jerked the trigger."

"Nerves," said Chesney. "You've no experience–"

"Blew in the window," said Billy, Clyde letting him talk. "Only I'm showing 'em how to heat the decoction when ... boom! ... a chunk hit the still, sent burning solvent everywhere–"

"Benzene ... and acetic ether," I said, with a low whistle.

"My chance," said Billy, "I chucked a beakerful at 'em ... kicked the open demijohn their way ... except the heat shattered another one, so the whole place went up. I jumped back in the coal cellar, shut the door. They're pinned by the window till they realized they're cooking ... ran for it."

"Good shooting with revolvers," I said, "at that distance."

Chesney shook his head. "Carbines. No time to reload ... dumped 'em."

Clyde looked around, said to Billy, "You run this place ... by yourself?"

"Uncle helped me set it up, but yeah, mostly I do."

"You," Clyde said. "Thorn, is it? Wait in the carriage. I've got some private business here."

Thorn glanced my way and I nodded. Chrystal threw me a glance too, trying to work out what Clyde's up to. When Thorn had clambered over the gates, Clyde said to Billy, "Let's take a walk around, *I'd* like to know how this place works." Then to Kyd, "Keep a tight grip on Goad." To Chesney, "fetch the carbines, reload them."

Billy went over to Meigs' body, found a bunch of keys in the dead man's pocket. Tossed them in the air, snatched them on the way down with, "Gotcha!" as if he knew he'd get them back. As he and Clyde walked towards the hothouse, I said, "Mind if I join you? I'd like to know too."

"Why not?" Clyde said, as if it didn't matter. Which worried me more.

THE FIELD WAS two square acres end to end, the hothouse a similar oblong a quarter the size. The brick-and-steel boiler house was oblong too, half as small again. The area felt abandoned and neglected until we stepped into the hothouse, saw sunlight-clean windows and open skylights venting the summer heat. A warm mist drifted from jets in the roof, settling on rows of *Artemisia Chinensis* – spindly green bushes as tall as me, ripe with tiny yellow flowers.

"Don't look like much," Clyde said, tugging on a few branches, sniffing his palm. He stood tall surveying the room. "Impressive. Where're they from?"

"China," said Billy. "Just overgrown daisies, really."

"Huh! Nature hides her treasure in the unlikeliest of places."

The plants made a rich, camphorous atmosphere, both alluring and sickly. Mingled with the whiff of wet iron and stone it might've let you forget the drama outside. Might've, if Billy hadn't begun a patter about soils and temperatures and humidity and propagation.

The end of the hothouse was a kind of workshop for stripping and grinding leaves, stewing them in covered vats of solvent. When Billy paused to let us take it in, I said, "You emptied Henry's safe ... that's when they grabbed you?"

He looked at Clyde ... should he answer the black? Like asking if a dog's safe to pat. Clyde nodded, and Billy said, "No ... Uncle said if anything happened to him I was to bring it all here, hide it. They followed me."

"All?" said Clyde.

Billy nodded at the boiler-house next door. "It's in there."

On the way, I said, "You know Henry took his life, to protect you?"

"Protect me?" He spoke as if I'm mad. "Uncle kept his work

in the family. Wouldn't give the likes of Meigs the shit under his fingernails."

Clyde choked a dry laugh, and Billy said, "Beggin' your pardon, Sir."

The lintel over the boiler-house door was black where smoke had billowed out. Inside's a long, narrow room, a short alley with boiler doors one side, a coal cellar on the other. It's iron and brick, which is why the fire died down so fast when the solvent ran out. Iron brackets on the walls once held wooden shelves for evaporating dishes. The shelves are skeletons, ribs of smoking charcoal. The dishes lay scattered in pieces beneath.

The place stank of oil, like fumes from an ill-trimmed lamp.

At the far end was a metal workbench under the broken window. On the bench stood machines for pill making, bottling and labeling, lots of broken glass.

"I'll get a brush," Billy said, "clear the bench."

He swept a patch clean, took out his keys to open a strong box under the bench. Inside's a hefty leather satchel which he set on the clean patch. Then he rummaged in the satchel and passed Clyde a series of items.

"Notebook," he said. "Process in the front, accounts at the back."

"Meigs see this?" Clyde asked. Billy nodded, and Clyde passed it to me.

The labelled sketches are beautiful, showing every step from sowing the seeds to bottling the medicine.

"Leather money purse," said Billy.

It was weighty, closed with a drawstring. Clyde opened it, tipped a shower of golden Mohurs – Company guineas – into his palm.

"Thirty pounds Stirling," Billy said. "More or less. Part of what Uncle got to furnish this place and do the trial in Calcutta."

Clyde funneled the coins back in the purse and tossed it on the bench.

Billy passed Clyde four stoppered jars, keeping up his patter.

"This one's crystals," he said, "the pure medicine. Then you've got your pills made with sugared gum. This one's a solution of alcohol, taken by mouth. Then there's a vegetable-oil solution for hypodermic injection."

Clyde ran a thumb along the final jar's white label. In small italics it said, *Artemisia Chinensis,* in big bold type below, 'BULLOCK'S REMEDY'.

"Modest, he wasn't," I said.

Clyde stood the jars on the bench. "No one in Calcutta was curious about a new malaria cure?"

"Uncle added a bittering agent," said Billy. "Tasted like quinine."

Henry didn't miss a trick, not when it came to money. "Company paid for this place?" I said, "When Loddiges shut."

"S'pose so," Billy said, "Uncle never spoke about money, 'cept the banks wouldn't lend him any ..."

"What about India, with Elijah Doyle?"

"What about it?" he said. "You're very nosy for–"

"What?" I got closer, looked down with the salad face. "It's me found out you're Henry's kin, worked at Loddiges ... or you'd be dead."

"Answer him," said Clyde, leafing through the notebook accounts.

Billy looked away. "Uncle hardly spoke of India ... well, one time, he's sitting in here, drinking beer, after that bloke ... what's his name, the one blew his own brains out? Uncle knew him, see–"

"Colonel Peach?" said Clyde, studying a column of figures.

"Yeah, Uncle had supper with him and the Prof, said they argued like hell about Jesus, converting the natives, Day of Judgment ... all that."

Clyde shut the notebook. "Ever mention rifles?"

"Nope."

I said, "How about grease ...?"

"Grease ... ah, you mean tallow? Yeah, hog and beef fat ... something about natives being superstitious. Uncle didn't get it ..."

I glanced at Clyde. Sounds like they quarreled over the cartridges: Doyle wants them withdrawn, kept quiet; Peach just the opposite. I said to Billy, "What about a dispatch ... or maybe a letter?"

Billy nodded. "Yeah, that's what I tried to tell yer. Uncle'd had a few beers, starts moaning he'd done all the work when they first got to India ... 'cos the Prof's so ill. See, they went ashore at this port, something like ... a jewel ..."

"A jewel? Ah ... Diamond Harbour?"

"That's it. Uncle says it's a filthy place."

"Customs office in the Bay of Bengal," I said. "Forty miles down-river from Calcutta. I helped O'Shaughnesssy lay the telegraph line in fifty-one." The name usually jogged a little respect from the likes of Clyde.

"Well, soon as they're ashore, the Prof gets the shits so bad he nearly died. Laid up for weeks. Anyway, he tells Uncle to go on to Calcutta alone, get things started. But he needs the Company's say-so, that's Peach. The Prof's got a letter, only he won't part with it ... so Uncle copies it out, and the Prof signs to say he'll bring the real thing, when he's well."

"So that's it," I said to Clyde. "They need to start the trial, but Doyle's got dysentery. Sounds like he never handed over the original."

Clyde tapped the notebook. "What did Uncle tell you to do with all this if anything ... *happened* to him?"

"It's mine ... we'll, me and mum's. Actually, Uncle said I should bring the notebook to you ... ask a good price."

Clyde took the satchel. He put away the notebook and jars, then nodded under the bench at four demijohns. "More solvent?" Billy nodded, and Clyde said, "Who else knows about *Artemisia Chinensis,* how to make the drug?"

Billy shrugged. "Uncle kept it all secret. Now it's just me ... well, I showed those men ... so there's Goad."

Clyde took up the purse. "Let's be clear, Billy," he said, "this place was paid for by the Company, we own it–"

"But it's my job, I–"

Clyde held up a hand. "You're a clever lad. How'd you like to work for me, earn more than any gardener ... or chemist?"

"I'd like that a lot, Sir," Billy said. "But this place–"

Clyde bounced the purse. "Thirty pounds Stirling," he said, "more or less. What if we said it buys your share?"

"Well ... yeah ..." Billy reached for the purse.

Clyde clenched his fist, drew it back.

Billy said, "About this job ..."

Clyde shook his head. "You need some self-respect, Billy. That man out there, Goad ... drove Uncle to suicide, said he'd cut you up ... would've killed you. It's a matter of family honour ... trust ... see what I mean?"

Billy looked uncertain, but he nodded.

CLYDE LED US out to where Kyd's guarding Goad, stood Billy less than six feet from the prisoner. "Give him your revolver," he said to Chesney. The officer's big eyes swiveled at Clyde, then Billy. He tucked his carbine under his left arm, drew a Colt. 31, a London Pocket. Flipped it so he's holding the octagonal barrel, offered Billy the walnut grip. He took it clumsily by the frame, no idea how to handle a gun.

"Show him!" Clyde said. Chesney used his free arm to fit the Colt in the boy's hand. "What's this?" said Goad, suddenly afraid. "Shut up!" said Kyd, jabbing his carbine Goad's way. Chesney lifted Billy's hand to shoulder height, arm outstretched, gun aimed at Goad's heart.

Goad said, "Wait ... no, look ... what-yer-want? I–"

Billy shrugged Chesney off, wanting to do this by himself.

"Hold on!" Chrystal said, "this is-nae justice–"

"Keep out of it!" ordered Clyde.

Seemed quite like justice to me, but I kept quiet.

Chesney shouldered his carbine, aimed at Chrystal.

Clyde said, "This isn't some piddling intrigue, Sergeant. It's the Company, Imperial rule."

Chrystal held his ground, knuckles white on the empty musket.

Chesney cocked his carbine.

With a nod to Goad, Clyde said to Chrystal, "A killer, torturer, traitor ... you can take the credit," – he got closer – "or go out feet first, with him."

"You'd better believe him, Chrystal," I said, Shiva singing in my blood.

"No ... NO!" Goad screamed. "I did nothing ... I ..."

No one listened. Chrystal stepped back, jaw clenched, eyes fixed on Clyde.

"Thumb on the hammer," Chesney told Billy, like he's aiming at a lump of wood. "All the way, two clicks ... steady, squeeze ..."

"Listen," pleaded Goad, "I'll tell yer ... 'bout them forceps ... Meigs said it's not Slegman ... it's that slut of a mistress, she's the one–"

"Get on with it, Billy!" said Clyde. "Shut his filthy mouth."

Billy licked his lips, gathering his nerve. Goad's eyes bulged. He lifted his hands against the lead, opened his mouth to speak ...

The shot echoed *PER-TISH!* off the boiler-house bricks, blowing a hole in Goad's right hand, spotting his chest. He fell on the grass, eyes glazed. Looked disbelievingly at the dribbling hole in his hand. Billy stepped closer, lowered his arm rigid as a crane jib, cocked and fired again. Goad seemed to fall asleep without closing his eyes, light fading away as he slumped over on the grass.

"That did it!" gabbled Billy. "That showed him!"

"Good shooting, boy," said Chesney.

Clyde stepped in. He took the revolver and passed it to Chesney who stuck it back in the holster. Clyde took Billy's hand, slapped in the purse.

I'm shaking. Still riding Shiva, angry with Billy more than Clyde.

In a wild threat, I said, "What about me, Clyde? I can make Bullock's Remedy."

"You're not making anything," he said. "You're under arrest."

I turned to Chrystal. "What ...?"

He's glaring at Clyde with a look of utter loathing, wondering how you'd bring him to justice, if justice applied to such a man. With obvious regret, he said, "Aye, he's right, Khan–"

"For murdering Lady Beatrice Motcombe," said Clyde.

Chesney spun the carbine from Chrystal to me, knew this was coming.

"There're two witnesses," said Chrystal. "Swear you threw her in the river last night, saw you do it."

"Why in God's name would I do that?"

Chrystal shook his head as if he didn't want to say it.

"You were lovers," said Clyde. "Weren't you?"

I said nothing, just stared trying work what he knew.

"Her husband wanted a divorce, said he'd expose you ... make a scandal." He turned to Chrystal. "You see? Doesn't even deny it."

"I didn't kill her."

"Oh, you killed her all right," said Clyde. "Tell them why, Khan ... why you had to get rid of her body."

I felt their disgust at the sly native, the seducer. I stared back – two Company soldiers, armed and lawless. I'd been here before, torn by anger and impotence, taught my place in the world of men.

Clyde's words droned on – *"Drowned in the filthy Thames... with child... a dark-skinned, thick featured half-caste... proof of your animal lust"* I didn't listen. I knew the rhythm of imperial scorn too well, the ease of a grotesque lie. Kyd too levelled his gun at me, and Clyde said, "Put the Darby's on him, Sergeant."

As Chrystal went behind me, I said, "We're not enemies, Clyde–"

"A murderer?" He came close, his face a foot from mine. "Slegman's waiting at East India House, wants the dispatch. Then you're going to gaol, no wriggling out of the noose this time."

Chrystal was convinced. He pulled back my arms, began screwing on the cuffs. I stared ahead, trying to make sense of what I'd heard. *Clyde doesn't know his niece took the dispatch. Slegman doesn't know either. Why's Adelaide Doyle holding it back, keeping it a secret?*

Out of habit I asked myself what O'Shaughnessy would do. But the question rang hollow ... the Director of Telegraphy, physician to the Governor General of India, just knighted by Queen Victoria. Sir William never stood where I do now, was never spoken to like this ... he wouldn't have a bloody clue!

But I did. Sir Reginald didn't lose a minute's sleep for the men dying in his service. That's progress by free trade, the civilizing force of capital. Irresistible as gravity. God's will. But an unreturned book on a library table's a crime against gentility ... so discomforting he puts it back himself.

"If I'm a dead man," I said, "why would I give Slegman anything?" Clyde didn't answer. I'd wrongfooted him. "He told you I killed Beatrice Motcombe, didn't he?" In the silence I didn't need to say, *"See? He doesn't even deny it."* So, I continued, "She was kidnapped from her apartment in the Adelphi," – I nodded at the bodies on the grass – "by them, on Slegman's orders. Shall I tell you why?"

Clyde stepped back. It's against his instinct to be lectured by a native Indian, to cede a grain of his authority. But he wants to hear what I've got to say.

"He meant to force the dispatch from me. Knew Beatrice and I were lovers, that she carried our child. I don't deny *that.* He locked her in a sewer at York Stairs before the rising tide, met me on the steam pier at Hungerford Bridge. When he didn't get the dispatch, he threw me the key ... marked YS. By the time I opened the iron gate, a flood of rainwater swept her into the Thames."

My tone and the look in Clyde's eyes said this wasn't some feeble attempt to wriggle out of the noose. Clyde drew breath to speak, but I cut him off. "At first, I thought he meant me to find her alive, hadn't counted on the storm. I was wrong ... it was about avoiding scandal

... but not by me."

When Clyde just stared, I said, "Slegman's good friend ... Shapton Sands. They were at Haileybury together, writers together in Calcutta. Sands was Beatrice's husband, until he abandoned her for a native wife, had two kids. Now he wants the Motcombe estate and the money ... planned to divorce her in the new year, cite me as correspondent. But if he dragged up her affaire in court, she'd expose his bigamous marriage, his other life in India. Mightn't matter for a commoner, but she's a peer of the realm, a noble lady. How much easier if ..."

"She's dead and you're blamed," murmured Clyde. His stare turned to an angry scowl, almost like paralysis.

"Oh yes," I said. "Slegman's endangered the Company and your business for his own profit ... duped you into arresting me for his crimes–"

"But ... if her life was at stake, why in God's name didn't you give him the dispatch?"

"I didn't know it was," I said, "at stake."

"You wanted more money?"

"Yes ... more money." I couldn't tell him I didn't have the dispatch.

"You'll get none ... only a rope. Slegman says he followed you over the bridge, saw you drown her. That's what he'll tell a court ... and there's another witness says the same, saw you from the bank. Put that with the affaire ..."

"I think desperation's changed his plan," I said. "Now it's my life for the dispatch ... I hand it over, his eye-witness testimony goes away ... Beatrice's disappearance becomes an unsolved mystery."

"And you trust him?"

"Of course not ... it'll be a game of wits."

Clyde sucked his lower lip. The others watched. They wanted a verdict, a lead on who to believe. Clyde might still have dismissed me but for his acid indignation, his sense of betrayal. My story rings true,

Slegman's name scratched on in like a signature, too clear for Clyde to deny his own conscience.

He turned his back to me. Strolled a few paces. We watched him fold his arms, take a deep breath, gaze at the distant platform of Hackney Station a quarter of a mile away. I kept thinking about Adelaide Doyle, why she hadn't given her lover a document that could destroy him. In a while, Clyde turned to look at me with his tongue shoved in his cheek like a boiled sweet.

"Tell me the truth ... does Green have the dispatch?"

I shook my head. "He doesn't."

"Has he seen it?"

"Nope."

He flicked a hand at Chesney and Kyd. "If these men escort you to the docks, put you on a Company ship to a far port of your choosing, if I instruct the captain and pay your one-way passage ... convince me you'll never come back, Khan ... you'll tear up that damned dispatch, never speak of it again."

I hadn't come this far to sail off the edge of the world. In any case, I'd got what I wanted ... more, in fact. Chrystal knows I'm no murderer. I'm not thinking of escape. I'm not thinking of Slegman or dispatches. I'm thinking of a girl called Bibaha on a bright morning in the Bengal jungle, at a tree by a well.

THE WELL TREE was just that – a tall Sal by a well, both about six feet in diameter. The well's mouth had lips of baked clay. Its water was black. No one knew how deep it was because no one could swim down that far. The tree was over a hundred feet tall. It was old, part buried in ivy and creeper with bark so craggy you could climb it. Further up the arthritic branches jutted this way and that, mostly leafless. The huge trunk bent like an old man's back. Which is why, at the very top, it hung over the well.

If you hugged the trunk, looked up, you'd see it puncture the sky like Jack and the Beanstalk. Except Sal trees really are magic – they'll do anything from cure your ills to fry your lunch to build you a home. This one tried your courage. Early on summer mornings we'd gather there, the kids. The girls picked flowers to make chains, sat in the grass or by the well cooling their feet in the icy water.

The boys perched in the tree by age – older meaning higher up – like little troops of monkeys smoking Sal leaves. I was one of the youngest, just weeks before my fateful trip to the river Mor. If I climbed above my station, the older boys would kick me back or whip me with their Sal lathis. Only one way past was understood: to say you'd never come back down; a one-way passage.

Bibaha. She was the *Ojha's* daughter, a girl I'd always known. But lately she'd begun to speak a different language. Not in words but smiles and glances, by graceful movement, in gestures with her hands and eyes. She'd always been my girl, even if she didn't know it. When I was the *Manjhi*, the chief, who else but the medicine man's daughter could be my wife?

Khagan had other ideas; a year older, a fast runner, already expert with a bow and arrow. He too walked with Bibaha and drew her smiles. One morning we'd both fallen in next to her on the way to the well tree. If she thought one's too few, he thought three's too many. We fought in the dust for five minutes, wrestling and punching, breathing hard. He won the tie, sort of. I couldn't get the better of bigger boy, not least because I'd no idea how to fight.

But I thought she understood that bigger doesn't mean braver or more faithful.

And so I watched. Noticed his too careful movements as he climbed to his perch. The glances down, the taut smiles. Khagan didn't like heights. The Sal tree could be his nemesis. Because the fate of men lay a hundred feet above, and in the black depths of the well below. We'd seen it. Watched in silent thrill and anguish, as others tried their courage, took their place in the world to come.

My first day alone at the well tree, I got just twenty feet before the ground abandoned me. Adrift in space, my hands held on too tight, sweat trickled on my back. My first grip of fear. I looked around to take the measure of courage, what lay between me and Khagan. Yes, or no? The next time I got up fifty feet, measured each foot and handhold, sat in the canopy of birds eyeing the solid trunk. The fixed point. If it held, I could hold.

The third time I passed the magic point where the trunk split into three boughs, each as thick as a man's arm. I stood on the edge, above the forest and the wheeling birds. When I looked down, I almost fell. My limbs were jelly, the sky tilted and sweat popped from my hands like hothouse sprinklers. Yes, or no? Far below, the world urged me to jump, pulled me with a coward's gravity.

I couldn't do it. Not the final steps.

Until that bright morning when I walked hand in hand with Bibaha to the well tree. Khagan met us there. As he climbed, he said, "She'll come back with me Shalpu," thew me a sneer. I said to Bibaha, "You'll wait for me, later?" She said, "We'll see, Shalpu, shan't we?" Then gave me a glance that made it my decision, a moment to impress her. Yes, or no?

That's when I knew. *I can do it. I'm ready.* No matter I'm small, just seven years old. *I can do it.* The conviction tingled in my hands, the excitement in my stomach, a kind of madness that normally lives in dreams. I climbed quickly to the first troop of boys. When they leaned out to whack me down, I said, "I'm going up!" They laughed, took a few swipes till harder heads said, "Let him pass," meaning they'd punish my hubris on the way down.

I climbed, knowing each branch and notch, let the work fill my mind, kept my eyes on the next grip. Look up, not down. Up into the cozy canopy, then out into the void with the three slender boughs. Each was parallel to the ground. I stood on the first bough with the second a little above my head. The third was higher still, a couple of feet further into the abyss.

So far so good. I'd done it before. But one more step and there's no turning back. That's when the fear broke through, pulled me like a

Bonga spirit hissing from the tree below, *"Come back ... come back you fool!"* My mind and body unhinged: flesh tingling, heart chugging like a piston; mind holding on – *I can do it ... just let it be done* – keeping it all together with measured, squeezing breaths.

I knew the drill: keep moving. I'd rehearsed in my mind, done it on similar boughs near the ground. Nothing to it. NOTHING TO IT!

I fixed my eyes on the third bough, studied its mottled bark. When a bird glided by, I sucked in its airborne ease. Nothing to it. Stepped onto the lower bough, grasped the upper one in both hands. Then my right hand went a foot to the right, the left followed, same with each foot, again and again, easing out into nothing. Over and over until you saw the crick in the bough, the spot.

I saw it to the right, getting closer. Kept my eyes on the mottled bark until the crick was in front of my nose. The spot. My gaze wandered to the far horizon, the infinite sky. I'm standing on nothing, holding nothing ... giddy, no strength in my hands. I've got to jump ... no, not jump ... more like a step to grab the higher bough ... nothing to it.

Then it's done. I see my knuckles gripping hard, sense a gentle swing from the step. I must be still; hold fast till I'm hanging like a plumbline, ready to drop straight and true. Now I lower my head to look down past my legs that don't feel like my legs, past my feet hanging improbably a mile above the ground.

Tiny faces in a circle stare up. They've gathered round the well, none left in the tree. But instead of a victory smile or whoop, I get my final slash of fear. Is the well directly under me? I can't tell. Worse, it looks too small, like a pail of water. I'll never fit inside. I look up, check the crick, check that my arms an even foot each side. Reason says it's right. My body says, *hang on!*

But I can't hang on, can't go back.

I cheat fear by springing open my hands, falling, weightless, trees racing by at a speed I've never known, faster than a galloping horse.

My arms whirl in little circles, knees bend to stop me flying into the well like an arrow.

The drop never ends. Now I'm falling, now I'm in icy, black water. Alive. But which way's up? I turn in a flash of panic till I see the dappled surface far above, strike upward with powerful kicks. Suddenly there's air and noise, a mass of faces staring in relief and admiration. Two older boys pull me out, stand me on the earth. Bibaha steps forward, gathers the folds of her sari to dry my face. When she kisses my cheek I feel the triumph, the joy.

WHICH IS HOW I felt now. Not joy, but the kind of elation that says belief is triumph ... climb upwards, don't look down.

"I'll not convince you, Clyde," I said. "I've an appointment with the Chairman at East India House, whether he likes it or not–"

"Don't be an idiot, Khan," said Chrystal. "Save yourself while–"

"Come with me! Arrest Guy Fawkes ... the man who blew up the British Empire."

"He'll send you to the gallows," Clyde said.

"We'll see. Let's take my coach."

Clyde looked at me for a moment, wondering what madness possessed me, just how dangerous I am. Then he shrugged. "Very well. Take him to Slegman, as arranged. You too, Sergeant Chrystal. Billy and I have work here."

I held out the cuffs, but Clyde shook his head. "If you're going to Leadenhall Street in that mood, I think you'd better keep those on."

I hadn't counted on that.

Twenty-Five

IN THE CAB I sat with my back to the horses, Kyd and Chrystal bookending the seat opposite. Kyd had a carbine butt resting on his knee. Chrystal held his empty blunderbuss. Chesney got up on the box next to Thorn, giving orders. By the time we set off, Clyde and Billy were lugging demijohns of solvent to the hothouse. As we raced over the watercress fields, I saw the first billows of black smoke, all traces of Bullock's Remedy vanishing for good.

We went south down Cambridge Street, Thorn pushing the pace, slanting westwards into Whitechapel, cutting through the eastern metropolis to hit the City at Aldgate. No one spoke.

I went over every step since trotting into Henry's basement, like hand and footholds on the well tree. Turning down Clyde's offer was as good as a confession to Kyd and Chesney. If I'm not cooperating, I'm a prisoner, especially as we're on our way to the Company Chairman ... their master, the man who says I'm a murderer, who I've had the nerve to call a traitor.

Chrystal's another matter. He's just seen Company brutality as few white men outside India have. Heard Clyde fail to deny the Chairman's a liar and murderer. But he won't arrest Slegman. Once we're inside East India House, military trumps civil law. The lieutenants will make short work of Chrystal if needs be. But he's the card for the right trick.

All the while my eyes keep straying to the chemical cabinet by me on the seat ... a little hiss of Shiva ... just enough to keep me invincible for one more hour. At Aldgate I fetched the glass tube from the cabinet and took a couple of snorts straight from the jar. I looked up, wide-eyed at the astonished faces, said, "Medicinal ... like snuff."

That's what I told them ... it's what I told myself.

THE GAME BEGAN before we got to East India House. I'd imagined us pulling up at the grand façade in Leadenhall Street, me striding in like a gladiator. But here I am in cuffs, swerving down Lime Street through a warren of lanes to the tradesman's entrance. Chesney let us into a courtyard and relocked the gates. Clambering out it felt like prison – three towering stone walls and the arse of East India House with its tenement windows and peeling paint.

Kyd and Chrystal stood behind me as guards. Chesney grabbed Thorn's slender arm and dragged her from the box seat like a child. "Inside," he grunted. "You're his man."

Thorn just nodded, fell in next to me.

We went in a side door and snaked our way past rooms of every Imperial office. Chesney led, followed by Thorn and me, then Kyd and Chrystal at the back. If a clerk glanced through an open door, he quickly looked away.

We're ghosts. Not to be found on any agenda.

The corridors smelt of wood polish and cigar smoke, echoed emptily except for the Directors' room. In there a few waited in dark suits for the meeting at four, chatting with the air of a filling theatre. I glanced, reminded myself I'm here to stop the show. A steep staircase took us to the first floor, to a uniformed custodian by a door. Chesney nodded, straightened his tunic, and rapped on the woodwork. There's no reply but the custodian turned the handle to let us in.

THEY SHOVED ME in first, like an offering, then filed in behind. The custodian came too, shutting the door after him. We stood in wary silence like tourists at a holy shrine.

It's an airy hall with two archways, one going right to a library, the other straight ahead to a museum. The hall itself was both: one wall solid with books, the others with display cases stuffed with exhibits. The high roof was vaulted like a church and topped with a glass cupola that let in a slant of afternoon sun.

We seemed alone at first, but then we felt a presence. Just inside the museum, among stuffed tigers and Indian saddles and musical instruments stood Nathaniel Slegman ... still as an exhibit, smart as a soldier on parade. His tailored blue frockcoat hung to his knees over a pair of pale-grey, fine-striped trousers. Black shoes glinted, bright as fresh pitch. A tan bowtie sat on his starched collar like a nervous butterfly. The contrast with the ugly head on top was hypnotic, like a turd on a neatly set dining table.

He watched me as if the others weren't there, surprised by my beaten face and the red bandana on my head, like a dacoit sprung from Jungle Terry. Then, he said, "You've arrested the wretch, Sergeant ... well done." He spoke in his public voice, like an orator, leaving a soft after-hum in the hall. With a fake smile, he beckoned me, said, "Here ... come in here," like talking to an imbecile.

I didn't move. I wish I knew what came next. Nathaniel Slegman invited me here. Which means he's afraid, he's vulnerable, desperate to know where the dispatch is. I'm climbing the well tree, moving up. It's only my confidence says I'll make it to the top and find the nerve to finish the job. And I don't even know where the top is or what job awaits. So I just keep climbing.

Slegman came through the arch into the slant of sunlight. I sensed the others shrink back a little. Not me. Even in handcuffs I stood tall and square.

"You're a dead man, Khan," he said, "But a quiet word or two, in confidence ... perhaps we can come to an agreement?"

An agreement? That's how fake his confidence is.

"About who drowned Beatrice Motcombe? I think we know that."

"We do indeed. I saw you from the bridge, hurl her from York Stairs." He sighed for the others' benefit. "I take some blame myself for telling you her husband meant to expose you."

"You're a liar Slegman ... and a murderer."

"Bennet," he said to the custodian, "fetch the other witness, there's a good fellow." Bennet hurried out. More familiarly, he said, "Come Doctor Khan. Let's stroll in the museum ... or would you be brought at gunpoint?"

Kyd and Chesney still held their loaded carbines. I stood my ground, but I knew he wouldn't talk in front of witnesses. So in a while I shrugged as if suited me to go. Into India, but not the one I knew. This was the Company's private India – the Museum – a doll's house of relics, an anatomy room of dismembered lives.

We walked past vitrines and cabinets of spears and tapestries and tusks, model canals, opulent homes full of idle Hindus. Each label reaffirmed our degradation: our knowledge rude, our artists blundering, our craftsmen useless, our musical instruments made in ignorance of acoustics. Now and then the grotesque became the bizarre – the golden throne of Maharaja Ranjit Singh, the Nawab of Lucknow smoking a hookah under a crimson awning ... like walking in a bad dream after too much ganjah.

Slegman paused at a case of effigies, Hindu gods. There were figures impaled on bamboo spikes, others threading string through their flanks or hanging by iron hooks. "These people," he said, "worship lumps of wood." He pointed at some rusty nails. "Stick them through their tongues," – he stuck his out, jabbed it with an imaginary nail – "like this. The degradations of a heathen creed."

The next cabinet stopped me dead: the doll's house of the Santal, hung with the drum and flute, the bow and arrow, a sprig of the Sal tree. Fragments of life with my mother, stolen and put on show as trophies of war. It stunned me to see them in London amid the jumble of India.

Slegman wanted a reaction. When he didn't get one, he said, "What kind of people grub for a living in the forest ... fight wars with bows and arrows?"

I looked at the mouldy Sal branch. "Their wealth's in the soil ... a drop of rain. It will be still when London lies in ruins."

"From flutes and arrows?" he scoffed. He nodded at the window to Leadenhall Street below, choked with fancy carriages and fancier people. "Ruins? A city of three million ... the heart of civility and trade? Half the world would be in London–"

"There lies its destruction, from within–"

"Your jealous insults–"

"Not at all ... the Thames fetid with nitrogenous waste from three million eating bread, stripping the vitality of English fields. You pay Chinese coolies to dig bird-shit from Pacific islands, sail it to England to feed the tired soil. Until it's gone ... until you can't rob Peter to pay Paul."

My vision startled me, conjured from the world-girdle telegraph and Liebig's *Agricultural Chemistry:* a dead world of barren land and poisoned seas. It startled Slegman too ... that a black should turn his world inside out ... make the museum reality, the street below a precarious dream.

His wary stare said, *"Who are you?"* as if I'd voiced his deepest fears. As if he saw the Bank of England crumble, a tide of rats flooding down Threadneedle Street. He pointed at me. "If it's Christ's will I hasten the end of things, so be it. Let him come in glory." The words bolstered his resolve, but he quickly changed the subject. "I want that dispatch, Khan."

"Ask Adelaide Doyle ... your mistress. She knows where it's hidden–"

"Miss Doyle!" He raised a hand to slap my ugly lips ... thought better of it. "How in God's name could she–"

"You think you know her schemes?"

That hurt him. Whatever his affection for Adelaide Doyle, I saw he didn't trust her; not a woman who's her own intelligencer, the niece of Sir Reginald Clyde, the stepdaughter of the late Professor Doyle.

"Fetch her," I said. "She's in the building. Ask her."

He licked his lips, pointed to a small door behind the display cases.

I'd seen others like it on our way here. "Passageways," he said, "stairs to storage vaults beneath the House, to the sewers and the Thames." He pointed. "If you deceive me, Khan, falsely embroil Miss Doyle in this affair, you'll be thrown in those vaults ... never see the light of day again." His black eyes glared.

Then he turned abruptly, led the way back through the galleries.

IN THE ENTRANCE hall he ordered Bennet to fetch Miss Doyle. I barely heard because I was staring at the witness he'd already fetched. The one who'd been on the riverbank, who says she saw me drown Bea.

It was Jane Muckalt, though it took me a moment to know it.

Her dress was lilac silk, close-fit and frilly, the skirt bell-shaped in layered crinoline. A corset pinched her waist so thin you'd think she'd suffocate. Her hair was a horseshoe of brown ringlets set in bonnet tied under her chin. Pretty, but not quite right; the way a maid who longed to be a lady might dress, or a prince might dress a courtesan to remind him she's no lady.

Not that Jane lacked beauty. It's her stance that gives her away: too solid, too masculine, too shaped by a maid's long days fetching and carrying. And she showed her feelings too much: an ugly scowl aimed at me.

Without a prompt from Slegman, she pointed a finger. "That's him. He's the one!" She told how I burst into the apartment last night, accused her mistress of ensnaring me in a reckless affaire to spite her husband. How I laughed at her declarations of love, at the accusation I'd raped her, swore the child couldn't be mine. Finally, in a blind rage, I'd dragged her from the apartment by the hair and hurled her into the swollen river.

The only truth in the outburst was Jane's anger, so venomous it left a mist of spittle buzzing like midges in the sunlight. Then she strode forward as if to strike me, might've done but for a silver purse gripped tightly in both hands. It's sewn with coloured beads like the one I gave Bea. Too like it to be coincidence. She stood in silence, glowering at me.

Kyd and Chesney are convinced, it's written in their eyes. Chrystal isn't, but he's wondering who this angry woman is.

I said, "Who gave you that nice purse, Jane?"

Taken unawares she clutched it tightly, glanced at Slegman. Catching her mistake, she looked away.

As if in defeat, I said, "You saw me ... from the Adelphi?"

"Yes."

"Hurl her into the river ... in the storm?"

"Yes!"

I stepped right, between her and Slegman. "Where did I throw her from?"

"What? From the ..." She tried to look round me, but I moved again.

"The Terrace," I said, "into the river?"

"Yes–"

"Impossible. Even at high tide the river's a good four or five paces."

We did the little dance again. "The jetty, then–"

"On the left of the Terrace," I said.

"Yes–"

"The Chairman says from York Stairs, on the right ..."

Slegman shifted from my shadow. "She's confused ... aren't you, Jane?"

"Yes. That's it ... York Stairs ... I remember now."

No one believed it. Slegman's integrity fell another step, his black eyes darting round the room. I didn't know what came next, perhaps a move with Chrystal, but it didn't happen. Right then Bennet ushered in an irritated looking Adelaide Doyle. She's a striking woman on any occasion but her appearance immediately sucked the attention from Jane Muckalt.

Adelaide wore a black dress like a frockcoat – V-neck and wide lapels, buttoned down the front. Beneath it was a white shirt and a black cravat. The dress hugged like a pelt, hung in a straight drape to black boots. It's what you'd get if a Parisian seamstress styled a woman as a city capitalist. She'd even drawn her hair up under a black top hat. It made me think of a huntress stalking the Directors in their native costume.

She moved gracefully into the room, carrying a smart leather satchel under one arm, taking in the people, wondering what'd happened to leave us standing like this.

"Adelaide," said Slegman, answering the question in her eyes, "Khan here claims you know the whereabouts of a Company document I seek."

"The one from my stepfather?"

"Indeed!"

She gave me a stare that mirrored mine an hour ago – *why's he accusing me ... what does he know?*

"He's given it to the Home Secretary," she said, "that's all."

"You know nothing of it?" Slegman asked, as if her answer would be final.

Nothing? She hesitated, turning the question in her literal mind.

A quiet voice near me said, *"Who's that?"* When we came in, Thorn faded into the shadows, stood still as a wax exhibit, the way she does.

I half turned, angling my head. "It's Miss Doyle–"

"Not her–"

"Jane? Muckalt, Lady Beatrice's maid."

Thorn's eyes narrowed. "I know her ... from the Sans Sauci."

Which didn't surprise me. I'd always thought Jane led a spicy life.

"Oh, she knows something of it," I said. Then, to Miss Doyle, "You want to know how your father died ... who killed him?"

"Suicide," said Slegman. "The man–"

"Nathaniel! How can you say that? He'd *never* end his own life, the idea's ... preposterous!" She turned to me. "Yes, Hyder ... I want the truth."

"Then we've things to trade," I said, "haven't we?"

Thorn leaned close to me again. "Why don't you tell 'em, Boss?"

"Tell them?"

"Where the dispatch is ... we know, don't we?"

Our eyes met. I understood. I glanced at Miss Doyle's satchel and saw the risk. I went to a floor-to-ceiling bookcase by the library arch, nodded into the world's largest collection of books on the Far East. "It's here," I said.

"Here?" echoed Slegman.

I nodded again. "In that very room."

Everyone looked, like hide-and-seek.

Slegman strode abruptly into the library, turned a circle holding out his arms. "What the hell do you mean ... here?" He knows what I mean. It's exactly where Miss Doyle would hide a valuable document: among a million books. To be found sooner or later or never, just as she wished.

"Adelaide," he said. "If you know where it is ... for God's sake ..."

She looked at me, cottoning on, understanding what I wanted.

"What do you suggest?" she said.

"I'll exchange the dispatch for my trunk, provided it's still full."

"And my stepfather?" said Miss Doyle.

"The truth ... exactly how it happened."

Slegman's trapped. Chesney and Kyd could bundle me down a back corridor to the Thames. Thorn too. But not Miss Doyle. He couldn't have two lieutenants with that over him, let alone Sergeant Chrystal and Jane Muckalt.

"Fetch the trunk," I said to Slegman. "I'll tell Miss Doyle the truth. Then we give you the dispatch. But first," – I took a pace into the archway between library and museum, held the cuffs to one side – "I want these off."

It's a risky plan for everyone, especially me. But seeing the trunk and getting my hands free are important steps. Risky for Slegman too, but he's got two loyal soldiers armed with loaded carbines. And a desperate man does things he ordinarily wouldn't do. His eyes roved the solid walls of books, knew he's chasing a lost leaf in an autumn forest.

"Bennet," he said. "Fetch Khan's trunk."

The custodian went to a low door in the paneling across the hall, one you wouldn't notice. He crouched and waddled inside, came back a minute later dragging the trunk to the centre of the hall.

"Open it," I said.

When Slegman nodded, he unbuckled the leather straps, lifted the lid. It's all there – photographs, journals, affidavits – the lot.

I lifted the cuffs again, said, "Well?"

Slegman nodded to the lieutenants. They came closer till we're in a tight triangle, the carbines inches from my chest. Kyd stood to my right, Chesney to my left. The others came closer too, drawn by the books and the hide-and-seek. Slegman stood behind me in the library; Jane Muckalt, Thorn and Miss Doyle in a triangle to my left. Jane's just out of Chesney's line of fire, Thorn and Miss Doyle behind her. Bennet stayed by the trunk.

"Undo the cuffs, Sergeant," Slegman said.

Chrystal walked to my left. His outrage at Clyde inciting Billy to murder Sam Goad still boiled off him like a nasty scent. Mix that with the struggle to square his conscience at the present charade and you've got a match for Slegman: another man angry enough to do things he ordinarily wouldn't do.

"Watch him!" Slegman said. "If he tries to run, shoot him without compunction ... understand?"

Both lieutenants nodded. Chrystal took a wrist and slotted the screw in a cuff. Over my shoulder, I said, "Like last time ... in Millbank?"

Chrystal looked around as he wound the key, checking the angles and the odds. If he grabbed Chesney's carbine, I'd get a moment's diversion to take Kyd. Moving the key to the second cuff he gave the tiniest nod. No one noticed ... except the person closest. The one who really hated me, who's so incensed she'll do things she ordinarily wouldn't do.

Jane Muckalt. She whipped her bag above her head to strike at Chrystal screaming, *"DON'T LET THE BASTARD GO, YOU FOOL!"*

Twenty-Six

YOU COULD WRITE a book about a gunpower explosion: the chemistry and physics, set it out in diagrams and equations. But nature just goes BANG! Which is what happened – a flash of hate and surprise and panic and loyalty and incompetence and misfortune and good luck ... BANG!

Jane swung at Chrystal who lunged at Chesney whose shot would've hit me if Thorn hadn't shoved Jane in the way. I grabbed Kyd's carbine as it fired, then hooked a left to the side of his head, threw him cross-buttock on the wooden floorboards. Fell on him to a gasp of decompression and a cracking of ribs. Tearing off the bandanna, I bound his hands behind his back.

Chrystal's sat on Chesney whose hands were cuffed behind him. "Old man," hissed Chrystal, "you've no experience."

Thorn looked blankly at Jane who lay on her back staring lifelessly at the cupola above. There's a ragged hole like a belly button in the lilac silk, except it's over her heart in a bullseye of blood. Her purse lay open next to her. Slegman's propped on an elbow on the library floor, gripping his right leg, face pinched in agony. Kyd's bullet hit him above the knee, severing the femoral artery. Bright blood pulsed between his fingers in time with his heartbeat.

Bennet dithered by the trunk awaiting the Chairman's orders.

Adelaide Doyle was different. She'd dropped her top hat and satchel as she bolted into the library, stood ten paces inside by a table with a lamp.

The air stank of gun smoke that curled in the sunlight. My ears rang with the double shots. There's an unstable feeling, as if the action is only half done.

Chrystal restarted it by taking Chesney's gun from its holster, striding into the library to Slegman. The Chairman looked terrified – as if the law's about to deal his just desert – tried to crab away. Chrystal quickly caught him, knelt, and put both hands to his throat with evident intent. Slegman made a grab for his wrists but fell on his back with a yell of pain. I was ready to pull Chrystal off till I saw he's only undoing the Chairman's tie.

He looped it round the leg above the wound, wrenched it tight like a garroter and tied it off. Then he knotted the gun barrel above. Slegman yelled again, a long, "Erg!" as Chrystal twisted the barrel like a windlass, cutting into the leg until the pulses slowed to a rhythmic ooze, then died away altogether.

The Sergeant looked up. "He needs a surgeon, soon."

Miss Doyle said, "No, not yet!" She stood by a lamp someone had used to melt sealing wax. It was still burning. She turned it up too high so orange flame and black smoke flickered from the glass chimney. By the flame she held a sheet of white paper. "One step towards me, Hyder, I'll burn it ... I swear I will."

Slegman leaned his head back, seeing her upside down. "Do it, Adelaide," he grunted, "burn it, now!"

Shaking her head, she said to me, "Tell me how my stepfather really died, Hyder. If you lie again ... I'll turn this to ashes."

This had to be the dispatch, though I couldn't be sure from where I stood.

"Adelaide ... my dear," Slegman groaned, "for God's sake destroy it. Think of our world intelligence ... the investors we need."

She tightened the paper over the chimney till the underside blackened and a visible scorch on top threatened imminent fire.

I held up my hands. "All right ... all right!"

She lifted the paper clear, but I wasn't sure what to say. I couldn't tell her it was suicide, not yet. I needed proof she couldn't deny. With no time to plan, I followed two thoughts – *Slegman doesn't know we've read the dispatch; two nights ago, Elijah Doyle went to a bank vault with despair in his heart.* I hoped together they'd lead me to my goal.

I pointed at Slegman. "Last year this man sent your stepfather to Calcutta with Henry Bullock. He carried a forged dispatch to James Peach, Chairman of the Military Board–"

"Never!" Adelaide said. "My stepfather wouldn't–"

"That's *exactly* why I'm sure he didn't know. He thought the Company and Parliament authorized a drug trial. But at Diamond Harbour he went down with dysentery, sent Bullock with a copy of the dispatch to Peach ... promising to bring the original when he recovered. But he never did. He kept it."

Everyone listened. Even the prone lieutenants had their heads turned my way. Slegman too. "Guesses," he groaned. "You can't *possibly* know–"

"Elphinstone," I lied, keeping Billy out of it. "Turned up at the Military Hospital asking questions for the Governor General. That's when Doyle realized the dispatch was fake, panicked ... cleared out so fast he left evidence in the preparation room." I pointed at Slegman. "Two nights ago, Doyle came here to confront you. Demanded you paid Bullock's price for the drug, made it cheaply available in India as you'd promised. When you dismissed him, he left in utter despair, went straight to the locker at his bank on High Holborn. Why?"

"How in God's name would I know? The man's a dreamer ... as though you could fight the devil with medicine and kindness."

I looked at Miss Doyle. She'd heard the admission the meeting took place. Now she stared, willing me to continue.

"Oh, I think you know," I said. "Why not tell Miss Doyle?"

"ADELAIDE!" he growled. "BURN IT!"

"When Peach went on about cartridges greased with beef and pork fat, Doyle saw the two of you in league ... fellow evangelists ... suspected you'd informed him in the dispatch ... a man who preached on parade, threatened to force Hindus and Muslims to become Christians. He feared you'd told Peach to say the Sepoys were defiled ... a prelude to mass conversions. But Doyle couldn't be sure ... couldn't read the cipher."

I turned to Miss Doyle. "Your stepfather said nothing ... hoping it wasn't true. He'd urged the Company to grow cinchona in India ... now he'd an alternative, a native plant. Cheaper. Better. If Slegman's deceit was a means to that end, he'd swallow it for humanity's sake."

"And to protect the Company," she said. "My stepfather abhorred scandal and unpleasantness." She'd lowered her arm, held the dispatch at her side well away from the flames. Which was just as well given what came next.

"The rumour started by Peach went up country like a thunderbolt ... unrest turning to alarm. The more the British denied it, the truer it seemed, uniting every faction hostile to Imperial rule. Insurrection became mutiny at Barrackpore ... then Colonel Peach's apparent suicide. Your stepfather's conscience tormented him. Then, two nights ago came news of rebellion ... Delhi fallen, the British massacred, their rule under threat ..."

I looked down at Slegman, at Chrystal beside him gripping the tourniquet. "Doyle didn't confront you about a febrifuge," I said, "he wanted to know if you'd sent him like a match to light the fuse of rebellion." I pointed an accusing finger. "That's when you dismissed him ... and when he dropped the bombshell he'd kept the dispatch ... wanted to know what it said ... or he'd make it public."

I paused to let my words sink in.

Miss Doyle said, "But ... how can you know what passed in private?"

"Once Slegman knew the dispatch was in London he had to have it. So he sent Meigs to waylay your stepfather. When Meigs found he was dead, he sent you to the bank claiming the papers as Company property."

"Is that true, Nathaniel?" Miss Doyle said.

"It's fantasy ... a sly fabrication. How could this ... native, know the contents of an enciphered dispatch? It's slander ... to turn you against me."

Which is when I spelled out the keyword, letter by letter.

He gawped at me wide-eyed, hardly believing his own ears. Not even the agony in his thigh could divert him from this abomination.

"I didn't find it out," I said. "Miss Doyle recognized the cipher, found the trick of the keywords–"

He twisted sharply to confront her, wincing at a bolt of pain. "You shared the Company's most secret cipher with a native ... a damned–"

"Is it true, Nathaniel? Did you trick my stepfather into carrying a missive ... one that lit the very conflagration he sought to avert?"

Slegman turned to me, eyes spitting hatred. I'd found him out. Still glowering at me, he said to Miss Doyle, "It wasn't a febrifuge made your stepfather threaten me ... it was you! He demanded I break off our affaire, stay married to Lucy Ocklynge ... if not he'd give the dispatch to the Home Secretary, ruin me ... RUIN US!"

I said, "Expose your subterfuge–"

"SUBTERFUGE!" he shouted. "I court no subterfuge. The cipher was a mark of authenticity." He struggled with Chrystal's help onto his elbows, sitting up to face me. "What do you know of Christian responsibility ... a heathen only half removed from savagery? When Doyle came whining of rebellion–"

"Whining?" said Adelaide.

"–I reminded him a man dying unbaptized goes to eternal hell, that Christ brought a fire to this earth we're sworn to kindle. Doyle was weak–"

"Weak?"

"–scared by the flutter of his own banners, the clamour of his own trumpets–"

"Nathaniel!" she implored. "He believed our missionaries taught emancipation, our drugs the goodness of Christ the Lamb–"

"Against the tyranny of idols and barbaric rituals? We fight the devil with fire ... or let our missionaries be recalled, our churches dissolved ... OUR BIBLES BURNED ALONG WITH OUR OWN

SOULS!" Then, quietly but with utter conviction: "One eternal life outweighs a million lost souls ... ten million!"

That's when I knew any tender feeling Miss Doyle had for Nathaniel Slegman was dead. The affaire had come undone before our eyes. She hated him.

"Tell her what you told Doyle," I said. "The truth!"

"To hell with you, Khan! I answer to God alone."

Furious at his condescension, I strode into the entrance hall, put a boot on Kyd's arse as I wrenched his revolver from its holster. Back in front of Slegman and Chrystal, I aimed the gun at the Chairman's chest, drew the hammer to full cock. "Let him hold that tourniquet himself," I said.

Chrystal's mouth opened, but I jabbed the muzzle. "Do it ... or he's dead!"

The Sergeant grasped the gun with one hand, pushed Slegman into a stable sitting position with the other. Then he helped him take the stock and barrel in his own trembling hands. Slegman groaned at the effort, stared down at the bloody mess of his left thigh.

"Now get away from him," I said to Chrystal.

He gave me a warning glance, but he rose and took two paces backwards. Now Slegman sat alone on the floor in a pool of blood. I got closer, put my boot on his leg by the tourniquet, right on the lacerated muscle and splintered femur. He flinched, let out an "Argh!" of pain.

"Doyle left here in despair," I said. "Why was that?"

He looked down, shook his head. When I leaned more weight on the leg he shrieked, looked up at me in fear.

"The bank," I said. "The cigar-case, six letters. He tried places ... Bengal ... biblical words, hoping to read your mind ... why, Slegman?"

I pushed harder, felt the fracture bow.

"Argh! I don't know ... for God's sake, Khan ... ARGH! ..."

"God's sake?" I pressed till his screams filled the library, till I growled, "My friend Henry Bullock drank cyanide to end his misery ... my darling Beatrice drowned in a filthy sewer ... alone but for the baby she couldn't protect! YOU DARE TO CALL ON GOD'S MERCY?"

He stared up in agony, terror in his eyes. I aimed the gun at his forehead. "You want mercy, ask me to pull the trigger, Slegman ... BEG ME!" – I waited as he gasped and whimpered -- "Or tell me why Elijah Doyle spent half a night in despair." I pressed the barrel to his forehead, leaned on the leg till his screams echoed from the distant museum rooms. Kyd and Chesney rolled and bucked to come to their master's aid, but their bonds held firm. Bennet's hands wrung in anguish. Miss Doyle's stare was fixed and merciless ... waiting for an answer.

I said, "You told him his name was on the dispatch ... didn't you?"

I leaned the rest of my weight on the wound. "DIDN'T YOU?"

Eyes and mouth wide in shock, he screamed, "YES! HE CARRIED IT ... DELIVERED IT ... SIGNED IT!"

I lifted my boot, un-cocked the revolver and tossed it to Chrystal. Between Slegman's whimpers, I said, "You let him think he'd take the blame ... and he believed you capable of it ... had to know." I looked at Miss Doyle. "And just before the dawn he wrote his final words and put the gun to his head." She didn't speak. Tears dribbled down her face as she imagined the pitiful scene, the body she'd seen slumped in the vault. "He misloaded the gun," I said. "The shot ignited a second chamber ... two shots with one pull on the trigger."

The room was silent except for the whimpering. Everyone looked at Adelaide. She stared at me with the look I'd often seen before ... *who are you?* In a while she nodded, whether in a kind of gratitude or understanding I couldn't say. She pulled a lace handkerchief from her cuff, dried her eyes. Then she took a long, settling breath and put the dispatch above the flames, just beyond their reach. "Doctor Khan's leaving, Nathaniel," she said. "He'll do so with his trunk of evidence ... or this dispatch. It's your choice."

He didn't need to think it over. "Let him take it," he grunted at

Bennet. "Let him go … unimpeded."

I lifted the trunk to my waist by the rope handles, threw Chrystal a glance. He shook his head. Kneeling to help Slegman, he said, "I'm needed here, till the surgeon arrives". Bennet held the door. As we turned to leave, Adelaide made a show of pulling the dispatch tight above the flames, letting it burn till flakes of black ash flew up in the heat. In a few seconds only two tags of white paper were left, pinched in her fingers.

I MAN-HANDLED the heavy trunk down the corridor and stairs like a thief with the Company silver. Thorn opened the doors as we retraced our steps through the labyrinth. On the ground floor we made our way to the central corridor. It's nearly four o'clock. The Directors' Room had filled with mustachioed men in black suits and cravats, waiting for a Chairman who wouldn't come.

We hurried past.

We'd just turned right towards the back door when a voice called, "Khan!" It's Sir George coming in the front door with Vernon Smith. They hurried up looking angry until the trunk caught their attention. "You got it?" said Sir George. I nodded, said, "From the Museum. You might want to go up." Then, I added, "Does our deal still stand?"

"The dispatch?"

"Burnt … but I can tell you what it said."

He nodded at the trunk. "Your evidence …. it's all there?"

"Every bit."

"Meet me at the Home Office in an hour." When he turned to the museum stairs, I said, "There's a Sergeant Chrystal up there … saved my life, Nathaniel Slegman's too. Oh … and you need a surgeon, urgently."

"An hour, Khan," Sir George said as he hurried off. I swung the trunk in Vernon Smith's way. "Tell me," I said, "if Elijah Doyle brought the dispatch back to London, how did you know it existed?" The question had troubled me on the coach down to East India

House.

"Service rivalry," he said, pushing past. "The Medical Board was mightily put out the Military Board ordered a trial at the hospital ... complained to the Governor General. He quickly ascertained we'd sent no such dispatch."

He shrugged, chased Sir George up the stairs.

"Come on," Thorn said, "Before Kyd and Chesney get free."

WE RATTLED OFF down Lime Street sitting side by side on the box seat, then west along Eastcheap into Cannon Street, round St Paul's Cathedral up Ludgate Hill. It's a London sky, marble and overcast. Neither of us spoke. As the remnants of my fury ebbed, my mood spiraled down like a kite with a broken strut. I felt sweat on my skin, a black feeling of hopelessness creeping like fog through my being.

"Should've killed Slegman," I said.

"They'd have hanged you."

"Yeah, but still ..." I'd got the trunk, got the Santal name on the pink map, assuming there's anything left of British India. But Bea's gone. Adelaide Doyle had betrayed me in a wicked cause.

"He might die yet," Thorn said, "probably in pain the rest of his life ... in a wheelchair ... that's worse than death."

"Looking on the bright side, eh Thorn?"

She twisted her mouth in a sort of smile.

"You saved my life ... shoving Jane Muckalt in front of a bullet."

"You'd rather I hadn't?"

"Well ... no, but it didn't seem to trouble you much."

Halfway down Fleet Street, she said, "What was your plan?"

"Plan? I was playing by ear ... fetch Adelaide Doyle ... reveal she had the dispatch ... get the cuffs off. Which is sort of how it went."

"You think?" She glanced at me, chewed on her pipe. "So ... when I said tell 'em what we know ... about the dispatch ... what'd you think I meant?"

"Miss Doyle, like I told you ... it was in her satchel."

"Not exactly ..."

I looked at her. "What then?"

"Jane Muckalt had it–"

"Bollocks! Miss Doyle–"

"Nope."

"Pull over, Thorn."

We stopped at the arches of Temple Bar, the old city gate between Fleet Street and the Strand. Despair sat on me like a weight, as if my kite had hit the ground. I wasn't sure I could talk. But then the afternoon sun blinked under the central arch through a break in the cloud, sparked a burst of elation like a shooting star at midnight. I flew with it while I could.

"All right," I said. "Why claim the dispatch was in the room?"

Thorn tapped her pipe, stuck it in a breast pocket. "I didn't think Miss Doyle took it. But you said only four of us knew it was in your bag. So it had to be her ... until Jane Muckalt walked into the library. I recognized her from the Sans Souci ... saw her in the mirrors watching you put the dispatch away–"

"Why the hell didn't you say–"

"Didn't know her ... till you told me. Then she starts selling you for Lady Motcombe's murder, so I think, *which of 'em is it ... Jane or Adelaide?* What if you say you know it's in the room ... maybe one'll give herself away?"

"And?"

"Yeah, like a hot poker up Jane's arse. And the way she held on to that bag ... well, had to be something valuable in there."

"But we both saw Adelaide–"

"I grabbed the bag, pulled out the dispatch ... Miss Doyle snatched it and ran into the library."

"So ... Jane ... the Adelphi," – I put my face in my hands – "I left her in the front room while I fetched a brandy ..." It's so obvious. "The initialed instruments ... drinking with Henry of a Wednesday ...

but how'd she find us in the Sans Souci?"

"Not sure but ... there's got to be a connection to Slegman."

I looked up. "East India Club, next to the London Library ... of course. Adelaide Doyle went there from Waterloo ... told me so. Must've told Slegman where we're meeting ... which means he didn't trust her. He sent Jane to spy. But what's her link to the Chairman?"

"Mistress? Former maid to Lucy Ocklynge? Both?"

"Huh ... but then, why not give him the dispatch?"

Thorn stared at me till I saw the ugly answer. "Didn't want me to save Beatrice ... or stop Slegman hunting me ..."

"Gave her power over him. Still bother you she caught a bullet?"

The teacup in the kitchen came into my mind, the smell of peppermint ... but it wasn't peppermint. It was aconite, thought by some to be abortive. Jane meant to kill our child.

"She hated me, Thorn. You're right about that business with the Ottoman. They were intimates ... Beatrice's refuge from an empty marriage ... Jane's way out of servitude ... till I came along. But Beatrice never ..."

"Never?"

She must've confided the divorce ... the baby.

"Never realized Jane would betray her."

"And you never suspected ... never crossed your mind?"

"Worse than that ... in Millbank my only suspects were you and Bea."

She took out her pipe and began stuffing it with Navy flake from a pouch on her belt. It had a pleasant smell of rum and tobacco. "Nah, I'd never cross you ... it's too dangerous."

"Me ... dangerous?"

She lit the pipe. "Four men drove your friend Henry to suicide ... all dead ... Jane Muckalt, dead ... Elphinstone ... you beat him to death in public. Then there's Slegman, crippled for life ... tortured into confessing his dirtiest sins."

"Torture ... yeah, I suppose that's what it was. But ... I wanted the truth."

"That's what Elphinstone would've said."

"For God's sake, Thorn ... when you put it like that–"

"Like what?"

"Like I'm some kind of Bedlamite ... so why'd I feel like the victim?"

"Because you think you're right–"

"I damn well am! But ... I'd give it all up to have Bea back." Which I knew was ridiculous, but I had to say it. "Really, I would."

"Doesn't work like that ... the trunk had a price."

"I know that! If I'd done Elphinstone's bidding, she'd probably be alive–"

"Maybe ... but Billy Impey wouldn't ... Yashoda would've got no justice!"

"Yeah? You're the one worked out who had the dispatch. I'd have got nowhere accusing Adelaide Doyle–"

"You made it happen, Doctor Khan ... why won't you just admit it?"

I climbed down from the box. "Take us to the Home Office."

"Where're you going?"

"Inside. I need to visit Shiva ... just a hiss."

Twenty-Seven

Monday, 29 June, 1857 ... two days later.

BRUNSWICK WHARF'S A breezy strip of land between East India Docks and the riverfront. Three miles from London, it's a fashionable resort for day-trippers. There's a hotel, a tavern and a restaurant. A fine promenade. The river in front's chock-a-block with steamers. At the back, the masts of East Indiamen tower above the white-stone railway station.

I like it. The ships and smells remind me of Calcutta, and a black face doesn't signify amid the lascars and Indian traders. It's normally a gay atmosphere, but not today. Soldiers are drinking hard at the Railway Tavern, saying goodbye. There're off to seize back Delhi from the savages ... redcoats and bluecoats like Hooker's blooms, warring for monopoly of the imperial flower bed.

I'm sitting on a mooring bollard thumbing through a copy of yesterday's *Sunday Times* someone left it my railway carriage. The caption – *Police Sergeant Apprehends Murderous Kidnappers: Three shot dead in Hackney* – caught my eye.

The story ran that Sergeant Jeremiah Chrystal found the body of Henry Bullock in Ivy Lane on Thursday evening. Suspecting kidnap, he traced Bullock's abducted nephew, William Impey, to a vacant nursery in Hackney. There he confronted three armed kidnappers who refused to surrender. In the battle that followed, the villains set the nursery ablaze before being shot dead by the Sergeant. Commissioner Wilberforce recommended Chrystal for a commendation on the grounds of his dogged detective work and outstanding bravery.

I was wondering who'd cooked that up when I noticed, *Disgraceful Riot at the Cambrian Stores: City Police Officers Assaulted by Prize-Fight Mob.* I'd pushed the fight from my mind. Once Sir George assured me the Company's finished – if the rebellion doesn't do it, my evidence will – I collected my prize money and told Thorn the Lab's hers.

The rest is a blank, a seesaw of Shiva and handi and ganjah and self-pity; anything to stop me thinking about Bea. The memories are too difficult. I'd lost a dear friend, a lover, a companion. But was she using me to divorce her husband? Why hadn't she told me about the child? Did she really care for me at all?

Now I'm waiting for a steamer to Buenos Aires. The voyage will get me out of London. Out of the British Empire. I'm not waiting for Shapton Sands to claim Earlsacre and kick me out of the apartment. War in India won't trouble them in Argentina. I'll track down those coca plants and make a ton of Shiva. Maybe I'll ship it to New York, start again; take out patents and become a chemical celebrity.

Reading the *Sunday Times* piece, I saw the *riot* story was a ruse to cover the fight. They'd somehow dug out the juicy bits: *Tipu Tiger fought like a man possessed ... word has it the British Bulldog slunk off to India in shame to rejoin his regiment.* I was pondering that when I saw a carriage pop over the railway bridge on Dock Wall Road. It's the Lab, Bessie leaning back to stop it racing down the steep descent. Thorn horsed her over the cobbles to a space between the icehouse and the stables, pulled up sharp. I was so surprised I hardly registered Miss Doyle on the box seat next to Thorn.

But I stood up when Sergeant Chrystal stepped out in a smart brown suit. He looked irritated, as if his trousers were full of fleas. Thorn and Miss Doyle hopped down. They peered at the crowds looking for someone. Me? I'd half a mind to turn my back. My ship leaves in two hours. But I owed them better than that. They'd each risked a lot to help me in the last few days.

I waved above the bonnets and caps. They hurried over. Miss Doyle held her hat against the breeze, her green glasses flashing in the afternoon sun. The others squinted at the light dancing on the water.

"That cab stinks," said Chrystal, brushing at his suit. He looked older, less wide-eyed and open-faced than a few days ago. I'm sure he'd say the same of me.

"Like a chemistry lab," I said.

"Been looking for you," said Thorn.

"Brunswick Wharf was a good guess," I said.

"You said Buenos Aires, via packet steamer to Southampton."

I'd forgotten I'd told her.

Chrystal took out a fat envelope. "For you." He held it out. When I kept still, he said, "It'll nae burn yer." Then, impatiently, "It's my day off, you know?" He glanced at the newspaper in my hands. "What happened to yer face?" When I said nothing, he added, "Several coppers were hurt in the that riot."

"So the papers say." I held up the *Sunday Times.* "Should've bought tickets. Bare-knuckle's not illegal."

"Assaulting a man is–"

"British Bulldog didn't complain." I tapped the other article. "Well done saving Billy Impey ... killing three men with a single-shot blunderbuss deserves a medal. What happened to justice not vengeance, eh?"

Chrystal stared, furious and wounded at my barbs. He'd sparked my anger implying the riot was my fault, but it quickly passed. I guessed he'd been faced with an agonizing choice: take the glory or the blame. Neither Clyde nor the Company wanted any connection to dead bodies or burning conservatories. If Chrystal told the truth, Clyde would deny it. His new servant Billy Impey would back him up, so would Chesney and Kyd. So would the City Police Commissioner, come to that. So why shouldn't Crystal take the benefit of their duplicity?

More consolingly, I said, "No point kicking a good copper off the force."

Chrystal nodded slowly, accepting the truce. In the silence I noticed Miss Doyle was also holding an envelope. It was foolscap, blank on the front. Pointing to the one in Chrystal's hand, she said, "Sir George Green asked the Sergeant to deliver that. He consulted me–"

"She's an *intelligencer,*" Chrystal said, like I'm an idiot.

"Intelligence said to ask me," Thorn said.

"What is it?"

"How the hell'd I know?" said Chrystal.

"It's important," said Miss Doyle.

It was labelled, *For the attention of Doctor Hyder Khan. Private and Confidential.* I made to put it in my coat, but Miss Doyle said, "I think it's urgent ... you should read it at once."

"Green would'nae put it in the post," Chrystal said.

It crossed my mind it's a warrant for my execution. But I trusted Thorn, so I slipped a finger under the flap and tore it open. Inside's a bundle of documents tied with ribbon. On top, a covering letter. I sat on the bollard and read:

My darling Hyder, I pray you never read these lines for it will mean my darkest fears are realized. Some months ago, I resolved to divorce my husband. I hired an agent in India to provide proofs of his bigamous marriage. I offered him a generous settlement if he did not contest the petition. I have not troubled you in this matter as I expected a quiet and speedy resolution in the new year.

I was wrong. Shapton not only refused the petition but, hoping to deter me, set his friends to spy on us. When I made it known I would not be deterred, he said he'd sooner murder me than face divorce. I believe him. That is why my lawyers have drawn up a will that disinherits him. All my property and worldly goods are yours. Be assured he and his confederates will contest it. Chief among them is Nathaniel Slegman, an evil man to be treated with the utmost caution. But be assured others in high authority support my wishes. You will find the details enclosed.

This is not a love letter my dearest. Twenty years of marriage to

Shapton have robbed me of the power to speak of love or romance. Yet you should know this past year has been the happiest of my life. I trust I do not trespass on your affections when I say I hoped to be your wife. Do not weep for me. Rather realize our dreams at Earlsacre. I cannot think of a man more suited to the task or worthy of its fulfilment.

I remain yours in hope and admiration, Beatrice.

Gulls above me screamed ... halyards and jib sheets cracked in the wind ... a steamer's paddlewheel churned a torrential rain. My emotional damn nearly broke. I'd been in a dream since I found Bea's ring on York Stairs – through that night with Jane, the fight with Elphinstone, the scene at East India House. Now her handwriting, the taint of her perfume on the paper, her words from the grave dragged me into a new and bittersweet reality.

She's gone, like a candle snuffed by an evil gale. Our child too.

But she'd known what might happen. Faced it with a courage that let her speak from the grave. Was that why she hadn't told me about the child, because she feared for its life? Her mistake was to confide in Jane Muckalt.

I stared down the reach to Greenwich Hill ... far off, melting. *She'd felt the same, wanted to my wife.* The knot in my stomach rose to my throat.

Do not weep for me! I wouldn't. Not here, at least.

A hand touched my shoulder. Adelaide Doyle had taken off her glasses, looked down at me with a sympathy I never thought I'd see. "I hope it's not bad news," she said.

I said, "Miss Doyle ... you're wrong–"

"Addie ... please," she said.

Now I thought about it, she'd done me no wrong. Quite the opposite.

"Addie, then ... you're wrong about Lady Beatrice. *She* wanted the divorce, not her husband." Then with a swell of pride, I added, "She's left me her entire estate in Kingston."

They all stared, hardly believing their ears.

In a while, Addie said, "Oh ... congratulations."

Chrystal said, "Bloody hell!"

Thorn said, "Ah ... Lord Earlsacre?"

"It'll be contested," I said. "In any case, my ship leaves in two hours. I'm going to South America."

"Needn't have bothered, then?" said Thorn.

"What?"

"Couple of hours you'd have been gone, never known about the will."

I felt my plan evaporating, knew I wasn't going to South America.

Chrystal shifted uneasily. "Sir George said he'd like to ... discuss this matter with you."

"That means Palmerston's in favour," said Addie, "the Prime Minister."

I felt a moment's irritation that Bea'd forestalled my escape, left me to face this alone. But it wasn't so. She'd left me an estate and powerful allies, a chance to fulfil the plans we'd talked about together.

Addie said, "They say the whitebait's good at the Brunswick Hotel."

I was a nice gesture. But I wasn't hungry, didn't fancy sitting down for a meal. "Another time," I said, "but ... soon." And I meant it. "I've got to fetch my luggage from the Southampton steamer." I threw a glance at the Lab, wondering how I'd fit myself inside with my trunk and carpet bags on top.

Chrystal and Addie exchanged a glance. "We'll get the train," Chrystal said. "It's quicker ... smells better."

Addie nodded. Turning to me, she said, "Thank you."

"For what?"

"The truth, about my father." She handed me the foolscap envelope she'd been carrying. "I'm not wrong about this," she said. "It's a gift ... to use as you will." She quickly leaned close and kissed me on the cheek.

Before I could say a word, she'd turned and walked away. Chrystal made to follow her but stopped, turned back. Holding out a hand, he said, "I could nae have faced Elphinstone, bare knuckle, in front of that mob."

We shook. He took a breath to speak again but thought better of it. Whatever it was, it didn't need saying. Then he turned and hurried after Addie. Thorn and I watched them join the bustle into Brunswick station.

* * *

When we'd fetched my luggage from the steam-packet, Thorn and I found the Lab, Bessie lazily munching hay between the ice-house and the stables. Heaving up a carpet bag, Thorn said, "Fancy a couple in the Brewery Tap?"

I heaved up the other bag, shook my head. "Not now ... later maybe." Then, I said, "Reckon the stables will look after Bessie for a couple of hours?"

"Dare say ... if you pay 'em. What've you got in mind?"

We took a ferry upriver from Brunswick Wharf, halfway round the Isle of Dogs to Greenwich Pier. Thorn and I stood together in the bows, soaking in the summer sun and breeze. Little waves slapped the hull. Beyond the wide river and the marshes stood the far-away woods and hills of Kent: a rural panorama of bleak beauty that fit my mood.

Chugging along, Thorn told me what she'd learned from Chrystal, what happened next ... *Kyd and Chesney sent to India ... Slegman barely survived an operation by Sir James Paget, a cripple for the rest of his life.* I wasn't really listening. The last days had been the lowest of my life, kept afloat by artificial mood.

I'm still desolate as the view, but I feel its hope and beauty too. Thanks to Bea's letter. The last lines staggered me. How like her to put duty over love, to see one could save me from the other. Like a psalm. My shepherdess calling me to a new life, a promised home-coming nestled in those far-away hills.

I OFTEN CLIMB the hill to Greenwich Observatory. There's no better place to study the Imperial capital with a pocket telescope – the spirits of St Paul's, the City's moneybags, the clippers and steamers coming and going like water bees to London's honeypot. The Isle of Dogs bows towards you like a huge teardrop shed for humanity.

It's an awesome sight from our spot on the hillside. Thorn took out the tin of Navy flake, stuffed her pipe. She cupped a hand round the bowl to shield it from the breeze … sucked … shook and pitched the match. Squinting through a cloud of blue, rum-fruity smoke, she said, "Why here?"

I nodded to the east, to the blue ribbon of the Thames that weaved a border between Kent and Essex. "She's out there somewhere, Thorn. From up here the river looks peaceful. Clean and picturesque."

"Like fresh flowers on a grave."

I nodded. "Somewhere I can come to be near her." Then we sat quiet for a while, Thorn smoking, me tracing the river with my monocular telescope.

"S'pose you'll want the Lab back," Thorn said, "if you're staying?"

"Uh-huh."

"Risky … Slegman's a dangerous man."

"It's Mungo worries me. He'll want me to defend the Imperial Championship, set up some big paydays."

I shifted the monocular to Ferry Road on the west shore of the Isle of Dogs. Ran it south to Scott Russell's ironworks where they're building the Leviathan, the biggest steamship ever made. I've watched it grow over the months, like a black-iron monster. Addie told me it'll hold enough coal to churn its way to Australia, reckons it'll lay the trans-Atlantic stretch of her world-girdle telegraph. Even from here – a good mile away – it looks huge, the men like crawling ants hammering a million rivets into the hull.

Thorn followed my line of sight. "They call it the floating city," she said. "Could've shipped ten thousand soldiers to India, or a whole new colony and all their belongings in one go."

"You sound like the *Illustrated News*," I said.

"Biggest weight ever moved by men," she mocked.

I smiled. "Things like that used to make me think the British were invincible, the future ... men with steamships the size of the Chrystal Palace, talking to one another by electricity across the world?"

"Used to?"

"Imagine digging up the Leviathan's iron bones in a thousand years, wondering how ships ever got that size."

"Like dinosaurs ... you reckon they'll die out?"

"Yeah ... since I knew the likes of Slegman and Clyde. Greedy children playing with toys they can't control. One day the mechanism will snarl up like a broken watch, leave the rest of us to clear up the mess."

"Huh." Thorn puffed on her pipe, thought about what I'd said.

When I collapsed the telescope and stowed it in my coat, Thorn saw the envelope Addie gave me poking out of an inside pocket.

She nodded, said, "You know what that is?"

I shook my head. "Probably some self-justifying story of her deeds over the past few days."

"You think?"

I took it out ... cream plaid and blank except for a gold-wafer seal embossed with Addie's initials. Curiosity getting the better of me, I picked off the wafer and slid out five foolscap sheets, each headed by the name of an officer in the Bengal Cavalry, each with an extensive biography in copperplate. One name was marked with a cross, meaning he was dead. One lived in Bengal, three in Britain, two of them in London. I showed the top sheet to Thorn.

"What is it?"

"One of her portfolios."

"Oh yeah ... what about?"

"Don't know ..." I fanned out the sheets. Then I saw it. "It's about a hanging and a rape in Bengal, twenty years ago. Two of these men were responsible."

"How could she know that?"

"Libraries ... Company records at East India House. It's her business."

"Even so–"

"How many whites in the Bengal Cavalry in the early 30s, the right age?"

"Why give them to you?"

"I was there–"

"You ... but you were only–"

"A helpless child?" I got up, brushed a few blades of grass off my suit. "Come on," I said, "let's get the ferry back to Brunswick Wharf." I felt different going down Greenwich Hill from coming up, knowing those men were alive, maybe here in London. Is that what my mother wanted when she took me to the Nawab's school, vengeance? I wasn't a helpless child anymore. Far from it. Was it time to dig up the past or to let it lie?

Author's Historical Note

The Bengali Santal were divided when the departing British drew a border between present day West Bengal and Bangladesh. They continue a deadly struggle against corporate interests to defend their homelands and way of life.

Bullock's Remedy – known today as artemisinin – was found in the 1970s after the North Vietnamese Army asked its Chinese allies to find a cure for malaria. Ancient Chinese herbals recommended the plant Artemisia annua, soon found to contain artemisinin. First used to protect Chinese soldiers invading North Vietnam in 1979, it's now the world's foremost drug against malaria. The global anti-malarial market is currently worth over a billion dollars annually.

The plant hunter, Robert Fortune did experience a miraculous fever cure while living near Ningpo in 1853. He reported the event in his *A Residence Among the Chinese* (1857). The Herbarium at Kew Gardens has a sprig of Artemisia Annua (K000942071) collected from the garden of Colonel C.M. Wade (agent to the Governor General of the Punjab) in Ludhiana in 1844. The drug could easily have been extracted by the method used by Khan.

The keyword found by Doyle and Khan may be inferred from the story. I leave it as a challenge to the reader to decipher the dispatch.

Acknowledgements

It's a tricky thing giving credit for a new project. A decade ago, I was an historian of science getting interested in global history. But how to tackle a topic that big? Then there was the government badgering British academics to do public engagement, whatever that was. I thought I might square the circle by writing a thriller set in mid-Victorian London. My characters would let me skip historical boxes to find an organic and page-turning story of science and empire – and race, gender and capital – to breathe fresh life into my kind of history.

I blame the novelists. I've never met Lee Child or Michael Connelly or John Sandford, but their slick style, cool characters and tangled plots were seductive. How hard could it be? It took me a decade to figure that one out. They'd probably raise an eyebrow at using pulp fiction as an historical method, but the craft they honed opened a new window for me on narrative history. I thank them for that. I've never met the historian Ranajit Guha, but his 'Prose of Counter-Insurgency' changed my view of imperial history. It's an historian's bread and butter to treat primary sources with skepticism, but Guha exposed much of the East India Company's account of India and Indians as a grand work of literary fiction. He introduced me to the Santal and the uprising of 1855, opening the way for a leading man with a serious edge.

Then there are the folk I do know, all of whom are friends and very distinguished in their respective fields. I began this project in the United States while my partner was building her own career as an historian of science. At Notre Dame, Katherine Brading had enough faith to offer me the basics an historian needs: a first-class library, great colleagues and a lively seminar. The University's Hesburgh Library was well stocked on Victorian Britain and its Empire. I was inspired by the idea of muscular Catholicism and the fine collection on Victorian boxing. The folk in History of Science, Medicine and Technology at UW Madison were similarly welcoming. Their Memorial Library has an exceptional collection on the Santal and their way of life. I especially thank Robin Rider for helping me navigate rare books, and Pablo Gomez, Nicole Nelson and Florence Hsia for their enthusiasm and critical reading. The students in the honours section of HS/ILS 202 (spring semester, 2017) who read an early draft, convinced me my project could make gen YouTube curious about Victorian science.

A project strung precariously between academic and popular writing often needs intensive care. For offering more life support than I expect they realize, I thank Michael Gordin (Princeton University) for his erudition, my former colleagues David Edgerton (King's College, London) and Hasok Chang (Cambridge University) for their loyalty, and Myles Jackson (Institute of Advanced Study, Princeton) for his irrepressible, good humour. Each in their own way provided life-saving oxygen at critical moments. Special thanks in that regard are due to Brian Dolan (UC San Francisco), who not only shares my interest in fictive history but became my editor and publisher. Special thanks too to Erica Charters and Rob Iliffe for offering me a home in Oxford's Faculty of History. Rob and I have been in conversation about history of science for nearly four decades – every pint of beer fondly remembered – and he's been an intellectual inspiration and faithful supporter throughout. Erica's keenness to include my work in the international teaching programme was as inspiring as our attempts to work out what global history means.

I dedicate this book to all of those above in meagre thanks for their friendship and support.